WELCOME TO THE
LEGEND OF THE FIVE RINGS!

You are about to enter Rokugan, a land of honorable samurai, mighty dragons, powerful magics, arcane monks, cunning ninja, and twisted demons from the Shadowlands. Based on the mythic tales of Japan, China, and Korea, Rokugan is a vast empire, a unique world of fantastic adventure.

Enjoy your stay in Rokugan, a place where heroes walk with gods, where a daimyo's mighty army can be thwarted by a simple word whispered into the right ear, and where honor truly is more powerful than steel.

Legend of the Five Rings

BOOKS

THE SCORPION
Stephen D. Sullivan

THE UNICORN
A. L. Lassieur

THE CRANE
Ree Soesbee

THE PHOENIX
Stephen D. Sullivan
Available March 2001

THE CRAB
Stan Brown
Available June 2001

Legend of the Five Rings

THE CRANE

REE SOESBEE

CLAN WAR
Third Scroll

Cover art by Brom
First Printing: November 2000
Library of Congress Catalog Card Number: 00-101964

9 8 7 6 5 4 3 2 1

ISBN: 0-7869-1659-1
620-T21659

U.S., CANADA, ASIA,
PACIFIC, & LATIN AMERICA
Wizards of the Coast, Inc
P.O. Box 707
Renton, WA 98057-0707
+1-800-324-6496

EUROPEAN HEADQUARTERS
Wizards of the Coast, Belgium
P.B. 2031
2600 Berchem
Belgium
+32-70-23-32-77

Visit our web site at **www.wizards.com/fiverings**

For Jeff Oakes, who showed me how to dream,
and for Dolly, who taught me when to wake up.

ACKNOWLEDGMENTS

John Wick, whose creativity inspired a world,
and all the folks at AEG, for their continued support
and love. Also, a thank you to all the fans of Rokugan.
The Empire wouldn't be the same without you.

PROLOGUE

The tent was quiet, and only the hushed whisper of wind disturbed the sleep of the wounded. A rattling breath, and another— the occupant was still alive, despite the ravages worn on him by time and the swords of his enemies. Outside, two guards stood at respectful attention as a young man passed between them, carrying water and rice to serve his father.

The Crane Champion rested on his futon, his bandages covered in blood, seeping through from the wound that had torn apart his stomach. White hair, dyed in the style of the Crane Clan, hung limply on his pillow, and his wrinkled and calloused hands clutched angrily at the blanket that covered him. As he saw his eldest son enter, the man's weary face contorted with rage and hatred.

"I need no . . . nursemaid." Satsume's voice was shadowed, an echo of his brave war cries. He had led the troops that morning in the assault against the Scorpion. Now he had only the strength to cough sharply, and blood trickled between his lips as his eyes narrowed.

"You must rest, Father," the youth said, kneeling beside the low cushions on which his father rested. "You will need your strength to heal." Cautiously, he offered the small bowl of rice, lowering his head in respect.

Doji Satsume snatched the bowl and cursed once as he threw it across the tent. The porcelain shattered into shards on the wooden arm of his dai-sho holder. The aged samurai lifted himself to one elbow to face his son. "You will never lead the clan," he snarled, the white scar across his cheek twisting his mouth into a sadistic smile.

"I . . . never . . ."

"Bring me the shugenja. The Asahina. I must rename my heir. Where is Tomo? Shidai?"

"Father . . ." The youth knelt by the bed, the specter of the man that he would become hovering at his shoulder. "You need to rest. Shidai is dead. He died protecting you in the city, helping me get you to safety."

"Safety." Satsume coughed again and lay back. "What safety can there be in Rokugan while a Scorpion rests on the emperor's throne?" His eyes closed for a moment. Their lightning flames diminished as his anger passed. "The shugenja is dead . . . the emperor is dead . . . and soon, when I die, the Crane will die with me."

The young man's face showed no sign of the bitter pain caused by his father's words, and he reached to offer the cup of water from the small tray at his side. "You don't know what you're saying. Your wound is grave. They've gone to get the finest healers from Kyuden Seppun, to bring all the aid they can."

"Useless." The aged Crane Champion flexed his powerful hands. With a grunt, he pushed himself into a crouch. "Their magic will no more undo the poison in my blood than will your pathetic rice. Give me my armor and my sword, and I will kill this Scorpion usurper myself."

"Father, you have to lie still."

With a tremendous thrust, Doji Satsume slammed his fist into his son's jaw, knocking the gray-eyed youth back against the low table. Kneeling by the mahogany, the youth cradled a split lip. He looked up at Satsume.

"Never," the man hissed like a striking serpent, "dare to tell me what I can and cannot do. You are not the champion of the Crane yet. You are a mewling, pathetic infant, of no more use than your mother." The words were choked as Satsume rose atop legs bowed from years of riding. "If you had truly been my son, you would have done as I told you. Now, fetch my armor."

The son of Satsume felt an old anger rise in his belly, spreading like a thick fire of hatred and regret. He closed his eyes, and an image flashed in his mind: his mother, her blue eyes turned toward the sky as her blood spread into the ocean's shifting tide. Her body had been broken on the magnificent sea cliffs below Kyuden Doji. She lay still in death, her hair floating about her like strange seaweed. Her skin was pale, her golden kimono tattered by the rocks—a doll thrown aside by some giant hand. He opened his eyes. The image faded, leaving only the smile that had graced her face—a smile of triumph that had haunted her son since the day of her suicide.

He had been ten years old.

"No."

Satsume turned, leaning heavily on the low table that held his swords. His face reddened, his eyes black with fury. "Eh?" he bawled, surprised. "So, my son thinks to become the champion a few days early, does he? Is that it?" Doji Satsume's snarling lip twisted beneath the grinning scar. He took a staggering step closer to the youth. "Do you think the Scorpion have killed me, boy?" The champion of the Crane took another step, reaching toward his katana on the stand.

"Do you think that Shoju's bushi have done you a favor?"

Satsume was built as if by Kaiu engineers, his short form burly and well muscled even in age. Blood seeped through his bandages, staining the hand he kept on his opened belly. The dark roots of his bleached hair were slicked with sweat, but his hand was firm and steady upon the katana's sheath.

Undaunted, Satsume's eldest son rose. He bore no weapon, no sheathed tanto or arrogant punch. He simply stood, nearly a head taller than his father. A presence radiated from the youth's inner chi, and from the memory of a hundred other times when he had knelt to receive his father's punishments. The scars of such 'lessons' still laced his shoulders, and a single trail of white marred the otherwise perfect cheekbone of the young man's face.

In that moment, his father wavered. Uncertainty touched his hand. When had his son become so large? When had those pale eyes, so weak and gray, turned into chips of stone? Even as they had marched together toward the captured city of Otosan Uchi, Satsume did not remember his son standing so proudly. Still, he was nothing but a boy, a stripling, hardly old enough to be given the name of his manhood. His gempuku could not have been so long ago, and memories of the cowering, whimpering child still echoed in Satsume's mind.

The boy was so like his mother.

"Get my armor," Satsume's voice was low, dangerous. The naked katana hung at his side, needing only the swift flicker of his hand to cover itself in the blood of a worthless son.

"You are too weak to fight. Your stomach has been pared open by Shoju's men. Even now, your blood trails away from your wound." The anger in the youth's eyes did not fade. "I will not allow you to destroy yourself." *As you destroyed her.* Unspoken, the words hung between them.

"Where is your brother?" Satsume roared, falling to his knees. The pain of his wound had grown too much to bear. "Where is my son—my true son—Kuwanan? Kuwanan!" The command went unanswered. Doji Kuwanan, the youngest son of the Crane Champion, was in the lands of the Lion, his tutelage with the Akodo drawing to an end.

"Kuwanan is worthy of this clan." The words were as hateful as the wound in Satsume's body. "But they will not bring him to me. Even now, outside the clan, they call you 'Champion.' " Satsume spit the words. "Kuwanan should have been born first, should have been my heir. He is everything you are not."

"I am your son, Father, and all your words will not change that."

"No, it will not. But my sword could." A deep rumbling began in Satsume's chest. The cough that followed brought more than blood to the old man's lips. He knelt, sheathing the weapon and clutching it at his side as if trying to reclaim his strength through the cool smoothness of the enameled saya. After a moment, his eyes opened again, trying to focus on the young man before him. "Bring me my armor. . . . Let me die in battle, avenging the emperor I have failed."

"No."

Satsume cursed, falling back onto the sheets of the futon. "When I am dead, you will lead this clan into ruin. You are nothing. Worthless." Satsume clutched the sword tightly. His labored breathing rasped in the quiet tent. "Weak and untempered. I should butcher you here, with my last breath. I should take your soul to Jigoku with mine and throw you before the gates of oblivion rather than leaving you here to destroy all that I have built. I cannot kill you. That is my failing. You are a miserable excuse for an heir. You are . . . your mother's son."

The young man's response was quiet and bitter. "Yes, thank the Fortunes, I am." As he picked up the shattered pieces of pottery, he heard his father whisper one final time.

"I hate you, Hoturi."

"I know, Father." Hoturi said, lifting the flap of the tent and biting back his icy fury. "She loved me more than you."

1   WHISPERS OF THE PAST

Autumn had turned the leaves to red and gold, shifting in a wind that smelled of rain. Hoofbeats echoed like thunder through the woods. Birds leaped into the air as two cloaked riders passed.

The samurai ignored the chill, their silvery cloaks billowing over dark blue hakima pants and gi—wrapped shirts of thick silk.

The first frost had fallen, and the last grains of rice had been brought in. Fall meant festivals and celebrations of the harvest. It was also a time of remembrance, a season of death and remorse for the actions of the past year. Autumn winds blew the words of the ancestors to the listening ears of holy men. White blossoms of summer fell, foretelling the snow that would soon follow.

At the southern palace of the Kakita, decorations were placed high upon the towering gold of the open gates. The emperor's own mon hung beside the symbol of the snow-white Crane. Kobune boats sailed up the coast, carrying rice and sake for the great festival, and artisans from every clan traveled to the palace in their palanquins. The Festival of the Last Harvest was one of the grandest celebrations in the land, and those who were lucky enough to attend told stories of the glory of Doji halls, the beauty wrought by Kakita artisans. Guests whispered through the winter of the magnificent sights of the Crane Court.

To the champion of the Crane, though, Kyuden Kakita was home, and autumn was time to return to it.

Doji Hoturi rode with the grace of one born to hold the attention of others. Even astride a shaggy mountain pony, he had a presence that spoke of courts and celebrations, of command and dignity. When he moved, the way before him opened. When he spoke, all other voices fell silent. Such was the birthright of the Doji Lord, the Crane Champion.

These woods were his homeland. For twenty-eight years, he had lived among them, playing at battle in their thickly branched groves. Now he returned to them as their lord and master. Satsume's death, more than two years ago, had granted the title and responsibility of Crane Champion to his eldest son. Those years had aged Hoturi. Now his face bore the firmness of manhood as well as the responsibility of command. Although he was the youngest clan champion in the empire, already his fame had won him respect—and allies.

At his side rode his sensei, Kakita Toshimoko, gray hair flying in loose threads from his grinning face. The horses charged together through the wood, recognizing the roads of their homeland. Toshimoko lifted his hand and caught a low branch as it whipped past, snapping it back toward the tree with a merry flip. Though Toshimoko had aged more than fifty years, no man in the empire would dare suggest he retire to the monastery.

"Come, samurai," Toshimoko said roguishly, "put a smile on your face. We're nearly to the castle, and if you ride to those gates with such a gray frown, the Kakita will grab their swords and kill someone."

Despite himself, Hoturi broke into a weary smile. "Let them kill the bushi of the Lion."

Toshimoko's usually cheerful face pulled into grave lines. He slowed his pony to match the gait of Hoturi's steed. "Especially now that the Matsu and the Ikoma have begun to marshal troops near the Osari Plains." Then, as suddenly, the somber face was gone, and a twinkle shone in the man's eyes. "Is your sword ready for battle, student?"

Hoturi grinned back. "The only time it wasn't ready was when we fought the Shosuro, and then only because you kept tossing so many in my direction!"

"Bah," Toshimoko snorted, leaning back on his steed. "I wanted to be sure you weren't bored."

"Bored?" Hoturi scratched his chin thoughtfully. "Well, perhaps after the twentieth or thirtieth one. But that was because you kept all the difficult fights for yourself."

"That's what they'll place on my ancestral marker, you know. 'Kakita Toshimoko rests here, the ashes of a greedy man.' Ha!"

"Greedy, by Jigoku," the Crane Champion swore. "You just wanted to finish with the Shosuro so you could claim their geisha houses before dark."

"Lustful, then."

"And that's no virtue to a samurai. You should be praying in the Ancestral Hall."

"Bother with virtue. It gets in the way of the blade."

Hoturi laughed aloud. Toshimoko's hair was as gray as his steel, but his wit was sharper than the blade he carried. Hoturi felt closer to Toshimoko than to any man—his teacher, his mentor, his friend . . . his family.

Just after Hoturi's mother had died, his six-year-old brother Kuwanan had been sent to the Lion. Kuwanan had traveled often since then, from the Unicorn lands to the Mantis isles, and had finally settled among the Daidoji to the south. The two had rarely seen one another since childhood, but Hoturi knew his brother to be the serious, somber bushi their father would have wanted. Kuwanan had grown to become truly Satsume's son.

Far more than brother or father, Toshimoko had shaped Hoturi's life. The old man was more a grandfather than a sensei. As a boy, Hoturi had come home numerous times with scrapes and bruises from fights with other students, and he had expected his sensei to punish him. Toshimoko never had, only pointing out why he had lost the fight and what could have been done to prevent defeat.

Hoturi looked again at his mentor. There were more wrinkles and scars on Toshimoko's face, and there was a lot more gray in his long braid, but his eyes were still clear, and his broad shoulders were as well muscled as any bushi's in the Kakita Academy. The years had been kind.

"Do you think the Lion will attack before winter?" Toshimoko murmured thoughtfully, allowing his pony to choose its own path down the forest road.

Hoturi sighed, leaning forward to pluck a stem of grass from his beast's harness. "No. Tsuko is impatient, but our treaties and our command of the Imperial Court should keep the Lion from outright war."

"For now," Toshimoko amended.

Hoturi nodded. Soon, the snows would come, and after them, the warm spring rains, and Crane lands would be trampled beneath the thick sandals of the Matsu. It was inevitable that Tsuko should try to capture the Osari Plain, the richest farmlands of the empire, to feed her troops as they traveled more deeply into Crane territories. "But I suppose Uji-san will have thought of that," he mused aloud.

"Uji? That sour-faced rat. The Daidoji have inbred too much, my lord," Toshimoko chuckled deep in his throat. "They're turning into Scorpion."

Hoturi's swift anger flared. "Daidoji Uji and his men will turn the Lion if they should come, I assure you."

"Of course. The Daidoji are very resourceful with their traps and tricks." Unmoved, Toshimoko chewed thoughtfully on a twig. "The empire is grateful for their contribution to society. Without them to slaughter our enemies by the bushel, the ashes on Crane fields would not be nearly as thick, or the ground as fertile. A pity they don't duel."

"Irreverent wretch." Hoturi smiled.

"The empire has enough reverence. It needs a little sense."

"Hmmph. Tell that to Kakita Yoshi and his courtiers. I'm sure they'll appreciate your opinion after seventeen days of negotiations about the weight of a season of rice, or something equally ludicrous." Pausing, Doji Hoturi smiled. "No, my old friend. We need the courts of the empire. We need the duties, the coffers, and the politics. That is where our strength lies. Without the Crane, there would be no civilization. It was our kami's gift to the world and a power through which we shall rule the empire. Honor is our weapon, Sensei, as much as your Kakita blade."

"Well said," the old swordsman nodded.

Hoturi's pony suddenly shifted beneath him, its ears flickering to the front and rear. The other steed was restless too and bumped lightly against its neighbor.

Ahead, at the bend of the path, a man walked with a rag-wrapped crutch. His face was shrouded, his body thickly swathed in the robes of a heimin. A jingasa hat of straw shadowed his face. The brown robes had blended with the trunks of the damp trees until the man was quite close, and in the depth of their conversation, neither samurai had noticed him.

Hoturi was used to ignoring heimin. Peasants performed the day-to-day tasks and skilled labor that were the foundation of the empire. They flocked to the villages of the Crane in ever-increasing numbers, drawn by the wealth of the land and the dangerous times.

The horse began to fret, coughing in its stride and slowing its pace. Hoturi had to urge it forward with his heels. Irritated, he looked at his companion, but Toshimoko's beast acted no better.

"A ball of rice," the heimin hissed through broken teeth as he approached, "to ease a poor man's last days?"

"Move on, man. We have no food to give." Annoyed, Toshimoko gripped his pony's reins tightly, barely looking at the heimin as he spoke.

"Step aside," Hoturi commanded, but the heimin continued to shuffle toward them.

At first, the smell was slight, no more than an irritating tickle at the base of the skull. But as the peasant stepped toward the horse, the wind carried a smell of thick waste and dirt. The peasant lifted a shaking hand, and Hoturi could see sores that laced the fingers with blood and pus.

"By the Fortunes . . . !" The champion of the Crane tugged at his reins, but the horse needed no encouragement. Rearing to avoid the heimin's touch, the pony danced backward, its eyes white and rolling.

Whimpering meekly, the heimin remained still. The hat that had once covered his desiccated face rolled back as he looked up toward the riders. Yellow pus cracked at the corners of his mouth. "Pity, masters, have pity on a sick old man."

"By Doji herself!" The revulsion in Hoturi's voice caused his pony to rear, and the Crane Champion fought for control of the animal. "You are ill, man, and should go to a monastery. Let them heal you."

The heimin's face creased into a sickly scowl. "No monastery will take me. I am ronin, once samurai—and the plague spreads, even now, through your lands." Grasping the horse's reins, he continued. "The brotherhood at the monastery can do nothing for me. My lord died at Otosan Uchi, on the day his son betrayed him, and I travel the land of the Crane, bringing the same sickness and filth to the peasants that has come to the daimyo. I am Doji Asamu, son of Doji Hakara and lieutenant to the brave Satsume . . . and now, murderer of his son."

Keenly honed, the poisoned tanto flashed beneath filth-encrusted robes, darting toward Hoturi's leg.

Toshimoko's sword leapt from its sheath before the assassin's blade could move three inches. The Kakita duelist dropped from his horse and struck. The katana sang through the air with the grace of a darting swallow.

A beat, and Toshimoko stood a half-pace down the road, shaking the blood from his blade while the two halves of the ronin's body struck the ground.

Hoturi's own sword, partially drawn, dropped back into the sheath of its saya with a quiet click. His face, as white as chalk, lost its charming smile and became the icy mask of the Crane Champion.

"An assassin." Toshimoko turned as he sheathed his katana. "And plague-ridden." The master of the Kakita spat down at the shivering corpse. Pus, as well as blood, stained the road beneath the fouled robes, and the ronin's chest bore sores covered in lice.

"He said that a plague infects our lands." Hoturi said coldly. "We must ask the Asahina shugenja to discover the truth of his words. We cannot afford to have samurai or heimin die from sickness, with the Lion prepared to march across our border. Perhaps this is Satsume's revenge for his ill-timed death. . . ."

"Nonsense. And better a plague than the alternative," Toshimoko said grimly, throwing aside the twig that had still been in his mouth. Hoturi raised an eyebrow in question.

Toshimoko stared at the body of the dead assassin until the limbs ceased their spasmodic twitching. "Yes, better to have plague," he continued, stroking his chin in thought, "than the Taint of the Shadowlands. One can be healed, with time and prayers. The other rots at the land from the inside, cursing all who come near it with the infection of the Dark God of the South." Standing, Toshimoko moved toward his frightened pony.

"You suspect that the Shadowlands Taint spreads north through the Crab Wall?"

The old man's eyes were grim and unsmiling. "Suspect everything, Hoturi-sama. That is how to be sure you live another day." Toshimoko nodded once more, restoring his cheerful smile. "And you lived through today, eh, student?"

Hoturi nodded, looking back at the body by the side of the road. The knife had been meant to cause his death, destined to foul his body with the same plague that infested the ronin.

"Ride on, Hoturi," came the gruff voice of the sensei. "Pay no attention to the past. It is the future that should concern you, Crane Champion."

Hoturi paused, looking once more at what was left of the ronin, and then turned his horse to follow. Behind him, a brown and wilted leaf fell upon the ground, ignoring the single twitch of a ruined hand.

2   KYUDEN KAKITA

The higher peaks of the Doji Mountains carried snow all year round. Their white-crested tops shone in the sunlight on even balmy summer days, and their foreboding cliffs rose from the ocean shore like the cradling hands of Suitengu, Fortune of the Sea. From the highest cliff, the plains spread for miles, filled with the wealth of rice and grain, the heart of the Crane. Also from those cliffs, one could see the city that surrounded Kyuden Kakita.

The keep itself was far from the mountains, but it stood like a white pebble amid yellow and green sand. Land on all sides of the Kyuden was rich, producing enough rice each year to feed the empire. From the banks of the southern mountains to the sparkling blue ocean to the east, the wealth of the Crane could be measured each year in thousands of bushels of rice—thousands of golden koku from the emperor's own hand.

Doji Hoturi had no interest in the fields, or in the peasants that fell to their knees in the thick water as he rode past. He approached the golden gates of the castle, his face seeming chiseled from the purest white marble. Before the gates bowed a retinue of Crane retainers and courtiers, sent to greet their champion with polite words and appropriate offerings. Hoturi had seen it all a hundred times, yet he sat aback his panting steed as if the Kakita men had his full attention.

Behind him, Toshimoko drew the hood of his cloak from his graying head and idly fingered his obi. This was not his place.

Before them stood Kyuden Kakita's golden gates, which never closed. Though this was the southernmost palace of the Kakita family, located far beneath the mountains that split the Emerald Empire, it was nonetheless one of the most beautiful palaces in Rokugan. The ancient oak gates were covered in thin golden filigree, silver kanji, jade threads, and delicately twisted vines of jewels. The legend of the keep was depicted there, of the Elemental Master who had arrived only to find the gates closed and barred against a storm. As the wind raged, the ancient sage had demanded entry. The marks he had struck on the door, marring the carvings and blunting the oak, still remained. His cries had gone unheard in the howling of the cold winter storm.

If Satsume had been champion then, the gates would have been manned with ten guards, no matter how cold the night. Hoturi's horse shifted under him as the Kakita by the gate began the elaborate bows that marked their lord's arrival. Satsume had never allowed anyone to remain idle—not even in the face of a winter typhoon.

It was said that the master's curse still remained on the keep. The curse dictated that if any child born within the encircling wall of Kyuden Kakita were to lift a sword, the Crane would fall. Thus, the gates stayed open, that no child could be born 'encircled' by the walls. It was a popular story among the bards and tale weavers of the empire and would certainly be told at this year's festival.

In all the land, only one child had ever been born encircled by the gates of Kyuden Kakita. Once, when the Lion troops had assaulted the keep and the Daidoji could not drive them back, a single woman had given birth to her second son. That child's name was Yoshi, daimyo of the Kakita.

"Your Honored Excellency." That very man stepped to the fore, bowing low. Yoshi was a delicate man with thin fingers and a sonorous voice. The Kakita's white hair flowed past his shoulders, held back in a thin cord positioned to accentuate his perfect features rather than to clear his face of hair. "Your lands and your people are given much prestige by your presence among us. We Kakita remember our blood ties to our brothers, the Doji, and we gladly open our lands, our mon, and our arms to you."

"Yoshi," the champion began once his retainer's voice had ceased. "Are the lands of the Kakita prepared for the festival?"

"Of course, my lord," Kakita Yoshi bowed again, his blue vest rippling perfectly with the motion.

"Have our guests begun to arrive?"

"Hai, my lord. They have."

Then it was time for the final question. "Have the gates of Kyuden Kakita been closed?" He had heard his father ask the question a thousand times, and only once had the answer not been the same.

"Never, my lord."

Within the keep, servants waited to lead the ponies away, and Hoturi dismounted with a casual air.

Behind him, Yoshi stepped to Toshimoko, their eyes meeting for a fraction of a second.

Before the courtier could speak, Toshimoko bowed formally. "My daimyo," the Kakita swordsman said, "it is good to see that you are well."

"And you . . . Master Toshimoko," Yoshi said, returning the formality. "The students of the dueling school have missed your lessons."

Toshimoko barked a sudden laugh. "My students fear my

return, more likely, Daimyo. They know that their shoulders will ache tomorrow as if the sky itself rested upon them."

Laughter from the courtiers surrounded them, and Doji Hoturi stepped within the golden gates. He ascended the small steps that led into the first courtyard, irritated by his own dirtiness and the long hours of travel. This was not the way he should greet his guests. A bath, first, he thought. Then he would oversee the final preparations for the festival.

And then . . . he would deliver his greetings to her.

⋏ ⋏ ⋏ ⋏ ⋏ ⋏ ⋏ ⋏

The bath was steaming hot as if to scorch the impurity from his skin. There had been no good place to bathe along the road from Kyuden Doji, no deep waters other than the shore of the sea, and the bitter autumn winds kept such indulgences from being pleasurable. Hoturi removed his kimono and laid it aside, allowing a young heimin servant to wash his skin with the scraping sponge and ladle warm water over his shoulders to remove the soap. The washing came before slipping into the heat and comfort of the tub. Baths were for relaxing. Hoturi slid in. The servant bowed and exited the chamber, head lowered, kneeling outside in the hallway before sliding the thin rice screens of the bathing room closed.

Hoturi hardly noticed him. Such servants were commonplace in the palace. When he was young, he had tried to speak with them, encouraging them to tell him of their lives in the villages below the palace. Satsume had beaten him for it. That was how the eldest son of the Doji learned the complex social structure of the empire—through beatings and curses, through error and pain.

Father. Even the scalding water of the bath could not match the anger Hoturi felt when he remembered Satsume. His father had been killed during the treacherous coup of the Scorpion Clan, murdered by Bayushi Shoju as the Crane charged in the name of Emperor Hantei. Before that, Satsume had been the iron fist of the Crane, ruling the lands of the Doji, the Kakita, the Daidoji, and the Asahina from the palace of the Emerald Champion. He had two sons, Hoturi and his brother Kuwanan, and had adopted his only daughter after the death of Satsume's brother and wife, her true parents.

Satsume was not a pleasant man, but he was honorable, and he fought like the bravest Lion. Satsume allowed no man to stand between him and his duty as a samurai. He did not know compromise, and he did not remember how to love. To him, Hoturi was weak, a child in a man's body.

Hoturi's mother had been different. Of the three children of the Doji Champion, only Hoturi could truly remember her, and even those memories were few and scattered. Her name had been Teinko, Toshimoko's twin sister. She had been an artist of great renown, all but assumed by the Imperial Court to marry the lord of the Doji and bear his sons. Hoturi smiled as he fought to remember her face. Laughter on the beach as a child brought back flashes of it. Hoturi had loved her. After she had died, he had told Satsume he was going to be an artisan in her memory, to keep her alive in his heart.

Hoturi still carried the scar of his father's anger, white and faint, above his lip. "My son will be a samurai," the Crane Champion had snarled. "A warrior. I will have no son that turns his back on that duty."

Satsume would have killed him that day if he had not agreed to join the Kakita Dueling Academy. It had been a simple choice for the father: a dead son who had failed him, or a living son who obeyed his responsibility to the clan. The decision had been harder on the son. Although Hoturi was now one of the foremost students of the Crane style of iai-jutsu, he had never been able to satisfy his father's demand for perfection.

At times, it seemed Satsume wished to burn all traces of Hoturi's mother from his soul, to crush all that was left of her gentleness. Satsume never remarried, never took a lover or a concubine, and never allowed Teinko's name to be spoken in the lands of the Doji. The only person exempt from that ban was Toshimoko, whose love for her had equaled Satsume's.

Teinko's suicide had left Satsume a shattered man, with only duty to guide him. That sense of duty had been passed on to both of his sons.

The bathwater rippled as Hoturi moved, trying to change the direction of his thoughts.

This was the dawn of peace between the Crane and the Lion. Peace had been Hoturi's goal since the day his father burned on a pyre in the emperor's city. It would be Hoturi's legacy to the Crane. Toshimoko occasionally chided his student for it, and Satsume would never have settled for peace, but this was not his father's time. Satsume's ashes lay scattered over the battlefields of the empire. He was no longer Crane Champion.

"I am," Hoturi said sharply, listening to the echoes on the water.

Satsume's voice echoed in his mind: You will never prove yourself worthy. Not to me.

Hoturi rose from the water, long white locks clinging to his shoulders. His gray eyes burned with resolve. Slipping on his kimono and reaching for his swords, he moved the shoji screens apart. As he touched the hilt of the ancestral sword of the Crane, it gave a faint, ethereal chime to welcome him.

For more than nine hundred years, it had made the same noise whenever its true owner placed his hand on its hilt, recognizing the authority and honor of the Crane heir. The sound gave Hoturi pause. He looked with pride at its enameled saya. The sword had been his companion since his gempuku, the day he became a man. It still served him well, as it had served his ancestors since the birth of the empire. One day, he would give it to his own son, and it would ring for a new Doji boy and never again for Hoturi. He looked forward to that day. Placing the ancient katana gently in his obi beside his grandfather's wakizashi, Hoturi stepped into the corridor.

The servant, still kneeling patiently outside in the hallway, bowed his head to the floor and pressed his palms to the mahogany wood beneath him.

"Tell my wife that I will meet her in the gardens after I have dressed," Hoturi commanded as he passed.

The servant nodded a brief, "Hai," and leaped to the task.

The Crane Champion had returned home, and all would be well again.

▲▲▲▲▲▲▲▲▲

In the garden, flowers blossomed despite the oncoming frost. Crane gardeners, skilled beyond normal measures, used humble magics to encourage the last few buds to spring into beautiful blossoms. Though the plum leaves changed through the year, the flowering vines retained their color and rich scent until the first snow. Outside the palace, forests warred with paddies of rice, struggling to reclaim lands the Crane had tamed. Inside, the courtyard gardens blended wilderness and domestic peace. Every detail, from the small blight on a leaf to the great stone lanterns in the willow-shrouded pond, was shaped to embody peaceful meditation.

Artisans sat among the garden's curving paths, practicing their arts outside the palace libraries. There would be only a few more perfect days this year. Best to capture their image and remember their beauty, to live the moment rather than allow it to escape. The Kakita halls were a place of perfection, where all the arts of Rokugan were studied and appreciated. Students from across the empire came here to learn the delicate magic of the artisan—the maya of imagination and expression. They were not shugenja, like the spell-crafting priests of Rokugan's Phoenix and Dragon clans. Still, the arts of the Kakita artisans were respected in the emperor's court and through the land.

A pair of soft cushions rested beside the path, dark gray

against the green grass. Two women sat there, trading stories and whispering of the visitors who had begun to arrive for the Festival of the Last Harvest. A white-haired head bowed low to a darker one, and gray eyes laughed into green ones, but the women's features were very similar. They were alike enough to pass as sisters.

". . . she is the prettiest of his legitimate daughters, so of course he hopes she will marry well."

"Well, perhaps, but a Crab? They're barely articulate." The banter was kind-hearted. Shizue, daughter of Satsume, plucked a small white blossom from a nearby bush and tested its fragrance delicately.

The dark-haired maiden sighed. "I wish she would simply fall in love." Her features were long and thin but held a certain sweetness that caught the eye. Although none could call her a creature of perfection, Doji Ameiko was a beautiful woman in her own right. Petite, she had a slightly crooked smile that hid gleaming white teeth, and her almond-shaped eyes danced behind dark lashes.

Shizue laughed. "Ameiko, women don't marry for love. You should know that. Love comes later."

A sigh. "No?"

"Did you love Hoturi when you married him?"

The answer was lost in a flutter of Unicorn maidens who pursued a puppy around the path. Their chatter echoed across the lake and resounded from willow trees. Behind the trees strode a tall figure, his eyes searching through the shading branches.

"Here he comes," whispered Doji Shizue. Her eyes sparkled, and her turned-up nose crinkled affectionately. "I'll leave you two alone. I'm sure Yoshi could use my help with the arrangements for the Phoenix Clan arrivals." As she spoke, she rose from her pillows with a graceful bow.

"Shizue-san . . . ?" Ameiko whispered, and the storyteller half-turned. "Thank you, for keeping me company." She bowed her head slightly."

Shizue smiled. "For you, Sister, anything."

Ameiko watched her sister-in-law step toward the Crane Champion, her walk shifting but graceful. Had it not been for her clubfoot, Shizue would have been one of the most sought-after women in the land, as her title and her talent warranted. Still, she remained alone, assisting Kakita Yoshi with his courtly duties and passing her evenings in story-telling and song. How sad for her, Ameiko thought, not to know love.

As her husband drew near, Ameiko lowered her face and bowed, her hands pressed to the ground. "Husband."

"Wife." Hoturi's voice was rich and friendly, as befitted her station by his side. Ameiko waited until he had performed the half-bow expected by decorum, and then raised her eyes to his.

For a moment, there was only silence between them. Then, training and polite manners intervened, and Ameiko gestured to the cushion at her side. "Will you do me the honor of resting with me, Hoturi-sama? I would be grateful for your time."

"Of course, Ameiko-san," Hoturi said quietly, removing his sword from his obi so that he could kneel upon the hill-side. "So," Hoturi began, his eyebrow raising in polite interest, "have you been comfortable here, among the Kakita, in my absence?"

"Yes, Husband," Ameiko's voice was soft and pliant. "I have spent much time preparing for the festival."

"Tell me." Hoturi smiled. Ameiko blushed, and nodded, and Hoturi continued, "Will you have a dance to perform?"

"Hai, my husband." Ameiko was an accomplished dancer, trained by the Kakita from her sixth birthday. It had been one of the reasons she had caught Satsume's attention as a bride for his errant son. Despite her lineage as a poor daughter of the Fox Clan, Ameiko had the instincts of a Crane.

"The Lion and the Crab have arrived together," Ameiko said. "Although the Lady Matsu sends her regrets, Hida

Kisada has sent his brother, Tsuru, to honor our house."

"A clever plan. Tsuru is no friend to the Crane." It was natural for Hoturi to speak of military matters with his wife, though rarely in detail. Her observations were often useful, and it was here that he felt the need for her most important function: absolute trust.

Not all men trusted their wives. Some arranged marriages were no more than the insertion of a permanent spy into a powerful household. Yet as he spoke, Hoturi looked at the sheen of sunlight on his wife's dark hair and the adoration in her eyes. He was familiar with the tricks of the court, the motions of head and hand to feign belief and trust, but Ameiko needed no such enhancements. She had loved him all her life.

"Will there be war, my husband?" Ameiko said quietly, unafraid.

"Perhaps. When Toturi ruled the Lion, I had no such fear. The Doji and the Akodo had an alliance, and my brother fought at Toturi's right hand. When I became champion, I believed the alliance could still hold. I hope Matsu Tsuko will see reason. Her greed and arrogance are boundless, but she must have some common sense. Toturi promised a charter between our clans to resolve the ancient feud. Perhaps she will agree."

"The promises of Akodo Toturi have died with his honor." Ameiko whispered. A sudden chill froze the words. Hoturi's eyes turned to ice. Sunlight crept a finger's width across the pillow between them before she spoke again. "Toturi . . ."

"Do not speak of it," he snapped in bitter command, and Ameiko fell silent. Hoturi considered, plucking a leaf from a flowering branch. "Still, I will watch my words with this Ikoma. I am certain he will speak with the courtesy of a Scorpion, but a Lion always has the heart of an overbold fool. It should be simple to tear apart his ruse." Hoturi reached for another leaf, and then paused to brush his fingers against the wilted petal of an otherwise perfect flower.

It hung from the branch with tenacity, refusing to drop or hang its head.

"There is one thing more, my husband."

"And what is that, my lady wife?" he said with a sudden gentleness that surprised her.

His tone only made it more difficult to continue. Ameiko reached in the folds of her obi and drew forth a letter sealed with the imperial mon. "This arrived for you three days ago. I have not allowed it out of my presence since the moment it came."

Hoturi's hand froze above the flower as he turned to look at the folded page. The seal was intact. "I see." The mark on the outer page bore the symbol of the empress.

Kachiko.

Hoturi took the note with the hand of a soldier, his faint calluses feeling the smooth weave of the rice-paper folds. After a moment, he placed it within the sleeve of his blue kimono. "What did the messenger say when he brought it?"

Ameiko's face was a parade of shrouded emotions, each stronger than the last. "Only that you would be expected at the palace three days after the festival."

Hoturi stood, placing his katana back between the cords of his obi.

Doji Ameiko sat silently. With a quiet movement, her hands folded in her lap. The wife of the Crane Champion did not look up as her husband prepared to take his leave. "It will be dangerous for you to go, my love." For a moment, her facade shifted. A single tear touched her golden-green eyes. Deeper words stood behind those eyes, but they were words she could not say. Ameiko remembered the whispers, the insinuations about Hoturi and Kachiko. Those times had passed long before Ameiko's marriage to Hoturi, but she could always feel his heart. "You must forget the past, Hoturi," she whispered. The pain in her voice could not be covered by her softness. "She is the empress, and she is a Scorpion."

"There are no more Scorpion, Ameiko-san," Hoturi countered flatly. "The emperor has killed them all."

" 'You cannot catch the moon in a lake,' Hoturi. You cannot destroy what you cannot find."

"You quote the words of Shinsei for me, Lady Doji?"

"If you will not hear my words, perhaps you will listen to his. If you go, she will destroy you. Hoturi-sama, I beg you, find another way."

Golden-brown eyes haunted his memory. A silken laugh echoed in his thoughts. Kachiko. "No."

"For more than a decade, and she has not spoken to you. All those years, and now, this? Hoturi-sama, you are the champion of the Crane, the destroyer of her family. She does not . . ." Unspoken, her words hung between them. Ameiko's face caught a hint of sunlight. Her delicate features spoke of woodlands, and her eyes glowed like a misted glen. "I love you."

"It is my duty." He met her gaze stoically. Behind his eyes, emotion and remembrance were folded together in the forge of a samurai's heart. "And I will perform my responsibility to the emperor's family. As all Doji must, I remember my obligations to my cousins in the Hantei line . . . and their families."

Hoturi's face did not betray his emotions as he bowed to his wife. Before he turned away, he plucked the wilted flower from the branch and dropped it to the ground. "Do you know why the Crane hate to see imperfection, Ameiko-san?" Watching until she looked up at him, Hoturi continued, "Because it reminds us of the nature of our souls."

With that, the Crane Champion turned and strode down the garden trail alone.

His lady picked up the discarded blossom and pressed the wilted petal to her tear-stained cheek.

3 TOSHIMOKO

Generations ago, between the palace and the gardens of Kyuden Kakita, cherry trees had been planted. Flowering branches shaded the paths, and wide trunks carried the weight of centuries. Pastures of green grass rolled merrily past a bubbling brook. In the distance, the willow pond glistened in the morning sunlight.

It was just after dawn, but already the palace was alive with movement and laughter. Mahogany floors gleamed, and busy heimin carried trays laden with food to the apartments of the guests.

The Crane palace was not designed for siege, but for pleasure. Inside the kyuden's whitewashed walls, gold arches separated the inner courtyards from the circling balconies and paths of the inner keep. Beautiful carvings and elaborate figurines adorned low alcoves and caused many guests to cease their speech and simply admire. Warmth spread through the building from fires lit deep beneath the stone foundations. Their heat was carried through the castle by a series of cunning shafts. Even in this cold autumn, flowers had been arranged in every room and hallway. Their sparse beauty reflected the turn of the seasons and the happy peace of the festival.

The highest chambers of the palace opened onto a great stone balcony overlooking wide forests. Below the balcony, banners swung gently over soft blankets of earth and a dais of wood. The practice ground of the Kakita duelists today would become a tournament ground for those who wished to prove themselves in swordsmanship. The academy of artisans, nestled in the groves to the south of the palace, had been bustling with activity for hours—if it had ever ceased during the night. When the Kakita held a festival, they expected the finest creations of their artisans to entertain their guests. From delicate origami and flower arrangements to plays of Noh beauty that would cause the harshest samurai to weep, the artisans labored to produce perfect offerings for the Festival of the Last Harvest.

The duelists were the most famous of those artisans, practicing day and night to satisfy their demanding masters. The Kakita believed swordsmanship was an art, and their intricate studies with the katana occupied the thoughts and efforts of a lifetime. Although outwardly they were no more revered within the academy than the dancers, poets, or storytellers, the duelists stood at the heart of the teachings of Kakita, the first swordsman of the empire. They were trained in the grace and beauty of swordsmanship, the courtly airs of the Crane, and the history of the empire. The emperor himself, for more than seventeen generations, had been trained by a swordsman of the Kakita. It was an honor to watch the students of the school perform, and the life's wish of many men to train among them.

Toshimoko had always liked festivals. This year's added amusement was the bitterness between the Lion and the

Crane. Toshimoko saw it as a fine diversion, a chance to teach the Matsu a lesson about the cost of too much pride.

Yawning hugely, he ran callused fingers through his wet gray hair and sat down atop the tangled covers of his cushioned futon.

The formal bath had been filled with visitors. Unicorn courtiers had visited the warmth of the bath gratefully, as had gruff and burly Crab guardsmen. One particularly promising Phoenix had broken into line in front of the sensei and several others, claiming that his sword was "as keen as Shinsei's wisdom."

After dropping him for an icy dunk in the river outside the palace, Toshimoko had thoughtfully informed the arrogant lad that sometimes even wise Shinsei became confused.

It had been a good morning.

Placing his swords into his finest obi, Kakita Toshimoko chewed at a bit of cinnamon bark as he braided his long gray hair. It was an affectation, really, but one that the old man could easily get away with. Many men boasted they would cut his braid, but as yet, none had even come close.

Without thinking, his hand fell to the hilt of his katana as if bidding good morning to an old friend. It was time to join the celebrations. He stepped out of the chambers.

"Konbanwa, Toshimoko-sama." Nodding her head in ardent respect, a young daughter of the Shinjo simpered the greeting. Her father, a plump man with silvering locks escaping from a poorly dressed topknot, paused to glance at his daughter's greeting and then bowed low.

"Konbanwa, Master of the Academy," he greeted Toshimoko respectfully.

"Kon-wa," Toshimoko said informally, not pausing to make small talk. Unicorns were amusing, he thought to himself, catching their whispers as he passed. But only in small amounts. It was a shame there would be no more Scorpions in the empire. Their small treacheries were a delicate form of Kabuki that he would miss. Best not to say that aloud, though. Toshimoko's brow furrowed. Too many politics these days.

"Concerned about today's matches, Toshimoko-sama? Perhaps you should leave the worried faces to your students and keep a wiser smile on your chin." Laughing, the story-teller stepped up her pace to match his.

"Who are you, impudent squirrel?" Toshimoko asked gruffly, tugging at a lock of her white hair.

"Do you not know me, Uncle? It is Doji Shizue. If your eyes are weary, I can have a maidservant guide you to the bal-conies so that you can hear the fighting." Her impish smile betrayed the teasing words.

"You are not Shizue-chan. Shizue is a little girl, only this high." He held a hand to his knee and winked at her. "You must be the maidservant."

"If you keep throwing the Phoenix in the river, we will both become maidservants."

Toshimoko grunted. "Not my fault. The boy wanted a bath. I gave him one."

"Tell me, old father, do you still remember the way to the dueling grounds? I seem to have lost my way." Shizue grinned shamelessly.

"Go past three mountains, and turn left," Toshimoko pointed at a line of burly Dragons, facing away from them and blocking the hallway ahead. "Better yet, let me move the mountains for you." Stepping forward with his best sensei shout, the old man barked at the gathered samurai, "What are you doing!"

Two of the Dragons jumped to the side, landing in mar-tial stances. Instantly, they had readied themselves for com-bat, legs wide and hands in fists to block or strike. The third simply lifted an eyebrow and looked back over his shoulder at the man with the young girl at his side.

Toshimoko stood with an almost bored expression, his hands clasped behind his back.

"Watching the Lion prepare himself," the third Dragon

said peacefully. On his sleeves hung the mon of the Mirumoto family, a very high-ranking name within the Dragon Clan. He still stood in the doorway at the edge of the practice field. Beyond him, the Crane practiced their swordsmanship. He pointed across the field at a knot of retainers dressed in the brown and orange of the Lion.

"Watching Lions?" Toshimoko scratched his head thoughtfully and reached into his vest for another part of the cinnamon twig. "That could be interesting. We'll join you."

The jumpy Dragons looked at each other sheepishly and lowered their hands, noting that Toshimoko seemed to be ignoring them.

"Since you seem better informed than your companions and significantly less eager—" Toshimoko's glance scalded the defensive samurai— "you can tell us about this Lion's technique." He bowed politely to the Dragon. The burly guards stumbled slightly backward, forced by decorum not to touch the sensei or the swords that protruded from his blue obi. "Come, Shizue. I wish to hear the Dragon speak."

The third Dragon smiled at his compatriots' obvious discomfort as Shizue stepped neatly between them and joined her uncle in his bow. "Honorable Dragon-san, I am known as Doji Shizue, and this is my uncle, Kakita Toshimoko. It is our pleasure to meet guests of our house, and we hope that you have enjoyed the hospitality of our Lord Hoturi." Her voice was smooth and polite, with just the proper touch of deference.

"Noble Lady, I am well aware of both your name and that of your honored uncle. Allow me to introduce myself. My name is Mirumoto Taki, son of Mirumoto Sukune, general of the Mirumoto family of the esteemed Dragon Clan." He bowed in return, his broad shoulders moving beneath a green silk kimono and golden haori vest. Brown eyes smiled from a round face, and twin swords hung at his side.

"Taki?" Toshimoko smiled genuinely. "I know your father. Good man and should be daimyo. Damn thing, that." When

Taki did not respond, Toshimoko pointed again at the Lion contingent aiding their lord into his complex armor. "Tell me about that one."

"The Lion is an Ikoma named Jushin. He is the son of Ikoma Ijode, once Akodo Ijode, and still lord of the Tenkai province. Their lands stretch beneath the Lion palace of Kenson Gakka."

"A farmer?" Toshimoko snorted.

"No, he is the third son of that lord and was sent to the Akodo War College when he was young."

"That explains the torn mon on the armor, then." Shizue said quietly. As the Lion's elaborate shoulder plates were fastened by three samurai retainers, the clear impression of a golden mon appeared. The gold had been scratched away and repainted with care but was still visible on the enamel of the laced plates.

"Now he and his family serve the Ikoma, since the Akodo were dishonored when the Son of Heaven declared their death. Some say the Scorpion were the lucky ones."

"Some do not speak of it at all," Shizue warned carefully.

"Mmm," muttered Toshimoko. "And some men are fools."

Unsure of the dueling master's intent, the Dragon samurai shifted in his stance. "Perhaps. The Lion certainly aren't. Not this one, at least."

"He came alone to the Festival of the Last Harvest. What does that speak of his foolishness?" Shizue prompted.

Taki chuckled. "Less than it says of his courage."

Toshimoko's grin twinkled in his eyes. "Poor Ikoma Jushin. I'm certain that when he returns home, he'll help the plants grow in the fields of his father's house."

Taki looked at the cheerful old man with a curious gaze. "You think Tsuko will strip him of status?"

"Bah," Toshimoko replied. "She'll send his ashes to fertilize the ground!"

"He has friends in the Imperial Court. Dangerous to send, and more dangerous to lose."

"One might say, invaluable," whispered Shizue thought-fully. "We thank you, Mirumoto Taki-san, for your insight and valuable time. My uncle and I are pleased to have spoken with you on this beautiful morning. Perhaps we might meet again, over the days of the festival?"

"Of course." Taki smiled, bowing politely and gesturing his men aside. "I am at your disposal, gentle sister of my host."

Shizue smiled, returning his bow. Smoothly, the two Crane stepped from the doorway down the stairs of the palace, and into the grassy pathway that divided Kyuden Kakita from its inner courtyards.

"You speak too much to the Dragon, Uncle," Shizue said, as if commenting on some small flower by the path.

"The Dragon are our allies, Shizue-chan. Taki was trying to help us." Toshimoko said jovially, eagerly walking toward the tournament fields.

Shizue sighed, shaking her head. "You play too many games, Toshimoko-sama."

"The same games you courtiers play, squirrel, but with swords and not fans."

The samurai on the dueling ground before the dais were resplendent in their gleaming armor. Lacquered plates shone purple, blue, gold, and green. The mon of the Six Clans waved on banners that hung from every corner of the field.

Toshimoko had always liked tournament days. Although he had long ago ceased to compete—it would not have been generous for the Crane to sponsor a tournament and win every prize—he lived the excitement of the bouts through his students, encouraging them to succeed and shouting in disappointment when they were beaten. This year, four of his best had entered the competition, two in the grand kenjutsu melee, and two more in the single-duel bouts.

Across the field on the wooden dais stood Doji Hoturi, surrounded by courtiers of all clans. Although the young man's face was stoic, Toshimoko could see the envy in his eyes as he watched the dueling. Hoturi had always done well on the iaijutsu field. Toshimoko sighed and spat out the tasteless cinnamon bark. All the good warriors were forbidden the competition of the ring. That must be why there had been so many wars lately.

Taking a pair of practice bokken lying by the field, Toshimoko strode toward one of his students and gruffly pelted him with a shomen strike.

The boy, a Kakita of good breeding but slow wit, fell to the side from the blow. "Hai, Sensei!" he yelled.

"Ho! Hoturi-sama!" Toshimoko called from the field, bowing and motioning to the student beside him. Hoturi looked toward them with interest, recognizing his old friend's voice. "This one needs to work on his ma-ai—his timing."

"Oh?" Hoturi called. "Tell him to step forward before he steps forward." It was an impossible task. The joke was an old one, and several of the Kakita students on the field smiled.

"I think Kakita Moshi needs to be shown before I can allow him to represent his school on the tournament field. Can you assist me?"

Although Hoturi seemed to weigh the request against his courtly obligations, Toshimoko could see that it was only a political maneuver.

Shizue knelt beside her half-brother and whispered polite words of greeting.

"Please, Lord Hoturi," she smiled. "Allow me to entertain your guests with a story while you aid your fallen cousin in his studies."

Good girl, Toshimoko thought, smiling. No matter how arrogant or impatient, no guest could refuse a story from the emperor's own tale spinner.

Hoturi nodded seriously and smoothly stood from the cushion. Removing his elaborate vest and headpiece, he offered them to a nearby Daidoji bodyguard for safekeeping. Taking the proffered weapon from Toshimoko's hand, he stepped from the dais and motioned for Kakita Moshi to stand. The two bowed formally to each other and settled into position.

Warily, the youth took a solid stance. He shifted the sword in his hand to a defensive shite position and awaited Hoturi's attack.

Toshimoko strode around the two for a moment, well aware their actions were being watched by half the samurai on the practice field. "Moshi!"

"Hai, Sensei!"

"You are too old to be reminded of your timing." Behind his back, Toshimoko shifted his fingers, knowing Hoturi could see them. "Ma-ai, the essence of superior timing, is critical. Your opponent will not warn you of his strike." Toshimoko's voice was deliberately rhythmic. He watched as the student absorbed each syllable. "You cannot expect the strike, for it will come when you least—" With a hidden movement, he commanded Hoturi to attack.

The Crane Champion responded with blinding swiftness. The single motion, feebly blocked, glanced into the Kakita's belly. With bokken pressed against the student's abdomen, Hoturi stood calmly. His face twitched, suppressing a grin.

"Who are you?" Toshimoko shouted to his student, invoking the ancient oath of the academy.

"Kakita!" the call resounded from twenty throats, echoed by the duelists in the gathering crowd.

Hoturi stepped back, lowering the bokken and nodding his head to the defeated Kakita Moshi. Echoing the shout, Hoturi raised his fist into the air and listened to the resonant voices of the gathered Crane samurai.

Some said a champion's place was not beside his men, but in front of them. The whispers of courtiers proved only that they had never touched the true sword of a Kakita duelist, never known the hand of a sword brother, or fought, eaten, and lived at the side of students, masters, and ancestors.

Remembering his years of study at their side, Doji Hoturi lifted his fist again, and again the name of Kakita rang in the crisp autumn morning. In that moment, Hoturi was only another member of the school, another brother who owed his life to his brothers' swords.

Smiling as the cheers faded, Doji Hoturi handed the bokken to his opponent.

"It was my honor to fight you, Lord Hoturi-sama." The young man said reverently. "No matter how I do in the tournament, on this day I have been defeated by the two finest swordsmen our clan has to offer." He turned, bowed respectfully to his sensei, and gathered the bokken.

Hoturi chuckled.

Toshimoko saw the stress fade from the champion's eyes.

A low voice from the crowd caught his ear. "Of course he does well against a half-educated boy. It is too bad we cannot see how the champion of the Crane would fight against a fully trained Lion."

Anger leapt into Hoturi's gray eyes, obscuring the pride that had filled them.

The words had come from the Ikoma. In full battle armor, he leaned arrogantly on the length of a wooden bo staff. His brown eyes were hard and cold, his gloved hands twisted about the bo, and his lips curved into a bitter smile.

"It is not the place of the champion to fight on the day of the festival," Hoturi said, and the words were made of ice. "This is a day of celebration, Ikoma. Let it be so."

Toshimoko watched as the Lion bowed slightly less deeply than protocol would demand. Behind them, courtiers of all clans watched in sadistic fascination, hoping to see the argument blossom into a political occasion. Toshimoko knew his student better than they did, and he understood the restraint necessary to keep from slicing the Ikoma's head from his arrogant body.

Hoturi returned the bow properly, only his eyes noting the fact that he had been insulted. "Sensei Toshimoko-san?"

"Hai, Hoturi-sama?" Toshimoko leapt forward as his champion called his name.

"Although it is not seemly that I join the fighting on this day, I would not want to see our Lion friend disappointed on the field of combat. I would like you to enter the trials, and ensure he has a fitting opponent for his . . . training."

Without the faintest touch of a smile, Kakita Toshimoko bowed first to his champion, and then to the suddenly stoic Ikoma Jushin. "As you wish, my lord," he said, raising his eyes to meet the Lion's. "It will be my honor to exchange lessons with a Lion."

Oh yes, thought Toshimoko. This was going to be a most excellent morning.

▲▲▲▲▲▲▲▲

The honorable daimyo of the Kakita was resplendent in his silver-blue kimono, leading his assistant, Shizue, and her three handmaidens into the grand hall. When Yoshi stepped through the sliding shoji screens of the main room, a faint sigh of appreciation wavered among the guests. Yoshi smiled.

The fighting had ceased and the armor had been put away, the swords were encased in colorful obi, and bushi of the six great clans feasted on delicate rice and fish. Elaborate fusuma screens festooned the palace's largest hall. Brightly colored paper lanterns cast a soft light around the room. The massive fireplace blazed, warming and brightening the stone chamber and reflecting from the white-painted faces of the ladies. Bowing like willows, the most beautiful women in the empire vied with the fire for attention. Their smiles sparkled and danced among boldly dressed samurai. Here gathered the highborn folk, those invited to the private festivals of the wealthiest clan in Rokugan.

This was Kakita Yoshi's battlefield, his home. The manipulations of the court were as natural to him as breathing.

Shizue greeted the Phoenix ambassador, slowing her pace to fall farther behind her master. Yoshi was delaying discussions with the Phoenix, and Shizue skillfully screened his escape. Her handmaidens fanned out, their dark blue robes sparkling with painted scenes of rivers and elaborate waterfalls. No expense was spared for the assistants of the Kakita Daimyo, and each movement was as precise as a master's calligraphy.

Let the shugenja have their spells and the swordsmen their weapons. There was no practice in the empire as dangerous or as exciting as this.

Now the games would begin.

Kakita Yoshi raised his fan from his obi. He smiled politely to the visitors who bowed before him and ignored his three Daidoji bodyguards. They growled and hovered like overprotective wolves. Among the courtiers, frankly curious stares greeted his choice of kimono. Beneath the silver-blue of the Crane, a second kimono peeped. Its golden tan reflected the color of the Lion Clan. Let them wonder, Yoshi thought, noting a gruff Ikoma Jushin resting his bruised ribs by the fireplace. Let them remember that silver and gold are the colors of the emperor's own heir. Bold, yes, Yoshi smiled, but effective.

One of the first to approach through the mingling crowd was the Crab Tsuru, who bowed respectfully and offered Yoshi appropriate greetings.

"My Lord Kakita," the Hida began, adjusting his obi as he bowed, "from the clan of the Crab, you have our gracious thanks for your hospitality and friendship. My lord offers his own, should you or your family be inclined to visit the lands of the Great Wall."

No chance of that ever occurring, thought Yoshi, but no sign of his emotion showed on his elegant face. The Crab had obviously practiced the greeting for weeks and, at least, had the inflections correct.

"My Lord Hida-san," Kakita Yoshi bowed gently, his form moving like a reed in the wind, "your words do us honor. The Crab Clan is known for their solid support of the empire, and their bravery upon the Wall of the South. We are the ones honored that your lord could spare you and your retainers for our humble diversions."

Confused by the faint implication that the Crab Champion did not need him, Tsuru nodded. "The battles at the Wall go well this season, and the creatures of the Shadowlands are few."

"So I have heard." The daimyo of the Kakita smiled, his sonorous voice carrying over nearby conversations. "It is well that your Lord Kisada keeps such a large standing army in his northern provinces, just in case the attacks at the Wall should begin in earnest. I would not want the empire to be overrun by the creatures, and your Lord Kisada's constant vigilance does your clan honor." A few eyebrows raised at the mention of the standing Crab army, but Yoshi's guests pretended not to notice the implications.

"Not at all, Yoshi-sama," Tsuru smiled, fooled by Yoshi's feigned interest. "The army of the Crab is fifty thousand men strong, trained in battle with goblins and oni. They are prepared to handle any threat."

"Any threat at all . . . save the threat of time." Yoshi's fan snapped shut carefully. "After all, your army camps over three days from the Kaiu Kabe, and the bushi do not carry jade for curing the Taint. Surely Kisada-sama does not believe Shadowlands creatures have slipped through Crab lines."

"No, of course not. The Crab serve the empire well. Nothing moves past us." Tsuru's chest puffed with indignation.

A matron of the Phoenix smiled mockingly at the man's ignorance.

"Of course not, Tsuru-san. Nothing at all goes past the Crab." Without a hint of amusement, Yoshi turned to his handmaiden. "Okasako?" He asked her, and she bowed beautifully. "Please show Tsuru-san our gift."

Reaching into her kimono sleeve, the Kakita maiden withdrew a small figurine of jade and diamond. Although carefully wrapped in tissue, the form of the statuette was clear through the coverings. Tsuru would open it later, when none were present to see, but for now, the point had been made.

"This is for you, my guest, that your house may grow and prosper in the absence of its enemies."

"Oh, no, Kakita-sama," Tsuru bowed politely as he began the customary refusals. Although the Crab was trying to make a good impression, his feet were too far apart—too much like a martial stance. The Crab would simply never learn. "It is too fine a gift for me, and I cannot accept."

"Good and honored Crab," Yoshi began, tapping the statuette lightly with the tip of his fan, "you have already stated that Crane lands are safe of any infestation from the Shadowlands, or your armies would know of such a danger. I am in no need of its protective qualities, but I know that when you return to your Lord Kisada, you will once more be upon the Great Wall, and will have need of it. Please, take it to guard your body from the Taint of the Shadowlands." Skillfully, Yoshi maneuvered the Crab's words, receiving exactly the answer he had expected.

"Oh, no, I will not be joining the armies on the Wall, but rather, the legions in the Yasuki provinces, just south of Kakita lands. There is little need for jade with no Shadowlands to fight, and your gift is too expensive and beautiful for my rough hands. I beg you, give it to some bushi more in need of jade than I."

Well spoken, for a Crab, Yoshi thought, but now you have told me where your legion will be camped after you have left the festival. Well spoken, but poorly played. "Humble Hidasan, your troops will not always be at the edge of the lands of the Crane." Heads turned slightly as Yoshi's voice rose. The pitch and timbre were gentlemanly, but to those who knew the language of the court, his intention was clear. "And when they move south—" a delicate emphasis on his last word— "you will again have need of this. As will your Lord Yakamo, so that he might live to see the day he will become

your champion." The hidden threat passed the Crab's dull
ears, and Tsuru smiled in pride at the mention of the son of
Kisada. "If you cannot take it for yourself, give it to him, that
he knows he has an ally in the lands beneath the emperor's
own heart."

Yakamo had an ally—Yakamo, not Kisada, whose troops
hungered for Kakita lands. Kisada saw an opportunity in the
Lion aggression to the north. Yakamo made no such threats
toward the Crane. The implication was deliberate.

As the Crab bowed and accepted the gift, guests clapped
politely. The fluttering applause in the chamber sounded like
the flight of birds, birds bearing messages to the other clans:
a warning that the Crane would not tolerate troops marching
upon its borders, a reminder that the Crane were the closest
in blood to the Hantei, and an assurance that the Crane enjoyed the adoration of the emperor.

As Tsuru accepted the small statuette, Yoshi bowed
slightly less than before and turned toward the far end of the
room.

Enough games with children. The Crab had been no
more than a ruse—an important one, but a ruse nevertheless. It was time to deal with the Lion and their "ambassador," Jushin.

Shizue and her handmaidens fell into place behind Yoshi
as he crossed the elaborate chamber. Brilliantly colored kimonos flashed as maidens bowed, hoping to catch the attention of the most eligible bachelor in Rokugan. Yoshi ignored
them. The attractions of love paled beside the whispers of
the court. Love, in Yoshi's estimation, was no more than a
tool to catch the unwary. Unlike others, he would never be its
pawn.

Hoturi had ordered Yoshi and Toshimoko to greet the
Ikoma samurai at this meal. The honor would help alleviate
any anger left from the abject beating the Ikoma had received
on the tournament field. How amusing.

Bowing to Jushin as he neared the Lion's table, Yoshi

turned to Shizue. "My lady Doji," he gestured toward the table, "would you be so kind as to entertain the Ikoma with a tale? They seem ill at ease, and I would not have such sorrowful faces in my house."

"Of course, Daimyo." She was beautiful, despite her odd foot, and her smile brightened the court. He knew the tale she would tell, and as she captured the Ikoma's attention, Yoshi stepped lightly away.

"Once, there was a great warrior named Akodo, daimyo of the Lion Clan and master of the sword. . . ."

"Is that wise, Yoshi?" Toshimoko asked peevishly as his younger brother approached the table. The two men were more than fifteen years' apart in age, their faces and bodies as different as their lives. Beneath their exteriors, though, twin fires of competition burned. The Kakita blood was strong in their veins, and it showed in Toshimoko's dedication to the school of swordsmanship as well as in Yoshi's ardent political conquests. The house of Kakita was strong.

"Of course it is wise, Brother," Yoshi said with a smile. "She reminds them of a former time of glory. Let them remember the Akodo as heroes and not as dishonored ghosts." Yoshi continued, "And it is at least as wise as breaking the man's bokken in tournament."

"Not my fault. He has a poor stance."

"Brother, you exaggerate. I'm certain the Lion's stance was as perfect as his school." The idle flattery turned to an insult on Yoshi's lips, despite his winning smile.

His brother laughed, pounding softly on the table. Passersby wondered what jest the Kakita Daimyo had made.

"Where are the Asahina?" Toshimoko asked. "If I have to suffer through this courtly babble, that old pacifist Tamako had better have to sit through it as well."

"Tamako sent his regrets, my brother. The Asahina are busy studying for the peace of their souls and fighting the demons that threaten their enlightenment. They pray for our prosperity, but they do not join us at court." Yoshi turned, bowing lower as Hoturi nodded his head. "Lord Champion."

"Yoshi-san. Join us."

"Of course, my lord." Yoshi sat nimbly, reclining on his knees.

"The Asahina." Toshimoko snorted. "They never come out of that dratted temple. All day, their daimyo, Tamako, prays and studies; studies and prays. Useless."

"They are the finest healers in the empire, old man." Hoturi's voice was gently chiding. "Their skills are unmatched."

"As is their foolishness. I hear they have refused to fight, even if the Crab and Lion attack," Toshimoko said.

"That is their way. They are servants of life and peace. They will not endure war." Yoshi whispered, raising his fan as courtiers approached the Crane Champion's table. Such talk was not for the masses.

Courtiers stepped up to the table, bowing and introducing themselves in an endless stream of pleasant words. Artisans danced, and musicians played soft tunes, but Hoturi's somber face did not change.

"It's Tsuko," Toshimoko said, as if reading Hoturi's thoughts. "She will stop at nothing to capture Osari."

"No talk of battle here, Brother."

"Why not? There is talk of battle all around us. The Lion sit with the Crab, and as far as the Unicorn are concerned, Jigoku can take all three."

"That makes it even more important that we appear unconcerned," Hoturi murmured as he saw the guests on the wide wooden floors begin to part with an appreciative murmur. "If our strength is questioned, it will be tested."

"Bah," Toshimoko snorted, rubbing a bruise the Ikoma had given him. "Satsume would never have cared. . . ." The rest of his sentence died as Hoturi's lips turned white. "The Crane have never been weak. We have the emperor's blood, and the Hantei's ear."

Hoturi had already stopped listening.

Faint applause rippled among the assembled nobles, and two maidens approached through a space that widened as they moved. One of them held a thick biwa, twelve-stringed and made of wood that had browned with extreme age. The other held her painted face high as she walked, every inch regal and exquisite in a kimono as blue as the sky. Her green eyes smiled into Hoturi's. Both maidens bowed precisely ten steps from his low table.

"My wife," Hoturi began, speaking loudly enough for the entire court to hear. "You do us honor with your presence."

"My husband," she replied softly, knowing even the farthest guest in the room would hang on her every word, "I would do you honor with a dance, if you would care to lose the time watching."

"Nothing is lost when you are here, Ameiko-gozen." The noble title was appropriate in such a large and formal group, though perhaps too esteemed for a woman with no noble blood. Still, as wife of the Crane Champion, Ameiko was entitled to certain indulgences.

At Hoturi's side, Yoshi smiled behind his fan, knowing the title had been noted. Many in the empire fancied rumors about Hoturi and his young wife. Let them whisper all they want about the lack of an heir, Yoshi thought. They cannot blame Hoturi for his father's weaknesses.

Placing the biwa on the floor, the second maiden pulled her kimono tight about her knees and knelt. With a masterful hand, she tuned the golden strings of the instrument.

The court gathered to watch. Firelight glistened from lanterns above them, which cast pools of bright color across the mahogany floor.

Motionless, Ameiko gazed adoringly at Hoturi.

The music began in the same instant that Ameiko reached for her fan. In a graceful, lingering motion, she removed it from her sleeve. The first, resonant notes matched her fan's slow unfolding.

Blue and silver, her kimono moved with each gentle step.

Her arms reached out and then drew back in a dance of love
and joy. The biwa's rich tones seemed to flow from every
inch of the hall, and Ameiko's face radiated emotions that
were rarely seen in court. Each movement was precise, yet
filled with passion. Her white hands flashed behind her fan,
first hidden and then revealed in an intricate dance of
shadow and illusion. Ameiko's slippered feet masked sound
beneath the subtle shifting of silk. Her body was as drawn as
a bow and as fleet as a deer.

She is a captured spirit, Hoturi thought as he watched his
wife dance before the court, something wild and untamed
that should not be held against its will.

She looked up at him behind a teasing fan, and her eyes
sparkled with love. It was not a dance of courts and courtiers
but a simple peasant's story of the fall of a bird, giving its life
to defend those it loved. The music told the story of a hunter
in the forest, chasing a wild boar. His hawk—the dancer—
flew in the sky above and watched as the hunter's spear broke,
as the boar began to stalk the man.

Bending the fan down, the dancer lifted her arm to mimic
the flight of the hawk into the winter sky. The image was so
real that several of the guests sighed in appreciation. Their
eyes rose from Ameiko's motion to the heights of the ceiling,
as if to see the bird vanish into the clouds.

With another movement, the creature fell to the ground,
stung by the hunter's call. Ameiko dropped to her knees. Unable to resist her love for her master, the hawk returned and
began to drive away the maddened boar, using her wings and
beak to stab at the creature's eyes. Her fan dropped lightly to
the ground, landing open and perfect at her feet as she
reached once more for the heavens, but again, the hunter's
call.

Each note echoed with fervor. The illusion was complete.
Enraptured, the whispers of the guests fell to nothing. The
music carried beyond the simple plucking of the biwa
strings.

At last, Ameiko stepped forward on one arched knee, reaching a hand as if for assistance, but the music died away. The hall was silent.

The hunter was safe, the boar was dead, and the hawk, fallen from the sky, would never rise again.

The dance was finished, but for several seconds, no sound rose from the chambers. Then, with a loud boom, the Crab pounded their hands on their table, cheering at the beauty of the simple country dance. Shortly after came the awed shouts of the Unicorn, and the polite applause of the Phoenix. Even the stoic Lion, refusing at first to watch, had been drawn into Ameiko's recital. Their applause was quiet but sincere.

"My lord," Yoshi whispered into his champion's ear as Ameiko and her handmaiden bowed to the applause. "It is time to meet with the Lion."

Hoturi looked across the hall. Jushin and his men were standing and glancing toward his table

The champion of the Crane nodded. Smiling at his bride, he stood and walked around the long table to her side. Without a word, he bowed before her, nodded to her companion, and gazed proudly into Ameiko's eyes. "Thank you, my wife. You were . . . perfect."

"Husband, you do me honor."

Though it did not seem much, it was enough. His compliment made her cheeks glow beneath pale makeup. Her green eyes narrowed in pleasure. To be called perfect was a Kakita artisan's fondest dream, and to be called so in public by the champion of a clan—even if that man happened also to be one's husband—was a singular honor. There would be talk through the land by midwinter, and Ameiko would again be lauded with gifts and invitations to travel to other courts.

Still, she would not go. She had never traveled from the Crane lands since their marriage. Though before their marriage she had been one of the most revered dancers in the empire, now she was content to be only his wife.

Hoturi looked at her beautiful face for a moment more, remembering each curve and line of her cheek and then turned to follow Yoshi.

It was enough.

▲▲▲▲▲▲▲▲

Hoturi stepped onto the wide balcony of Kyuden Kakita and looked down at the magnificent gardens beneath him. Three stories below, the grass shone with torchlight, and the rocks of the garden path gleamed like smooth water. The faint scent of blossoms drifted on the wind, mixed with the bitter aroma of pine and smoke from fires within the keep.

Already, the Lion had assembled on the stone balcony. As one, they bowed when Hoturi walked through their entourage toward the high seat that had been placed for him. Kakita Yoshi stood behind the ornate stool. He smiled pleasantly as his champion nodded to the Lion kneeling below him.

Beside Jushin, four samurai retainers knelt in support of his petition. Although their names were unknown to Hoturi, they each bore the Ikoma mon and seemed equally reserved. These were unusual Lion, whose very natures precluded emotional outbursts.

Hoturi took his time settling on the stool. He removed his swords and handed them to Kakita Toshimoko, who placed them upon a nearby dai-sho holder of soft cherry wood. The Lion would wait while their host took his time enjoying the autumn evening and the beauty of their surroundings. The pause was carefully planned, of course, and Hoturi waited for Yoshi's cue to begin. The courtier would instinctively understand when the Lion had exhausted their patience.

After a few moments, Hoturi saw the fan flutter slightly, indistinguishable to any glance save his own.

"Welcome, noble Lion, to the court of the Crane," Yoshi said.

Hoturi drew his attention to the Lion as if noticing them for the first time.

Again, they bowed politely.

Jushin rose from his seat and came forward. "It is my honor, Doji-sama." The Ikoma bowed, and rested on his knees before Hoturi's low stool. "We have much to discuss. The Lion are most concerned about the Crane's statements about the Osari Plains. By all the records, the plains rightfully belonged to Matsu Gusori, in the days of the Third Hantei. . . ." All the arguments were old, tired, and worthless, but the Lion insisted on repeating them each time the clans discussed the issue.

"Yes, for certain, Ikoma-san," Hoturi nodded, "but you forget that the emperor himself allotted those lands to the Crane more than six hundred years ago. Are you questioning his decree?"

"Not at all, Doji-sama. But the plains remain our property by claim of the kami and the rightful holder, Matsu Kojume, and by decree of the Celestial Heavens. We are certain the emperor would agree."

"Then we shall have to ask him." Hoturi snapped, his mock anger calculated to lead the Lion through emotional territory. If the Ikoma slipped during this negotiation, the Crane could easily report that his bad manners had insulted them and be perfectly justified in turning away his claims. "If you are here to discuss the emperor's business, you are sadly far from where you should be. Otosan Uchi and the Shining Prince are quite a ways north of Kyuden Kakita."

"Akodo Jushin is most wise. I'm certain. . . ." Yoshi said quietly, as if distracted.

"Ikoma!" The Lion said more loudly than was necessary, appearing uncomfortable with his own reaction.

"My pardon, noble Jushin-san. So sorry to have disturbed you. Ikoma. Of course. Please, continue."

The Lion seemed even more uncomfortable. His head nodded like a tree frog.

Red-faced, the ambassador continued. "The plains of Osari were given to the third son of Matsu, and their bounty was to be split among the clans. . . ."

"Matsu's third son was Kojume?"

"No, Gusori."

"But Ikoma-san, you said that the Third Hantei gave the plains to a man named Kojume?"

Flustered, the Ikoma rethought his words and tried to find his error. "No, Kojume is the current owner."

"No, Ikoma-san, Doji Reju is the current owner." Hoturi's fan snapped shut. He secretly enjoyed the Lion's discomfort. "By the decree of the kami of the Crane."

"The emperor . . ."

"Has left the plains of Osari in Crane hands for more than a significant amount of time. There is no reason for the Lion to mistrust that decision." Hoturi smiled. "Tell me, Jushin, do you have the authority to withdraw the Lion troops from Sayo Castle?"

"Lord Doji-san, I cannot withdraw the troops."

Ignoring the man's implication that he was unwilling to negotiate, Hoturi took the words at face value, nearly crowing with the closeness of victory. "Then why am I talking to you? Doesn't Tsuko trust you?"

"I do, of course, have authority. I am trusted by my clan and champion." The Ikoma's chest puffed up, and his anger swelled. He opened his mouth to speak again, his jaw widening into an **O** of provoked emotion, and Hoturi nearly smiled.

Immediately, Kakita Yoshi twisted the man's words again. "Then you can prove your trust by following your words. Withdraw the troops from the lands around Sayo Castle."

Before the Lion could reply, the world fell apart.

A brilliant flash of orange light erupted in the air above him. A thunderous boom followed. Sparks showered down upon the assembled samurai. The light flared too brightly to see.

Hoturi leapt, reaching instinctively for his swords. As he

drew the ancestral sword of the Crane, it sounded a pure bell-tone of anger. *Magic*, he thought, *dark magic has done this, and the cost will be bitter.*

Blinking rapidly, Hoturi saw old Toshimoko move in front of him, sword drawn and eyes closed.

One Lion shouted. His cry was cut off in a bloody moan. The orange light turned to serpents of flashing mist. Their bloody jaws opened and closed around the Lion samurai's arms.

Suddenly, at the edge of the balcony, four men appeared. They circled around to press their backs to the palace wall, cutting off the entrance to the court chambers. Dressed in the thin black gi of assassins, their eyes narrowed behind thin silk masks. One man motioned wildly, his voice hissing like a snake. The three others drew thin swords and leaped toward Jushin.

"Shinobi! Ninja magic!" Hoturi screamed, lunging toward them. "Toshimoko!"

It was too late. A ninja impaled Jushin from behind with a savage thrust.

Blood trailed from the Lion's mouth. He turned. Using his last strength, he cut through the ninja with a single katana strike. Staggering, Jushin stepped toward the next black-clad enemy. His strength failed, and he fell to his knees. More blood rushed from his open mouth.

Toshimoko's katana carved through a second man as he leaped for Hoturi. The ninja's poisoned tanto clattered to the floor. His body parted. The sensei shook the blood from his sword, whirling in a blaze of motion and taking another stance.

Still, the brilliant serpents of light flashed blindingly.

"Hoturi!" Toshimoko called, hearing another body fall. Was it Hoturi or another Lion? Toshimoko shielded his eyes with one hand, squinting past the shimmering light. White hair flashed, and a blue gi moved with a sword strike.

Hoturi still lived.

Whirs of motion through the air became stars of pointed metal. One cut through Toshimoko's gi and thrust into his arm. A second and third missed Hoturi by a fraction. They blurred into the wood support of the balcony and stuck through the beam.

"Sensei!" cried Hoturi as he leapt toward the third ninja.

Toshimoko drew the shard of metal from his arm and threw it disdainfully to the floor.

Seeing the third Lion crumple, Hoturi placed himself between Kakita Yoshi and the poisoned blade of the assassin.

Toshimoko spun toward the wall. His bright blade cut through two magic serpents and sheared across the stone toward the ninja leader.

This was no ordinary assassin but a spellcasting shugenja, who caused the bright lights and distorted images. His spell broken, he leaped away from the Crane's blade and shouted a guttural cry of retreat. Placing his hands behind him on the wall, the shugenja walked upward.

Toshimoko stared in horror.

The man climbed much as a spider. Threads of thick green silk hung from where his hands had been. The ninja's body twisted as he scaled the wall with impossible speed. He laughed, an inhuman sound, and vanished into the darkness above the palace.

The fourth and final ninja, faced with a furious Lion and the steel blade of the Crane Champion, looked once toward his leader. With a loud kiai shout, he leaped from the balcony, landing three stories below. The ninja staggered into a run, heading for the wide expanse of the Kakita gardens.

The Lion threw himself off the balcony after the fleeing ninja. As he landed, though, there was a sickening crunch. Within moments, the Lion had stopped moving, his body as still as a shadow on the ground.

Hoturi swiftly replaced his sword and reached for the wall, ready to jump into the darkness and follow the fleeing ninja, but Yoshi's fan swiftly intervened.

"We need you whole, and safe, my lord."

Toshimoko croaked, "I am in no condition to follow. . . . That foul thing's blade has poisoned me. It is but a scratch but enough to unsteady my mind. My sword will be little better."

"Call for the Asahina healers," Hoturi commanded the servants that huddled inside the palace corridor. "And send my brother into the gardens, after that man. He must be caught, at any expense."

The heimin scurried to obey, pressing their heads to their hands in rapid gestures of respect.

Hoturi looked down at the bodies of the three Lion. Jushin's lifeless eyes stared back. "There will be a harsh price for this dishonor on my house," Hoturi whispered to the dead.

4   A BROTHER'S DUTY

Rumors flew as if with wings, fluttering throughout the palace. They chased the Daidoji guardsmen that rushed to secure the entries and guest quarters. Whispers took form with eager speed, breaking the courtesy of shoji screen and rice-paper wall.

Lady Ameiko was dead, murdered in her chambers by a Lion militia. Hoturi had gone mad, insulting Kisada, and lay mortally wounded by a Hida guardsman's blade. The Ikoma had started a fire in the upper chambers and killed all the line of Doji Satsume. Matsu Tsuko herself had arrived, demanding the surrender of the Osari Plains—no, Kyuden Kakita—no, all the Crane provinces. The only thing anyone knew for certain was that something had happened to the Lion ambassador, and that Daidoji stood outside every door, their faces blackened by duty and anger.

With the anger of a caged oni, Doji Kuwanan marched through Kyuden Kakita. The storming steps of his thickly set legs shook the delicate paper of the screens. Behind him, three somber-faced Daidoji guardsmen paced with spears raised and ready.

"Word?" Kuwanan demanded of the two gate guards.

Swiftly, they knelt as he approached. "None, my lord. Nothing on the road, and nothing in the river. Either the fleeing assassin has escaped on foot, or he is still within the palace." Even for a member of the Daidoji family, the man's words were terse, with none of the courtly frills one might expect from a Crane. The Daidoji were the youngest family of the clan, formed from the children of Lady Doji and Lord Kakita and sworn to defend Crane land and honor with their lives.

Kuwanan nodded. Rage burned in his silent visage. Turning, he straightened his shoulders. "Send twelve men to check the countryside outside the palace. Keep the guards in place, and bring me another four to search the southern gardens."

The Daidoji lowered his head again and then stood. As he reached for his spear, Kuwanan could see the twisted snakes that laced his wrists in blue, tattooed coils. The marks of the Daidoji family were granted only to those who passed their trials of manhood.

Kuwanan's own hands tensed reflexively. Those tattooed serpents had nearly encased his own arms and marked his destiny, but his father had determined another course.

No time for memories.

Kuwanan's stride echoed heavily through the Kakita corridors. He was short, compact with muscle, and thick-necked, with a square jaw and a nose that curved slightly from being broken three times in his youth. Kuwanan was by no means the beauty of the Doji family, but he was its strength. In that, he had everything in common with the Daidoji at his command. Where Hoturi's white hair was long and elegant, Kuwanan kept his shorter, dyed white only out of protocol, and often pressed back with a brow band. No grace was spared in his step. No smooth courtier's voice flowed from his lips, but the trained and brutal commands of a soldier.

For the first three years of his life, Doji Kuwanan had been the younger son, forgotten in the shining light of the heir, his brother Hoturi. Then, his mother had died, and it had all changed. He had been sent to the Lion Clan to cement a treaty of peace between the two. His sensei had broken the boy and sent back a man. Kuwanan smiled at the thought. When he had left Kyuden Doji, he had been a small, angry boy whose tears could not be hidden. When he had next seen his family, he had been one of Toturi's finest students, a warrior of the Lion style, as cunning as their battle cats.

Then the Scorpion had come, and Toturi had fallen from grace. Matsu Tsuko had broken the treaty, and all the sons of the Crane had come home—including Kuwanan.

Now he served with the Daidoji, merging their defensive style with the aggression of the Akodo and the training of the masters of the Lion. The young man's anger had turned to strength, and he held two things close to his heart: the safety of the Crane and the strength of his own command.

Throwing open the palace doors, Kuwanan marched into the courtyard and approached the garden. The Daidoji guardsmen stationed in Kyuden Kakita's outer grounds would know more, and he intended to discover what they had seen.

"My lord?" a Daidoji's voice called softly through the branches of a flowering tree.

Kuwanan looked up to see a guard lying prone along one of the highest limbs, his form hidden by the shifting shadows and thick leaves. Kuwanan paused, and the Daidoji rolled nimbly from the tree, landing with no noise at all and lowering his head in a smooth bow.

"Lord Uji of the Daidoji wishes to speak with you. He says

he has found the trail of the assassin. I can take you to him."

Uji. Kuwanan's lips curved into an almost feral smile. "Good."

"Hai, Kuwanan-sama." Moving softly through the trees, the guardsman vanished into the shadows, leaving Kuwanan to rely on sound and movement rather than form. Trained in his methods but lacking his skill, the youngest son of the Doji nobility stepped forward through the brush.

Within moments, another form detached itself from a spreading bough, and then a third. Each of the Daidoji bowed to him, making their presence known as their daimyo's brother passed them by. When he moved on, they faded again, becoming once more part of the darkness and silence. Only the guide that led Kuwanan through the twisting garden paths made any sound—and only because he intended to be followed.

The sound before him ceased, and Kuwanan stepped out into a small twist in the path. The faint scent of smoke hung in the air where the stone lantern by the lake had been extinguished. The Daidoji guard rested lightly on one knee, his spear forming a pillar of steel and moonlight. As Kuwanan approached, the Daidoji rose, stepped back, and waited silently behind the Doji prince.

From the edge of the path, another figure slid down a tree. He held lightly onto a limb with one hand while placing his feet noiselessly upon the ground. His face was hidden by a thin leather mask that hung from his darkened helmet, and the serpents on his wrists were black with age. Dark hair trailed from beneath his helm, coiling like water snakes about his wiry shoulders.

"Kuwanan-sama," Daidoji Uji began in a voice that sounded like a hissing serpent, "less than seventy paces to the northeast lies a drainage ditch that carries the stagnant lake from the pond into an underground river. The rushes near it have been pressed to the ground, and the water runs slowly, as though blocked. We have found him." Uji's eyes were steel blue in the moonlight. The twin swords at his belt hung with care, wrapped in silk to prevent noise.

The daimyo of the Daidoji did not pause to be congratulated. Nor did he lower his eyes from Kuwanan's as he signaled for his guard to advance, moving silently and slowly. The guard bowed and vanished.

"Uji-san." Kuwanan smiled viciously. "Show me the way."

The Daidoji nodded and raised a hand to command his men. Without a word, he stepped in front of Kuwanan, choosing a bare path between flowering vines. Kuwanan followed, trusting the keen vision and knowledge of the Daidoji.

They reached the narrow path that led toward the lake, and it became necessary to step single file. Uji's hand flickered again in the moonlight, and Kuwanan heard a very soft movement to his right. They were not alone; the Daidoji guard paced them. Uji nodded in faint pride. With a curious gesture, he pointed forward and began to move again.

It was slow going along the edge of the lake, placing each foot into the sucking mud and withdrawing it silently, but Kuwanan had studied with Uji and his men, and he made little noise. The drainage ditch lay only a few short paces ahead when suddenly Kuwanan heard a shout of pain.

Leaping forward, he and Uji ran the last few yards through grasping willow branches and thick brush. The two Crane samurai burst out into a narrow ditch that ran downhill, away from the lake. Soft sounds came from just downstream. A thud and splash told them the fight had been as swift as it had been sudden.

They turned the corner again. Uji cut aside the hanging willow branches and saw a man kneeling by the ditch, his clothing spattered with mud. Over him stood a black-garbed figure, his sword cutting the flesh that had once been the Daidoji's neck. The head of the guardsman fell into the ditch with another splash.

Uji's swords leapt into his hands.

Before he could move, Kuwanan leapt atop the black-garbed figure and knocked him to the ground. Rolling swiftly to one side, Kuwanan heard a ninja-to, the blackened sword of the assassin, swing past his torso. The man had been well trained. Kuwanan twisted to his feet like some burly jungle cat.

Daidoji swords flash in the light of the crescent moon. The wakizashi cut into the man's leg, slicing black cloth and the flesh beneath.

It was not a killing blow, and the assassin leaped back onto his hands in a sudden flash of acrobatics. He rolled to his feet. The man was good.

"Don't kill him!" Kuwanan commanded.

Uji paused, lowering his swords into a defensive stance.

Kuwanan drew his own sword in a chopping stroke, wishing he had been taught the single-movement draw and strike of the Kakita Academy. With a battle cry, he thrust his sword toward the assassin's face, hoping to drive the man back into Uji's reach.

The assassin had kept his wits, however. He swiftly shifted so that Kuwanan's blow missed by a hairbreadth. The return assault was only a half-beat behind, cutting at Kuwanan's arm.

The Doji parried, allowing the ninja-to to slide harmlessly down the length of his blade.

Uji struck again. The assassin whirled and blocked. He kept the momentum of his attack and launched a fierce kick that pushed Uji back into the streambed.

Kuwanan swung an overhead blow.

The black-garbed man leaped aside, catching the force of Kuwanan's blade on his own and shifting his weight away from the strike. The tip of Kuwanan's blade crossed his own chest, tearing cloth but narrowly missing skin.

Kuwanan had assumed the assassin was a Scorpion and so had fought with directness, countering thrust with parry rather than moving aside. He had been wrong, and it had nearly cost his life. The assassin fought like a Lion, the constant footwork of the Akodo beneath the mask of the Bayushi. Enraged, Kuwanan shouted again and forced his katana past the assassin's thinner blade. He heard a sharp crack as the ninja-to snapped beneath ancient steel.

The assassin leaped back, but his injured leg failed him. As Kuwanan tore away the veiled mask, the assassin's eyes widened in anger and pain.

Kuwanan grimly lifted his katana for another blow. "Surrender, and your death will be swift!"

The assassin's eyes narrowed. Behind him, Daidoji guards approached.

"My death . . ." the assassin murmured. A trail of foaming blood trickled suddenly from his mouth. "My death has already been decided. You will make it no swifter." His voice failed. He writhed in agony, and he fell to his knees, choking.

"Uji!" Kuwanan shouted.

The assassin clutched at Kuwanan's feet. Kuwanan sidestepped the strike. With a gurgling laugh, the man lay still upon the ground. His last breath choked from his throat.

"Uji," Kuwanan snarled, "Send for the Asahina. We must know who sent this man!"

"I am sorry, my lord." The voice was cool, composed. Kneeling beside the assassin's shuddering form, Uji looked into the man's mouth. "He has swallowed a poison pellet. Nothing can be done." Turning away from the corpse, the Daidoji cleaned his bloody sword upon the damp grass.

Kuwanan's roar of rage echoed across the lake, frightening the sleeping cranes that roosted by its shores. They took flight above Kyuden Kakita, calling softly against the stars.

▲ ▲ ▲ ▲ ▲ ▲ ▲ ▲

Kneeling at the door to his brother's chambers, Doji Kuwanan waited for his formal request to be granted. At his side rested a bag containing three severed heads—a pitiful token of loyalty on such a dark night.

"Your petition has been granted, Doji-sama," the guard said as the screens were opened. "The champion bids you enter."

Kuwanan rose smoothly, grasping the bag by its silken neck, and stepped into the chambers. Maids scurried left and right, carrying away broken pottery and rice paper from shattered screens.

Hoturi knelt on the dais, a cup of warm tea in his hand and a bandage about his shoulder. Again, Kuwanan knelt, placing the bag at the edge of the dais.

Hoturi nodded to his brother, noting the tightness in his jaw, the tear through the chest of his kimono. Behind him, Ameiko motioned. An eta—the lowest class of peasant in the empire, trusted only to touch filth and the dead—stepped forward to open the bag.

"My lord," Kuwanan's voice sounded too loud in the small chamber, "I have brought you the head of the assassin who struck down Ikoma Jushin. Further, I bring you the heads of those guardsmen who allowed the assassin to enter the palace, as proof of their honorable seppuku and their final loyalty to the clan."

"Place them with the others on the spikes by the Western road, that all who travel toward Lion lands tomorrow may see our dedication to peace." Weary, Hoturi nodded. "It means only one of the men escaped us."

Kuwanan's head snapped upward. "Escaped?"

Nodding, Hoturi placed his cup on the low table beside him. An eta carried the heads away to be washed and prepared as he had commanded. "During the battle, one of the four assassins . . . changed. It was shinobi."

"Shinobi? The dark magic of the Scorpion?" Kuwanan's throat tightened with anger. "The Scorpion are involved?"

"Assuredly."

"The man I fought in the gardens did not use the Bayushi style, my brother. He fought like an Akodo." Kuwanan paused, wondering if his brash words had angered the champion of the Crane.

Doji Hoturi only nodded. He understood the implications of Kuwanan's discovery far more than did his forceful younger brother.

"Deathseekers."

Kuwanan's training at Toturi's side rose in him, and he remembered the proud march of the Akodo soldiers, the honor in their eyes. "An Akodo would never participate in such an attack. It would be an insult to their ancestors—they would rather die than play the thief in the night."

"The Deathseekers are Lion who have no reason to live, who have been stripped of honor. They beg to throw away their lives in service to their clan. They will die rather than surrender. That is their only duty." Hoturi nodded. "When offered only one way to die with honor, my brother, some men will take it no matter what the cost."

"Who has the authority to command such a thing? And to provide them with shinobi, to hasten their escape?"

"No, Kuwanan." The champion of the Crane thoughtfully rested his chin on his fingers. "Only one escaped. Only one.

"The rest were left to die."

In the quiet pause between words, Doji Hoturi looked up at the graying sky. The scattered clouds turned yellow with approaching dawn. They stretched across the window of his chambers like a veil of propriety.

"The dawn is clear, as all the other dawns have been." Hoturi's voice was calm. "As will be many more dawns to come. There will be no early snow this year. No respite from the Lion will come with the winter. Already, Jushin's retinue has sent a messenger to Matsu Tsuko, informing her of his death in our lands."

Kuwanan nodded. It was to be expected.

"My lord?" the guard at the door, a Doji, stepped beyond the shoji screen and knelt at the edge of the dais. "Another visitor. Shall I turn him away?"

"Who wishes to speak with me at this hour?" Hoturi asked.

"A Crab. Hida Tsuru, of the noble family. "

Kuwanan looked down at the floor by his knees, half-expecting Hoturi to command him to leave. The Crab were no friends to Kuwanan, and he detested their power-hungry champion. His thoughts were well known.

"Bring him in, but only for a few minutes. Ameiko?"

Understanding her duty, the lady nodded, stepping through the screens into their private chamber. If she was needed, she would be called.

Kuwanan bowed and then stood from his position before the dais, joining the two Doji guards behind the champion. Ignoring the mud that stained the knees of his hakima pants, he tightened his obi in order to hide the tear in his shirt.

Hoturi nodded respectfully at his brother. A faint wrinkle at the corner of his eye revealed good-natured amusement at Kuwanan's vanity.

The Hida, however, was in no way amused.

Tsuru stormed in, wearing only his hakima pants and no shirt over his bare, scar-covered chest. Dark, closely cropped hair clung to his sharp cheeks and long jaw, fighting for attention with the wild look in Tsuru's eyes. "Hoturi!-sama," he added belatedly, remembering his position and where he was. Kneeling awkwardly on a thin silk cushion, the Crab bowed to the champion of the Crane before lifting his head to bawl, "What in Jigoku's name is happening?"

All in all, a rather polite entrance. For a Crab.

"Good morning, Hida-san," Hoturi said, using the Crab's family name in order to remind him of the formality of their surroundings. "You are awake early this day."

"And you haven't slept, Crane Lord. They say a hundred assassins have attacked the palace, butchering your entire family." Tsuru's voice was filled with the gravel of sleep, but his body was tensed for battle. "My retainers say the Lion apartments are shrouded in the white of mourning."

Hoturi nodded, reaching to sip from his tea again. After a pause just long enough to incite the Crab, the Crane said, "Ikoma Jushin is dead."

Tsuru's jaw tightened. "Who has done this?"

"Three heads, belonging to the assassins, are on pikes along the western road. The Daidoji are efficient in their revenge."

"So they are. And the Lion will be equally efficient, I am certain."

"The Lion," Hoturi said, glad that his voice was cool, "are to be commended for their bravery." It was not the answer Tsuru had expected, and the Crab was silent before the dais of the Crane Champion. "Their emissary—a bushi of no particular skill—stepped in the way of an assassination attempt planned for myself and my Lady Ameiko." After the morning's tournament, Hoturi could not resist the faint jab toward the Lion. It was the least of the arguments he was about to create. "We thank his family for his courage and for his dedication to the empire. Arrangements will be made to see the body home for burial, with all the honor the Doji can give."

Now the Crab was starting to show his anger. "Honor? A man was murdered in your house. Your guards did not stop it. Their heads—"

"Their heads already rest on pikes beside the assassins."

Tsuru paused, thinking this through. "The Lion died here. Nothing can change that."

Hoturi nodded. "And so you fear for your own life, as I'm sure many of my guests do. I assure you, Tsuru-san, the guards have been doubled, and the assassins will not return."

Puffed up with irritated pride, Tsuru blustered, "Fear? Me? I served on the Great Wall of Kaiu. I have destroyed three oni by my own hand and slaughtered ten legions of goblins! Why should I be afraid of mere men, here in the heart of the empire?"

"Excellent," Hoturi smiled. "Then you will do us the

honor of returning to our other guests and informing them that they too have nothing to fear. I am certain they will trust the word of such an esteemed member of the Crab house."

Trapped again by his pride, Tsuru paused, his face reddening. He nodded. Bowing curtly, he stood and turned on his heel. As the Doji at the door bowed and opened the sliding screens, Tsuru muttered to himself, "I will tell them all. There is nothing to fear in the lands of the Crane."

Hoturi sipped his tea again, pretending not to have heard the insult. Kuwanan's face reddened with anger. Without glancing at his lord, the Doji closed the screen once more, standing in the hallway outside the doorway.

The red clouds of morning touched the corners of the sky, filtering the first rays of the Sun Goddess down onto the earth. As the windows brightened, Kuwanan stepped forward again, allowing his anger to cool into indignation.

"How can you allow him to speak that way? To disrespect your authority?"

Hoturi's demeanor changed abruptly. The last vestiges of his control slipped away. "Kuwanan-san," he barked with such fury that his brother took an involuntary step backward. Hoturi stood, raising himself from the cushion on the dais and stepping down to be level with his brother. In the early morning light, his face seemed carved from ice, the sharp cheekbones and strong jaw perfectly highlighted by the first rays of dawn. "If you believe I have allowed that low animal to have the better of me, perhaps your loyalty to your clan is misplaced."

Kuwanan, eyes wide from Hoturi's sudden assault, regained his footing and lashed out again. "He speaks to you as through you were barely his better—as though the attack was your planning."

"No doubt that is exactly what he has been led, by the Lion, to believe."

"Then why did you not contradict it?"

"If I had, would that not have been proof of its truth?" A

full five breaths passed between them before Hoturi spoke again. "Right now, Tsuru walks through the palace as if at my command, informing the guests that Kyuden Kakita has not been compromised. That alone will speak a hundred scrolls. What do you think the Phoenix and the Unicorn will believe when they see the Crab moving at my will, and despite his rough words, speaking of the safety of my house? I do not care what Tsuru believes. I care what the empire sees. What the houses of the empire believe becomes truth. The defense of our clan is not gained by convincing your enemies of your sincerity. Only of your strength."

Kuwanan glanced at the stoic Daidoji guardsmen that stood behind the dais, their faces as emotionless as stone. They had not questioned their lord, although his motives had surely been as strange to them as they had seemed to Kuwanan.

The samurai felt his face grow red with shame. "Hoturi-sama, forgive me. You are right. It is not my place to question you."

A smile wickedly spread across Doji Hoturi's lips as he placed his hand on Kuwanan's shoulder. "Kuwanan-san, if it is not your place as my brother, then it is no man's place at all."

"Hai, Hoturi-sama." The friendliness that had grown between them as brothers returned, and Kuwanan's broad face broke into a half-hearted grin.

"The Lion have taught you that wars must be fought on the battlefields. Now that you are home," Hoturi continued, walking toward his chambers for some much-needed rest, "you must learn that not all battles can be won with swords."

"Sleep well, Brother."

"Three hours," said Hoturi, watching the Crane guards slide the shoji closed as he stepped through. "No more. There will be much to do once our friend Tsuru has spread the news."

In the silent court chamber behind him, Kuwanan bowed

to the closing screen. For three hours, I will guard your court and house, my brother, thought the young samurai. And then, the battlefield will be yours again, complete with enemies and dangers that even the cunning Daidoji do not yet know.

I pray we have the weapons to fight them.

5   THE EMPEROR'S CITY

The final day of the Festival of the Last Harvest broke with light gray clouds and a bitter wind beneath the bright sunshine of Amaterasu. The waving banners of the Crane still hung in the air above the tournament ground. Within the palace, fires were lit to warm the festival halls. Artisans attempted to out-do one another with their cheer and cleverness. To the sight of a casual guest, it was a magnificent end to a strikingly beautiful four-day festival.

Hoturi stood in his private chambers, the letter still crumpled in his hand. Wind blew softly through open screens, carrying the scent of blossoms not yet touched by frost. The chamber was wide, artistically arranged to suit both convenience and beauty—the perfect room for the champion of the Crane. Yet still, standing in the middle of all this perfection, Doji Hoturi was having one of the worst days of his life.

In Otosan Uchi, four Crane ambassadors had been killed. All the deaths were blamed on 'accident of coincidence.' As accidental, he supposed, as the death of Jushin at the hands of those assassins.

Hoturi walked through his room, keeping his steps as light as possible. As a youth, he had often stomped, an attempt to imitate his father's burly stride. Now he walked with purpose, deliberately keeping his motions under control. With a faint push, the balcony door slid back. The balcony was high, with a view of the gardens unmatched anywhere else in the palace. From this view, Hoturi could see the gardens, the wide fields of the Crane, and the gates of Kyuden Kakita—gates now guarded by six Daidoji soldiers, their weapons readied for battle. So different, Hoturi thought, from the merriment of only a single day ago. Leaning on the ivy-covered stones of the balcony, he watched the wind blow through the trees.

Four Crane, four honest men of standing and culture, were dead by treachery and by the Lion Clan's misplaced pride. Let them burn, Hoturi thought, crushing the carefully written parchment that had come by urgent messenger. Let all Lion burn for their arrogance and their hatred. Since the first Matsu fell before the first Kakita's blade, all Lion have hated all Crane.

It wasn't like the Lion to be so underhanded. Their typical methods included brash attacks, calls for outright war, or insipid bragging to rally their brainless troops. But now, instead of the honest Akodo that once led the clan, a Matsu of no real lineage, no honor, and less courage had claimed the throne of the Lion.

Hoturi felt sick to his stomach over all that had been lost in the coup: the lives of the Scorpion, the honor of the Lion.

Toturi, my friend. What would you think of this, if you were here to make treaties and speak of peace?

He concentrated, remembering the words of Shinsei. "If you are willing to sacrifice yourself for all things, then you can be trusted with the world," read the words of the Thousand

Year Tao. One thousand years ago, the ancient Shinsei had come down from the mountains and taught the people of Rokugan the paths of enlightenment. His words had been carried on through generations of samurai. He had taught of peace and brotherhood, and the temples raised in his name still stood across the empire. Respect among equals. Peace between brothers.

It was time for peace to end, for the Lion to know that the Crane were no longer fodder for their blades.

It was time for war.

"I trust you are finished tearing that apart?" Toshimoko bowed lightly from the chamber archway.

Hoturi raised an eyebrow, surprised to see the sensei. He had not heard Toshimoko come through the main chamber. *Too tangled in my own thoughts*—Hoturi chastised himself. *What if the ninja had returned? Where would he be then?*

Stepping through to the balcony, Toshimoko picked a dead leaf from the thick ivy that obscured the gray stone wall. He wore his katana neatly by his side, undisturbed by death and clean of the blood that had covered it the night before.

Hoturi glanced at him. "Sensei."

"If you're finished," Toshimoko continued, "you can come inside again. It is going to rain today. Might start soon. You're wasting your energy, standing there and encouraging it."

"Four men, Toshimoko. Four men dead in Otosan Uchi, because I could not stop the assassin here."

"Four?" Toshimoko snorted, stepping back into the room and reaching for a half-empty bowl of rice. "Imagine four thousand."

"What?"

Toshimoko looked up. "Four thousand."

Before Hoturi could ask for an explanation, the guard at the door slid open the shoji screen. "My lord," the guard's boyish face was as pale as rice paper, "Daidoji Kugai-san, here to see you."

Understanding, the Crane Champion felt a great weight settle on his slim shoulders. Kugai, chui lieutenant of the scouts sent to the Osari Plains, would abandon his duty for only one reason.

The Lion had begun to march.

A look at the weary, bedraggled Daidoji who knelt outside his chamber confirmed his expectation. "Kugai-san," Hoturi said, motioning for the man to rise. "Speak."

"The armies of the Matsu gather . . . to the north of Osari, my lord." The soldier's words were weary from his rapid journey. Although Kugai was a veteran of many smaller battles, his scarred brow was drawn with tension, and his brown eyes refused to look up from the lacquered wood of the apartment floor.

"How many?"

"More than ten thousand, my lord. At first count."

"And how many Daidoji stand at Osari?" Toshimoko's question was almost rhetorical.

"Four thousand, Sensei. But we have five hundred more men just three days north of here, ordered to come to Kyuden Kakita for the winter. They could be turned northward toward Osari. . . ."

"How long until the Matsu attack?" Hoturi asked, preparing his haori vest and reaching for his swords.

"Fewer than five weeks, my champion. Sooner, if they begin to forage across the border to capture the smaller towns. Most likely, the Daidoji at the Osari Plains will see battle within two."

"How soon can Yoshi-san get an appointment with the emperor?" Hoturi asked Toshimoko.

"Four weeks. No less. For any normal man, even that would be impossible. But Yoshi-sama," Toshimoko used the higher honorific while in front of the Daidoji samurai, "always seems to do the impossible."

"Four weeks is still too long. Even if the emperor immediately grants Kakita Yoshi's request, the Lion will not hear of it until their troops have already marched through the northern fields—the villages of Gusai and Horjintu, and Sayo Castle, with all our winter reserves of grain. If they should get their hands on it," Hoturi clenched his fist with rage, pressing his hand to the low table and fighting to preserve his composure.

Toshimoko's voice was calm. "If they take Sayo Castle before the first snow, the Crane will starve through the winter, and the Lion will continue the attack in the spring. They could even launch a strike against Kyuden Kakita, if the first thaw comes early."

"Kugai-san," Hoturi commanded the kneeling Daidoji. "Rest for seven hours. Then, take forty men, and tell Daidoji Uji to go with you. If anyone can slow the Lion advance, it will be Uji."

"Fighting in the winter," Toshimoko shook his head. "The Lion are surely mad."

"A madman controls all battlefields, Sensei. Unpredictability is the gift of fortune." Hoturi's voice remained somber as he spoke.

"Kakita's words."

"And my own, Toshimoko-san." Hoturi turned again to the Daidoji warrior, "Go."

The Daidoji stood. Sharply bowing, he stepped into the hallway and was gone.

"Come with me, Toshimoko-san." Hoturi left the chamber, placing the ancient sword of the Crane in his obi and turning the hilt into a sparring position.

The corridors of the upper palace were empty of guests, although music filtered through the thin walls and heating corridors. Below, the festival was ending, and guests prepared to turn homeward to spend the winter in memories of the wonder of the Crane court.

On the Osari Plains, the Daidoji would prepare for war.

"Yoshi can speak until his delicate face turns blue, but he will not be able to change the emperor's schedule." Toshimoko said. "We do not have the men ready to fight the Lion. Our troops are lodged for winter. We've already placed them in reserve, and the snows are beginning in the far north. Changing those orders now will mean men die marching, before they ever reach the Lion."

"I can reach the emperor."

Toshimoko stopped in the middle of the hallway, hardly believing his student's confident tone. "How?"

Pacing down a long stairwell of delicately enameled paintings, Hoturi withdrew a starched letter from his vest. The letter sent by Empress Kachiko, its imperial seal still intact, lay pressed against his fingers as he strode toward the lower levels of Kyuden Kakita. "She wishes to see me."

Shocked, Toshimoko paused in the stairwell. After a hushed intake of breath, he nearly shouted. "No."

Hoturi strode on.

The sensei was forced to leap down the stairs to catch up. "You haven't even opened it. She could be telling you of a death at court. She could be . . ." At once lost for words, Toshimoko stepped in front of Hoturi, kneeling and forcing the Crane Champion to stop. "By Lord Kakita himself, Hoturi. Who knows what that viper wants? Burn the letter. Better yet, I'll burn it for you."

"No, Sensei." Hoturi's voice was firm.

"Hoturi-sama . . ."

"Don't kneel to me, Sensei. You've enough at stake here to stand."

Toshimoko nearly leapt to his feet. "It is a trap. She is mistress of lies. Kachiko has never forgiven the Crane for our part in the death of her clan."

"Those deaths were commanded by her husband, the emperor. She cannot condemn us for his orders. And now she controls his motions, keeping his schedule light so that he will not be further burdened by insignificant delays."

"Ten years, and more, Hoturi, since you and she . . ." The sentence trailed away as Hoturi's eyes turned to ice.

Toshimoko whispered, "What can she want with you now, if not treachery?"

For a moment, Hoturi looked as exhausted as Daidoji Kugai had, kneeling on the threshold of his chambers. His gray eyes darkened, and pale hair shook about his shoulders. With a precise, slow motion, he offered the thin parchment to his sensei, lowering the letter so the mon was clearly visible on the folded sheets. "Open it."

"Hoturi . . ." Toshimoko shook his head, the long braid thumping lightly against his muscular shoulder blades. "I know what happened between you, before Kachiko was married. Half the court of the empire knew. You didn't exactly make it a secret." The steel in Hoturi's back stiffened, and the young champion half-turned to leave. "Student, listen. Understand. What was between you . . . has died." Lowering his voice, the old Kakita nodded his head gently. "It died on the day we took Otosan Uchi."

"Open it." Emotionless. "She wants to see me. She will see me, and when I am there, I will speak to the emperor and force the Lion to retreat by the command of the Imperial Hantei." His eyes narrowed, and his hand clenched into a fist. For a moment, Toshimoko could see the boiling anger behind Hoturi's gray eyes. Then, as suddenly as it had come, it faded and was gone. "And once they have retreated, Toshimoko, we will destroy them."

It was a statement of fact, not a boast, nor merely the words of a man hoping for the best, and the sensei knew it.

"Go ahead, Toshimoko. It doesn't matter what it says. I do not have to hear the words to know her mind. And when you are done, burn it if you wish. It makes no difference to me." The letter began to fall from Doji Hoturi's hand, and Toshimoko reached to take it. "There is nothing you can say or do, Sensei, that will instruct me in this. I am going to Otosan Uchi, and I will convince her to let me see the Hantei emperor."

As his student pushed past him, Toshimoko felt the light

weight of the letter in his hand. For a moment, staring at Hoturi's retreating form, he felt age settle into his bones, shifting beneath layers of callused and weathered skin. The beat of his heart seemed distant, and he felt its echo in Hoturi's fading footsteps. For a moment, he considered throwing the letter into the fireplace nearby, watching its precise calligraphy twist and burn in effigy. Imagining her face charred by the fire.

Toshimoko shook his head, clearing it of anger and hatred. Those were not the ways to enlightenment, nor were they the virtues of the Kakita Academy that he struggled to uphold. Calmness replaced doubt. Years of discipline tore away the veil of emotion.

Patiently, Toshimoko opened the parchment, breaking the delicate seal and listening to the faint crumble of rice paper beneath his hands. Two lines of calligraphy blackened the white paper.

My Lord of the Crane,
Your presence is requested in the Imperial Palace at your earliest convenience.

No formal name had been signed to the thin rice paper, but the mon of the Imperial House had been imprinted into the delicate weave, marking its contents as the true words of a member of the Hantei family. It had to have come from Kachiko.

"Damn the woman," Toshimoko said, dropping the paper into the flames. "And damn the man."

As the paper blackened and curled, he could almost hear her laughter.

▲ ▲ ▲ ▲ ▲ ▲ ▲ ▲

Two days passed as guests made their way out of the Kakita provinces, two days of enduring courtly farewells.

When the last guests had gone, Hoturi spoke alone with Daidoji Uji, his most trusted lieutenant. It was time to leave, and Hoturi would not see a minute wasted. Each moment that passed was one more step for the Lion troops, one more heimin killed by the Matsu.

"Sir," Uji said as he saddled Hoturi's shaggy pony. "I feel I must warn you. There is danger along the roads to Otosan Uchi. The Lion may have heard that you are leaving. A troop of Daidoji guardsmen . . ."

"Would only make travel slower and more difficult," he cut in. "No, Uji-san, this is a journey I must make without your men."

Evening hung thickly about them, and Kyuden Kakita's white walls were shadowed in the first touches of twilight. Even the heimin servants had been dismissed. Only the lights of the castle gleamed palely in the night sky.

"I don't presume to judge your commands, my lord." The Daidoji shoved a lock of his unruly black hair behind his ear. Without his helm and the leather mask, Uji seemed almost common. His narrow eyes could be mistaken for those of any other samurai, but the serpentine movements of his hands as he talked gave away his true nature. "But you may be in danger."

"My sword is enough."

"For one, perhaps. Or three. But a command of troops? If you were to be captured . . ."

Hoturi checked the pony's gear carefully, tugging at the straps that held the thick cotton saddlebags to the wooden curve of the saddle. "If I travel with even ten men, the Lion will know it. I wish to reach the Imperial City without their interference. The only way to do that is to hide my passage."

"Yes, my lord." Uji's voice was sullen but contained. The silence in the empty courtyard was cold, and the open gates of Kyuden Kakita gleamed faintly in the dull light of the half-moon. Hoturi glanced once more at the palace, wishing

Toshimoko had come to bid him farewell. There was no sign of his old sensei.

Always clever, Uji nodded. "He left this afternoon, my lord. Claimed to be on his way to visit a sick relative."

Hoturi grunted, "Sick, by Doji's armor. He went to the geisha houses in Osuka village, and we all know it."

"As you say, Lord Champion. Have a good journey." Uji held the pony's reins as Hoturi stepped into the saddle, drawing his cloak and hood tightly around his face. The cotton was brown rather than the blue of the Crane, to hide his identity as he rode north. Although the lands between Kyuden Kakita and Otosan Uchi were controlled by the Crane, Hoturi would take no chances.

"Traitors hide behind masks and mon," he whispered, looking up once more at the palace.

Of course she was there. Her hair loosed for rest, she stood on their balcony and held a small fan in her ivory hands. She did not look down at him—it might have drawn attention from the few other visitors left in the days after the festival—but stared quietly at the moon above.

"Guard her for me, Uji-san."

"Yes, Lord Doji. She will come to no harm."

Hoturi looked toward his wife's silent form and thought, I wish I could love you. Then he turned his pony and pressed his heels to its furred sides.

As his pony trotted amiably along the forest path, Hoturi wished he had one of the rolling steeds of the Unicorn. Their tall legs and agile movements gave the Unicorn an advantage in battle, and they were far easier to ride than the stubby ponies the other clans bred. The sons of Shinjo were notoriously jealous of their steeds, and few were ever allowed outside their far northern provinces. A shame. With one of their kind, the ride to Otosan Uchi would have taken half as long.

Frustrated, Hoturi kicked the pony into a faster pace, hoping to arrive at a travelers' grove by midnight. From there, he would trek northward for a week, more if Lion agents watched the main causeways, and longer still if the villages along the way were infested with plague.

He rode in silence, allowing the pony to choose its path and settling into the gentle movement of a long night's ride.

Sometime later, a faint light spilled across the dirt road, casting twisted shadows from the trees. Hoturi paused his steed and slid from the saddle, checking his sword to be certain it was ready. Leading his pony forward, he glanced into the clearing, expecting to see a small caravan or a group of merchants resting for a long journey north.

Toshimoko's voice called from the fireside, "You're late, student, and your food's nearly cold. I expect you'll clear the pony after dinner, so come and eat while you can." Without even a trace of his whimsical smile, he held out a bowl of steaming soup and tapped the coals with a hickory branch.

"Old fool. If I'd known, I would have ordered you to stay at the palace."

"Perhaps I'm an old fool," the man smiled, "but I'm here to make sure you live to be one as well."

Hoturi accepted the soup, a resigned smile on his lips. "I could order you not to come with me."

"I'm not coming with you," Toshimoko said. "I'm going to visit my sick cousin, Yugoro. Yugoro happens to live in Otosan Uchi, of course, but what's the harm in that?"

"All right, Sensei. You win." Sitting by the fire, he lifted the soup to his lips and tasted the warm broth appreciatively. "But I'm not washing the bowls."

"You never do, my student." Toshimoko chuckled, lying back and placing his head on folded arms. "You never do."

The two men slept that night by the fire, listening to the sounds of the forest and the faint movements of their ponies. They were both tired when the sun rose, but Hoturi felt the need to put as much distance as possible between himself and Kyuden Kakita. Having consented to wearing the brown and gray of a ronin, Toshimoko pushed himself into the saddle of his wide-bellied pony.

They rode for two days through forest and glen, following the least-traveled Kakita roads. Hoturi's pony knew the way to Osuka village, and did not care for his interventions. Hoturi felt a kinship to the beast. For most of his life, he had been a samurai, bound only by the code of bushido and his duty to the Crane. Then, occasionally, he was reminded that he bore an additional burden—that of champion. It was like a rider on his back, driving him along the path with a steel whip and iron reins.

Unlike the pony, Hoturi wouldn't submit meekly to the demands. There was more to life, much more, and it was time that being Crane Champion proved its worth to him, as well as to the clan.

Kachiko . . .

He shook his head angrily. Enough of that. Hoturi patted the pony's brown neck and listened to the steady beat of hooves against hard-packed earth. "We'll need to stop for food," he commented, feeling the faint bulges in his bag. "I have enough for only three days, and the forest is barren this time of year."

"I taught you that," Toshimoko said grumpily.

"Osuka is within a day's ride. We can refill our bags before we cross the northern fields. At this time of year, we should be able to cross the Twisted River without trouble, so long as there is little rain. Until we discover how far the Lion have entered our land and where the plague has centered, we'll need to be wary." He looked northward, through the thick forest and overhanging growth.

Toshimoko nodded as they rode along the forest path.

The village of Osuka was a bustling place of commerce and prosperity, large enough with trade and the traveler's road to support two teahouses and a single geisha establishment.

"When we arrive, I must remember to say hello to Meiko." The sensei smiled. "She can sing like the Fortunes themselves, and her lineage is good. She was an Isawa before her bankrupt father was forced to sell her to the geisha Oba-san.

Now she lives with her song, and a more beautiful girl I have not seen since . . ."

"Since the one before her. If you believe that fable, I'll sell you the Scorpion lands. You're a romantic, Toshimoko."

"Perhaps I am," the old man laughed, pounding his pony's shoulder gently. "But I am a lucky man."

"You are. . . ."

His comment died away as rapid hoofbeats came from the woods ahead. They were wild, scrambling madly across the rocks. After a moment, the white-eyed pony crashed through the trees. Its hooves and legs were covered in thick red mud, and the Daidoji on its back clung with the last desperate strength of honor. As Toshimoko and Hoturi reined in their startled animals, the third horse reared suddenly, nearly throwing its injured rider.

"Hold! Hold!" cried Hoturi, sliding down from his steed and calling to the man on the frightened pony. There was no response. With a swift movement, Hoturi leapt to grasp the fluttering reins. He drew the rearing pony into the center of the road.

The soldier had been tied to the pony's back with a length of torn silk banner. Its blue was stained with crimson blood. The bushi's eyes rolled back into his head with the effort of staying conscious. "Osuka . . ." the soldier gasped. "Lion . . . have reached Osuka. Must tell the Kakita. . . ."

"By Shinsei." Toshimoko's oath was softened by disbelief.

"His wounds have been bandaged," Hoturi spoke rapidly, "but this man won't live another day. The belly wound is deep, and there's blood all through the wrappings." Looking up at the sensei he said, "This was a quick wrapping, not meant to last."

"Only to get him to Kyuden Kakita."

Hoturi nodded.

"We can reach the village in two hours if we push the ponies." Toshimoko handed Hoturi the reins to his mount as he turned away from the Daidoji's horse. "We cannot help this man. But we may be able to help the troops at Osuka."

Smacking the frightened horse's flank, Hoturi sent the Daidoji toward Kyuden Kakita. "The pony will carry him home, and that will be message enough for Uji." Striding to his own beast, Hoturi leaped into the saddle with a practiced motion, clearing his katana and wakizashi. "We are needed elsewhere."

Their steeds were only too grateful to be away from the smell of the dying man and his terrified mount. They leaped to the path with swift hooves.

▲ ▲ ▲ ▲ ▲ ▲ ▲ ▲

Toward the middle of the evening, the two men reached Osuka. Their ponies staggered with fatigue. The valley was filled with flowering cherries that had lost their leaves and stood bare in the autumn twilight. It seemed almost peaceful from the hill on which the two men rode, but beneath the calmness of the evening hung the tension of war.

Pines spiraled down into a fertile valley, its rice fields drained and empty for the winter. Yet where the village should have been, there were no lights, no bustling passage of latecomers seeking a teahouse in which to rest. Instead, they saw only a thick mist that shrouded long groves. As they approached, the stench struck them with the force of a gloved hand. Bitter, the "mist" was smoke, filled with the scent of charred flesh.

The two men cautiously rode downhill, watching for any sign of movement. The air was still. The silence was broken only by the harsh cawing of carrion birds and the crackling of fires within the burned buildings. A few black shapes stood where once there had been a prosperous village. The road into Osuka had been churned into acrid mud by the trudging of a hundred armored feet.

Through the smoke, Hoturi made out more distinct

figures—a house, broken and smoking beneath twin crags of rock, the shattered remains of blistered metal in what once had been a blacksmith's shop. Hoturi rode slowly through the village streets. Beside him, Toshimoko covered his face with a scrap of rough brown cloth, tying it behind his head to shield his nose and eyes from the smoke.

Hoturi's pony stepped through a broken torii arch. To one side, near a larger crevasse of rock, three more buildings burned. Bodies lay piled near the last, their blue armor scorched and twisted in the heat of the fires. Their blackened skin reeked.

Fire had destroyed the village of Osuka and trapped her brave defenders. Fire had been the killer, but the Lion were the cause.

"Hoturi-sama," Toshimoko called, motioning for his student to return. Toshimoko's pony stood beyond the perimeter of the still-burning village.

Hoturi approached and saw what had attracted the sensei's attention. A plain of rice paddies had become a battlefield, filled with blackened skeletons and more smoke and flame. The Daidoji had made a stand against their attackers, giving their lives to defend the holdings of the Crane. They had died for their valor, but perhaps somewhere in the surrounding hills and forests, some Osuka villagers still lived. They would make their way south to the castle of the Kakita. The Lion would surely follow.

There had been no siege, no pitched battle. Although the Daidoji had fought bravely, their numbers had been too small. They had been decimated.

Hoturi rode through the smoking field, trying to ignore the stinking bodies of his clansmen. The faces of the Daidoji leered through blackened flesh, their swords broken and their tattooed arms outstretched on the bloodied ground.

Amid the blue and silver of the Crane, an occasional Lion corpse remained. Drawing his horse up beside a dead Matsu, the champion of the Crane gazed with hatred at the mon.

"They aren't headed to Kyuden Kakita," Toshimoko called from across the field. "Their tracks head north." He turned his nervous steed. "The Lion will have more troops waiting there. Our Kyuden has over four thousand standing soldiers. The Lion cannot afford a siege." As he spoke, another curl of smoke rose beyond the forest.

Hoturi heard the sounds of clashing blades. "Toshimoko!"

Nodding, the dueling master spurred his pony. Together, they chased the sound across the field and into the nearby woods. Once in the forest, even the churning noise of hooves could not drown out the scream of soldiers in combat.

Between three large oaks, in a clearing just outside the village, a small group of Daidoji stood back to back. Around them circled a troop of Matsu, cleaning their blades. The body of a fallen Crane lay among them.

Looking up, the leader of the Lion scout party scowled at Toshimoko and Hoturi, mistaking them for clanless ronin. "Who do you fight for, ronin, or do you simply seek your own grave?" There were fifteen Lion, armed and armored in the colors of the Matsu, and they growled at the interruption of their sport.

"Ride on, ronin," called the leader of the Daidoji warriors, bravely ignoring the blood that stained his broken shoulder plate. "This is not your affair."

Hoturi recognized him as Daidoji Tashima, youngest son of a minor lord in the far southern lands of the Crane. He spoke with the confidence of a man who was not afraid of death and the calmness of a samurai who would not die alone.

"What's this?" Hoturi growled, lowering himself from the pony. "Fifteen men against three? The Lion have lost their honor. Let me find it for you."

Red-faced, the Lion lieutenant stepped toward Hoturi, his hand reaching dangerously for the hilt of his katana. "I am Matsu Hotakura, son of Matsu Demasu, third son of the General Ayoda. I served the Lion at the Battle of Kyu Pass, when the goblins of the Shadowlands slipped past the Wall and dared threaten the village of Kien-shu. It was I," he began to shout, "who killed the ronin Hametsuda when he dared insult my lord. It was I who cut down the bandit lord Yugoro, and scarred his face so badly that his own children will not touch him for fear of receiving a similar wound. Who are you, filth, to question my honor?"

Stepping lightly away from his pony, Toshimoko shook his head in mild amusement.

Hoturi rocked from his toes to his heels as if pondering the Lion's question. "Who am I? I am the man who will kill you."

The silence that followed Hoturi's bold remark lasted only a single sharp moment. The Lion drew his sword.

Two strokes followed. Hoturi's blade slid past Hotakura's. Amazement grew on the Lion's face as a trickle of blood stained his lips. The Lion's hand crept through the open wound in his chest.

Pausing to shake the blood from his weapon, Doji Hoturi looked back at his opponent. Hotakura fell.

The other Lion scouts roared in fury. Together, they leaped forward. Two were dead before their hands could reach their weapons. Toshimoko spun lightly back toward the others, a smile on his lips.

Raising his sword in a vicious blow, a Matsu guardsman charged Hoturi. Twisting his blade, Hoturi slid it along his opponent's weapon. As the swords met, Hoturi lodged a solid kick between the man's ribs. The Lion staggered backward.

Two more took his place, their katanas shining in the scattered light.

Stunned into action, Daidoji Tashima raised his sword and screamed a fierce kiai shout. "You do not fight alone!" With a vicious slash, he struck the legs from under a charging Matsu.

The other two Crane samurai attacked, their faces pale. Even with the help of the unknown ronin, the odds were more than two to one.

Three Lion fought Hoturi. Leaping back, the young prince used terrain to his advantage. He parried one sword and then another, dodging beneath the low limbs of a pine. Behind him, the Lions' ornate armor was caught in the sticky sap of the evergreen. They were forced to cut through the low-hanging limbs.

Toshimoko meanwhile bickered cheerfully with another two samurai, correcting their movements.

"Too slow. Were you two trained by Matsu Kioda?" The Crane sensei smiled, deflecting a blade with a lightning-fast snap of his katana. "The man is old and weary. He has taught you to fight like old men!" Disarming one of the Matsu, Toshimoko slapped the other Lion on the rump with the flat of his blade. "Faster!" Pausing to stare angrily at the confused soldiers, Toshimoko pointed at the fallen blade. "Pick that up!" The Lion stumbled for his blade as his companion stepped back in shock. "Now, boy," Toshimoko took his stance and resheathed his blade, "try again."

Hoturi sliced through the shoulder straps of a Matsu's armor and lodged his sword in the samurai's throat. There was no rush of emotion as the Matsu fell, no overwhelming sense of right or wrong—only the knowledge that ten thousand more waited to the north.

Leaving a man screaming on the ground, Tashima spun. His blade rushed through the chest of another Lion. The cut was too deep, and the katana stuck, torn from Tashima's hand.

One of the last Matsu charged the disarmed man.

Toshimoko lightly turned aside the Matsu's strike and, with a single massive blow, killed the Matsu.

Tashima stared, wide-eyed, at the blood trailing down the old man's arm. "I know you," he whispered, glancing at Hoturi as he drew his sword from the fallen Lion. "I know you both."

One Lion still stood, his sword lowered defensively. He pressed his back against a pine tree and glared at his opponents. "There are fifty more men on the other side of this ridge. They have heard our screams. They will come for us, and when they do, they will kill you."

Tashima responded, "They will come for you, Lion, but when they do, you will be cold and dead."

"We are fifty. You are four."

The stroke was swift. Hoturi watched a thin trail of red trickle down his blade as the last Matsu fell.

"We are four," he said quietly, "but we are Crane."

"He was right, Honorable Lord," Daidoji Tashima said, using a scrap of silk to bind an open wound in his left arm. "They are fifty, and we are four. We cannot stop them before they reach the next village."

"What is the next village?" Toshimoko asked, sheathing his katana.

"Haikeun, my lord."

Hoturi shook his head. "No, Daidoji-sama." The Daidoji's eyes widened at the honorific, and widened more as Hoturi and Toshimoko both bowed low. "We are but traveling ronin, once employed in the service of the Crane."

Their eyes wide, the two Daidoji glanced at each other warily. "If my lord says so,"

"Your lord says nothing," Toshimoko grumped, kneeling to look down at the dead Lion. "But this mad ronin does. Perhaps it would be better if you forgot your lord, and showed the ronin where the Lion march."

"Of course . . . of course." Bowing, the Daidoji pointed to the north. "Leave your horses here. It is not far, and we know the path. Master Daidoji Ukamo-san had sent us to scout the armies to the north. When we returned to Osuka, we found that the village had been destroyed, no more than a day ago. There is something else. The village of Haikeun still has travelers from the Kakita Festival. A young Phoenix there bragged of his swordsmanship—"

"Phoenix?" Toshimoko asked. "Was he a young man, rather pale, thin eyes and a twisted smile?"

"You knew him?"

"Ah . . ." Toshimoko looked away. "We met at the festival."

"He was challenged to a duel by a passing Crane," Tashima continued, "and because of his injuries, has been forced to remain in the village."

Toshimoko looked almost sheepish for a moment. "Keen as Shinsei's wisdom, indeed."

Hoturi glared at his sensei. "Show us the way, Tashima-san. We will follow."

6 ARMIES ON THE MARCH

Matsu Gohei marched at the head of a small legion. He watched Crane heimin leave their fields and houses, running in terror from his troops. The path behind them was strewn with Osuka villagers. Ahead, another village rested in soft green valleys. Its roofs shone in the bright sunlight. Gohei smiled, testing the shoulder plates of his armor. Battle would be a welcome reprieve from the day's march.

"My lord," a scout ran from the rear of the small army, bowing low. "The last group of scouts from Osuka have not returned, and several soldiers report seeing a party of ronin traveling through the woods toward Haikeun."

"Ronin?" Gohei's dark eyes flashed beneath his large golden helm. He was not a large man, but his thick shoulders and wide stance conveyed the impression of a towering mountain. A mane of silk tassels upon his family armor shook as he signaled orders to his second-in-command. The army would continue its march toward the village. In a grating voice, he said, "How many ronin?"

"Fewer than ten, my lord. The reports are mixed." The Lion armies made good use of their scouts, sending them ahead and behind in order to maintain steady information. They knew the lessons of the first Akodo, master of war: Know the terrain, and you will know the enemy.

"Even ten ronin are no match for us." Gohei spoke to himself, but the scout bowed and agreed with a soldierly shout. "Continue the march on the village. We meet with Agetoki-sama's troops in fifteen days, and we need the provisions this Crane stronghold will supply."

"Hai, Matsu-sama!" Bowing again, the scout leapt to rejoin his unit.

Gohei returned to the front of the legion and bowed to his commander. The mounted man was Matsu Hametsu, a member of the Lion's guard and a powerful warrior. Although he outranked Gohei, the younger man was well respected among the Lion.

Hametsu glared down at Gohei, suddenly angry. Too cocky, too presumptuous, and his name held few honors of its own. A prestigious lineage does not make a powerful warrior, but Gohei seemed determined to raise his fame within the empire—no matter what the cost.

Marching though Crane lands toward Sayo Castle was one way to achieve that goal. While the Crane chased these small legions, Tsuko and her larger force would continue relatively unmolested. The Crane could not rally their pitiful Daidoji legions in time and would not risk dividing their troops. They were, as always, predictable. They would rise up with childish voices in the emperor's court, begging the Hantei to force the Lion back.

Even the emperor could not command withdrawal of troops he did not know existed. The Lion marched legion by legion, preparing to meet at the palace of the Crane.

At the entrance to the village, a tall torii arch stood. Its red mahogany pillars rose over the hard-packed road. As the leaders approached it, another scout ran toward them. His white face contrasted with the brown and gold gi of the Lion Clan.

"My lords," he gasped, crouching to his knees before Hametsu's shaggy pony.

"Speak," Gohei snarled before the senior officer could reply.

The scout glanced up at Hametsu, and the chui nodded. "There is a samurai at the gates of the village, Lord Hametsu-sama. He says . . ." the scout winced, "He says the Lion may not pass through the village. If they do, he says . . . he says they will die."

Snorting, Gohei reached for his sword to kill the scout. "Fear? I see fear in your eyes at the sight of one man?"

Hametsu raised his fist before Gohei could draw. "Silence, lieutenant!" he shouted. Gohei dropped his hand. Addressing the runner once more, Hametsu said, "Where are the others in your guard?"

"I beg your pardon, Hametsu-sama, but they are all dead."

"Dead?" Gohei bawled, his sharp-nosed face turning red.

"Hai, my lord!" The scout pressed his forehead to the earth. "The man has killed them all."

This time, the Lion commander did not stop Gohei's blow. The runner's head rolled in the dirt of the village road.

Staring forward, Gohei saw a shadowed figure standing in the village arch. Wind blew dust through the empty streets behind him. Within their houses, peasants hid, covering their children's eyes and praying for the Seven Fortunes to turn away the Lion army. Another man, also dressed in the gray and brown of a masterless ronin, appeared in the arch. In two of the houses closest to the road, an unknown number of Daidoji archers waited. They had already cut down the Matsu scouts who had approached too closely.

Hametsu shouted, "Ronin!"

The echo rumbled through the army, and the soldiers ceased their march. Gohei raced up and down the lines, commanding the men to hold their ground upon the road. They would be ready to charge when Hametsu gave the word.

"Ronin!" Hametsu shouted again. "Approach me, and I will spare your life when I destroy this village. The battle between Lion and Crane is none of your affair. If you seek to prove your sword, prove it within my command!" The offer was a good one. Most ronin would gladly trade their skulking days for the life of a soldier.

But this man shook his head. "No, Lion. I have more honor than that. How much do you have, that you would face me with an army at your back?" The young man raised his arms, his hair wrapped in a hood that hid his features.

Angered, Hametsu yelled, "I am Matsu Hametsu, son of—"

Cutting off the commander's family line, the second ronin shouted, "Son of the dog that spawned you, Hametsu of the Matsu house." Picking a twig from his teeth, the ronin smiled. "Fight, or turn your troops and put your tail between your legs."

Roaring in rage, Hametsu leaped from his horse and reached for his family's blade. "When I have killed you, ronin, I will kill your old grandfather and feed his bones to the crows!"

The first man smiled. "You are a fool as well as a dog, Lion, to believe you will ever have that chance. But before you die, you must command your troops to leave this place and march back to Lion lands. If they stay here, they too will be killed."

"By the heimin of this village?" Hametsu laughed, placing his weapon in his obi. "I think not. You are the only fools here!"

Twin bows tensed above them, their arrows shining in the sunlight. "How many archers do you have, ronin?"

"Enough."

"Do you hear that, men?" Hametsu said, handing his reins to another samurai. "When I die, these ronin ask that you leave."

The soldiers laughed, trusting in their lord's prowess.

▲▲▲▲▲▲▲▲

Hoturi smiled bitterly beneath his hood. "I challenge you, Matsu Hametsu, to a duel to prove your worth. When your body is spilled upon the ground at my feet, the crows will pick at your entrails to find one single scrap of honor. But they will fail, and they will starve."

"My lord . . ." Gohei snarled, opening his hands before Hametsu in a gesture of obeisance before his enraged commander could respond. The two men spoke briefly.

Leaning toward Hoturi, Toshimoko whispered, "The Lion will never agree. He isn't angry enough."

"Ssh, old man. All will be fine."

"Hoturi, if the Lion attack, we can't hold them off alone."

Smiling, the champion of the Crane turned to his sensei and winked. "I spoke to Shiba Katsuda when we arrived in the village. He remembers you well, Sensei."

Toshimoko's ears turned red, but his voice did not change. "Katsuda is wounded and of no help to us."

"He has been more help than you can imagine, Sensei." Hoturi's lightly teasing voice was drowned out by the shouting Lion.

Gohei fell to his knees before Hametsu as the commander yelled orders to their men.

Toshimoko shrugged, his eyes hardly betraying the fear of a man facing fifty armed soldiers. He stepped back toward the arch once more.

In the road, Matsu Hametsu turned, stepping away from the body of the army and leaving behind a very angry lieutenant. "Ronin!" shouted Hametsu. "I, son of Matsu Akui, commander of the southern guard and honored by Lady Tsuko-sama, accept your challenge. Where do you want your ashes to rest after I have cut your head from your body?"

The Lion cheered their lord's bravery, raising spears and shouting his name as a war cry.

Hametsu grinned broadly before drawing his metal mempo across his face and attaching it to his helmet.

"Do not worry where to lay my bones, Lion," Hoturi grinned, enjoying the bloodlust that flooded up. "But what of your men, when you fall?"

"I have commanded Gohei-san," the Lion saluted his kneeling lieutenant, "to return to Tsuko, in the event that I am killed. He will not order the attack."

Glancing at Toshimoko, Hoturi nodded.

The Lion took a stance just in front of the village's gleaming torii arch and lifted his hand. "Come forward, ronin filth," he chuckled, eyes bright behind the metal fangs of his mempo, "and feel the claw of a true Lion."

Walking carefully, Hoturi moved toward the Lion commander, his hand light on the hilt of his sheathed blade. Tradition demanded that contestants in a formal duel be unarmored, unafraid to face death, but the Lion wore heavy battle armor. Hoturi had only his gi and hakima pants. Lighter, more able to move, it would seem Hoturi had the advantage, but the Lion's competence showed in his every step, and his armor could prove a mild deterrent, even to Hoturi's strong blade. Only time would tell the difference between a patient man and a dead one.

Hoturi felt anger rise behind his eyes, rage at the Lion for their greed, their arrogance, and the lives they had already taken. His gaze locked with Matsu, forcing him to relent.

The Lion moved into a martial pose.

Hoturi felt the world recede, narrowing to two men— himself and Matsu Hametsu.

The world itself stopped in the instant of a duel, to watch the hearts of the contestants. In the second before the strike, Hoturi could feel the Celestial Heavens watching, and he prayed that they were pleased.

The swords cut forward in the same instant, piercing each other's guard to thrust toward the throat. At the last moment, the Lion's courage broke. He turned aside Hoturi's blow rather than striking. The swords turned, racing down their steel blades and shifting apart to prepare for another assault. Without hesitation, Hametsu cut toward Hoturi's legs, expecting the sword to be deflected.

Hoturi allowed the strike to go through but stepped nimbly beyond the blade's length. He slashed upward with a stroke intended to cut the Lion's arm in two.

Reeling back, Hametsu raised his sword and cut toward Hoturi's body, but too late. Already, the other man's sword was within his guard, cutting sideways through his back and dividing the length of his spine.

The Crane Champion stepped back and watched the Lion struggle. A soft noise escaped the Matsu's lips. Before he could scream, dishonoring his ancestors, Hoturi's stroke parted the head from the body. One blow, and the great commander of the southern guard was dead.

The soldiers stared in shock, their spears frozen.

"Leave this land!" Hoturi shouted, lifting his eyes from his beaten opponent.

Confused, the soldiers milled about in their lines, looking toward their lieutenant for an order—any order that would bring sense to their commander's death. A roar of fury escaped some throats. Others, stone silent, only raised their swords and prepared for the charge.

"I cannot order the charge," Gohei shouted. His voice broke with anger. "I cannot command you to seize this village or to destroy those who have stolen our brave commander's life."

Toshimoko stepped toward Hoturi, his hand on his

sword. Now was the moment between life and death. The world had narrowed once more.

"But I can give you all a day's leave," Gohei snarled, fiercely drawing his sword from its sheath. "And while I cannot tell you how to spend it—" the soldiers' eyes gleamed as they realized their new commander's intent— "I can surely show you how I intend to spend mine."

Almost as one, the Lion charged.

Arrows sprang through the air, launched by the watchful Daidoji. For each arrow, a man fell, but the volley could not slow the charge.

Hoturi and Toshimoko raced into the village. Positioning themselves between two mud buildings in the village, they prepared for battle.

The sensei looked soberly toward his student as the first Matsu reached them. "Old times, Hoturi?"

"That's right, old man," Hoturi grinned. He parried the Lion's first slash.

"Stop grinning!"

"Never. Not while we're winning." Quickly cutting through a Lion, Hoturi began a series of intricate attacks. Blood glistened on his sword.

Toshimoko dispatched another soldier and then a third. "Winning?" he exclaimed loudly. He caught the sounds of heimin screams, and the faint smell of smoke as the first buildings were set aflame.

"Let's go." Hoturi and the sensei dodged through buildings, cutting down Matsu guards with swift strokes.

A pair of Matsu tore open the door to a large house. Within, a heimin man held his rake aloft, daring to defend himself against the samurai. Laughing, the Matsu chopped the rake in two, stepping toward the heimin and his young family.

Hoturi leapt toward the doorway.

One of the Matsu shifted his sword to catch Hoturi's charge.

Parrying with a swift stroke, Hoturi turned the Lion's blade into the wall. Metal thudded through packed earth.

The second man hurled a tanto toward the Crane's face. The tanto missed, but narrowly.

Hoturi caught the Lion in the face with a solid punch and sent the man staggering backward.

The other Matsu withdrew his sword from the wall.

Hoturi dodged for the door but saw three more Lion outside, lighting fire to another hut. There would be no easy escape. He parried the first Matsu's blows and kept him in the other man's way. The tactic would not last long. Already Hoturi's arms grew weary.

The peasant struggled to quiet her child as the three samurai tore at each other with brightly shining blades.

Hoturi kicked one Matsu, feeling the Lion's knee crunch.

The Lion staggered backward and fell. From the ground, he cut at Hoturi's leg. The sword tip sliced into Hoturi's thigh. Seeing blood stain the Crane's clothing, the Lion growled victoriously. He punched a gauntleted hand into Hoturi's wound.

Blazing agony shot through the Crane Champion's leg. Grunting, Hoturi stumbled. He chopped his katana through the Lion's body. The strike was messy, and the sword shivered as it reached the solid earth floor. Sweat dripped into his eyes. Hoturi tried to stand, struggling to draw his katana from the dead Matsu's body.

The second Lion stood above him. Mocking laughter rang from his lips as his katana descended.

Just before the blow could fall, Hoturi felt a presence beside him. Half standing, half leaping, Toshimoko fell through the open doorway. His blade twisted to parry the Lion's fatal strike. The Lion's blow ricocheted from Toshimoko's sword, sliding down the blade and sinking deep into the sensei's arm. Without a sound, Toshimoko's katana rose again, cutting the Matsu three times before he could fall. The Lion didn't have time to savor the wound he had given the swordmaster. His body struck the floor, and his eyes closed in death.

Outside, in the burning village, a horn sounded. Looking up from his bleeding shoulder, Toshimoko said, "More Lion?" He grimaced. "We haven't finished with these yet." Pain etched his face, but his voice and his sword were steady.

"No, Toshimoko." Hoturi stood slowly, testing his lightly injured leg. "That's not the sound of Lion troops. That's a northern troop cadence."

A shadow in the open street proved Hoturi's words. Three Lion lowered themselves into battle stances.

Hoturi stepped out of the hut.

The Lion soldiers roared to their companions and raised their blades.

A single Phoenix samurai-ko, her black hair shining over her flame-colored armor, stood wreathed in the smoke of Haikeun's buildings. She smiled peacefully, holding her sword gently in one hand. Behind her, two men stood, their robes shifting in the wind of the flames. As the Lion marched toward her, the young woman smiled and raised her sword.

At her cue, the men began to chant. The flames around her soared to the sky with the power of the kami. The Phoenix shugenja lifted the spirits of the flame to do their bidding. Chanting the mantra of the fire kami, they called to the blaze, summoning the heart of each flickering flame to life. Fire danced, arching higher above the street. It pulsed with the sound of the shugenjas' voices. It twisted across the dark road and glared from the sword of the samurai-ko.

The woman advanced through the shifting flames, stepping within the roaring inferno. As fire danced around her, the Lion retreated, their steps unsure.

With a powerful lunge, the Phoenix was upon them. Her bright sword was shrouded in burning flame.

The Lion screamed as its white-hot power struck through them. One was consumed in flame, and the other was cut apart by the samurai-ko's sword. As the third Lion fled from the onslaught, the woman smiled behind a thick veil of black hair.

"Honorable Hoturi-sama," she shouted over the battle sounds. "It seems you have a fight on your hands. Can we be of service?" Her eager grin belied the serious words.

"We would never begrudge you any kind of amusement, Tsukune-san!" Hoturi smiled at the staring Toshimoko for a moment, and then bowed in return to the samurai-ko. "Shiba Tsukune-san, this is my sensei, Kakita Toshimoko-san."

"Introductions can wait, my lord," Tsukune saluted both men. Her sword smoked from the heat of the Phoenix flames. Suddenly, through the smoke, Hotusi could see twenty more Phoenix bushi stood, confident and silent, behind Tsukune. With an eager smile, the samurai-ko said, "There are Lion to fight."

▲▲▲▲▲▲▲▲

The Lion retreated to the north, toward Matsu Tsuko's gathering armies. Their banners were torn and charred, but their golden mon still gleamed from more than twenty shoulders. Of the Phoenix, eighteen survived, including the two Isawa shugenja and their mistress. The village of Haikeun smoldered, but most of the buildings still stood.

Hoturi stood in the doorway of a heimin's hut and stared after the retreating Lion troops. They still had the upper hand. Tsuko still gathered troops to the north, threatening Sayo Castle and the winter provisions of the Crane.

Toshimoko lay on a mat within the huts. A young Isawa Yao bound his wounds and prayed to the spirits for the sensei's swift recovery.

"He was lucky not to lose the arm," Tsukune said, moving silently behind Hoturi and gazing after the Lion. As if she could read Hoturi's thoughts, she bowed slightly and continued. "Toshimoko-san will live to hold his sword for many more duels, Crane Champion. And, if his reputation correctly precedes him," her lips curved narrowly beneath a dark shock of hair, "to hold more than a few geisha as tightly as before."

Hoturi laughed. "Tsukune-san." Bowing, he admired Tsukune's athletic form. She had removed her armor and wore only the short gi of a bushi. It suited her, Hoturi thought. He looked away before she could notice how his eyes had strayed to the gentle curves hidden by the brightly colored plates of her do.

"Hoturi-sama." Her cheeks dimpled in the sunlight, and her eyes danced a dark brown. The wind lifted the sweat-dampened hair from her neck.

"What will you do now?" he asked.

"Katsuda is still injured, as are several of my men." Tsukune glanced at the village behind them. "This small town is not provisioned to feed my men for several weeks, nor can I move them far.

"Kyuden Kakita is only three days' march to the south," Hoturi smiled.

Tsukune nodded, and her eyes narrowed. "Tell me, Hoturi-sama," she said, looking north. "How long has it been since you traveled to the Phoenix lands?"

"Four years, my lady."

"Four years." She paused, straightening her obi and the sword that hung gently at her side. "And yet you would invite me to your palace, as if it were only yesterday." Tsukune looked up at Hoturi. Something moved behind her eyes, a memory of times long past. She had seen through his invitation—a legion of Phoenix, even small, would lend great strength to Kyuden Kakita's defenders. Trapped by early snows, they could be forced to remain through the winter—and reward their hosts with valor in battle, come spring.

"Come to my tent this evening, Crane Champion, and speak with me."

"You would discuss my offer of hospitality?"

"I would discuss your bargaining techniques." She smiled. "You have lost some of your wit since your marriage, Hoturi-sama. By now, you would have invited me to your tent, not waiting for me to ask you to mine." For an instant, she stepped toward him. He could smell the sharp scent of her athletic body.

A noise behind them disturbed their reverie. Toshimoko coughed, spitting something to the ground as he came toward the two bushi. He moved his arm gingerly. "Your healer is well trained," he said gruffly, bowing to the Phoenix samurai-ko.

"Thank you, Kakita-san," Tsukune smiled, turning. "If you wish to eat, there will be food at my tent in an hour. You are both welcome to test Phoenix hospitality."

"No, thank you, Shiba-san. I've already seen your hospitality when you fought the Lion." Toshimoko laughed. "I'd say the Phoenix make keen hosts." He indicated her blade and the retreating Lion army and laughed again. "I'll eat in my own tent, thank you very much."

She bowed, laughing, and turned toward her tent. "If you will excuse me, Samurai, I will go to bathe. The day has wearied me, and I must rest." Tsukune glanced again at Hoturi before she walked away. Her eyes revealed nothing of her inner thoughts.

Watching her retreat, Hoturi smiled. Though she was wearing only a simple rose-colored gi, it clung to her body with the sweat of the day's fighting. Trimmed silver patterns gleamed among the plain threads as a reminder of the Phoenix's wealth and prestige among the clans. Her silver rings, sign of her oath of fealty to her clan , were absent from her hands, but Hoturi knew that they were with her. Most likely, they had been hidden in her obi to leave her fingers free to wield her sword. Once she had bathed, they would return—constant reminders of the blood she had shed to become one of the chosen of the Elemental Masters.

Hoturi paused to make a proper bow to Toshimoko.

"You knew the Phoenix were coming."

"Yes," Hoturi said, "But I did not know the command would be hers. The Fortunes have made me a lucky man."

"You know her?"

Hoturi smiled. "Once, I knew her . . . well."

"And now?" The sensei grunted.

"Now . . ." The champion of the Crane paused, his smile fading. "She is a tool to secure allies for our clan."

Toshimoko stretched his arm again, testing its strength. "Do not forget your position. It is dangerous to play these games."

"Dangerous to lose, perhaps, but not dangerous for me."

Toshimoko glanced after the Shiba, watching as she stepped behind the silk flap of her large tent. The silver and rose banners of the Phoenix were being lifted by a young soldier, placing the pole of the mon firmly in the ground before the samurai-ko's tent "Very brave. I approve." Toshimoko winked at Hoturi. "But never underestimate your opponent, Hoturi. Nothing is ever as it seems." With a somber nod, the old sensei lowered his arm.

It had been four years since Doji Hoturi had spent the winter months in the cold northern lands of the Shiba. He still remembered the beautiful mountains, covered with snow and ice, waterfalls trickling slowly down the slopes. She had laughed then, when he approached her, laughed with cheeks reddened by the bitter winter wind. Tsukune had been more than a dalliance. She had been a lover. Hoturi stared after her, watching lanterns within the tent cast shadows on the walls.

Ameiko knew about the others, of course. She forgave him for them. Marriage did not imply faithfulness. Only loyalty. Hoturi would never harm Ameiko—but he could never love her. She understood that his duty to the clan came first. Watching the shadow of Tsukune's body slide across the silk walls of the tent, Hoturi smiled gently. His duty to the clan was to provide it with protectors against the Lion, to ensure that the Phoenix would travel to Kyuden Kakita.

Hoturi bathed in the river nearby, washing the sweat of battle from his skin. Though the mark on his leg still bled lightly, it was only a slight wound. The scar would be faint, and his leg could bear the weight even now. He dressed in a clean brown gi and hakima, the casual dress of a ronin. Though the Phoenix knew his true name, there were no other robes to wear.

The guard at the tent door saluted. His armored helm nodded in a deferential bow. "My lady is waiting for you, Doji-sama."

"Yes," said Hoturi. "I'm certain that she is." Confidently, he pushed aside the flap and stepped inside.

The tent was clean and sparse, ornamented only by the gleaming suit of armor on its stand and the dai-sho in their holder to one side. Golden glows emanated from three lanterns that hung from the arched ceiling, and the coals of a small fire glistened in the center of the earth floor. The Phoenix were wealthy, but such a display was almost certainly designed to impress. The Phoenix had intended to meet with him—but not, he suspected, in a small village under Lion attack.

"Four years, Hoturi," Tsukune said. She was kneeling beside her armor and cleaning the plates with a small scrap of oiled cotton. She lost no time before leaping to the subject— there was no polite banter or solemn conversation. Only a soft bow, demanded by protocol, and the curious tilt of her head. Tsukune rubbed at an imaginary speck on the smooth plate of her do. Beneath her calm demeanor, she was angry, and that was all the information he needed. "Four years."

"My lady," Hoturi bowed gracefully. "You have not yet asked me why I have come." Hoturi watched Tsukune place the enameled plate down, reaching for another and beginning the ritual of cleaning once more.

After a moment, Tsukune looked down at the armor in

her hand and indicated a nearby cushion on the ground. "Rest, my Lord Hoturi-sama. You must be weary from the fighting."

"No more than you, Lady Tsukune-san." Formal titles, formal poses, as the two samurai considered their opening moves. No, thought Hoturi. Not opening moves. The true game belonged in someone else's hands. This was merely a diversion, a test before the true contest of wills. That would come when he reached Otosan Uchi, when he saw Kachiko again.

Tsukune was still speaking, and her voice drew him out of his thoughts. " . . . to be the greatest Shiba bushi of his generation, but now he spends his time creating armor for the simplest samurai of the clan." Her voice smoothly covered the distance between them. She had not noticed his lapse. His eyes had not wandered, despite his racing thoughts.

"But you are not the simplest samurai, Lady Shiba." As he spoke, one of the heimin entered through the flap, bearing cups of rice and a warm pot of tea with two cups. She knelt on the floor just inside the tent, bowing low before placing food in front of the two samurai. "Your beauty shines as brightly as your blade. You are cherished among your clan, and we Crane are pleased to have you in our lands."

The faint reminder was enough to furrow her brow. Despite the debt he owed her for her assistance, these were Crane lands, and he was lord of the Crane.

Using the heimin's entrance as a convenient distraction, Tsukune smiled and set aside the metal plate and laces. "Ah, the food." Tsukune was not a courtier but a bushi, and her movements lacked the simple grace of a woman born to the highest court. With callused hands, she poured tea into the two small cups. The heimin bowed and backed through the tent flaps, her eyes lowered to the floor. With no such humility, Tsukune caught Hoturi's gaze and offered him one of the steaming cups. "Your land is bountiful, Crane Lord," she smiled, "but your heimin are frightened."

Lifting the tea to sip, Hoturi responded, "They know that the Lion may return."

"And they'll be murdered if you aren't here to defend them."

"That stone has not been turned."

Tsukune smiled, curiosity in her eyes. "Yet you are concerned enough to dress as a ronin in order to sneak to the emperor's city?"

Damn the woman, but she was still clever. "My journey is a secret, my lady." Let the cunning of the Phoenix be their own trap.

"Secrets?" Tsukune set down her tea and lifted her chopsticks. "I thought secrets were for Scorpions."

Allowing the jibe to pass, Hoturi took a long swallow of the tea. "There are no more Scorpions, Tsukune-san. Someone must carry their burden." Tsukune nodded in approval, and her smile grew. Hoturi continued, "And their burden leads me to Otosan Uchi, as you have already guessed."

"You can defend only one land, Hoturi-sama," Tsukune said forthrightly. "The emperor's city, or the palace of the Kakita. It is certain that both are in danger. Where will you stand to fight?"

Lowering his cup, Hoturi stared at the samurai-ko. The game had taken a turn. "What do you know of Otosan Uchi?"

For a moment, Tsukune seemed trapped by her own cleverness. "The same as you. The emperor's health is not good."

"Not good." Hoturi repeated, sipping his tea. "How kind of the Phoenix to take an interest in my cousin's well-being. The affairs of the court are, as always, widespread." He moved closer to her.

The memory of their past lingered in her eyes. She was beautiful, still as lovely as the day he first saw her, performing the dance of the sword among Phoenix snow. "Hoturi . . ." she said severely. "Our clans have always been allied. Through ten generations, the Phoenix have stood beside the Crane—"

Hoturi grasped her hand. "Then stand with us now against the Lion."

"No." Tsukune attempted to withdraw, surprised into honesty by his forward gesture. "We cannot risk being drawn into war. Please believe me. If I could aid you, I would."

"For the sake of old times, Tsukune-chan?"

"For many things," she said evasively. "I've come with a message to deliver to you from the masters themselves." The Five Masters, guardians of the elements, were the empire's most powerful shugenja. Together, they ruled the enigmatic Phoenix, rarely traveling from their high mountain peaks. Instead, they sent their oath-sworn to deliver messages of importance—some written, some told through blood and visions. Hoturi did not pretend to understand their ways, but their power demanded respect.

"And after you deliver it, what then?"

"I . . . am to do as I am bid by the champion of my clan. The Master of the Void has said that my path will become clear to me in time."

"The Elemental Masters use their power to manipulate their clan. How will they use you, Tsukune?" He drew her hand to his face, touching it lightly to his cheek and feeling her pulse beneath his fingertips. "How will they grant you death?" On her right hand glistened the twin rings of the Phoenix oath-sworn.

"They command me, Hoturi-sama. . . ."

"You, of all people, do not need to remember my title."

She leaned toward him. "Hoturi. I have a duty." Her voice was rough, tested by steel and desire.

"I know duty." He touched her lips softly with a finger, bidding her to silence.

"No," her eyes were haunted. "There is something else. I must deliver a message to you. The masters have made me their herald for a message they cannot trust to writing."

"Tsukune . . ."

"You must believe the message," she whispered. "It speaks

of danger and blood, Hoturi. I fear for you. I heard them speak, before they ordered me to leave the Shiba lands. They said that you must make a decision between duty and honor and destroy a part of yourself to face the future." Her eyes grew faraway, and he sensed the presence of an alien force. "It is time." Clutching Hoturi's hand, Tsukune leaned back and closed her eyes. "It is time."

Suddenly, Hoturi grew chilled. The Elemental Masters were watching, using their oath-sworn as a servant to their power. Her hand grew cold in his touch, and her heartbeat slowed. "Hoturi-sama, Crane Champion," she whispered, and her voice became the voice of the Five. Hoturi had seen it before, but only in times of great danger. Once, when Satsume's life had been threatened and once since then, on the day the Scorpion attacked the Emerald Throne. To see it again here chilled his blood and turned his stomach to ice.

Her eyes became as white as snow. Her pulse seemed to cease beneath his touch. Tsukune's features grew pale, animated by a celestial intelligence. The masters spoke with Tsukune's voice, and the echoes held five new tones. "Champion, you will be tested, as we all must be tested. The writings of Shinsei have long foretold your coming, and it is time that you learned of your future."

Hoturi swore softly at the sudden change. "By the Fortunes!"

"The Fortunes will not aid you. Your only resort is to destroy yourself. The stars have foreseen it. It has been told in the Tao. You, Hoturi, will be the death of your clan. Your men will overrun the land, and your sword will cut a bloody swath in the province of the Crane. The Lion are not your true enemy, Doji Hoturi. Your enemy is yourself." The Shiba samurai-ko shivered, her voice dropping to a low rasp. Another master spoke. "Follow the present, Hoturi, and you will destroy your future."

"I do not fear you, Phoenix. Keep your prophecies to yourselves."

"All men forge their own destinies, Hoturi, this is true." A third voice emerged. "But know that even jade cannot protect you from the burden of your soul. Forget your duty, and you will be lost. We tell you this as allies of the Crane, even as we foretold your father's failure on the day your mother died. He did not fear us either."

Snarling, Hoturi jerked Tsukune's nearly limp body toward him and stared into the empty white eyes. "I will go to Otosan Uchi, and I will face that future. And if I must die to defend my clan, then so be it. But I will not fail."

"The cost of arrogance is blood and dishonor. Remember that. If you are determined to continue, remember the price of friendship."

The samurai-ko's eyes began to flutter. Shaking, she clutched at Hoturi's shoulders. The brown of her irises gradually returned. The unseen power of the masters faded and as their presence receded, Tsukune shook violently.

"Have . . ." she coughed. A thin trail of blood formed a single tear from her eyes. "Have they gone?" Her voice was a bitter rasp.

"Yes, Tsukune-chan," he whispered, awed by the power of the transformation. "They have come, and they have gone."

"I have fulfilled my duty to my masters." Her eyes closed in relief, and her pale face began to gather some of its lost color. "My purpose is finished. Now my only duty is to await their next command."

"Your duty demands that you deliver your message. You have. But it says nothing of your men or of their duty. Their duty is to you, Tsukune—and they will go where you lead them. The masters cannot argue. They have sent them with you for this purpose. Kyuden Kakita is not far, and the snows have already begun in the north. In all they had to say, they did not tell you to return." His roguish smile returned for a moment as her brows furrowed in understanding.

"Hoturi—I have no reason to remain here, either."

"No?" He lifted her hand to his lips, his gray eyes holding hers. "Then let me give you one."

Her dark hair fell like a shadow over her face, touching the high cheekbones and brushing lightly against shoulders that trembled beneath her silk kimono. The muscles in her arms tensed, uncertain whether to reach for him or to move away.

"Tsukune," he whispered, "you have become a commander in the Phoenix armies—a leader of honor and of courage. But still . . ." His touch raised the hairs on the back of her neck. Gently, he breathed on her hand, not quite touching the palm with his lips. "Still you are a woman."

"And you are champion of the Crane."

"Not tonight."

She smiled, at last allowing her hand to travel to his cheek. She touched the smooth, pale skin and felt the soft bristles of a day's growth of hair. "Who are you tonight, Hoturi?" Her voice was low and full.

"Only a samurai. Only a man."

"And if I stay with you tonight, where will I be tomorrow?" she murmured against his forehead as he bent forward to kiss the hollow of her throat.

"You will be safe, Tsukune-chan. Safe within the palace of Kyuden Kakita, where your men can rest from their wounds, and where you can rest from your burdens for the long winter."

"The night is cold this time of year, Hoturi," she whispered softly, a lock of dark hair falling into her brash eyes. "Do you remember how the Phoenix keep warm in the winter?

"My lady," he smiled, kissing her lightly, "I could never forget the warmth of the Shiba fires."

She smiled as he drew her close, and the shadows of the lanterns played upon the silk walls of the tent. For a while, the entire world was empty of all but warmth and the pleasure of two souls, glad to be alive.

7   DEADLY GROUND

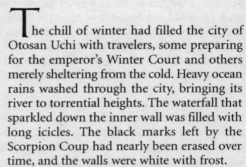

The chill of winter had filled the city of Otosan Uchi with travelers, some preparing for the emperor's Winter Court and others merely sheltering from the cold. Heavy ocean rains washed through the city, bringing its river to torrential heights. The waterfall that sparkled down the inner wall was filled with long icicles. The black marks left by the Scorpion Coup had nearly been erased over time, and the walls were white with frost.

The southern gate to the city, known as the Gate of Dawn, shone in the noonday sun. Golden kanji, enameled into the highly arched stone, protected the city's inhabitants from ill luck and bad fortune. Above, the sun shone sporadically between the thick clouds, peeking through in long, slender beams that dotted the city's elegant streets. Heimin, covered in thick cotton cloaks and heavy straw hats, roamed through the city, enjoying a day without rain. The ocean roared in the east, crashing against the wall of the city, and the banners of the palace snapped above curling rooftops. Their enameled shingles gleamed green above bare trees and icy ponds.

Riding his pony down the southern road to Otosan Uchi, Hoturi looked over the seven hills of the city. From this distance, he could see the faint indentations in the northern mountains where the palace of the Emerald Champion stood. It was uninhabited now, empty of all save a few Seppun samurai and heimin. The emperor had not needed a champion since the Scorpion had been destroyed, since Satsume had died.

Hoturi grimaced, feeling his pony stumble over rivulets caused by the heavy rain. To him, the city was not beautiful. Though it looked white and clean beneath the sun's bright gaze, he could not forget how it had appeared when he had last seen it, surrounded by the tents of the six clans. Nothing could burn that image from his mind. The white walls had been covered with the blood of Scorpion bushi. High banners had burned. He could still see the city smoking and in rubble.

Opening his eyes to the bright morning, Hoturi drew in a long breath of cold air and tried to see the city as it truly was. Now, Otosan Uchi was the home of the 39th Hantei, Favored Child of Amaterasu, Goddess of the Sun. The Seppun, servants of the emperor, boasted that Otosan Uchi had become a city of renewal, reforged since the blood and rage of the Scorpion Coup. The city belonged to a new emperor—and his chosen bride.

Kachiko.

"Come on, boy!" Toshimoko called. His pony cantered ahead toward the city. "You're falling behind. This trip is your idea, remember? At least try to look as if you are excited to be here!"

Hoturi waved at his sensei. His pony continued down the sloping path. When last he saw this city, funeral pyres had surrounded it. He could still see the bodies of his friends placed into the flames. Hoturi remembered trying not to be afraid as his father died in the tents of the Crane, as the armies of the Doji, Daidoji, and Kakita looked to him for leadership. He remembered trying to be worthy of their trust. . . .

Trying not to be afraid for a woman that was not his to lose. Kachiko. She had been inside the city when the clans gathered for war. Hoturi remembered her smile, seeing the softness of her shoulder beneath her silk kimono. He had met her on a winter's day like this one, just before her engagement to the Scorpion Daimyo had been announced. She had been but fifteen years old and he only seventeen. That was nearly fifteen years ago. Since then, she had changed, growing cold and distant. For more than ten years, no word, no message of love or hate. Nothing at all except the emptiness of a love they had once shared.

Slapping the reins against his steed's neck, Hoturi rode toward the city's streets.

⌄⌄⌄⌄⌄⌄⌄⌄

Despite the evening's chill, the garden was full of blossoms. Gardeners tended the soft petals through the winter, encouraging the flowers to bloom despite the season. In preparation for an imperial announcement, they worked twice as hard, and the gardens put forth a last-second effort, overgrowing the path with exaggerated prosperity.

Yoshi stepped through the hanging branches of the imperial walkway. Ah, the magic of the artisans. Even here, in the Imperial Palace, their efforts did not go unnoticed.

Ahead of him stood the empress's guard. Her handmaidens were arrayed beneath silken hoods of gold and green. They circled like birds around the bench where another figure sat, as still as a garden statue. Around her, the flowers had closed with evening. Their petals whitely gleamed like early snow, but they still spread their fragrance upon the wind. Stone lamps glowed with soft fire.

Three burly guards parted as Kakita Yoshi passed. They looked stoic, as if they were trying not to stare at the lithe man in the dark-blue kimono. Yoshi's white hair fluttered like a banner in the breeze. More than one of the handmaidens sighed softly beneath her concealing cloak.

Kachiko had been true to her word: there were no other courtiers present—only the handmaidens, and his own attendants. This meeting was to take place between the empress and the foremost Crane courtier, and no others. No doubt, because of its very nature, it would be swift. Yoshi had known the empress would keep her word. All eyes in the palace followed her, and many belonged to her spies.

The handmaidens bowed first, a bevy of wilting flowers followed by the smooth flutter of fans. Behind him, Yoshi could sense his attendants' response, perfect and effortlessly sincere.

"Great Lady," he said, bowing gently. "I am honored by your audience. My prayers go to speed your husband to health, and may you both reign over the Emerald Empire for another thousand years." Of all the courtiers in the empire, only Yoshi could precisely manage the perfect blend of sincerity and politic that made such an elaborate greeting possible. Words, after all, were his specialty.

She kept her hood above her face, her hands carefully tucked into the sleeves of her gold and purple kimono. Beneath the golden hood, the perfect silhouette of her mask curved lightly against the dark cowl of shadow. Her dark hair was pulled back. Only a few long wisps escaped to trail across the silk that covered her high breasts. She said nothing, only inclined her head gently in appreciation of his greeting.

Yoshi quietly held out a hand, watching as the handmaidens peered toward him. At his side, one of his three attendants stepped forward, trying to glimpse the note he held.

The Scorpion smiled, a gloved hand sliding from her kimono's thick sleeve to accept the plainly wrapped message. "I am pleased to tell you that his Excellency, Lord Doji-sama, will be attending the emperor's formal announcement." The words were too straightforward, but he had been advised to keep formality. "As always, the Crane are honored to have received the invitation."

Kachiko smiled, slipping the acceptance note into her sleeve. Nodding, she stood. Her handmaidens clustered to her side. Even beneath the concealing cloak, her firm hip curved gracefully as she moved.

One of the maidens stepped forward, bowing again as she began to speak. "My lady respectfully tenders her regrets that she is unable to continue your earlier conversation. Her grief over her husband's illness has robbed her of her ability to speak."

Yoshi almost smiled. It was a clever ploy, one Bayushi Kachiko used infrequently. It saved her the dangers of conversation, reaffirmed her status as empress, and reminded of her husband's ailing health. A magnificent tactic but not enough to fend off a keen eye and sharp perception.

Allowing Kachiko to step aside, her handmaiden bowed respectfully. Beneath the hood, the handmaiden's face peered. For a moment, Yoshi caught a glimpse of a delicate veil of silk. A Scorpion's mask. The few Scorpion allowed to freely wear their masks were those in the direct retinue of the empress. No simple handmaid, this, but one of Kachiko's most loyal retainers.

The empress is frightened, he realized suddenly. *Or she wishes me to believe she is. She has no fear of me—I am no bushi who could take her life. If she were to fear me, it would not be here that she showed her true face. What business does she have that her own assistants are not trusted enough to carry out? The Seppun sworn to her side would die for her, regardless of her past. It was not their business to question— only to serve to the death. Something more was at stake here,* something even Kakita Yoshi's expert glance had nearly missed. The mask beneath the hood . . . something about the way the empress held her hands in her sleeves . . . the slow movements of the handmaidens, as if screening their mistress—all became signals identifying the fox to the hunter.

Watching the empress and her handmaidens retreat into the gardens, Yoshi noted something more—a figure standing in the shadow of a statue. Yoshi's eyes narrowed. He signaled his attendants to precede him into the Imperial Palace. From his sleeve, he withdrew a small mirror, just large enough to be covered by a curved palm. He walked toward the palace and glanced down into the mirror, catching sight of the empress and her maidens. The shadow detached itself from the stone as soon as the Crane were a safe distance away. The figure moved silently to the path and knelt before Bayushi Kachiko. Something gold glistened in the faint light of the stone lanterns. Then, the Crane were too far away to see clearly. Kachiko's three retainers moved to encircle the kneeling figure and the willowy empress.

Yoshi put the mirror back into its secret pouch within his sleeve. Something was wrong—terribly wrong. Yoshi did not believe Kachiko's pretty lies. She was his oldest enemy in the court—and the only true challenge left to him since the Scorpion were destroyed. No matter whom she plotted against, a few well-placed whispers would shortly turn the matter to his advantage.

Soon, he swore, resisting the urge to glance behind him, he would master her treacheries as well. When he did, the Imperial Court would belong, truly and without reservation, to him.

"Thank you, my lady," he whispered to himself as his assistants opened the thick wooden doors into the palace, hearing the inner rice-paper screen slide aside. "You have given me a weapon against the Lion, and you don't even realize it." Yoshi allowed himself a single smile of victory, and then moved on.

▲▲▲▲▲▲▲▲

A few short hours after dawn, the court of Hantei the 39th gathered at the Imperial Palace, their robes and kimonos thickly bundled about them. The emperor had not directly addressed his court in several months, and the implication that he may be well enough to receive the courtiers of the six clans sent a ripple of excitement through the palace. The wide corridors were festooned with ivy and boughs of pine. Delicate flower arrangements artfully decorated every corner and alcove of the tremendous building.

As Kakita Yoshi walked the halls, he could feel the age of the walls. The elegant architecture of a thousand years ago still stood proudly within the gleaming central city of the empire. For a thousand years, the line of the Hantei had ruled from this palace, giving the empire form and structure and guiding the clans.

The new Hantei was no great emperor, though. He was too young, too impulsive, and too angry. His arrogance was not curbed by wisdom. Why else would the boy have chosen to wed the poisonous wife of his father's murderer? To end the Bayushi line? No. He had done so because the woman was beautiful. Hantei the 39th was useless, impressionable. The throne was in the hands of an idiot.

Yoshi smiled. The emperor's ineptitude gave power to the Imperial Court, and thus to Yoshi. His command of the court hinged on favors given by the Crane Clan over the years, and a hundred lesser debts owed to Yoshi alone. With Hoturi as his banner, the way was easy.

Hoturi had brought a fire to the clan, a balance between the aggression of the Daidoji and the politic of the Doji and Kakita. He also wisely left the Asahina, fourth family of the Crane, alone on their wide plain, discussing peace and meditating on the Tao. In every way, Hoturi had proven more a champion than his father. Tall, strong, courageous, and handsome, his image reflected everything Yoshi needed the

Crane to be. Hoturi's strength of character did not matter—only his charisma and the appearance of sincerity. It was a simple matter to gain loyalty from those who could see only with their eyes.

Down the empty hallway came the sounds of a samurai practicing, the gentle chants that gave rhythm to the practice kata. Good. Hoturi and the old sensei were awake and preparing for the day. Yoshi's pale hand fluttered through his notes as he remembered all that he had seen in the garden. He had memorized all the faces, ensuring he knew what to say to everyone he would meet.

Know your enemy—he thought, quoting the First Kakita ironically—even when your enemy has never touched a sword.

This morning, the court whispered of a battle with the Lion to the south, in which Shiba Tsukune was said to have aided the Crane. Yoshi smiled. He already knew ten times more than the others did, firsthand from Hoturi. Yoshi knew even more than his champion. Though no one else had seen Kachiko for days, Yoshi had met with her last evening. The strings he had pulled to arrange the meeting had damaged his strength in the court for days. Still, the meeting had given him weapons against the Lion ambassadors. A small army of Lion destroyed in Crane lands by the Daidoji guard and a troop of traveling Phoenix—more than anything, it cemented the public opinion of an alliance between the Phoenix and the Crane. It was an alliance Yoshi was eager to ensure.

Yoshi entered his chambers and waited until the Crane courtiers had gathered, including Hoturi and Toshimoko. After studying each in rapid appraisal, Yoshi led the Crane to the gardens. At his side, Doji Shizue and his other attendants walked silently. They had all been informed of their duties, but the tension of the court would shortly begin to fray their nerves. It was always so when the emperor spoke.

Servants scampered through the hallways, and Toshimoko straightened his obi for the ten thousandth time.

Good Fortunes, Yoshi thought as he watched his brother walk. After nearly sixty years, the old Crane still hadn't mastered the ability to look casual. With Toshimoko, it was all or nothing—and court and courtiers, as far as he was concerned, were nothing.

Two servants slid back the shoji doors into the imperial courtyard. Courtiers raised their heads from conversation. They looking up from behind colorful fans and took in the beauty and glory of the Crane.

Yoshi smiled gently, aware he was being studied, and looked up at his lord.

Hoturi stood calmly. He appeared every inch the lord of the Crane, with a gleaming silver kimono over a silk tunic of darkest blue. The silver was just close enough to white that it reminded one of mourning, Yoshi noted. Well enough, that too could be used to their advantage—the lord mourned for the men lost under his command. He remembered those who had died fighting the Lion.

A bell rang in the courtyard, announcing their arrival.

Yoshi and his retinue bowed politely to the assemblage. Allowing Hoturi to step forward, Kakita Yoshi positioned himself at his lord's right elbow, completely prepared for the day's events.

"We are honored to have the Crane Champion among us today." One of the Unicorn bowed. Instantly, Kakita Yoshi recognized the man as Ide Tadaji, foremost Unicorn courtier.

"No, Lord Tadaji," Hoturi smiled and bowed as he recognized his Unicorn friend. "We are all honored to have been invited to the emperor's court. The day is pleasant, and surely, the emperor's health must be much improved, to see Amaterasu herself gracing the garden." Indeed, sunlight streamed around them, piercing the clouds effortlessly. The morning had deepened, and the budding flowers had begun to open in the early sunlight.

"If the emperor grows healthy once more then surely the land will follow," the Unicorn said hopefully. Though the Ide was simple to read, he was difficult to predict. "The plague that burdens the northern lands—I have heard that it has spread to your own, my lord."

"Yes," Hoturi said carefully. He motioned for the Unicorn to walk with them, and seemed glad to see the gentle Ide once more. The two had been friends before the coup, when Hoturi spent much of his time in the Imperial Court. Time had lessened their companionship, but the two men still exchanged occasional letters. "Four villages have reported it, but it grows slowly. We have every reason to expect that our lands will be spared that particular pestilence."

"We traded one plague for another." Toshimoko said rashly, and then blanched at his own words. "My pardon, my lord," he mumbled, picking a bit of lint from his twisted obi.

The Unicorn seemed glad the ice had been broken. "My lord Hoturi-sama, if you have time while you are visiting your cousin, I should like to speak with you about the plague . . . and other matters."

Yoshi pulled a flower from a nearby bush, watching the dance of courtiers around them. Hoturi was handling the Unicorn's persistence well.

"I will gladly meet you in the gardens while I am here. In a few days, perhaps?"

"You are too kind, Lord Champion," Tadaji said, bowing again.

Politely, Yoshi bowed to Tadaji, interrupting their conversation. "Tadaji, if you have the time, I also wish to speak with you about certain issues. The Unicorn are in need of rice, I hear, to feed the peasants in your southern provinces. With the battles among the minor clans, the Falcon will most likely not be able to return their usual tithe to your borders."

Tadaji's face fell.

Pity the Unicorn, Yoshi thought smugly. They cannot even tell you how they plan to feed their heimin from day to day.

"The Falcon are at war?"

"Oh, yes. Wasp brigands are attacking them, it is said. A village has already been lost near Kyuden Toritaka. Had you not heard?" Yoshi would have been surprised if Tadaji had said yes, considering the first battle had begun two days ago. He raised his fan conspiratorially and led the Ide ambassador away from Hoturi and Toshimoko. "Some Lion say the Unicorn secretly attacked the Falcon in order to provide a false reason to invade Ikoma lands. Of course, that isn't true. . . ."

"Not at all!" Tadaji's features quirked.

Noting Ikoma Ujiaki, the Lion courtier, marching angrily through the court, Yoshi stepped closer to Ide Tadaji. "See how angry the Lion are, simply because you and I are speaking? The Unicorn are unappreciated, your ways so badly misunderstood—"

"Not here, Ryobu," Ujiaki said nearby, his hand touching another Lion's chest warningly.

The young man blanched at his superior's touch, insulted by the public reprimand. His too-pale face reddened under a shock of dyed golden hair. "My brother is dead. His name was Hametsu. Matsu Hametsu."

Stone-faced, Hoturi watched the confrontation. "Your brother died attacking the Crane." It was both a declaration and a response. Nearby courtiers raised their fans, pretending to ignore the simmering ferocity behind Hoturi's words. "He deserved to die, for breaking the emperor's edict against war."

"The battle was fought at Haikeun village, rightfully a Lion holding. Half of Crane lands are rightfully the property of the Lion. Your people have expanded into our territory for a hundred years, hiding behind words and edicts!"

Yoshi remained beside the Unicorn, his lips moving softly behind the wide fan. Tadaji muttered something about Lion arrogance. The Kakita smiled. This test could not have come at a more perfect time.

"I have no quarrel with you, Matsu," Hoturi stepped closer to the Lion, ignoring the ranking ambassador to stare directly at the red-faced Matsu Ryobu. "But if your people believe they can march through peaceful lands and destroy our prosperity for the sake of your pride, I will turn your arrogance against you. Your brother is dead. Do you wish to see your entire house join him on the pyre?"

Flinching, the Matsu reached instinctively for his blade, but the Ikoma's restraining hand became a shove. "Ryobu!" his master barked.

Shaking with rage, the samurai lowered his hand, releasing the tsuba of his sword.

Hoturi had not even moved. His shoulders were tensed, his legs spread, but his hands remained at his sides.

"Ryobu-san, would you think to insult the emperor by bringing war into his very garden?" asked a woman's voice. It was soft, but its command was clear to all. As she spoke, the courtyard bell tolled belatedly, as if in apology. Even the heimin had not noticed her smooth entrance—designed to embarrass courtiers too engrossed in politics to pay attention to the Imperial House.

The empress had arrived.

With a swish of silk, the empress moved, her attendants spreading out around her like the spokes of an elegant fan.

Immediately, the Lion fell to his knees. His face showed rage and humiliation. Heads bowed. Heimin lowered knees to the ground. Even the stammering Crab fell silent.

The empress walked among them, ignoring them as befit her station. By law, her commands were no more than the requests of the emperor's wife—but in reality, they were far more. Every word she spoke carried the weight of an imperial command.

Hoturi bowed slowly, allowed by station to keep his head above the rest of the court. For a second, the honey-colored eyes behind the lace mask flickered in his direction. A soft smile spread across her perfect features. "Rise, honored guests," the empress said, moving among them with a delicate motion of her hips. "And enjoy this rare day." She paused near

Hoturi, eyes delicately lowered behind the mask that flattered rather than hid her features.

Warmth spread through Hoturi's chest. "Thank you, my lady."

She smiled and said nothing, but a hint of her perfume drifted to him, breathing of spice and exotic lands. She lifted a single finger to brush back a strand of hair. The polished nail slid down her cheek to pause at her neck before she glanced up again with a faint smile. Her features were perfectly formed. They fit her heart-shaped face, flattered by large eyes the color of honey. Her lips were full and ripe, and always held a hint of her smile. She was a creature of perfection such as any Kakita artisan would give his or her life to create—proportioned to catch the eye and capture the heart.

Though Kachiko is empress, Hoturi reminded himself, she is still a Scorpion. She is beautiful and deadly. The combination had always awed him, and now, she used both to her advantage.

"What game are you playing?" he whispered as she stepped away.

She said nothing, only shifted her hips in a dance of silk and gold, and walked away. The time was not right for words between them, but soon . . .

Ikoma Ujiaki, leader of the Lion, also bowed before the empress. "My lady, will the emperor be joining us?" His obvious concern was overshadowed by his desire to divert attention from his disobedient attendant.

Kachiko paused, turning to look over her shoulder with a silken glance. "The Shining Prince will attend us as his health allows, Ujiaki-san." Her musical voice was rich, carrying clearly through the garden. "Until his arrival, I have been entrusted with carrying out his traditional duties."

The Lion Ryobu scrambled to his feet. "Empress Kachiko, the Crane have struck against the Lion. My brother has been killed. I have the right—"

"You have no rights at all!" Hoturi stepped forward, causing the Lion to drop into a martial stance.

"Noble samurai," Kachiko said sweetly, "cease your arguments. This is a day for celebration, not for battle." She stepped toward a low stone bench by the path and motioned for Hoturi and his retinue.

Indicating a nearby go board, Kachiko turned to Kakita Yoshi and Ide Tadaji. "A game, nobles?" Something hid in her eyes.

"No, thank you, my lady." Tadaji replied, bowing. His motions were stilted, and he kept his eyes low. Something flickered between them with the cold flame of hatred, but then was as swiftly hidden behind a silver smile.

Though Tadaji had refused, others were willing. Courtiers wheeled through the garden. Their kimonos shone in the pale sunlight like flocking birds. They whispered and laughed. Their fans fluttered in pale imitation of hovering wings. The nobles of Rokugan's court played their elegant games.

Discussions of fashion and love were overshadowed by whispers of war. Yoshi spent his time maneuvering the Lion and the Crab into discussions they could not win. He listened to tales of armies maneuvering through the empty Scorpion lands, and of Crab marching north along the Crane border, heading for Lion lands.

Beiden Pass was the frightened whisper among the Unicorn courtiers. Beiden Pass would be the meeting point of armies, the deciding confrontation in the Crab-Lion alliance. The Hida hinted constantly that they had intentions to seize the empty provinces to the south of the pass. The Ikoma only added to Yoshi's discomfort by implying that their alliance with the Lion would hold until they had finished with the Crane.

Already, the Crab had faced a ronin army in Beiden Pass; already, they had been driven back. The question behind every lying face at court was whether the Crab would retreat or would attack the troops that held the pass. The Crab threat could not be ignored even if the Lion roared more loudly.

The only bright spot in the afternoon was a solid alliance with the Phoenix. Repeatedly, Yoshi found that the Isawa and the Shiba had coaxed the Lion into his palm, waiting only for the Kakita to close his fist. It seemed the Phoenix wished an alliance as much as did the Crane.

Midway through the afternoon, two Seppun guardsmen opened the stout wooden doors of the throne room. A small man in the golden robes of an imperial advisor stepped into the garden. Moving to the empress's side, he whispered a few words into her delicate ear. Kachiko smiled.

Yoshi whispered to Hoturi, "That is Bake, the emperor's favored mentor. When he speaks, he speaks for the emperor."

The champion nodded.

Kachiko stood and followed the hunched little man into the imperial chamber. As the doors slid shut behind them, the voices of the courtiers lifted again, filling the silence with an expectant buzz.

Moments after she had left, the empress returned. Her Seppun guards positioned themselves to either side of the screen entrance. Radiant and regal, she lowered her eyes respectfully as Seppun Bake began to speak.

"Samurai, nobles all, the 39th Hantei, Lord of the Seven Hills, Emperor of the Emerald Empire and favored son of the Goddess Amaterasu, awaits inside to hear your council. May the light of the Shining Prince never fail, and may the light of the Celestial Heavens illuminate the empire through his wisdom and guidance." Bake shriveled into his fine robes, slinking back into the throne chamber.

Kachiko nodded to the assembled court. Stepping back into the mahogany chamber, she moved gracefully to the edge of the dais, bowed, and stepped to her place behind the young emperor.

Stepping into the throne room, Hoturi was awed once more by its sheer grandeur. Ornate enamel adorned the broad beams of the ceiling. A magnificent tapestry depicted the fall of the kami from the Celestial Heavens. On the dais, between Kachiko's kneeling form and that of Seppun Bake, a glittering Emerald Throne rested. It was wide enough to support two men, and stood taller than any other chair in Rokugan, carved from a single emerald during the first days of the empire.

When last Hoturi had seen it, the throne room had been covered in blood. For an instant, Bayushi Shoju's still form lay on the dais, his broken sword shattering the pristine emerald of the throne. Then, the vision was gone,

Hoturi bowed along with the others of his station.

Kakita Yoshi moved to the dais, kneeling and lowering his head in obeisance. He too held great favor in the court, and was allowed to sit upon the platform with the Seppun and the emperor's advisors.

On the throne rested Hantei the 39th, Lord of Rokugan.

Hoturi sank to his knees in the front row, trying not to stare at his emperor.

He was smaller than Hoturi had remembered, young for his age. Though slightly over twenty, the emperor had the wan face of a boy five years younger. The hollows under his eyes had been powdered, but his face still appeared sunken with weariness. Gloves covered bone-thin hands, and golden slippers covered his feet, barely peeping out from beneath thick green and gold robes. The emperor wore at least four layers of clothing, plumping his form from a frail boy to a more solid man. Still, he only just covered the Emerald Throne. His father had seemed part of the stone itself.

For a moment, Hoturi felt a great sorrow.

No one in the court could miss the signs of the emperor's failing health. No wonder the Lion did not fear the Crane; their connection to the emperor was now as shallow as his health. If the Hantei died without an heir, the bloodline of the Doji would no longer be a part of the Hantei line. Already, with his Bayushi bride, the emperor had broken the age-old tradition of marrying a Crane. Soon, the empire could shift into full civil war. It all balanced on the health of one very young man and one failing peace.

After the court had settled itself, the emperor lifted his eyes from his lap and placed one hand on either of the throne's arms. His gaze slid slowly over the court. Occasionally, he nodded as he recognized a favored courtier, but his gaze never paused, never changed. With a gloved hand, he reached into a golden box held by a kneeling Seppun Bake, pulling forth a carefully penned scroll. Though his voice was faint, it still held the unmistakable aura of an eternal lord. Despite his ravaged body and his trembling hands, the Hantei was still emperor.

"Noble Lords," the emperor began. "For too long, our throne has stood without a protector. It has come to my attention," a pause, a shuddering breath, and a glance at Kachiko, who sat quietly on her cushion at his side, "that with the plague that destroys our land and the violent incursions of numerous Yobanjin bandit tribes, the position of Emerald Champion must be filled."

Faint murmurs rose in the gathered crowd.

Hoturi clenched his fist beneath his kimono sleeve but kept his face stalwart. Behind him, Toshimoko's faint exhalation told that he realized the game afoot.

The emperor continued, raising his head to increase the strength of his fading voice. "My lady wife has nobly agreed to carry out the duties of the arbiter of the tournament. Seppun Bake will be on hand to ensure the faithfulness of those who choose to attend."

Both bowed, respectful of the responsibilities given them by the Hantei.

Hoturi saw Yoshi's fan tap once, and then twice on his knee. In the far back of the room, there was a soft movement. Doji Shizue slid into the open hallway, vanishing before the assembly noticed her. Something was occurring, but Hoturi could not see it.

The emperor continued his speech for a few more minutes, and then raised his hand above the crowd. Bowing as one, the courtiers began to clap. Hoturi too applauded the emperor's announcement.

"Imperial Lord," a soft voice pierced the room, "I stand for the Dragon, in acceptance of your tournament. I need no formal announcement to ask for the chance to serve you, nor any astrologer to tell me that this is my time to step forth." A young woman knelt in the aisle at the rear of the chamber, her green robe spread around her knees. The Dragon mon shone from her back, and the symbol of the Mirumoto flashed on her sleeve. She raised her head. Black eyes shone in narrow sockets. A thin nose sliced through a sharp-featured face. "My time is now."

The Hantei nodded, surprised by the woman's forward speech. Raising a hand to Seppun Bake, he coughed. The sound was like ice grating on pine boughs. Despite his stoic control, Hoturi flinched.

Twisting forward like a slithering snake, Bake smiled. "It is so noted, Hitomi-sama. The Mirumoto Daimyo of the Dragon stands for her clan." Picking up a brush, the Seppun marked elegantly upon a roll of blank white paper, noting her name and rank.

Several of the Lion glanced at one another across the aisle of the court. Hitomi's sudden acceptance of the tournament created an unthinkable precedent. Those who wished to challenge for the position would have to speak now, or appear unconfident and weak.

On the far side of the court, a Lion stood. He bowed deeply, first to the emperor and then to the others on the dais. "My name is Kitsu Motso, daimyo of the Kitsu family, son of Kitsu Ariganu, son of the Lion Clan." His bass voice was proud, and his back was stiff with pride. "With the permission of my lady, Matsu Tsuko-sama, I will stand for the Lion. As your right hand, we proudly request the chance to serve."

Others stood, their voices raised one by one as they told

of their lineage and their bravery. Three Lion, in all, and then two samurai of the Crab. Suddenly, Hoturi realized who had brought Mirumoto Hitomi into the chamber, and whose command had begun this hasty roll call of duelists. Carefully, he glanced toward the dais, but not at the grand Emperor Hantei.

Kachiko's eyes were closed in pleasure, listening to the chaos of the court. She knew Hoturi could not deny his clan the right to compete in the tournament of the Emerald Champion. His own father had held the position, and if he did not at least attempt to regain it, the Crane would lose favor in the Imperial Court. Yet, if he tried and failed, the Crane would appear weak. They could lose their tentative alliance with the Unicorn, or worse—they could lose the respect of the emperor.

Well played, Lady, Hoturi thought. Still our game of go has not finished. You may have set out the board, but I choose when and where to place the first stone.

Hoturi glanced swiftly at Kakita Yoshi, looking for some sign of encouragement. The Kakita Daimyo shifted his legs, twisting his fan and lowering the tip. Remain on your knees, he entreated Hoturi with the secret signs of the Crane. Tension clenched the corner of Yoshi's mouth. Obviously, if he were to accept the challenge, it would be disastrous for the Crane. Behind him, the rest of the Crane were silent—all of Yoshi's attendants were courtiers, not soldiers. None could possibly represent the Crane in a duel of this magnitude.

The letter had been sent to him, addressed to the champion of the Crane. Kachiko had planned to force him to accept, trapped by arrogance into believing she wished to see him privately.

The Fortunes and simple wit were on his side. He had not come alone.

Nodding faintly to Kakita Yoshi, Hoturi shifted upon his cushion, tapping the man behind him with one toe. It was all the encouragement needed.

"I, Kakita Toshimoko, master of the Kakita Academy and lord of the twelve provinces of Kunankei, will stand for the Crane. It is our honor and duty to follow the tradition so nobly set forth by our family, cousins of the Hantei from times long past. We will fight, and we shall serve." He bowed nobly.

On the dais, the emperor's eyes lightened as he recognized the sensei. "Master Toshimoko, your dedication to our family is well known. We look forward to seeing your skills tested in our tournament."

"Thank you, Your Imperial Majesty." A slight smile crossed Toshimoko's face as a mutter passed among the Crab at the back of the room. As all masters of the Kakita Academy, Toshimoko had once been the sensei to the Hantei. The Crane were connected to the imperial line through more than blood. It was time the Crane's place in the empire was remembered.

"My lords," the emperor said over the whispers of the court. "I grow weary, and . . ." his hand reached for the arm of his throne. Another cough spasmed through his thin chest. "I must rest, and the tournament must be planned. I look forward to seeing our greatest duelists compete on the field of honor. For your clans, my lords—and for the honor of your houses."

Beside him, Kachiko stood, bowing and saying softly, "We shall have strength for you, Your Majesty."

The Unicorn courtiers murmured approvingly. A whisper of agreement from the Crab affirmed her ploy. The courtiers were dismissed.

Even as she assisted her husband into a golden palanquin, Kachiko's eyes lingered on Hoturi.

In time, my lady, I will tear away all your masks and silk, and there will be nothing left but the truth of your heart. Hoturi smiled, feeling in his pocket for the smooth black stone of the afternoon's go board.

Hoturi approached and bowed to the emperor. To Bake,

he said, "My lord Seppun, someone seems to have dropped this. I believe it was part of her Imperial Majesty's go board. Could you return it to her?"

Bake bowed, confused, and took the stone. "Of course, my lord," he said handing it immediately to Kachiko.

Without waiting to see if she accepted the piece of black glass, Hoturi turned and followed the Crane ambassadors from the room. He knew what would occur behind him. He had no need to stay and watch.

The board has changed hands, my lady. Now it is your turn to place the stone.

8   SMOKE AND DRAGONS

Kyuden Kakita shone with frost. Thin trails of icy dew covered its stone towers. Though the chill air turned her breath into white plumage, Ameiko knew the cold was not enough to slow the armies on the march.

Even so, she had left her chambers in high spirits, carrying a sprig of fresh-cut pine. Its scent cheered her as she walked the long corridors of the palace. The fireplaces burned dimly in the early morning, not yet rebuilt from the long sleep of a winter's night. Ameiko didn't mind. She was warmed instead by the secret message hidden within Kakita Yoshi's letter to the Crane court.

As she continued down the corridor toward the Kakita libraries, Ameiko reread the missive.

First it gave praise to the Seven Fortunes for Hoturi's safe arrival at Otosan Uchi. The imperial lords had met, which meant the court would be in an uproar over who would speak with the Hantei first—if at all. The emperor's health must have been improving for him to summon his court.

Yoshi had not done badly, Ameiko told herself as she gracefully descended the oak staircase, but she wondered what truths remained uncovered in his letter. Pondering the real intent behind the master courtier's carefully couched phrases, Ameiko gazed at the heimin cleaning the corridors of the palace.

Most nobles never remembered the faces of their servants, ignoring the lower classes as one would ignore bricks in a wall. Ameiko knew each of them by name. She whispered polite greetings as she passed their kneeling forms. She was well loved here. Each samurai in the guard would gladly have given his life to defend the lady of the Crane.

There were those who believed ambition had caused Kitsune Ameiko to climb her way through society's ranks. She had been the daughter of a minor noble house, but one day became the bride of the Crane heir. Over the years of their marriage, her beauty and wit had earned her friends in every corner of the empire. Those who knew her understood the true reasons for her unfailing loyalty to Hoturi.

Love alone had raised her to his side.

In the libraries of Kyuden Kakita, Ameiko reached for the ink stone and brush to compose a reply. Three servants aided her, lifting the scroll cases to their proper place and gathering rice paper and ink. Yoshi had arranged a meeting with the ambassador of the Unicorn. The Phoenix, as well, were willing to consider an alliance with the Crane. Within the cadence of the phrases lurked another message. Scouring the parchment and unrolling even the finest edges of the letter scroll, Ameiko reread Yoshi's delicate calligraphy. The symbol of messengers, and allies, and a faint Phoenix mon. Something unusual was stirring in the emperor's court.

Shaking her head softly, Ameiko sighed. She placed her cheek in her hands. The treachery and intrigue of the court were second nature to the Doji and the Kakita, but Ameiko had been born in the Fox Clan, a small group from the southern forests. The court was not her friend, though it had often proven the Crane's finest ally. Perhaps Yoshi's manipulations and Hoturi's sheer strength of will could gain something that war could not. She prayed to Shinsei that it would be so.

Still, Tsuko's armies gathered to the north, and three villages had already been burned. The future grew dimmer with each sunset. Soon the palaces of the Crane would shake, and be broken.

Footsteps approached beyond the paper screen. "My lady?" a low voice called out. A moment later, one of her heimin knelt by the door and slid back the screen. In the hallway beyond knelt the daimyo of the Daidoji.

"Dear Fortunes," Ameiko said, standing from the low table. She composed her features. "What happened, Samurai, that you should look so pale?"

"My lady, there has been another message," Uji replied grimly.

Straightening her shoulders, she asked, "From Lord Hoturi?"

"No, my lady. Actually, yes, my lady, but not in that way."

"Come here." Ameiko knelt once more on the cushion behind the library table.

Uji walked into the small stone chamber. Behind him, the door obligingly closed, slid by the hands of heimin.

Signaling for the servants to leave, Ameiko turned to face the growing light of the window. She arranged her kimono so that the folds spread gently on the floor. When the heimin had gone, Uji knelt beside her. "From the look of your face, Uji-san, the Daidoji have been wounded once more."

"Yes, my lady. Haikeun village has been burned, but the casualties have been light." Uji paused, his dark face becoming sallow and his shoulders tightening.

"Yes?" Ameiko prompted, noting the man's stubborn jaw.

"The messenger asks to stay the winter in Kyuden Kakita.

The first snow will fall soon, and the roads will become treacherous."

"A samurai carried the message?"

"No, my lady." Noting her confusion, he continued, "Eighteen samurai, my lady, and three shugenja. They are Phoenix, of the Shiba family, asking your hospitality."

"Phoenix." Ameiko repeated. How could Yoshi have known this would occur? His letter had mentioned Phoenix allies, but had given no details of their arrival. "Are they injured?"

"Yes, my lady," Uji snarled. "By Lion blades." Nodding his head in polite deference, he stood angrily. "The Lion march through our northern province, just to the west of Sayo Castle. It is obviously their first target in our lands. We . . ." His face darkened as he realized that he spoke to the lady, not the lord, of the house. "I'm sorry, my lady. You have much else to do, and the Phoenix are in need of comfort."

"Uji-san," Ameiko said sharply. "In my lord's absence, you will speak to me of all things concerning the clan. As his wife, I care for the house and finances of the Doji—and as the wife of the champion, I care for the entire clan. Do you understand?"

Uji blackened visibly. "Hai, my lady. Forgive me."

"No, Uji-san, you will not be simply forgiven," Ameiko cautioned with a faint smile. "You will tell me what you know of the Lion troop movements and will explain my lord's wishes regarding these Phoenix. Then, I will write to Kakita Yoshi of our plans so that the court can continue to turn on the will of the Crane."

"Hai, Ameiko-sama. Hai." Uncomfortable, the soldier bowed again.

He turned to the window to compose his thoughts. With narrowed eyes, he watched the artisans in the gardens below, discussing the festival of days past and preparing for the winter to come.

Ameiko turned again to the table, preparing the ink stone

with a small amount of ground kohl. Tipping the water vial, she filled the reservoir of the stone with liquid and smeared the kohl to paste with her brush.

The brilliant light of dawn crept across the windowsill. As silent moments passed, it began to illuminate the small chamber with glorious light.

Uji waited patiently for her to command him to speak. He was a broad man, and his shadow clung to the wall. Even without his armor and the well-known black mask, the daimyo of the Daidoji was a dangerous man. Bound to the Crane through ties of blood older than the empire, the Daidoji were the strength of the clan, and Uji was the strength of the Daidoji. He had served the Crane for fourteen years without truly speaking his mind, and this time would be no different. Every word was colored by anger, every action dictated by a hatred of anyone who dared defy his command of the Crane provinces. Where Hoturi ruled through lineage, Uji commanded through strength. The Crane had good reason to fear Uji if his loyalty ever turned. He knew every inch of the lands they controlled, and he had the strength at arms to seize them.

At last, Ameiko nodded. She was ready to hear his words.

"The Lion," he began, "are gathering to the west of our border. Tsuko's force is a few days past Sayo Castle. Smaller legions have already entered our lands. We have harassed them as much as we can, but our troops are light in that area. With hostility from the Crab to the south, we are spread too thin to provide direct support against a large force. I'm keeping three hundred men here at Kyuden Kakita, but the Phoenix could prove more than useful. Their shugenja, in particular. We have none here—the Asahina are secluded in their monastery, and even if they wished to join the battle, they could not arrive before spring."

"Who commands the Phoenix at our gate?" Her fingers paced the table restlessly, idling with the calligraphy brush as if eager to release her thoughts.

"They are commanded by Shiba Tsukune, who has defeated Kitsu Koji, on the road just west of Kyuden Kakita."

Ameiko looked up, concerned. "They have already faced the Lion?"

"Twice. Once, in the village of Haikeun, and once against the Kitsu troops."

Tsukune. Ameiko remembered the samurai-ko, lingering impressions of a small, dark haired woman in bright armor shading her eyes. Hoturi and Tsukune.

"The Phoenix will prove good allies. We are fortunate they have chosen to ask our hospitality," Uji pressed his hands to the table, leaning forward over the scattered rice-paper scrolls. "If the Lion take Sayo Castle, we will need all the aid we can get. The winter is nowhere to be seen. Our skies are clear, and not a cloud passes the southern mountains. Even the foothills of the Beiden Mountains are free of snow. The Lion could march any day. If they come to Kyuden Kakita, your life will be in danger. Hoturi made certain that the Phoenix came to us in order to protect the Kakita. To protect you."

"I am certain my lord's duty is near his heart, as always." Ameiko's green eyes were clouded, her hands stilled by thought. "Tell me, Uji . . . how did he convince them to stay?"

"Katsuda-san, one of the bushi, is injured. They needed—"

"No, Uji-san." Ameiko placed the brush on the paper, ignoring the smear. "This is not about what her men needed. It is about the needs of the Crane." With a calm exterior, Ameiko folded her hands. "Tsukune is a beautiful woman, deadly on the battlefield and trained in the rituals of the Phoenix, our allies. I understand need, Uji-san. I understand too well."

"Lady Ameiko, you should move to Kyuden Daidoji. It is on the peninsula, away from the Crab and too far south to be threatened by the Lion troops. The Matsu are going to siege the walls of the Crane as soon as the snows lift in the spring. Sooner, if the winter is light."

"Leave?"

"Three hundred Daidoji troops, eighteen Phoenix samurai, and three shugenja—that's not enough to defend the province from the full force of a Lion assault. When they have assembled the Matsu troops, they will have nearly ten thousand men."

"The Kakita have their duelists, and whatever small magics can be created by the artisans. Then, there are the Asahina."

"The Asahina are pacifists. They will not aid us in war, even if their champion commands it. And origami will not protect you from a Lion's blade." Uji declared, twisting his hands into fists. "I'm a fool to think a woman could know anything of war."

Ameiko's eyes flashed. "Nevertheless, you will send word to their daimyo, Asahina Tamako."

"My lady, we have already sent three messengers. All have been turned away with a blessing and a prayer to the Seven Fortunes. Tamako has never responded to our earlier messages about the war. The Asahina will not leave their library. They will not fight, even to save our lives."

She watched as he stood from the table, pushing a thick black string of hair from his face. "You will do as I command. And I will stay in Kyuden Kakita."

"Kuwanan will make that decision."

"No." Ameiko stood, her voice as sharp as broken glass. "Uji-san!" He straightened at the sudden command, jaw tightening beneath darkly tanned skin. "I will make that decision. In Hoturi's absence, I am in charge of his house."

"Ameiko-sama,"

"You forget your place, Uji!"

"Do I?" he snarled. "Then remind me. Tell me how to defend the Crane from three times their number. Give me what I need to keep our land safe, and to destroy those who would destroy us. If you wish to command as a samurai, Ameiko, then you must be ready to die as one. The clan needs you,

Lady Ameiko. You must go to Kyuden Daidoji. If needs be, I will lay my life down to get you there before the first snow of the season."

"I am ready to die." Her chin straightened. "When I swore to be Hoturi's wife, I swore to be a Crane. And if I must die, I will die as one."

Uji looked at her for a long moment, seeing the strength behind her words. If there was any weakness in her pale face, any sign of uncertainty . . . but there was none. Bowing humbly, Uji lowered his eyes. "My apologies, Ameiko-gozen." He held the bow, waiting for her to return the gesture as a sign of understanding.

For a moment, Ameiko considered turning her back and leaving the samurai in shame. "You have spoken to the wife of your liege with anger, Uji-san," she said coldly.

"No, my lady." He replied. His voice was emotionless and sincere. "I have spoken to my lady with honesty."

Understanding rushed through Ameiko. Uji's status as a high-ranking daimyo gave him the right to question his lord, and his responsibility to the Doji house gave him the obligation to do whatever was necessary to defend that house. "Uji-san," she said quietly, "I thank you for you concern, but I will remain here."

"Hai, my lady."

"Give the Phoenix the rooms in the west wing. It has the best sunlight for the season. The shugenja can use the large chamber for their rituals to the kami."

"Hai."

Ameiko bowed slowly, staring into Uji's eyes as he raised his head. He stepped lightly backward, straightening.

"Uji-san, one further thing." The daimyo of the Daidoji turned, his hand on his obi. "Does he love her, this Phoenix samurai-ko?" she murmured, her voice silken.

"No, my lady. It is said that he does not."

She nodded, lifting the blackened brush from the table and feeling its soft, wet bristles with her fingertips. "Do not fear for my safety in this palace, Uji-san. The Lion cannot harm me, no matter how many men they command."

"Ameiko-sama," he said, drawing a sheathed tanto from his belt. "Please, keep this with you. It was my father's, and it will keep you safe."

"No, Uji," she smiled. "It is too beautiful, and an heirloom of your family. It should be kept in the house of the Daidoji, not given to a daughter of the Fox."

"You may have been born in the Fox lands, Lady, but you are now a Crane. This dagger has defended the Doji for a hundred years. Let it continue its duty, and protect you from the Matsu, if they come."

"Only love can destroy me, Uji. Believe that." A faint smile touched her features. For a moment, even the cynical Daidoji Daimyo understood how truly beautiful she was. "No dagger can protect me from that death, no matter how noble or how honored the weapon may be."

"Doji Ameiko-sama," he began, offering the dagger a third time. The golden hilt shone lightly in the growing light of the morning. "I would not give this to your husband, nor to his brother. You rightfully deserve the protection of the Daidoji, as a lady of the house, and as one of the bravest souls I have had the honor to know. The dagger does not honor you. You honor the dagger, simply by being its guide."

Nodding, Ameiko smiled and took the dagger in her small hands. "Thank you, daimyo of the Daidoji. I only hope that if the time comes that I must use it, I will have as much courage as those who carried it before."

Uji nodded respectfully. The screen of the library slid open again, and he left the room.

Alone once more, Ameiko knelt behind the low desk. Her blackened fingers gently touched the hilt of the ornate tanto. Though small, its gleaming blade was well oiled. Ameiko knew nothing of weapons, and the little martial training she had received had been for the art of dance. Light glinted down the edge of the blade like fire on water, shining with all the colors of the rainbow and reflecting an orange sun on the gently curving golden hilt. Raising her eyes to the window and the forests beyond, Ameiko sighed. The forests called to her, but their song would wait. Now was not the time to leave the safe walls of Kyuden Kakita. Even if her blood begged for release, she had to remain.

Placing the dagger on the table and removing the stained sheet, Ameiko dipped the brush into the ink and began composing her letter to Kakita Yoshi. As she wrote, she heard a faint scrabbling at the window—scratching claws and whuffling breath. A fox raised an eager yip outside. It barked again, encouragingly.

Knowing the source of the disturbance, Ameiko closed her eyes. No, Sister, she thought softly. Today, I must be the Lady of the Crane. Tomorrow, we can run through the forests, but not today. Though Ameiko longed to join her true family, she knew her mind and heart must remain with the Crane.

It was not right that she leave Hoturi now—not even if all the laws of the spirit world demanded she return. He needed her. He loved her.

Outside the window, a mournful bark sounded. Paws scampered across the garden, lightly brushing the trees.

Beginning the first strokes of an elaborate kanji symbol, Ameiko tried to smile.

9 TOUCH OF A BLACK HAND

Four days later, news of the tournament of the Emerald Champion had spread throughout the city. Entrants from the minor clans had begun to come forward. Each clan was allowed only three entrants, and most sent fewer. To enter more samurai would imply that the clan's faith was not fully behind their entrants. Fond of appearances, the Imperial Court spent its days discussing the samurai who dared to challenge for the position.

The Emerald Champion was foremost of all the Emerald Magistrates, keeper of imperial law and title, and general of the armies of the Hantei. It was a prestigious and powerful position. With his standing guard of Seppun, the Emerald Champion's duty to the emperor and the empire was unquestioned.

"Make sure that old man remembers how to use a sword," Yoshi mocked lightly as Hoturi and Toshimoko sparred.

Toshimoko snarled. The days were passing slowly. The Lion still marched. Crane brothers still died. As he practiced on the tournament field near the emperor's palace, Toshimoko tried to keep his mind from returning to that fact.

"I'm not concerned that he knows how to fight," Hoturi said seriously, assuaging Toshimoko's gruff humor. "I'm more worried about that arm. Sensei, you're slower than usual."

"Slow? I'll show you slow, by Shinsei!" The wooden bokken blades crashed together once more, sliding effortlessly through their kada. Each kada was a practice lesson, one following another with simplicity and grace. The movements were precise and natural, made through the centuries by a hundred thousand swordsmen, each a child of the Crane.

From the side of the practice field, Yoshi watched Toshimoko and Hoturi test their blades. Those who passed by had eyes only for the sparring duo, allowing Yoshi a blissful respite—one he could use to the Crane's advantage.

He pondered the passing of the last few days. The emperor had made no more appearances, nor had Bayushi Kachiko stepped out of their chambers. Despite Yoshi's considerable skill, he could not keep the Crane within reach of the emperor. Each time he arranged a meeting, it was put aside by ill health and careful machinations.

The winter remained bitter cold, but no clouds dotted the horizon. No snow came to grant the Daidoji a reprieve from Lion forces. The little news from Sayo Castle was not good. Tsuko's legions gathered, harassed by the Daidoji but still strong.

Yoshi watched Toshimoko and Hoturi leave the field. The empty practice ground was covered in half-hardened mud, scarred by the tread of eager feet. It would not look this way tomorrow. Tomorrow, the field would be filled with bright banners and courtiers.

Tomorrow, the true battle would begin.

▲▲▲▲▲▲▲▲

On the morning of the contest, Hoturi wrapped a bandage around Toshimoko's arm, and a heimin helped him into a gi and hakima of fine soft silk. Yoshi stood nearby, relating the latest news.

The Crab had arrived only yesterday, telling of a battle at the southern pass.

"Beiden," Hoturi sighed, leaning back on his heels. "They fought at Beiden Pass, as we thought they would." If any place in the palace was safe for them to speak, it was here. The Crane chambers had long been held by the clan, protected by the most trusted Daidoji guards.

"All the court will have heard of it by now," Yoshi thought aloud. "To the right, Toshimoko-san, or you'll make a fool of yourself out there." Toshimoko twisted the obi again, cursing softly as Yoshi continued. "It is said that the actual battle occurred nearly a twelve-day ago, on the day of the Horse. Runners from the pass have only just reached us with news of the battle. It will be some days more before the results of the combat are known."

Considering, Hoturi stood. "I will speak with the Unicorn today, during the competition. Tadaji has always been a kind man, and I know him well. Their horses travel significantly faster than our own, and their news is often more advanced. We could use them as our allies, for that alone if not for the strength of their armies. I would be glad to fight with the Unicorn by our side—and better, to have Tadaji's strength in the court allied with you, Yoshi."

"If you must speak to the Unicorn so unprepared," Kakita Yoshi knelt upon a scarlet cushion and nodded thoughtfully, "be sure to talk to him frankly. The Ide are still very much the gaijin they were when the Unicorn returned to the empire two hundred years ago. Sometimes, where they will not respect sincerity, they will respect open emotion." Looking up into the shocked faces of the other two Cranes, Yoshi snapped his fan shut with a precise clap. "Crude, yes, but it will be effective. Do you doubt my advice?"

"No, of course not, Daimyo-san," said Hoturi, smoothing down an impatient lock of white hair. "I'll remember your words when I meet with him this afternoon."

"You're going to miss the duels?" Toshimoko burst out, annoyed.

Hoturi grinned charmingly, offering Toshimoko's swords to the older samurai. "Of course. I already know the outcome. But I will miss only a few rounds, my friend. I want to see you give the Lion what they deserve."

"Again." Mollified, Toshimoko took the swords with a bow, and placed them firmly in his belt.

They left the Crane chambers one by one, following the step of their champion. Hoturi walked through the corridors of the Imperial Palace, ignoring the scuffling heimin and the guards that bowed low as he passed. Behind him, Yoshi, Toshimoko, and the Crane guard strode sharply, their banners waving beneath the high ceilings of the palace.

Before them, the doors to the tournament field opened to a blaze of brilliant color.

What had once been a muddy field was now a well-tended tournament ground. Daises lay beneath the brightly painted mon of the six great clans. Heimin hurried throughout the field, making final preparations before the courtiers arrived. Across the field, the Crane banner flapped in the morning sun. Beneath the banner, two artisans bowed low to their champion. Doji Shizue was among them. She smiled and lowered her head. Her fan fluttered two times, closed with a snap, and spread slowly open once more. Even in a largely empty field, the Crane practiced caution. Enemies were never far away.

Yoshi whispered behind Hoturi, "All is well. We should proceed. Tadaji is to meet you in the gardens. You will not be missed here for some time, and the empress will not arrive until a moment before the contest."

Nodding, the Crane Champion entered the tournament grounds with his retinue. Beyond the fighting ground, he passed alone into the palace gardens.

▲▲▲▲▲▲▲▲

The gardens were empty except for one man. Ide Tadaji waited on a stone bench, a strange look of sorrow on his face. Hoturi approach and exchanged pleasantries, but he instinctively sensed that something was terribly wrong with the Unicorn.

"Her gracious lady has yet to grant me an audience," Hoturi began. Whatever was troubling his friend would come out in its own time. After all, Tadaji had requested the meeting. "I hope she decides to see me soon. Grave business requires my attention elsewhere."

"I had heard that a Lion army was headed for Crane lands. . . ." Tadaji said.

Hoturi nodded and reviewed the basic strengths of the Crane, from their Phoenix allies at Kyuden Kakita to the possibility of southern snows. Hoping to draw out his interest and encourage a smile from the gentle Ide, Hoturi played to the man's clan pride. "I tell you this because you are my friend, and you are a Unicorn whom the Crane trust. Many of our samurai are dead or dying from the plague. The heimin have fled to the countryside. Villages have been destroyed by plague and pillaging Lion. Kyuden Kakita is guarded by only a tiny army, less than a third of what is needed against the Lion near Sayo Castle."

Tadaji's face lightened with realization of the trust being placed in him. Friendship began to overcome nervousness. Tadaji nodded briefly, as if trying to organize his chaotic thoughts. "The Lion are that strong?"

"Ten thousand and more."

Tadaji paused, considering "And when you arrived, you

discovered that it was not the emperor but Kachiko you must deal with." The Unicorn shifted on the uncomfortable stone bench, wrapping his lame leg about the body of his cane.

In some ways, Tadaji had much in common with Shizue, Hoturi thought, remembering his sister's shifting walk. Perhaps that was why Hoturi had liked him from the beginning. Both had overcome their defective births to follow the path of their Tao. The thought made him smile. Then, also thinking of his talented sister, he allowed the smile to fade from his features.

Hoturi nodded, speaking of emperors and politics while his heart ached. Kachiko would not see him—her game, whatever it was, still waited. Enough, he thought angrily. "I have men in Otosan Uchi—Daidoji soldiers. They are anxious to return, and it is unwise to leave Kyuden Kakita undefended for so long."

Tadaji stared earnestly into the younger man's worried face. "Of all the clans of Rokugan, the Unicorn know the fear and desperation of standing alone in a fight. Seek an alliance with the Unicorn Clan, Hoturi-sama. We too stand against the storm of war that rumbles in the darkening sky. I can speak to Shinjo Yokatsu. He will agree to a meeting with the Crane if I request it."

"An alliance with the Unicorn," Hoturi said softly. Looking at Tadaji and letting real hope shine in his face, Hoturi bowed toward the ambassador to thank him. "I can think of no other clan I would rather trust at my side in these uncertain times."

May the Fortunes bless you, Yoshi-san, Hoturi thought. Your advice has brought allies to our cause. Your advice, and this good man's friendship.

Someone approached down the path, a thick-bodied man in a deep scarlet gi. His was a familiar stride, the sound and carriage of other days. Beneath a silk mask lurked a blackened face and the pale brown eyes of an assassin.

Hoturi touched his hand warningly to the hilt of his

katana. Every nerve in his body strained to kill.

The man was Bayushi Aramoro, Kachiko's brother-in-law and an enemy to the Crane.

Tadaji grasped the handle of his cane in dislike.

"Honorable Doji Hoturi-sama," Aramoro said, his voice oiled and slick. "Empress Kachiko requests that you do her and the emperor honor by attending her in the royal chambers in one hour."

"Please tell the lady that it is I who will be honored to appear at her request." Watching the tournament from the empress's private balcony could prove the opportunity he needed. Kachiko knew well that their conversation would go unheard from that vantage, yet she must also know that they would be watched from the courtyard below.

Aramoro bowed silently, his hands never leaving his sides.

Hoturi watched him, aware that a single movement could send them both to their deaths. Of all the samurai of the fallen Scorpion, this one was the most dangerous. The most dangerous, Hoturi corrected himself as the man began to leave, other than his mistress.

▲▲▲▲▲▲▲▲

Eight bushi still stood on the emperor's tournament field, eight samurai in gleaming hakima and gi, their clans' mon embroidered in glittering thread. The last duelists included two Lion, one Unicorn, one Crab, two Dragon, a member of the Fox Clan, and one Crane.

Toshimoko still stood, Hoturi noted with relief as the heimin guided him along the interconnected balconies. The imperial viewing chambers were directly above, in perfect position to see each strike and parry of the shining katana.

The next two opponents were called forth by Seppun Bake, the master of ceremonies. "Matsu Mori, son of Matsu

Agetoki, come forward and hail the throne. Mirumoto Hitomi, daimyo of the Mirumoto, come forward and hail the throne." The man's voice was as spindly as his raised arms, which flapped in the breeze like winter branches. He snorted a cone of mist into the wintry air.

The two samurai stepped onto the tournament field. They bowed toward the emperor's balcony, some ten feet above them. Then—far more shallowly—they bowed toward each other.

On the balcony, the mon of the imperial family waved in a faint breeze. Golden chrysanthemums decorated intricately carved wooden rails. Two cushions provided a commanding view of the entire battlefield and each dais below, but one of the pillows was empty. The emperor, too ill to attend the gathering, had sent his blessing. And his wife.

Hoturi gazed across the balcony and bowed formally.

Reclining on the golden pillows, Kachiko gazed at the duels with a careful eye. Her rich kimono shone despite the relative shadow of the balcony's cloth sunshades.

Hoturi rose from his bow, uncertain if she had seen him.

A servant knelt before him, touching her head to the ground. This was no heimin, but a very young woman of noble house, servant to the imperial family. She had probably not even passed her gempuku, and she bore the mon of the Crane.

"I am Kakita Kaori, Master Hoturi-sama, servant to the Imperial Court and fostered to the care of Seppun Kossori. It is my honor to direct you to Her Imperial Majesty. She bids you meet with her and tell her of the battle, that the emperor will be well informed of each technique on the field of honor."

Clever Kachiko, Hoturi thought as he nodded. With such an excuse, he could stay on the balcony indefinitely—and he would be seen as serving the emperor. Very clever.

The attendant stepped to the side, motioning Hoturi forward. Beyond her skirted kimono, Kachiko rested, stirring the breeze with a waving fan. Though the day was cold, the habit seemed to be her way of passing time.

Hoturi paused to watch her for a moment before bowing again. "My lady Kachiko-sama," he murmured once they were alone.

"Hoturi, thank you for attending me," she smiled. Her reddened lips curved gently as her fan slowed in the air. Without looking in his direction, she indicated the pillow beside her own. "Rest, Lord Champion. The tournament reaches its height." As she spoke, her silken kimono slid gracefully across an outstretched arm, sheathing the pale skin in scarlet and gold.

Below the balcony stood Aramoro, his arms lowered at his sides and his legs spread as if to leap over the rail to defend his lady.

Noting the staunch guardian so much on edge, Hoturi chanced a faint grin.

Kachiko caught the implication and raised an elegant brow. "My lord, you do me much honor in attending my summons. Tournaments such as these often grow boring to a lady. Your observations are of much interest to me." Her voice was soft music, the delicate tones of a biwa.

"It will be difficult to turn my thoughts to blades when my eyes are caught by brighter stars."

She hid her smile behind the fan. "Look there, Hoturi, if you can draw your eyes away for a moment." She pointed toward the tournament ground.

Two samurai took their stances. The Dragon woman crouched low, her hands covered by the long sleeves of her haori vest. Her opponent leaned forward in an aggressive Matsu stance.

A shout pierced the still air, and the two opponents drew in a single arching strike. Their blades chimed against one another. The bright flash shone in the winter sunlight as they moved, shifting their balance. Within another breath, it was finished. The Lion fell to the ground. Blood began to stain the man's kimono, spreading crimson against the bright orange of the Lion Clan.

"She injured him?" Hoturi was shocked.

"She has yet to gain full control of her capabilities." Kachiko's artfully placed fingers were only inches from Hoturi's own. "She fought with the Crab in Beiden Pass, only a few days ago. Just before she came to Otosan Uchi."

"Days . . . ?" Hoturi laughed softly. "You had her brought here for the tournament."

"Perhaps it should be seen more as pity to a wounded samurai in great need of allies. You have not looked very closely, Hoturi-sama." She leaned forward to whisper in his ear, and her warm breath brought shivers to the young man's spine. "Look again."

The field was clearing as the Lion's men came to carry him from the ground. Blood from his wound stained the soil beneath Mirumoto Hitomi's feet. She watched impassively as he was taken away. Suddenly Hoturi saw what lay beneath her long sleeves. Her right hand shone of stone and glass, the flesh changed to cold rock.

"Shinsei's blood," he swore.

Kachiko leaned back, laughter rippling from her pale throat.

"A gift from you, I expect."

"A gift from the emperor, of course. Little Hitomi was injured at the battle with the Crab, her hand severed by a Hida. What else was I to do for a loyal samurai of my husband's empire?"

"Where did you find it? What is it?" Hoturi shifted on his cushion, allowing a trailing lock of hair to brush against his hand.

She pretended not to notice. Silver bells tinkled from her obi, their echo as compelling as her laughter in the air. "It is Shosuro's Hand, an artifact of the fallen Scorpion." Beneath the bitterness of her clan's destruction, lay the pride of hard-earned triumph.

"Lost in the labyrinths of the Bayushi, beyond remembrance. You have my admiration, Empress, on your treasure-finding skills."

She laughed again, and placed her fan on the ground, delicately brushing his fingers with its sandalwood spine.

On the field, two more opponents were called, but Toshimoko was not among them. Again, the pause, the strike, and the blazing speed of master samurai. Before Hoturi could draw a breath, the last Unicorn in the tournament had fallen to his opponent's blade. This time, there was no blood. The strike was clean, and the duelist withdrew his blade before injuring the Shinjo. The applause that had been lacking after Hitomi's duel danced delicately through the crowd.

Hoturi struggled to stay focused on his task, on the tournament, on anything except the burning in his chest. After more than a decade apart, he had thought the emotions dead, fallen to three thousand days. As he looked at her, the jeweled amber eyes smiling down from behind her delicate lace mask, he knew it could never be so. There had been others since Kachiko, nameless and faceless save his wife, but nothing in the empire touched him as did her smile.

Kachiko lowered her chin. Her voice sank, becoming timid with grief. "You are staring, Lord Champion."

"I am blinded by the sun." The old compliment came easily to his lips, remembered by his heart more than his mind. For a second, he saw not an empress on silken pillows, but a maiden whose dark foxtail of hair cascaded across the green grass of a summer day. Forgotten laughter came to her eyes, and her lips curved into a maiden's blushing kiss.

As if reading his thoughts, she turned away. "I have grown old, Hoturi. I am not the girl you once loved."

"I never loved a girl, Kachiko. I loved you, for all you were. And I love you for all you have become. You have beaten them."

"Have I?" Her regal robes stiffened. A faint breeze shivered through the balcony. The tinkling of silver bells seemed almost somber, a temple's call to evening.

On the field, Bake screamed out another call to the samurai, but Hoturi did not hear it. "Your people have died, but you live. With me, you can be granted all that you have lost."

"Hoturi . . ." She nestled closer to him. Her fingertips slid down the length of the fan to brush against his. "I asked you to meet me because I have found something. Something very important." It was impossible to think with her eyes staring into his, her body so near. Silk rustled as she moved. He longed to carry her from the balcony. Her breasts moved softly beneath the thin fabric of her kimono, and she raised her fan to cover her lips from inquiring eyes. "I have no clan to turn to and no family to help me. . . . I need you to meet with me, tonight, in my chamber. I found something else in the labyrinth where my family had hidden Shosuro's Hand. I believe it can help us both. . . ."

It was painfully simple to agree.

▲▲▲▲▲▲▲▲

On the field below, Toshimoko dispatched his opponent with a ringing shomen strike. The blade cleared the ground by a half-inch after it had carved the mon from the other man's sleeve. Stepping back to the edge of the crowd, the sensei bowed toward the high balcony. He glimpsed Crane-white hair next to the ebony tresses of the empress. Toshimoko knelt to compose himself.

His beaten Crab opponent stormed angrily from the field, muttering curses about duels and the thick clubbed iron of his tetsubo club. Stuffing the sword he carried into his obi, the Hiruma stormed through his clansmen, punching them aside with righteous anger.

Another angry child, Toshimoko thought, trying not to look up at the empress on the balcony.

Hoturi, don't be a fool for her.

"Two more, brother, and the position will be yours," said Yoshi, standing nearby. "Watch for the woman. She is more dangerous than you believe."

Snorting, Toshimoko rose. He drew and oiled his blade. "Which woman? The Dragon or the Scorpion?"

"There are no more Scorpion, first son of Toshimo. Have you forgotten that?"

"Save your platitudes for those who believe them, second son. There is more to this than pleasant words."

"You've seen her hand." It was a statement.

Toshimoko nodded. "What dark magic has been done to the daimyo of the Dragon's largest family?"

"Five days ago, Hitomi was in a battle at Beiden Pass. Now, she is here, with a strange hand of black glass." Yoshi paused. "I must speak with her. She knows more about the Crab forces than we, and despite the danger, that information is too valuable to lose."

"Do it soon," Toshimoko growled. "She has already defeated her next opponent."

The woman stood once more on the field, and the Fox samurai knelt on the ground before her, clutching his hand to his bloodied chest.

Soberly, Toshimoko said, "If I also best my match, the final battle will be Dragon against Crane."

On the tournament ground, Mirumoto Hitomi swung her blade to clear it of blood. She bowed, first to the empress's balcony and then to her opponent. In an unusual show of arrogance, Hitomi turned next to Toshimoko. She raised her sword in salute, her black eyes as hard and cold as the obsidian hand that held the blade.

"Best hurry, half-brother," Toshimoko breathed. He nodded solemnly, returning Hitomi's salute. "Destiny is waiting."

Kakita Yoshi turned and sliced his way through the crowd, moving with the precision of a samurai's blade. The Dragon gathered close to the edge, watching as the last two duelists fought for the right to challenge Hitomi's victory.

"Honorable Lady, it is my earnest desire to wish you well in your next duel," Kakita Yoshi said brightly, his caution concealed by sincere interest. "Your fighting style is an honest dedication to the great two-sword stance of Mirumoto. I have been honored to see such a master of the Dragon style. Tell me, my lady, do you find the Crab style difficult to contest? Their brutal strikes would seem in opposition to the delicate strokes of Mirumoto Niten."

Hitomi nodded bluntly, unable to ignore the Crane's question. Other Dragons paused to hear their lady trade words with Yoshi. A breeze from the east blew the banners around the field, ruffling the colors in a vivid display.

The Dragon quietly ordered her retainers to remain at rest. "My lord," she spoke clearly but with a rough rasp in her voice. "There is no style that can master the Mirumoto Niten. It is the sovereign strike of the matched blades, parallel to the sword of the soul."

Yoshi paused to watch as Toshimoko and Kitsu Motso squared their shoulders, preparing for the first blow.

"Lion fights Crane. Don't you think that's more interesting than discussing the Dragon technique?" As she spoke, Hitomi moved behind her banner and pulled her sleeve down over the joint of her thumb.

Yoshi affected not to notice the glint of stone. "Not at all. The Dragon, like the Crab, fight with strength and power. The Crane fight with skill. One sword, one stroke, and no more."

Hitomi grunted savagely, "The Crab fight with cowardice."

"I'm certain Kisada-sama would disagree," Yoshi said cheerfully, deliberately baiting her.

The samurai-ko spun on her heel, nearly reaching for Yoshi's tunic. Her hand stopped only inches from Yoshi's chest, trembling, and spun into an obsidian fist.

The Kakita never moved, but simply smiled.

"Kisada," She hissed, slowly withdrawing her hand. "Can die along with his coward son."

"I don't see how that can happen, Hitomi, if you are here and they are at Beiden Pass."

Almost snarling, she responded, "The Crab have retreated from Beiden Pass, only five days ago. Yakamo's army of Shadowlands filth was not enough to defeat the army of the Dragon. But this," she tore away her sleeve and held out the stone hand. It was grafted to her flesh like a thing alive, creeping over her forearm with long tendrils of black, glossy stone. "This the Crab took from me. I will take more from them when I see them again."

"Where will you see them, Hitomi-san?" Yoshi whispered, hoping her anger was enough to spin the tale.

"When they are done with you, Crane. I will destroy them when they are done with you."

A chill struck Yoshi's spine, the like of which he had never before felt. Suddenly, for all his courage and mastery of the political empire, he felt deeply and totally afraid.

"The Crab march on Kyuden Doji, Crane, to restock supplies and heal the wounded that our blades have given them. Even your foremost scouts will not catch Yakamo's men. But with this," she flexed the obsidian hand, and veins of stone shifted within the obsidian, "I will destroy them."

Remembering his duty, though his heart failed in his chest, Yoshi asked one final question. "How do they travel, that the Daidoji cannot see them pass?"

"They travel with demonic oni, creatures of fire and acid, with claws of iron and teeth that break katana—and Cranes." She cursed. "The very ground moves for their passage." Lifting her sword to her obi, she bowed curtly.

On the battlefield, Toshimoko's blade sliced open Kitsu Motso's tunic from side to side, leaving the golden fabric twisting in the breeze. Not a mark showed on the Lion's chest.

The crowd broke into wondering applause.

Hitomi stepped onto the field without being called. A cold breeze followed her. On the far side of the courtyard, a panting Toshimoko slowly raised his blade.

As one, the duelists bowed gracefully to the emperor's balcony. Yoshi glanced up at the high pillared area, seeing only Aramoro's shadow as he stood on the ground beneath the mahogany rail. True to his word, the Bayushi guard would never leave her side.

The two samurai bowed to one another, turning toward the center of the courtyard as if pulled by a single cord. Their eyes met, the old sensei and the young daimyo. They paused in the center of the motion, respectfully saluting both the samurai and their house.

On the dais, two heads bowed to each other, the black and the white, moving slowly together behind a wooden fan.

The courtyard grew silent and still, awaiting the stroke of a single sword, the master's attack of iaijutsu.

Yoshi listened to the stillness, hearing each whisper of silk, each shifting slipper and tinkle of ivory charms.

Toshimoko was a silent statue, his gray braid moving quietly in the breeze like the tail of some great, chained cat. Opposite him, Hitomi's hand gleamed in the sunlight, as cold as ice and as devoid of soul.

At last, a bird fluttered between them in dreamy slowness. The samurai moved. With ringing whispers, two swords slid free of their sheaths. Only one sword struck.

Twisting free from her stone hand, half of Hitomi's katana clattered uselessly to the ground. She was pushed bodily backward by the force of the strike.

Sliding effortlessly down the shattered katana, Toshimoko's blade rang against Hitomi's obsidian hand. The sword leapt up to point at the hollow of her throat.

For a moment, frozen in time, Yoshi looked up at the faintly concealed dais above the mesmerized court. The two heads behind the fan parted, their lips opening in faint smiles. His heart fell to the ground in fear. Hitomi's words rang once more in his mind. Parallel to the sword of the soul. . . .

Hitomi's face, contorted with rage, shone up from where she lay upon the ground. Above her, Toshimoko removed his blade from her neck. Stepping back into the shadow of the courtyard, he raised the steel katana in front of his face in salute to the valor of the fallen.

10 A DAIDOJI'S WILL

The wide field should have been empty. Instead, it was filled with soft movement. Tents rustled. Horses stamped in broad swaths of grass. The Lion encampment seemed peaceful enough from afar, but within the orange tents, murderers rested.

These Lion—their helmets doffed and placed in neat rows beside sleeping soldiers—gathered not to face honorable battle, but to destroy and pillage Crane villages. Already, three more had been razed to provide food for the marching horde. Three more villages filled with Crane, set to the torch.

Like the flames that blazed behind them, the bright orange and yellow banners of the Lion snapped in the strong wind of a stormy midnight. Around them, the darkness trembled with the weight of sleeping souls. Matsu Suzemeri led more than five hundred men—a full command to prepare the way for Matsu Tsuko's armies to take Sayo Castle.

In the forests beyond the Lion encampment, silent shadows moved.

On other nights, the Lion would have set sentries and allowed the rest of the soldiers to sleep, but tonight, the Lion troops camped in Daidoji territory. Ten men on guard was not enough. The Matsu commander had posted thirty.

In high trees, two Daidoji men raised their hands, wound willow branches around their wrists, and slid gently to the ground. Beneath them, four more crept from the low brush. It was a simple matter to remain hidden in the thick Crane woodlands, a much more difficult thing to stay silent over the dried autumn leaves that covered the ground.

Daidoji Uji glanced at his lieutenant, the black kohl on his face dimming reflection. The man's blue-gray eyes glittered in the open moonlight, watching as his daimyo flickered his fingers against his stocky chest. Smiling, the younger man nodded. The raid would come soon.

Samurai were expected to be straightforward, honorable, loyal to their lords, and servants to the code of bushido. Crane, in particular, held themselves to high standards of honor and to Kakita's lessons, known collectively as the Sword. They were duelists, masters of defeating one opponent with one strike.

Uji scowled as a branch snapped somewhere behind him. The Kakita knew nothing of using few men to defeat ten times their number. Victory came to those most prepared to take it. Let them call the Daidoji honorless. Let them decry their hidden ways and revile their dangerous and dishonorable methods. Because of the Daidoji, the Crane lived to speak such things.

Three of his samurai crossed an open patch of ground, their dark blue gi covered by patches of darker brown. Uji smiled. These men, forty in all, could destroy five hundred Lion tonight, if the Fortunes favored their strike.

Already, five of the thirty sentries had been killed, their

passwords learned, their helms worn by Daidoji that marched in their place through the woods. The ground of the encampment itself . . . Uji almost laughed. Like a snake through vines, he scaled a tall tree. The very ground would be the death of the Lion.

The maps of the Daidoji showed every tree, every bush and rise. Uji knew them all as if they were brothers. Though the Crane lands were wide, every plot had been covered by Daidoji troops. Now that knowledge was being put to the test.

Lord, one of the Daidoji signed, kneeling before the tree where Uji surveyed the Lion encampment. Nodding, Uji summoned the man into the tree. While the samurai climbed, Uji studied the battlefield.

The Lion were camped in small clumps for warmth. Their fires blazed high. They would be blind to the night around them, once the sentries had been breached.

How do the Lion rest? Uji asked without speaking, his fingers moving lightly against the bark of the tree.

Deeply, sir. The right flank has been opened, and the pits and spikes are prepared.

Ten months ago, Uji had known the Lion would march through these plains, known they would be forced to camp in this valley, if harassed by his men. He had been correct, and now the preparations were about to pay off. A lot of brave Daidoji samurai were about to die, but if they succeeded—if Uji had accurately predicted the Matsu's strategies—Sayo Castle could be saved. Ten days of constant harassment, of killing scouts and sentries, of using firecrackers to terrify the Matsu supply horses, had served the Daidoji well.

Now was the time to strike.

Tell them we are ready. It begins.

Two simple movements, no more, and the other samurai slid down the tree in perfect silence, motioning to the others that the time had come.

▲▲▲▲▲▲▲▲

"What was that?" A Matsu samurai raised his head, wishing the campfire were warm enough to keep away the bitter chill.

"Nothing. The fire crackled. The sentries are fine. You are dreaming again, Mosu-san."

He lifted his head from the thin woolen blanket. "Something else." A sharp crack, the whinny of horses. Mosu reached for his sword and drew it to his side.

Yelling erupted from the edge of the encampment.

Even Mosu's weary companion could not ignore the summons to battle. "Daidoji!" he cursed, leaping to feet bloodied by marches across stone-covered ground.

Men raced among tents that suddenly blazed with fire.

"There!" one shouted.

A Crane samurai leaped ahead of them. He threw something into the fire. A sharp series of crackling pops showered the men with sparks. They howled as the fire burned through clothing and singed flesh. More firecrackers detonated, sending out charcoal, ash, and flame.

Mosu charged relentlessly past flailing Lion, determined not to be turned back by his pain. He spotted the saboteur crossing the encampment. Screaming, Mosu pursued. He raised his sword to slash another Daidoji across the back. The Crane fell, cut in two by the massive stroke.

Mosu shouted, "They are not ghosts!" He cuffed a fallen Ikoma. "They are men, and they can be beaten!"

Screaming Tsuko's name, four more Lion joined Mosu.

The saboteur wove through the camp, leaping over horses and tossing more fireworks into the bonfires. Smoke erupted along with screams of pain and fury—some cut short by death. The man dropped a flaming torch into stacked bundles of rice. The sudden flare showed his dark blue gi.

"Daidoji!" Mosu snarled.

The man turned to run.

Mosu and his men gave chase, screaming for blood. "After him!" Mosu yelled ferociously, holding his father's sword before him as he began his swing.

The Daidoji leapt into the woodlands and turned, reaching for his sword. His smile was as feral as winter.

Suddenly, the ground collapsed beneath Mosu. The screams of his followers echoed in dumbfounded ears. His feet flailed without purchase. A shower of earth and thin balsa wood scattered across his eyes and face.

Then he landed upon the spikes, and knew no more.

▲ ▲ ▲ ▲ ▲ ▲ ▲ ▲

"What's happening?" Matsu Suzemeri came out of his tent, girding his sword to his side with an obi of orange and yellow cloth.

"The Daidoji, sir," a nearby guard fell to one knee, his face blackened by soot.

Suzemeri saw fire among the supply tents. His men raced through the night, screaming for their commanders. Flames spread through the dry grass on which they camped.

Striding through the chaos, Suzemeri shouted, "Mosu! Mosu! Where in the twin furnace of Jigoku is that man?"

"My lord, he went to the forest, chasing some of the Daidoji saboteurs."

"Damn him!" he shouted with frustration. "I'll have his head for this!"

Horses screamed as they charged through the encampment. Firecrackers whirled and hissed, tied to their stubby tails. Hooves tore through tents and shattered posts.

"I'll have his head!" the commander repeated.

Another group of samurai fell, clutching their throats as if to remove the Daidoji arrows that had sprouted beneath their chins.

"As you wish, Matsu," a voice shouted from the safety of a

high tree branch. "We've pulled it from the pit for you." Something flew from the saboteur's outstretched hand and rolled across the blazing clearing.

Mosu's head.

At that moment, grass fires reached the strings of powder buried just beneath the ground. The entire plain exploded into flame.

▲▲▲▲▲▲▲▲

"The nearest troop of Lion are seven days from Sayo Castle," Uji reported, kneeling in the wooden court chamber of the Kakita. "Our troops have gathered the local heimin to transport the rice from those silos farther south."

"Seven days," Ameiko echoed quietly, looking at Doji Kuwanan thoughtfully. Hoturi's brother made no reply. His eyes were dark and lifeless, but beneath their stony façade, intelligence burned. She asked, "Will that be enough time to empty Sayo Castle's reserve?"

"No, Lady." Kuwanan's deep bass voice rumbled through the room. "It would take twice that, or more."

Ameiko sighed, placing her chin on her hand. "So sorry, Kuwanan-san, but seven days is all the time we can give you. Use it wisely."

He nodded. His broad face lowered. "And what about the rice we cannot get out of the keep before the Matsu arrive in enough force to capture Sayo Castle?"

"Burn it, Kuwanan-san."

Uji's swarthy face darkened with anger.

Beside him, Kuwanan bowed curtly, disliking his orders but knowing nothing more could be done. Many Daidoji troops had died during the conflict with Matsu Suzemeri. Kyuden Kakita could spare few more men.

"I received a letter from Yoshi-san today." Ameiko lifted a folded piece of parchment from her sleeve. "He tells me the tournament for the Emerald Champion is finished. The emperor once more has a champion. And that man," her voice lowered dangerously, "is a Crane. Toshimoko-san has become the emperor's hand."

Blotches of color appeared on Uji's cheeks, and his hands clenched.

Kuwanan smiled with pride. His thick face brightened like the sun through clouds.

Ameiko placed the letter on the dais before her knees. After a moment, she stood. "Kuwanan, you should be on your way to Sayo. They will be in need of you."

Kuwanan bowed, took a single stride backward, and turned to pace through the sliding shoji doors. He walked with pride. For him, the news meant honor to the Crane. His father's position at the emperor's side remained in the clan most worthy. Even more than Hoturi, Kuwanan could be blind to the deeper machinations.

"Uji, remain." Ameiko stood from the dais and motioned for Uji to follow her. She led him onto the wide stone balcony overlooking the Kakita forests.

Silently, he followed, his mood black.

"You do not approve of the appointment, Uji-san?"

He rested his hands on the stone railing, feeling ivy crush beneath his fingers. "Do you wish my frank opinion, Ameiko-sama?"

"Do you think I would ask you otherwise?" Green eyes leveled sharply, and her fan tapped once on the stone.

Uji nodded, running a hand slowly over his unshaven face. The black kohl he wore to assault the Lion still darkened the shallow slopes beneath his eyes, clinging to his cheekbones in a thin gray smear. There had been no time for bathing—Uji had far too much to do to waste time with fashion. His clothing was clean, his hands washed. It was enough.

Calmly, the Daidoji Daimyo considered his lady's question. "Toshimoko is a brave fighter, if a chaotic one. His valor is unquestioned, and he was certainly the most qualified to win the challenge."

"I want your opinion, Uji-san. Do not repeat the babbling of the court."

"His appointment takes one more Crane away from Crane lands, and gives us an obligation we cannot possibly fulfill. Toshimoko will be alone, and we will be without his assistance when the Lion come. No doubt, the empress has several errands that the great and honorable Hantei must have completed. The Emerald Champion will become her handmaiden." The scorn was thick. Uji's snakelike face contorted in barely controlled anger. "We cannot afford to lose more samurai. To lose one such as Toshimoko. . . ."

"If the Emerald Magistrates could be called, they could be of great use to us," Ameiko noted. "We must pray that the spirit of our ancestor, the First Doji, has watched over us. Perhaps we can turn Toshimoko's victory to our cause."

"The Magistrates are useless. Worse than ronin. It will take more than a Crane with a strong arm to turn them from raiding villages and hiding like dogs."

"It is all the hope we have, Uji-san," Ameiko said unwillingly. She pointed beyond the forest, over the faraway hills of the Kakita provinces. "We have already turned back the Crab, though after their defeat at Beiden Pass and the plague that roams our southern lands, they will no doubt assault our provinces for provision. The ronin army at Beiden Pass cannot keep them back forever, nor can the Unicorn harass them enough to send them home to their Kaiu Wall. They have attacked one of the lesser palaces of the Kakita. Who is to say they will not return and do so again?"

A string of lights illuminated the distant hills, sparkling like stars against the velvet night.

"In seven days," Uji paced the balcony like a caged animal, his footsteps padding against the stone. "The Matsu legions will take Sayo Castle. There is nothing we can do to prevent them. We must allow Kuwanan to do what he can, and then withdraw all of our troops to Kyuden Kakita and prepare to defend ourselves against Tsuko's assault. War will come to us whether we wish it or not, Ameiko. It will come, and we must be prepared."

"Something is about to happen, Uji. Something that could destroy the Crane."

Somewhere in the forest, a fox yipped softly, its mournful note echoing against the hills.

A chill ran down Uji's spine at the sound, his usually stoic stance hollowing with unease.

"I feel fear, Uji. A darkness spreads from the north. It touches the hidden places in my heart."

He was silent for a moment. "The Lion march toward Kyuden Kakita. That is what you feel." Whispering, he tried to soothe her strangeness, concerned for the shadow that had suddenly come over her features. "It is the thing we all fear."

Gathering her cloak closely about her, Ameiko did not reply.

11 SHATTERED MOONLIGHT

He came to the empty chambers as he was bid, late in the night, after the moon had hidden his face beneath clouds and darkness. The wooden floor made no sound beneath his careful footsteps. The door slid open softly at his touch. Starlight drifted faintly though the open windows, illuminating the wide room.

"What is left for us, my love?" The silken whisper drifted to his ears. "Now that the war has come, and time has destroyed us both?"

"Nothing has been destroyed, only forgotten," he replied, searching the shadows to find her. Hoturi sighed, brushing aside the gauze that veiled the view of the gardens.

A light rustle of silk caught his attention at the far side of the room. "Am I, too, so easily forgotten?" Kachiko's form separated from the shadow, a moving piece of the darkness, as soft and smooth as water in a lake.

"Never, Lady," he breathed.

"Years ago, Hoturi, you loved me. Before Shoju came—before I was forced to be the wife of the daimyo of the Scorpion, you told me you would give up anything for me. Have you ever wondered what it would have been like," her fingertips slid softly down the thin cords that tied her obi at her waist, "if we had left the empire behind, as we once planned?"

"How young we must have been to think that responsibilities could be so easily lost." Hoturi moved behind her and smelled the scent of lilac and mist. He wanted to touch her as he had once before, but something in her eyes stopped his fingertips a mere inch from her ivory cheek. Without touching, Hoturi traced his fingers along her face, her shoulder, her breast. "We were lucky to have such dreams."

"You never dreamed of me?" Her voice lowered, and her face turned away from the light.

"I did not say that, Kachiko."

The cool winter wind surrounded them, brushing aside a lock of her hair. It slid from the ivory clips that held it, drifting down beneath her shoulder. Kachiko walked across the room. Her scarlet kimono shifted about her. Silk spread down over long, slim legs, silhouetted in the window light. Each step she took called softly to him.

There was no other sound in the palace save the soft chirrup of frogs from the great pond in the garden.

"Hoturi," Kachiko murmured, shifting against the window's glare, "not a day passed that I did not think of you." The truth of her words shone in her luminous eyes.

"And I of you. But I didn't turn you away, soft kami. It was your word that kept me from your side. When I came to the palace, Aramoro threatened my life—and said you would not see me again." Pain and sorrow, so long concealed, began at last to surface. "I came to you, as I had come to you a thousand nights since your marriage, and by your choice, I was turned away." Slowly, he made his way to her side. "Why? After four years, Kachiko, you didn't even tell me yourself. You had that ape, that vicious assassin, tell me that"—Hoturi felt again the bitter sting of loss—"you didn't wish to see me."

Without answering his question, Kachiko slid a manicured fingernail through a long strand of his hair, pulling it free of the topknot that bound it. "Your clan destroyed my family."

"On the emperor's orders, and more than ten years after you left me."

"Was it so few?" she asked thoughtfully, her voice low. "You are right, I suppose. It seemed like many more."

"Kachiko, tell me." Hoturi suddenly grasped her shoulders, his hands warm through the kimono. Pulling her tightly toward him, he felt the garment fall to one side, baring her shoulder at his touch. "Why did you leave me? Did you stop loving me?" Breathing the scent of her neck, he whispered huskily in her ear. "When did our game end?"

Gasping softly, the lady of the Scorpions twisted her fingers in his hair, drawing him near. Her bare cheek pressed against the warm hollow of his throat. A single tear raced down her cheek, unseen by any save the shadow and the starlight. "It did not end, my love," she murmured, trembling. "I simply changed the rules."

▲▲▲▲▲▲▲▲

Far away, in a quiet corner of Kyuden Kakita, three green-eyed foxes crept through an open window, seeking the source of the mournful wail that had broken the night. The palace slept, each guard walking his post without disruption, unaware of the tremors that shook the half-world between spirit and man.

▲▲▲▲▲▲▲▲

The silk cords of Kachiko's obi untangled beneath his fingers, slipping to the floor as he twisted the knots free. "You have haunted me." His breath warmed her cheek.

She smiled, hands touching the crest of his shoulders and lightly brushed his collarbone. "Ten years ago, when I turned you away, I did it for your own good. There was a secret that I held, more important even than your love."

"More?" The silk was soft, catching at the nap of his fingers as he brushed his hands against her sides. "There was nothing more important to me than you."

"Liar." She smiled. "Your duty was always more important. Even when you lay beside me, I could sense your thoughts returning to your house."

"And what of you? Married to the daimyo of the Scorpion, what future did we have?"

"Oh, my love. We had all the future in the world. We simply didn't have the time to find it. I went to the mountains of the Bayushi, and when I returned, you were married as well."

Shuddering at her touch, Hoturi closed his eyes. Ameiko's face swam before him and then was gone. "Ameiko was my father's choice, not mine. I married her to please him."

"As I married Shoju, to escape the Shosuro house." Her arms slid around him. "Do you love her, Hoturi?"

The question seemed innocent, but Hoturi was loath to answer.

▲ ▲ ▲ ▲ ▲ ▲ ▲ ▲

The stars hung low in a thick black sky, twinkling like the tears of the Fortunes. Silently, the foxes nudged open the shoji screens of the chamber.

Seated upon the futon was a maiden, her hair disheveled around her shoulders, spreading out in a dark cloak upon the floor. She wept, rain sliding down her cheeks. The foxes circled, their red tongues lapping at the salt water, kissing away her tears.

Do not cry, Sister, they pled. We are with you.

▲▲▲▲▲▲▲▲

"Five years ago," Kachiko whispered, her warm breath tickling the inner lobe of Hoturi's ear, "I sought beneath the labyrinth of Kyuden Bayushi. What I found there was as ancient as the empire itself."

"Shosuro's Hand?"

"Yes."

Images of the black stone fist flashed before Hoturi, and then were driven away by Kachiko's touch. "What is the hand?" Hoturi asked, trying to assemble his thoughts. Her scent, the warmth of her body near his made him remember nights long forgotten.

"It is the hand of the first Scorpion Thunder, the ancient hero who followed the prophet Shinsei into the Shadowlands. Of all the Thunders, only he emerged from that dark place." The ache of the days past seemed to fade as she touched his hands to her cheek. She continued, softly, "It is one of the most powerful artifacts of the ancient days, when spirits and kami walked the land, when the power of the Celestial Heavens remained in the empire."

"And you have found something else beneath the lost palace of your clan?" Hoturi pulled her against him, heart beating like a taiko drum.

"Something even more wondrous than you can imagine. I will show it to you," she promised.

"I want you to show me a great many things." He drew away from her, wanting to see her face:

Shadowed and mysterious, her lips parted in a remembered smile. Her eyes were large and bright, the color of golden honey in a sunlit plain.

"Hoturi—" Kachiko murmured, her lips trembling, so near his.

He wondered how any other woman could possibly have replaced her. The warmth of her body burned brighter than any other fire in the land. She was the moment before sleep, when all the world was peaceful and silent and nothing could be wrong. His strength had been no more than anger. For over a decade, he had fought against the life he had been given—his father's bitter words, his lost love for Kachiko. He had been no more than a stone on a go board, unable to deny the hands that moved him.

Pulling her close, he vowed to change it all. To have her once more, to right the wrongs of his arrogance and blindness . . . It was time to change the world.

▲▲▲▲▲▲▲▲

She lifted the dagger to her throat. Her mournful wail broke the silence of the spirit world.

Around her, the foxes yipped and danced, pleading with their sister. Come with us, they begged her. Come with us, and we will take you home. You were never meant to be here for so long, never meant to stay.

Tears fell to the floor. "I love him," she mourned, "And he loves me. He must."

The kitsune leaped from side to side, their fox faces twisted in sorrow and in fear.

▲▲▲▲▲▲▲▲

"Do you love her, Hoturi?" A single tear ran down Kachiko's cheek.

He caught it on the tip of his finger. "No," he admitted quietly. "Of all the women in my life, all those with whom I have shared a moment, or a night, you were always there with me when I fell asleep." The wind blew softly through the gauze curtains, stirring the thin sheets into motion at the corners of the room.

He lowered his head, lips just above her own as he whispered, "I have always loved you."

▲▲▲▲▲▲▲▲

The knife cut once, twice, slicing through softness and bringing light in straight, bitter lines. Darkness fell to the floor, cut free from ties and bonds.

Ameiko dropped the tanto with a grief-stricken howl. She stood, her shorn hair pooling around her feet. The knife fell with her tears, landing softly upon the torn and forgotten tresses of humanity.

▲▲▲▲▲▲▲▲

Hoturi's mouth pressed against her own, sealing his love for Kachiko in a long, tender kiss. Her hands reached to hold him. A strange fire flooded his veins, rushing to his mind with the power of intimate poison. For a moment, he believed it was no more than the return of emotion, the sensation of his heart opening to her once more.

As his eyes began to blur, though, he knew it for what it truly was. His heart shattered into a thousand shards.

Kachiko stepped back, careful not to touch her tongue to her poisoned lips.

The champion of the Crane fell to his knees. His breath shortened in dreadful gasps.

"And I love you, Lord of the Crane."

The room twisted in strange patterns. The gauze curtains became ghosts of the past. Satsume's voice echoed in Hoturi's ears. "He will never prove himself worthy," it roared in his ears. "Not to me." Hoturi could not tell if the laughter he heard was Kachiko's or his father's.

Blackness grasped his mind and dragged him beneath the waters of conscious thought.

A shoji door slid aside, and another shadow entered the room. Kneeling before his lady, Bayushi Aramoro awaited her command.

"Take him below, to the dungeon cell we have prepared." She smiled victoriously. "Let him live with the rats and snakes for a while. Let him know the blackness our clan has endured because of the Crane. When I am ready, I will come for him."

"Your performance was excellent, Kachiko-sama," Aramoro said dangerously, rising to fulfill her order. He was thinner than Hoturi, but muscular, and he easily lifted the fallen Crane. "For a moment, I almost believed you, myself." When she did not respond, he bowed slightly and left in silence.

As the screen closed, the first rumble of thunder prowled through a blackened sky. Kachiko retied the silk cord of her obi and turned back to close the open windows.

When the rain fell, she could blame it for her tears.

▲▲▲▲▲▲▲▲

On the distant fields of Kyuden Kakita, four foxes fled into the wide woodland.

Lost forever to the world of men, one turned for a last long gaze at the lights of the distant palace. For a moment, the wind ruffled her shorn hair, reminding the young kitsune of all the things that would be left behind.

That place is not yours, Sister. One of the other foxes nuzzled away her tears and barked encouragement. You should never have stayed as long as you did. The ways of man are not the ways of the spirits. Leave them to their own destiny: it is not for us to change the will of fate.

I loved him.

We know.

The barren branches of the forest rustled wildly in the high wind, groaning with the coming storm. Then, following the others with a single mournful howl, the kitsune vanished forever into the Crane forests, leaving behind only memories and pain.

12 THE IMPERIAL FAVOR

"Kakita-sama?" The servant kneeling in the doorway was a minor son of the samurai caste, most likely a Seppun or Otomo.

Yoshi idly wondered what he was doing in this area of the Imperial Palace. Regardless, Yoshi would finish his calligraphy before responding to a servant with such atrocious manners.

The midmorning sun slanted quietly through the window. Beside him, Shizue remained silent. Ink glided delicately onto the thin sheet of rice paper. The Crane chambers were silent as the two of them rested in tranquil study. Only the faintest sense of tension rose from the servant kneeling in the doorway.

After a few more sweeps of his brush across the paper, Yoshi spoke. "If you wish to paint a bamboo tree, Shizue-san," Yoshi placed the brush in a cup of clear water, and ink spread blackly through the water, "you must first study the tree, be one with the tree, memorize and become every inch of the tree. Then, you must forget about the tree, and simply paint."

Bowing, the young storyteller smiled, pleased to share the dawn with her mentor.

"Yes, Seppun-san?"

The servant bowed more deeply, and Yoshi assumed he had guessed correctly.

"Forgive the intrusion, Great Lord, but the emperor has decided to honor your request for a meeting."

"Excellent."

"You must come with me now, if you please."

The implication shocked even Yoshi. "Now?"

"His Imperial Majesty feels well enough to have visitors. That condition may not last, and his health is failing. If you wish to speak with him, so sorry, you must come while he is feeling well enough to receive your presence."

Yoshi nodded. "Of course." His mind racing, Yoshi set his thoughts to the task before him. The latest word from the Crane strongholds spoke of Crab marching toward Kyuden Kakita. Daidoji assaults had slowed the Lion to the north, but the Crab continued forward unmolested, driven before Toturi's armies at Beiden Pass. Already, the battles there had been vicious. The Crab were backing away from the mouth of the valley.

Gathering his things, Yoshi stood swiftly. He motioned to his assistants to clean up the paints and brushes. The painting would have to wait. "Shizue-san," he said as he followed the servant out the door, "if Lord Hoturi comes while I am gone, please tell him to wait. This meeting with the emperor will be of great interest to him, I am certain."

"And Master Toshimoko-san?" she inquired politely, bowing in agreement.

Yoshi paused, "No. He has other duties to perform."

Shizue nodded and began to wrap the brushes in a piece of wadded cotton, placing them in their ornate box.

▲▲▲▲▲▲▲▲

The door to the emperor's chambers was guarded by a dozen armed and armored Seppun, their brown-and-gold mon shining in the weak light of the winter sun. They bowed slightly to Yoshi, recognizing the white-haired courtier as one of the emperor's most trusted advisors.

The young servant knelt before the door, pressing his forehead to the ground. Behind him, Kakita Yoshi knelt on the smooth wooden floor of the hallway, his eyes resting on his folded hands.

The servant gently moved aside the painted paper screen, touching his head to the ground once more before he spoke. "Honored Master, Lord of the Seven Hills, your servant, Kakita Yoshi-sama, has come at your command."

A faint cough came from behind the screen, and then a soft assent.

The servant bowed again and moved smoothly to the side, sliding the screen door open to reveal Yoshi.

The Crane bowed from his kneeling seiza position, touched his head to his hands, and murmured the appropriate greeting. Yoshi's motions and words were absolutely perfect. Perfection, he reminded himself, was something at which the Crane excelled. "I thank you, Great Master, for your time."

"You are . . . welcome, my servant." The young Hantei's voice was even weaker than it had been before the tournament.

Looking up, Yoshi saw a low futon, raised six inches from the floor and covered in blankets to keep out the winter's chill. The gold pillows that surrounded it contrasted with the rich cherry of the shining floor. A blazing fire heated the chamber from a low stone fireplace in the eastern wall. Two servants prepared tea over the fireplace, keeping it warm for the emperor.

"Come here, Yoshi-sama," the Hantei said, raising one blue-veined hand to summon the Crane forward.

Rising just long enough to take four steps forward, Yoshi saw the emperor truly. Without the powder and the thick robes, his condition was all too apparent. Thin limbs barely made ridges beneath numerous blankets. The emperor's skin was pasty and white, showing blue veins beneath every inch. The sores of the plague were not apparent on the young man yet, Yoshi thought gratefully, only too aware of the plague-ravaged Crane in the south.

"Rest, my friend. Have tea with me."

"You do me honor, Hantei-sama."

Barely able to lift his head from the thickened pillow, the emperor smiled.

Yoshi was struck by the Hantei's gentle blue eyes, his fine nose and thin lips—the imperial line's long Crane heritage. For generations, the Hantei had always married a Crane. Only this young man, infatuated with Kachiko, had broken that long-standing tradition.

A door near the fireplace slid open. Bowing, the Seppun servant knelt just on the other side of the screen. "Your wife has arrived, Imperial Majesty, with your medicines."

Kachiko bowed gracefully from a kneeling seiza, the tray on the ground before her. The emperor smiled. She rose, carrying the stained wooden tray in her perfect hands.

Damn the woman, Yoshi thought.

"Kach-chan," the emperor said, burying a cough beneath a too-thin hand. "You are kind, to remember my illness."

"Your Majesty," the empress's lips curved in satisfaction, "you do me too much honor, complimenting me in front of your noble guest. How could I possibly forget my duty to the Light of Heaven?"

As she set the tray down and lifted the cover on one of the plates, Yoshi caught the scent of warm, wet cloths.

The emperor smiled at Yoshi's casual glance. "She has proved you wrong, my friend."

"Your Majesty?" Yoshi asked.

"Her dedication and devotion has proven her nature,

despite the incessant whimpering of the courtiers. I'm certain half the court still believes she is going to kill me." His chuckle became a cough, racking the emperor's body with relentless spasms. When the cough had passed, the Hantei peered up at his bride, wincing slightly as she placed the warm cloths on his forehead and wrapped them about his hands.

"I am certain she has proved a fine wife, Your Majesty."

"Oh? Are you? Yoshi-sama, I have something you can do for me."

Yoshi bowed, honored by the emperor's request. It did not surprise him that the emperor had not yet spoken about the Lion or the Crab. The Hantei knew Yoshi's purpose. He would attend to it, in time. "Your will is my heart, Majesty."

"Kachiko." In that single word, the emperor's voice retained the ring of authority. "Show him."

She froze for a moment, surprised, and then reached to untie the strings of her golden obi. Yoshi stared frankly, wondering what treachery the Scorpion woman was trying to accomplish. Turning her back, she lowered the right shoulder of her kimono. An ornate, stylized tattoo of a scorpion covered her shoulder blade and back. The scorpion tattoo was magnificent, but the emperor pointed at something else.

Just below the sting of the carefully drawn creature, a white scar marred the perfection of Kachiko's smooth back.

The emperor continued, "A few weeks ago, an assassin came into my chambers. The guards along the corridors had been killed. The man had entered by a secret passage known to only those of my blood. I do not know how he was able to enter. Kachiko was by my side. With her shout, the Seppun were summoned. However, not soon enough to prevent his blow."

Kachiko held the kimono deliberately, peering back over her shoulder with faintly concealed curiosity. Her skin shone as pale and exquisite as old ivory, delicately touched by the scarlet fabric that brushed her waist.

Yoshi wondered if she was looking at him, and then realized that every man in the room was thinking the same thing.

Foolish, he chided himself, foolish and dangerous.

"The assassin struck at me, but the empress took the blow herself, risking her own life to save mine." Pride rang in the emperor's tone. He paused, distracted by Kachiko's beauty, and then whispered, "Enough."

The empress raised her kimono, demurely tying the obi about her waist.

"You will tell them, Yoshi-san, about the attack, and about the bravery and dedication of my wife."

"Hai, Majesty."

The Hantei nodded. "And while you will defend her honor and her loyalty to the court," the very words made Yoshi ill, "I will be able to find the time, free of worry, to send a message to the Lion. I find it necessary to remind Matsu Tsuko that the Kakita are my cousins. If the Lion wish to visit Kakita lands, they shall need to speak with me before they continue."

Effectively, the words were an imperial command, informing the Lion to remove their armies from the provinces around Kyuden Kakita.

Yoshi's mind raced, assessing the offer. To order a Lion withdrawal from Kyuden Kakita would infuriate Tsuko. Her honor would demand another strike, potentially against Kyuden Doji, or the warmer strongholds to the south of Beiden Pass—the Daidoji lands, or those of the Asahina. Still, it would give Toshimoko and Hoturi a chance to ally with the Unicorn and drive the Crab south again. It would allow the Daidoji to array their weapons against the Lion. Possibly, Fortunes prevailing, it would give the Crane time enough for the snows to come.

Yoshi nodded, bowing once more. "Your Majesty, this tale of courage and bravery has touched my heart deeply. It would be my honor to be the empress's liaison, and to further her reputation in the court." And, if cautiously done, he could make it appear he was as close to the Hantei as the Scorpion woman. Such apparent reliance could only serve Yoshi's purposes, no matter how it was gained.

"Good." The emperor smiled, his thin lips drawn and his face weary. "I fear the assassin was a ronin. My reign has earned . . . certain enemies." The Hantei sighed, pushing himself back into the lavish pillows of his futon and gazing at his doting wife. "An irony, considering all my wife has done for the empire, that it would cause her harm. Did you know that she has retained an entire unit of Lion Death-seekers, each descended from the First Akodo himself?"

Kachiko's face did not change, nor did her hands falter in preparing the Hantei's herbal mixture, but Yoshi glimpsed tension in her shoulders.

"Truly?" he said carefully, sipping a cup of exquisite tea brought to him by the Seppun servants.

"So unfortunate." The Hantei sighed ruefully, inhaling the rich steam of the green liquid. "The empress has given them a chance to die honorable deaths under imperial command. What more could they ask? My lady Kachiko-san gives her entire life to the empire, and the empire repays her with . . ." Another racking cough spawned a seizure. The Scorpion clutched his hands until the spasm passed. ". . . with deceit."

"Your empress is most brave," Yoshi nodded his head toward the woman, trying to ignore how she touched the Son of Heaven.

"Hai," whispered the emperor. "Yoshi-san, I am tired, and the sun is going down. I wish to see the sunset with my wife."

"Of course, Your Majesty." Yoshi bowed from the waist. He politely finished his tea and set the cup on the servant's tray. "May your evening be blessed, Hantei-sama."

"And may your people know the peace . . . that I have been forbidden."

Yoshi bowed again. He backed three steps from the emperor before turning to go. Outside the sliding paper door, he knelt once more, touching his head to his hands as the Seppun servant slid the door quietly closed. Lifting his eyes a fraction of a second before decorum would dictate, he glimpsed the empress's cold, caramel-colored eyes, burning holes into his own.

The empress. The empress employs Akodo guards. One of the ninja that attacked us at Kyuden Kakita used Scorpion magic. The rest fought with Lion techniques, taught by the Akodo from time immemorial. Yoshi fought to put it all together as he was escorted back to his chambers.

The empress's guard, eager to die beneath imperial orders. It was the only way the Deathseekers could restore their honor. The command of the empress would do. Death was death, and even the fires of Jigoku could be forgiving.

The Lion would retreat. That news, at least, was worth dying for. Yoshi's brows knitted as he reached for his fan. The empress had sent the assassins, it was certain. With no way to prove her guilt, the matter was closed.

For now.

13 TRIAL OF THE EMERALD CHAMPION

Crushing the small piece of parchment in his hands, Toshimoko scowled. He had held the title for only a few days, but already the emperor demanded that he move out toward Unicorn lands and gather the ragtag group of magistrates granted him.

"Yoshi!" He yelled through the wing of the palace, not caring about formality. "YO-SHI!" He stormed into Yoshi's private audience room, ignoring the Crane servants that scurried out of the way. This was Otosan Uchi. The servants who survived the Scorpion Coup knew the fine art of vanishing.

"By Shinsei, Toshimoko-san," Shizue scampered from a gathering chamber just outside the audience room. She held a soft cloth in her hands and wiped away whatever paint she had been using. "What's the matter? Has my brother returned?"

"No." Gruffly, Toshimoko threw the wadded paper into the fireplace, looking around for his half-brother.

Servants scurried across the impeccably polished floor. Crane house banners waved with their passage. The sliding screen doors in each wall stood open. Toshimoko peered into one, then another. Stepping around Shizue, he shouted Yoshi's name into the small Crane garden. Still, there was no answer.

"Damn the man!" Toshimoko stomped back through the room. Drawing another breath to bawl once more for his half-brother, Toshimoko was interrupted by a sudden sharp cough.

Yoshi stood, unruffled, in the arched doorway to the gardens. In his hand he held a sprig of winter violet that had only just begun to bloom.

"Yes, Brother-mei?"

"I must go. The emperor—"

"The empress, rather." Seeing Toshimoko's reddened face at being interrupted, Yoshi strode gently to the fireplace. "Come, now, Toshimoko-san, don't stand on formality. You're to head to Unicorn lands to bear the emperor's message to the Unicorn, under the guise of gathering the Emerald Magistrates, now under your care."

Flustered, Toshimoko nodded. "Curse you, Yoshi! You knew about this? My own brother, and you didn't warn me about the command?"

"We may have the same father, Toshimoko-san, but our mothers were of distinctly different breeds. That means I am your half-brother, and as such," Yoshi's eyes twinkled, "I have an obligation to tell you only half of the truth."

"By Kakita himself, you're a slippery snake."

"You're confusing me with Uji-san, Brother."

Shocked, Toshimoko laughed out loud. "I suppose I am." His anger faded into amused remorse. He knelt by the fireplace, watching the message-paper burn. "I have a duty to perform. I must go. Where is that boy?"

"Our esteemed champion, you mean?" Yoshi's face darkened. "Leave that to me. He's only a few hours missing, and he has no appointments until this afternoon. Most likely, he has taken after his sensei." A guarded look. "I only hope the young women he has been spending his time with are . . . discreet." Morning sunlight shone off Yoshi's pale white hair and reflected in his too-blue eyes.

They are the eyes of a predator, thought Toshimoko. That much, at least, we have in common.

Yoshi wore a brilliant kimono of shaded blue, shifting from the palest sky-gray through the darkest blue of a tempest sea. The wide sleeves parted to show thin arms, pale with lack of exercise but not in any way weak.

Toshimoko felt like a hen beside a peacock. His faded kimono had once been blue, but was now gray. The only bit of brightness was the shining handle of his katana, in an obi of twisted silk. "I must leave immediately."

Yoshi nodded, suddenly serious. "I know. But there is a bit of business you can perform while you run this fool's errand. Ide Tadaji spoke of an alliance with the Unicorn. As Emerald Champion, your voice will carry a great deal of weight."

"Only the weight of politics. I am a champion without a legion. The magistrates have fallen to rubble during the last three years."

Nodding, the Kakita Daimyo placed the strip of violet into a thin vase, arranging the flowers carefully. His visitors today would be Phoenix, and they would understand the significance of a flower that bloomed despite the winter's struggle. "You must travel to Shiro Shinjo and speak with Shinjo Yokatsu, the Unicorn Champion. The arrangements have already been made with Tadaji. Bring back allies, Toshimoko. The Lion will retreat from Kyuden Kakita, but the Crab travel north to fill that gap. Soon, Tsuko's arrogance will take her to our door once more. Already, my spies among the Ikoma have given me her battle plans. They have taken Sayo Castle, and their next march will be toward the ocean, and Kyuden Doji."

Standing, Toshimoko nodded. "Have the Asahina pray for me. I leave within the hour."

"If they will come down from their silver pillars, I will tell them just that." Yoshi looked up from his flowers and watched Shizue bow to bid her uncle good-bye. "Be cautious, Toshimoko. A title will not protect you from danger on the roads of the empire. Without a guard, you will be at great risk."

"Yes, Yoshi-san." Formally, Toshimoko bowed, resting his hand on the hilt of his katana. "But this, and Kakita's blessing, will be all the guard I need."

▲▲▲▲▲▲▲▲

The road twisted high through the Dairuken Mountains, twining among hills and curving over glens. Late in the day, the cool scent of water and thick forest drifted from below. Rocky slopes gradually gave way to thick grasslands and clumped trees—the Shinjo hills.

Three men camped near the roadside. Their fire burned quickly through small twigs. The glow faded, fell, and then rose again as one of the men knelt by the circle of stones and puffed.

"Ten men on that last caravan, and all they gave us was three lousy koku," one of the men snarled, tossing more wood toward his companion on the ground.

"Wasn't their fault. Refugees from the Crab lands. What you think they got in their pouch?" The dialect was poor, obviously from far southern lands. "Shouldn't have come this far north. Not much up here but Ikoma, and through them, Dragon and Unicorn. Nothing to farm, nothing to field.

"Barely got the koku to be traveling. They din't have much for us to take."

"Hai," the third man snarled, running a rough hand over his unshaven face. Thickly muscled, he stood a head taller than his companions. The worn cloak bundled about his shoulders bore a thick crust of mud over its faded mon. He was dark-haired, his thick cotton gi tucked tightly into padding around his ankles. The hakima pants clung snugly to his bandy legs, and his hair had not been washed for days.

His companions were little better. A few teeth missing, with clothes as much patched as worn, they hurried to build the small fire against the evening's chill.

A rustle in the bushes caught the leader's attention. He reached for his sword, tucked in its battered saya.

A weary pony strode down the road, seeking shelter in the thick trees. On its back rode an old man in a green cloak, his head lowered as if asleep. The pony whickered in appreciation, seeing the firelight ahead.

"Hey, old one," the unshaven man shouted gruffly, standing and reaching for the pony's reins. "This here's a toll road. Emperor's orders. You got toll?" He eyed the thick cloak that covered the rider's gray hair.

"Toll road?" The voice was surprisingly strong, despite the wrinkled flesh. "Who says?"

"Emerald Magistrates." The burly man smiled, showing brown teeth. He spat on the ground in front of the pony's hooves. "You know? We're law here, now that the Lion left these lands to go cut up the Crane. We say there's a toll, there's a toll."

Winking conspiratorially, one of his companions chirped, "Toll road, yeah. Keeps the bandits out of Ikoma lands."

"Well, let me off my horse, then, and I'll find your toll." Shifting brusquely, the rider swung down onto the hard-packed trail and reached into his cloak. "How many koku you want? Two, or three?"

Pleased at the old samurai's willingness to offer money, the three men clustered closer.

"Yeah, three." The laughing voice was the leader's. He pushed back the filthy cotton cloak around his neck. "And your cloak. That'll look mighty pretty on me, 'stead of you, gray-hair. A waste, a good cloak warming your old bones."

"I'm afraid I can't give you my cloak, boys." Blue eyes flashed beneath the hood, and a swift hand slid the ancient Kakita blade free of his obi, but left it in its sheath. "But here's your three each."

Toshimoko jabbed with his blunt saya, pounding one man. This was not a battle to the death, but a sensei's first lesson to his students. The blow knocked the wind from the man. Toshimoko turned in a fluid motion to strike him behind the head as well. A third blow caught him beneath his chin, knocking him unconscious.

As the first magistrate fell, the old man spun. His green cloak whirled in a wide circle around him. The second barely had time to draw his sword. The saya caught his knee and sent him sprawling.

The third, leader of the scruffy bunch, had his weapon out and struck the old man's midsection. His katana tore through the swirling cloak. The magistrate staggered forward, but caught only cotton and silk beneath his blade.

Toshimoko parried the leader's blade on his saya and stared at the gaping hole in the new fabric. "You tore my cloak!" He punched him squarely in the sternum.

Flustered, the ronin staggered back. He clutched his chest and gasped for air. The second man struggled to rise.

The sensei shoved his saya lengthwise beneath the man's armpits, hauling him up and hurling him toward his leader. "The emperor himself gave me this cloak, and you have the audacity to tear it!"

The men fell backward, sprawling on the road with an audible thud. Shoving the hood back from his head, the Crane sensei held out his cloak to reveal the long tear.

"Who in the name of Jigoku are you?" The ronin panted, shoving his half-conscious companion from his lap.

"I'm the new Emerald Champion, your lord." Jerking the cloak over his head, Toshimoko stared mournfully at the rift.

"Your first duty is to wake up those filthy friends of yours and remind them who they work for."

The ronin stared at the badge of office that hung, carved in jade, around the old man's neck. He nodded in shocked understanding.

"Your second duty," Toshimoko continued, throwing his cloak in the fallen man's face, "is to sew that up."

▲▲▲▲▲▲▲▲

Many of the towns between Otosan Uchi and the Shinjo lands were the same: poor and cold. What few magistrates Toshimoko found were scruffy, often drunk, and little better than ronin. Three years without an Emerald Champion had driven those who wished to succeed into the ranks of the armies. In Rokugan, a man without a lord was a forgotten man.

The leader of the first three magistrates was named Wayu, born of the Badger Clan. His story was simple, repeated by many of the ruined magistrates. He had served the Emerald Champion when Doji Satsume had held the post. Magistrates had been stationed in the back forests and highlands of the empire, with little news of coup or war or plague. Though they knew the Scorpion Clan had been destroyed, several of the men Toshimoko found carried their masks packed deep in their bags. It did not matter, thought the wiry old Crane. Students are not judged by the lessons they have learned, but by the lessons they teach to others.

Slowly, Toshimoko's retinue grew. The forgotten magistrates flocked to his side. Few had horses—indeed, most did not even have sandals—but all remembered the reason they had joined the Emerald Champion so many years before. They remembered honor. It alone had given them hope through the empty years.

"Sensei," Wayu said several days later as the men marched toward the foothills of the Dragon Clan.

Toshimoko's sturdy pony whickered, pushing its head against the man that walked to one side. "Yes, Wayu-san?"

"One of the men," he indicated a wiry youth, no more than sixteen, who bore the emperor's mon as if it were a shield to guard his honor, "says he knows a shorter route through the mountains. If he is correct, it could save us three days."

Toshimoko raised an eyebrow. Fourteen men followed him now, from aging investigators to young toughs, all tested by time but forgotten beneath the empire's gaze. "What's his name?"

"He calls himself Toku, Sensei. Hometsai found him in the east village, just beneath the cliffs."

The name Toku meant honest. "Bring him to me. We'll discuss it."

Wayu bowed, pacing to the rear of the marching men. He stepped toward the boy and cuffed him on the back of his neck. Faintly, Toshimoko heard Wayu chastising the other samurai as he urged him forward. "If you lie to him, boy, I'll have your ears for the eta."

Toshimoko laughed. He called a halt. Breaking a soft branch from a nearby birch tree, he began to peel the bark from it with a small tanto.

Wayu strode toward him, pushing the boy to his knees as he reached Toshimoko's side.

"Toku, hmm?"

Dark brown eyes peered from beneath a shock of black hair. "Hai, Champion-sama, hai."

"Call him sensei," Wayu punched the boy again, lightly but with enough sting to make him tilt to one side.

"Champion is for formalities," Toshimoko agreed, chewing on the birch twig. "Sensei is for a teacher, which is what you men need now."

"Teacher? I do not need a tea . . . ow!" The boy shouted as Wayu cuffed him again. "I'm a samurai. Samurai." He pointed to the jade token that hung around his neck.

"So?" The Crane looked at his Badger lieutenant. "Tell me about this pass through the hills."

Staring belligerently at Wayu, Toku began to scuff up dirt with his hands. Forming a crude pile, he reached for some of the scraps of bark that lay at Toshimoko's feet and lay them in twisting lines through the heaped dust. "Here is the mountain. Here, the river. Here is a bridge. It is small, wooden," Toku squinted up past his uneven mop of hair. "But it can carry your men, one at time. Better than going around the river. That way takes four days, and then you have to go through Matsu lands."

"Matsu, hmm?" The old man looked at Wayu thoughtfully and continued, "What are the women like in Matsu lands, Wayu-san?"

"Cold as the Dragon mountains, and with fewer peaks."

The sensei's laughter echoed through the glen. Even Toku smiled. Toshimoko said, "Then we'd better trust the boy. Toku-san, lead the way."

▲▲▲▲▲▲▲▲

In the foothills of the Dragon, snow twisted down the mountain in white spirals. Higher still, it made sweeping plains of ice. The weather slowed Toshimoko and his men to half their previous pace. Even the Crane lands must be covered in snow, he thought. With no news, he could only hope—and continue his march.

After three weeks, they neared a small village at the edge of the Shinjo lands, below the frozen mountains. Toshimoko sent Wayu ahead to find the village. The rest of the magistrates marched along the bitter, stone-covered Dragon roads, wrapping their thin cloaks tightly at their sides. Even Toshimoko's pony shivered in the bitter wind that ruffled its thick winter hair. The men groaned with the weight of the cold.

Wayu returned. His breath turned to white mist in the

bitter chill. "The village is to the southwest. The road passes by a river where we can bathe. You can see the Shinjo plains from there. Not far now, Sensei." Wayu seemed pale, unsettled by his trip, but this was no time to discuss strategy or danger. Not in front of the gathered men.

It had been hard enough to kick them into the journey, and would be harder still to tell them that there was danger ahead. Toshimoko snorted, watching the mist from his nostrils trail away like the smoke of a dragon. Half the men would charge forward, their swords open and their heads empty. The other half would shiver in fear and wait for his command. A far cry, thought the sensei, from the bravery of Satsume's Emerald Guard.

Toshimoko nodded, noting that Wayu still awaited his response. "River, hmm?"

"Hai."

"Good." Looking over his ramshackle group, Toshimoko smiled. "Plenty of time to bathe, then. Toku-san!"

Many of the men winced at the thought of bathing in an icy river, but the alternative was to enter Unicorn lands stinking like the worst heimin. Mismatched garments of gray and brown covered most of their bodies, patched together with bits of red, gold, and blue.

"Toku, I want you to find walnuts." Opening the water bag at his waist, Toshimoko drank a long swallow from its mouth.

"Walnuts? You hungry, Sensei?" The cheerful young man grinned up at him, one eye squinted shut against the brightness of the sun.

"Many walnuts, Toku. Ten helmets full, or more. Take the others with you."

Toku hopped from one foot to the other, his padded legs dancing in the snow. "There's a forest to the north. I know it. I'll find them, Sensei, if I have to steal them from the squirrels." Bowing awkwardly, he bounded among the other men and collected their battered helms.

Toshimoko took another swallow of water. He corked the bag and tied it to his wooden saddle once more. The shaggy pony snorted, eager to resume walking.

"Wayu and the sensei say follow me." Toku said proudly to the other magistrates. "I'll show you the way." With curious glances, the men followed Toku into the woods.

Wayu watched his sensei's long fingers impatiently tap the wooden pommel of the saddle. When they were alone, Wayu bowed once more. "There's something else, Sensei."

"I know. What is it?"

"Two men, on stakes near the village's arch. Their heads are removed, placed on top, their bodies spread out on the stakes to feed the birds."

Grunting, the sensei said, "Heimin?"

"No, Sensei. Samurai, by their hair and garments." Wayu's voice dropped. His nut-brown eyes grew even more concerned. "One of the bodies bears the token of an Emerald Magistrate."

"Signs of plague?"

"Hai, Sensei, but no banner warding us away."

The men would be horrified by this treatment of their companions, but they were bushi, and they were samurai. It would not turn them back. Toshimoko caught the attention of three of the men as they headed toward the forest. "Keep your swords ready," he ordered.

"Hai, Sensei."

As soon as the men returned from gathering walnuts, Toshimoko started the march back down the road. Soon, he saw what Wayu had reported—a small village, no more than forty huts and barns. Steep hills clustered tightly around the town, and thick snow drifts piled beside narrow, twisting village roads. Any number of bandits could hide here, ready to destroy the unwary. At the entrance to the village stood a torii arch, between two large boulders. To either side of the road, a pike had been buried deeply in the ground.

The bodies they held were less than ten days old and seemed lashed against the torii arch. The cold had preserved them despite the animals that picked away flesh and sinew. The samurai had been hamstrung. Their feet dangled beneath the thick hemp that tied them to the stakes. Their chests had been torn by several sharp wounds, which sagged open beneath the stumps of rotting necks. Above, their heads leered down with lidless eyes.

The men marching on the road made no sound other than the hiss of breath, trying not to stare up at the bodies splayed before them.

Only Toku said anything at all. "Shinsei . . ." he whispered. "Poor bastards."

Around the necks of each of the two men hung the small jade tablets of the Emerald Magistrates. Even in troubled times, the peasants feared to pillage the tablets, lest they draw the emperor's wrath.

Toshimoko rode his skittish pony near the bodies and used a tanto to cut the tablets free. They fell to the ground, sinking into the thin crust of snow.

Wayu lifted his arm to point at the village. "Master, there's someone coming."

Toshimoko looked up and saw four heimin standing in the door of one of the huts. In their hands, they held hoes and other farm implements—tools better saved for the spring thaw.

"Turn back." One of them shouted with a thick Unicorn drawl. "You aren't wanted here."

"There's plague," another added, thumping his scythe on the ground. He pointed at a small boil beginning on one of his hands, and then to the black ribbons that adorned one of the larger huts at the edge of the village.

Toshimoko glanced at his men.

Their eyes shifted nervously from the village to the staked bodies.

"No plague," Toshimoko shouted. "Only dead magistrates."

"No samurai in this village," a heimin yelled arrogantly. "No more. Go home."

"Who killed these men?" It was a command, barked loudly. The heimin instinctively ducked behind their crude weapons. When they gave no response, Toshimoko shouted again, tugging his horse's reins and riding beneath the high torii arch. "Who killed the servants of the emperor?" He signaled Wayu to prepare for a fight. Keeping one hand on his sword, Toshimoko urged his pony toward the heimin.

"I did." It was a quiet assertion, resigned and calm.

Toshimoko looked to his left, at one of the smaller huts. In the doorway stood a man in the tattered hakima of a samurai. His hair was shaved except for a small topknot perched easily on his head. His face was browned by weather and age, his swords hung loosely in their battered saya. On his left cheek, a boil had begun, leaking its pus down the man's jawbone.

Toshimoko cleared his throat. "These men were the emperor's hand in this region."

"They were murderers, rapists, and brigands. They brought the plague into this village, and they murdered the people who lived here." The man seemed well educated, his clear syllables rolling from a swollen tongue.

"Your name?"

"I am Daidoji Kensen. You are Sensei Toshimoko-sama. Yes, I know who you are. I was wondering how long it would take you to bring your brigand band to our village."

Surprised, Toshimoko swung down from his horse. "What testimony did you have against those men?"

"My own," he managed in a faintly strained voice. "And that of the heimin." Gesturing toward the clump of peasants holding their farm tools in white-knuckled hands, the samurai nodded. "You're the emperor's hand now."

"I am." Toshimoko walked toward the Daidoji, stepping over the drifts of snow that lay in the road. When he was three strides away, the sensei stopped. Caution flared in his old veins. His eyes narrowed.

"Then take this." Drawing a token of jade from his gi, he pulled the string over his neck and threw it at Toshimoko's feet. "Five years ago, I was posted here by Doji Satsume, with those men, to preserve the emperor's law upon this land." But I will no longer serve an emperor who will not heal his people."

Behind Toshimoko, several of the men growled, sensing the disrespect in Kensen's words.

The sensei lifted his hand, quieting his men. Glancing around at the village, he estimated that two hundred men and women could live here. If even a fourth of them were men in fighting condition, with scythes and pitchforks, Toshimoko's band could be overcome. Heimin, the sensei thought. It was ironic to come through all this only to be attacked by a plague-ridden Daidoji and rotten dogs. "Speak your mind, Kensen."

"I don't have to. This village and thousands like it speak for me. The empire is dying, and the emperor has no will—no strength—to heal its wounds. Look around you, Toshimoko-sama. Tell me. What has the emperor, with all his politics and power struggles, done for us?"

"You have no right to question the emperor!" Though he remained at the arch, Wayu's hand instinctively reached for his sword.

The Daidoji did not flinch, nor even look at Wayu. He only stared into Toshimoko's blue eyes with solid brown ones. "Kill me, Emerald Champion. Kill us all, for what we have become. But do not kill us because you believe it to be your duty. Strike because it is time to be rid of the plague upon this land. The wound that Satsume was given at Oto-san Uchi has spread, leaving boils in its path. He did not even die honorably, but wasted away in his tent like the pitiful champion he was. And when he died, the Emerald Magistrates died with him. We are the corruption from Satsume's wound, Toshimoko-sama. We are the foulness that has spilled from his failures."

Shuffling on one putrid foot, the Daidoji stepped closer.

He reeked of rotting flesh. "Kill me, Sensei of the Crane, because it is your duty. Follow the commands of an emperor who is dying of the same disease that slaughters his empire. There is no honor anymore."

"Kneel," Toshimoko said slowly, "and I will give you the death you deserve. Honorable seppuku, to pay the Fortunes for your dishonorable words." He stepped closer to the Daidoji, moving within a sword's length, unafraid.

The Daidoji shook his head. "I will die fighting, old man, not on my knees. I will die knowing that I have served my duty by killing those who believed the emperor was more important than the empire." Drawing his sword in one stroke, the samurai called, "How will you die, Champion?"

Instinctively, Toshimoko drew and struck. His blade passed effortlessly through the samurai's body. Toshimoko looked back over his shoulder as he completed the stroke. His cloak whirled slowly past the falling Daidoji.

The magistrate had not even bothered to swing his blade.

"Well done, Sensei!" His men cheered, raising their fists in salute.

From the doorway, a comely young peasant maiden rushed, kneeling beside the fallen Daidoji. Tears fell from her expressive eyes. Toshimoko took a step back as she clasped the man's tanto. She buried it to the hilt in her own throat. She fell beside him. Small plague boils on her hands wept angry fluid across her swollen belly. Blood gushed from the wound in her throat.

Had it been the Daidoji's child, ill-gotten on the woman? Toshimoko wondered. And how had the heimin girl learned to claim an honorable death—a samurai's death? A peasant willing to die like a samurai. . . .

Toshimoko cleaned his blade on the Daidoji's weathered gi and sheathed it. There was more to this corruption than he could see with his eyes. "Take no food from this village," he ordered his men, commanding them to move on. "We want nothing of this to carry with us."

The men grumbled. It meant another three-day march with little provision. Still, none of the men wished to risk plague simply to ease their rumbling bellies. They would follow his command.

Toshimoko mounted his pony and rode away. He looked back at the heimin who clustered about the body of the fallen magistrate.

If only it were so easy to leave the Daidoji's words behind.

14 BLOOD AND SHADOW

Chains.

Cold stone wall pressed angry wounds into his spine. Iron manacles tore the flesh of his wrists. Chains bound him, stretching from taut arms up toward a ceiling hidden by darkness. His silk gi and vest had been taken from him, leaving him half naked against the chill of mortar and rock.

Hoturi's eyes stung with salt. Blood trailed down his wrists. For how long had he been confined—two days? Ten? Somewhere above him, the Crane must believe he had taken another of his anonymous journeys. Somewhere, far above him in wooden hallways and gently arched rooms, Kachiko played her courtly games. The emperor labored, breath to breath, and the Crane battled with Lion and Crab.

Their champion was a fool, and he deserved to die in darkness and chains.

Stone grated on stone, and a faint light shone against the floor. Footsteps, soft and delicate, whispered behind flickers of torchlight. Two figures approached. Their forms were blackened by shadow, framed in halos of gold.

Aramoro. One was Bayushi Aramoro, with eyes like black chips of stone behind his veiled mask. It clung to his lower jaw, shielding his nose and lips from sight while leaving his eyes free to shine with hatred. He lifted the torch above his head and lit another that hung from a nearby wall. As it burst into slow, sparking flame, the other figure moved closer.

Her body slid gently beneath the rich silk of her kimono, weaving like flame against the pale light. In her hands she bore a heavily ornamented golden box, which shone with an inner light. Even its brightness did not match the radiance of her smile.

"Good morning, Hoturi-sama," Kachiko whispered. Her musical voice echoed through the chambers and labyrinths of Otosan Uchi's deepest heart. "How well you look, my lord. How the night's rest has suited you."

Her hair, pinned up by ivory clips, coiled like ropes of silk. Setting the box on a low, spiderweb-covered table nearby, Kachiko stepped toward him and placed her hand on his cheek.

Hoturi shuddered from the unwanted touch. Her warm hand felt violating, and yet soothing. Reflexively, he tore his face away and tried not to hear her tickling laughter.

Behind her, Aramoro lit another torch. The room slowly took shape. Spiders had owned this space for years, covering its low ceiling and thick walls in their white canopies. Chains hung from thickly mortared stones nearby, and three low tables were the only other furnishings.

Aramoro lit a third torch and placed the one from his hand in an empty iron bracket on the wall.

"How the mighty have fallen," Kachiko murmured, using one delicate red fingernail to touch the chains that bound him. "How low have you become, Hoturi, and how it suits you. The higher you fly, my lord, the farther you have to fall. . . ."

Hoturi struggled against his chains, trying to reach her pale shoulders. "I will kill you, woman. This treachery is beneath even you. What game are you playing with me, Kachiko? What will this do for you, when you have killed me?"

"Killed you?" Her laughter pealed like cascading bells. She lifted her hand to the golden casket, her fingers outstretched in a gesture of triumph. She touched the elaborate catch, the lid, and the burnished gold. "Oh, no, my love. There will be no death for you. Nothing so simple to repay you for your brave deeds. We have something else for you." Raising her hand from the small chest, she reached toward Aramoro.

Aramoro bowed at her command. From a pocket within his gi, he drew a balsa wood box and gave it to his mistress.

The box was thin, but wide, and as Kachiko opened it, a sweet scent of decay struck Hoturi's nostrils. Something inside had been crushed to a powder and wrapped in delicate leaves, left to rot over time.

Kachiko smiled. "My brother makes such wonderful gifts. This was for your father, Hoturi, but the old man died too soon to be of use, and so I kept it for you. Such a delicious irony."

Breaking open one of the leaves from the box, she touched the greenish powder within. Her long fingernail cut a fine line through the dust. Hoturi watched as the red enamel of her nail turned first to purple and then to black. She raised her eyes, fascinated by the change, and looked deeply into Hoturi's own. Her chin dimpled with a brooding smile. She placed the edge of her fingernail to his throat, lightly scratching his neck and leaving behind a thin trail of blood.

The pain was intense. As the powder on her nail mixed with his blood, the scent of sulfur and decay flooded Hoturi's nostrils. Kachiko stepped back. Her form swayed in his vision, blurred by agony and his own anger. Still, the lord of the Crane did not cry out, though his body tensed within the chains.

"Aramoro remembers the day he last saw you, before I became empress, Hoturi-sama," Kachiko whispered into his ear, relishing his anguish. Drawing another fingernail across his chest, she watched as her powder boiled within the wound. It turned to black, the edges of the scratch deepening and tearing open beneath the acidic corruption. "Do you remember it?"

"I . . . told you," Hoturi said through clenched teeth, "the day you turned me away."

"No, Hoturi." She smiled again, drawing her fingernail once more through the residue within the broken leaf. "Perhaps you do not remember, because it was such a simple thing. The day your forces assaulted Otosan Uchi—and the Crane captured the northern wall of the city?"

Hoturi remembered, biting back a wail as another cut burned across his muscular arm.

Her warm hand caressed the tension of his upraised limb, brushing through his pale hair. She did not pause in her discussion. "The day you fought the Scorpion that defended the Forbidden City was the last day I loved you."

Ashamed that she would speak of such things in front of Aramoro, Hoturi murmured, "Take me from here, Kachiko. Let this be between us. Your people have suffered, but I have offered you aid. This torment does not suit you, and it does not benefit your clan."

"My clan?" she whispered with hatred. "You forget, Lord of the Crane. I have no clan. They are scattered, destroyed by your blades and your empire. All that I have loved has died—except you, Hoturi. But I plan to change that small fact." Brushing her fingernail across his lips, she smiled with pleasure as they began to blacken and burn. "But not tonight."

Her smile faded into hatred and her claws slashed five rents across his pale chest. Pouring some of the powder upon each wound, Kachiko backed away to see Hoturi struggle in anguish.

His flesh smoked as black blood trailed down his torso. He could barely suppress a shout, and his face twisted into a mask of pain. Hoturi closed his eyes, shaking with the torment of a thousand small agonies.

Kachiko turned to Aramoro. "You may begin now, Brother. I am done with his first lesson."

Aramoro drew a coiled whip from his obi.

Hoturi's head lowered like that of a charging bull. His blue-gray eyes opened and shone with hatred. The poison that laced his wounds flooded through him. Aramoro lifted his weapon. After the first strike, Hoturi's blood-filled eyes began to fail. The room swam in a haze of colors.

Beneath his black mask, Aramoro wore a victorious smile.

▲▲▲▲▲▲▲▲

In a drug-filled pain, Hoturi felt time pass around him. One by one, the long empty days sealed in stone were followed by nights of agony and whispered lies. Visions swam through Hoturi's mind. He wondered if Kachiko was trying to drive him mad. Each morning before the empress retired to her chambers, she placed cool rags on his wounds, pressing his hair back upon his head and smiling as if to comfort him.

Always she returned in the evening and bore the strange golden box. It shimmered and glowed to be near him, something inside lending a strange radiance. The box shone twice as brightly as she carried it away each dawn, as if its glow had grown from his suffering.

Hoturi did not know how many such days passed, only that she was always near him, giving agony and pleasure with the same hand. Her touch burned with memory. Hoturi began to dream.

"Do you remember love?" she whispered. Nights of passion, her body moving beneath his own, her kisses like sweet rain upon his face. Once they had known love. In his memory, he moved his hand upon the soft flesh of her breast, but felt only the chains that bound his wrist to stone.

"Kachiko . . ."

"Think of the battles, Hoturi, when the Scorpion fell." The face of his father leered at him, cursing him for his weakness and his foolishness. Toshimoko, too, stood before Hoturi, but the old sensei turned away as Kachiko's fingers brushed against his spine. "Remember my boy . . ."

Dairu. My first duty. The only son of Bayushi Shoju, heir to the throne of the Scorpion clan.

Kachiko's son.

Images turned to blood and fire. Otosan Uchi reared up before him once more in dream. Satsume's roar from horseback, spinning a tall pony through the twisting streets. Beside him, Hoturi ran with the other guardsmen, cutting down the Bayushi soldiers as they fled through the burning city.

Later, in the palace, Hoturi stepped over the broken body of a Scorpion samurai-ko, turning toward a young boy filled with pride and anger.

Remember the boy. Among a contingent of guards, Dairu stood proudly, blocking the Crane from passing into the inner chambers of Otosan Uchi. They defended the last sanctuary of the Scorpion, preventing the Crane from freeing the hostages held there.

The image spun. Faces swirled together—Dairu's, his own, Satsume's. . . .

"Is that why you are doing this?" Hoturi heard himself whisper. The words were brittle on his swollen tongue, on lips charred by poison kisses. Dairu's face moved like water, focused and then lost in the Crane Lord's mind. "Because I killed your son."

No longer was he in the corridor of Otosan Uchi, but on

the street where Satsume had fought his last battle against an enemy that had dishonored his name.

In the vision, Hoturi's own sword moved. Cut. Killed.

He was in the palace once more, and Dairu's belly tore apart. . . . Dairu. . . . Satsume. . . . Blood spilled onto the ground. Hoturi heard his own voice—"Tell your father hello when you see him in Jigoku. . . ."

The boy's black hair tumbled beneath a fallen helm.

Kachiko's lips brushed his skin. Her body, her voice whispered beside him in the dark. Shoju never knew, never suspected . . . or never cared.

"I loved you. . . ." Who had spoken? She? He? Or was it just the memory of her voice, so real in the darkness.

Her laughter rang again, echoing through stone chambers and the corridors of his mind.

"Your son . . ."

Rain washed over him like the tears of a broken man. Rain, and a vision of the Bayushi palaces. Aramoro stood at the gates, his sword drawn. "Go home, Crane. It is done. She will not see you now." It is done.

Her silken body rose like the tide.

It is done.

The dead boy's face. . . . Shoju's corpse, cradled beneath the throne of Otosan Uchi, Toturi's katana through its chest. . . .

Hoturi's mind struggled to put the pieces together, fighting to understand. "She will not see you now." Shoju's scream, behind the closed oak doors of the chambers. Toturi's victory. The boy's face, his eyes wide as Hoturi's sword cut through his chest. Dairu . . . my first duty. Pain lanced through Hoturi.

My first duty.

The boy's face, his blue eyes wide beneath a Scorpion's mask.

"Remember," she whispered. Her words kissed his scorched and bleeding skin. "Remember."

Bayushi Dairu on the floor of the emperor's palace. His eyes were as pale as the sky above the city.

The long years rushed forward to envelop Hoturi, and Aramoro's voice echoed in his mind once more. "It is done. She will not see you anymore."

Dairu. Kachiko's son.

Another voice spoke, that of a Crane soldier, on the day of Satsume's death. "Your sword has struck a great blow against Shoju . . . you have taken away his heir, and destroyed the future of the Scorpion. . . ."

My first duty. Dairu. Crane-blue eyes stared up at him from beneath scarlet blood and a black mask.

Hoturi's son.

This time, the scream was his own.

▲▲▲▲▲▲▲▲

"No, Brother," Kachiko smiled as Aramoro lifted the stinging lash once more. "Enough."

Hoturi hung limply in his chains, blood trailing from numerous wounds. His pale skin shone white against the gray stone. Kachiko touched him once, feeling the skin shift beneath her fingers. He did not move, nor rise, nor speak. The silence was her victory.

"Look at me, Hoturi."

Something in her voice forced his head to lift. His eyes were swollen from days of agony and pain. She was still beautiful, more than a decade later—her face, the gently curved red lips and smooth skin.

"What you have seen is the truth. But now, I will show you a lie greater than any in the empire."

The golden box opened beneath her questing fingers. A shimmering glow eclipsed the dim torches of the dungeon cell. From within the elaborate container, Kachiko lifted an object of such beauty and perfection that its very existence hurt Hoturi's heart. It was shaped like a great egg, golden and gleaming with intricate wires twined through its form. Each golden wire seemed a thread of a great skein. They wove among themselves, pulsing slowly. Within the threads, Hoturi could see red and black, gemstones of such beauty that they gleamed with an almost feral light. The egg swelled and shimmered in Kachiko's soft hand.

Somehow, it almost seemed alive.

"This, my love," the words were smooth but bitter in Hoturi's ears, "is the prize I promised to show you when we spoke on the emperor's terrace. The last gift of my fallen clan, stolen from the caverns beneath Kyuden Bayushi as a child is torn from a dying woman's belly."

It gleamed and glowed as if alive, and some sentience within it reached for Hoturi's mind. The golden threads of the egg's shell continued to move in Kachiko's fingers. It was larger than her hand and throbbed with a bloody light that reflected from the chamber walls. Hoturi could hardly move his eyes from the gleaming surface—perfect in every way. As he watched, the threads twisting into faces, screams, and images of his own past.

His sole thought was, it knows me. . . .

Kachiko stepped closer to Hoturi, holding the egg before her womb. Her hips moved with a seductive sway, teasing Hoturi's tortured gaze. "Pan Ku is the name that the First Bayushi gave to the Dragon that bore this. Have you ever heard the tale, Beloved? Let me tell you its tale so that you can appreciate its true value before I reveal its secret.

"Once, long ago, the First Bayushi's eldest son was murdered by treachery and the deceit of the Dark Lord of the South. Bayushi's wife was inconsolable, and her tears watered the ground until the mountains of the Beiden Pass grew from her sorrow. At last, unable to see his wife in such pain, Bayushi swore to bring her a Dragon's tears, to properly mourn their son. Only through such grief could his tortured soul rest in Jigoku. He went to the Dragon of the North, and of the East and West, and to the Dragon of the South—but none would hear him, and he could convince none to shed a tear, even to save the life of his lady."

Moving in small, swaying steps as she told the tale, Kachiko stood close before Hoturi. Soon, their bodies were only inches apart. The golden egg throbbed with eagerness between them.

She continued, "Only one Dragon from the far off Celestial Heavens, calling himself 'Pan Ku,' listened to Bayushi's tale. Together with Pan Ku, the First Bayushi made an oath. The Dragon would give Bayushi a tear to save his lady, but in return, Bayushi would murder a child of the Dragon's choice. Bayushi agreed. Pan Ku gave him the shell of a golden egg, that he could carry the blood of the slaughtered child into the heavens to collect his prize. "

Murder a child . . . his son. Her son.

The haze around Hoturi's mind flowed gently, encompassing her smell and the glow of the golden orb into a vision of gentleness and love. Almost forgetting his pain in the vision of her, he whispered Kachiko's name. Again, the egg shifted and glowed, pulsing with lust and desire.

The egg . . . was feeding on his pain, on his memories. Feeding his desire with its own.

"The child that the Dragon chose, Hoturi, was the youngest son of the First Hantei, and Bayushi murdered him without regret. The blood of the child was caught up in this egg and turned to stone. Bayushi carried the egg and its precious contents to the Dragon in exchange for the life of the First Scorpion's beloved." She smiled, relishing Hoturi's reaction to the golden bauble's lustful emanations. She watched him flex against the iron chains. He struggled to reach her, cursing at himself for a desire that was not his own. In her hands, the Egg of Pan Ku pulsed, growing stronger as Hoturi's will weakened.

"But the Dragon my ancestor served was not a Dragon at all. Pan Ku was nothing less than Fu Leng, the Dark God of the Shadowlands in disguise, testing his brother's loyalty to the empire.

"A test," Kachiko purred, "that Bayushi failed."

The Egg of Pan Ku swirled in her hand. For a moment, the face of a child formed, screaming as his life was destroyed, and his blood was drained into the ancient artifact.

"Sealing the blood of the murdered innocent into the golden shards of this egg, the First Bayushi cast a terrible curse upon it. One day, he vowed, another child would come forth from the blood of the Hantei and the tear of the wicked Pan Ku. That child would be as evil as the deed that formed it, and its rise would break the very mountains that had risen from his dead wife's tears.

"This egg, Hoturi, will be our child."

Kachiko lifted the golden globe from her belly, holding it delicately before his face. Smiling at the ruined lord of the Crane, Kachiko whispered his name again. Her breath blew green and gold mist from the strange object. The tendrils of smoke began to drift more thickly, wrapping them in a soft cloak of forced desire.

Hoturi moaned, trying again to free his hands, not sure if he wanted to choke her or embrace her. The mist shrouded them both. Thick arms of smoke held them close. Slowly, as if to kiss him, Kachiko lifted her lips to his. She held the egg between them, pressing its smooth golden shell to Hoturi's lips. Then, with a soft sound, she pressed her own to the opposite side of the shell.

The mist condensed. A terrible wind tore through the small stone room. Aramoro leapt to his feet to defend his mistress, but could see nothing.

"Kachiko-sama!" He shouted in fear, reaching for his weapon.

Her laughter pealed within the clustered mist that blocked his sight. Strange red eyes glowed through the cloying smoke. Kachiko stepped back. She was safe.

Then, within the smoke, a second figure appeared.

Holding the hilt of his sword, Aramoro leapt between his Bayushi mistress and the Crane Lord, now free of his chains and without any sign of wound.

"No, Aramoro," her voice was sleek in victory, purring with a kitten's throaty pleasure. "You do not understand." Kachiko stepped forward, running her fingertips over Hoturi's chest and shoulders.

Aramoro glimpsed another figure, still chained to the wall of the cell.

"Two . . ." Aramoro's sword fell back into its saya, his numb fingers slipped from its hilt.

"Yes, Aramoro-san," Kachiko purred softly. "One for me, and one for his honored clan, to repay them for their part in the fall of the Scorpion." Reaching beneath one of the low tables, Kachiko pulled forth a long chest. Inside lay Hoturi's clothes, fan, and sword.

The false Hoturi stared into the Crane Champion's eyes, every inch a perfect replica. Even the small scar on Hoturi's cheek, given to him by Satsume long ago, was reflected in the beast's image.

"He has your eyes, Hoturi," she cooed softly, touching the replica's chin and turning his face to hers. "You'll also note that he has much more than your appearance. He has your memories, your darkest thoughts and desires—and none of your honor," the word was a slap, "or your sense of duty to constrain him. He is perfect, my beloved lord of the Crane. Perfect to take your place and bring your clan to ruin."

"Here, little one," Kachiko lifted the ancient sword from the sleek chest and offered it to her creation. "You will carry this. Bring to it all the honor it deserves." The weapon made no sound, unable to rejoice in the grip of a wielder that was not the true heir of the Crane.

The beast's red eyes faded as it touched the sword, turning as pale and blue as those of the Doji Lord. It looked once more at Hoturi, smiling a feral grin as it shoved the katana into its obi. Carefully, Kachiko dressed the false Hoturi, placing the rich garb of the Crane Champion on the creature that had sprung from the magical egg. When she had finished, Hoturi felt as if he were looking in a mirror. The beast's hands, face, movements, even its voice as it whispered to Kachiko—all were identical. All made this double indistinguishable from the true lord of the Crane.

The only difference was the madness behind its eyes.

15 MADNESS RELEASED

Kakita Yoshi knelt on the high dais of the emperor's throne room, enjoying the silence of the evening. The huge chamber was empty, its floor shined to a reflective glow. Below the dais, two lanterns glowed. The lord of the Kakita rested on a fine cushion, enjoying the gentle fall of twilight.

In his hand he held a small figurine of jade, a woman carved in resemblance to the Lady Doji, first of the Crane among the Celestial Heavens. The token brought him peace when his mind was troubled, and it was never far from his side. With the recent troubles in the court, Yoshi had taken to carrying it even when he was alone. It was his way of asking for Lady Doji's blessing and that her watchful eye be never far from her noble sons.

In the somber twilight, his battlefield was silent. The samurai of the court had stepped into their chambers to prepare tomorrow's strategy. Soon, Shizue would come, ending her discussions with the Phoenix. Then, she and he would return to their chambers to prepare the next day's strategy. For now, the silence filled him with restful quiet.

Ten days had passed since Toshimoko was named Emerald Champion, and already the court revolved around the Crane and their war. All the houses of Rokugan feared the strength of the Emerald Champion. They remembered Satsume's legions, clad in shimmering green and gold and marching at the side of the Crane. It was good that the great clans of the empire knew fear. It made them more malleable—easier to control.

A sudden disturbance in the hallway caught Yoshi's attention, destroying his reverie. A servant shouted and fell prostrate, begging forgiveness in a broken whisper. The painted screens of the emperor were flung wide, and the stark light of the corridor chased the shadows into distant corners of the room.

A large figure broke the light from the hallway. He leaned arrogantly on one of the doors. "Yoshi-san," a mocking voice echoed through the mahogany beams of the council room. "I knew I would find you here."

Hoturi? The man strode into the room with a warrior's steps, wide and stalwart.

Deeply surprised, Yoshi stood from his cushions to greet his lord. "My lord Hoturi," the courtier's voice did not betray his emotion, "I had not expected to see you here. Your note said you had left for Kyuden Doji, to see that the palace was prepared for Lion attack. We have readied the men to follow—those that can be spared from Otosan Uchi's Daidoji guard."

"Thoughtful." Hoturi smoothly smiled, his eyes bright in the dark room. Hoturi's gaze drew Yoshi's attention as a serpent's draws in a wren.

Something inside Yoshi recoiled. "My lord," he whispered, "there is great need for you in the lands of the Crane. You should not have returned."

"You think to command me, Yoshi?"

The lack of formality seemed sinister, echoing though the emperor's own courtroom. "No, no . . . not at all, my lord. It is only that . . ."

"Iie." The biting retort churned in Yoshi's stomach. "You will be silent." Hoturi stood on the edge of the dais, his hands balanced on the hilt of the ancestral sword at his side. For a long moment, the champion of the Crane looked around the wide chamber. His flickering eyes rested on the painted screens, the wooden dais, and finally, on the throne of carved emerald at the center of the high chamber. "Come here, Yoshi."

The Kakita Daimyo bowed, moving smoothly from his seat on the dais.

"Kneel."

Confused, the Kakita Daimyo fell gracefully to his knees at his lord's side. The figurine was clasped tightly in his hand. The edges of the statuette bit into his soft palm.

Hoturi stepped around him, a smile playing on his lips. He moved like a cat, circling the pale daimyo as he spoke. "The world around us has changed, Yoshi. There is no time for mistakes or for pleasant games. The Lion and the Crab have struck their first blow against us. We must repay them in blood." Sinister threads wove their way through the Crane Champion's words, implying murder and destruction. "You whisper gentle words with the courtiers here while Daidoji and Doji die on the field of battle. The earth drinks their blood as you drink your pretty sake."

"The Crab have turned away from our southern lands, due to our efforts here. . . . They have—"

"Iie!" Yoshi heard a faint click as Hoturi's sword slid from its saya. The blade gleamed red in the light of colored lanterns. Blood trailed down the edge of the ancient weapon, tingeing its shining soul with madness and fury. "You have not done enough! You have failed to keep the Crab from our borders. They will return, and the Lion still slaughter our men without pause!" Hoturi's voice shook from the force of his anger. For a moment, Yoshi heard Satsume's voice instead of his son's. "The Crane are done playing your games, Yoshi! It is time to fight and to give our enemies the brutal deaths they deserve.

"There will be no more mercy from the Crane. We must strike without regret. We must strike without thought. And those who fail us," the sword slid fully from its sheath. "Die."

The sword blow stunned the Kakita Daimyo, sliding through cushion and dais and sinking deep into the cherry wood below. The blade protested as Hoturi wrenched it free. He raised the ancestral sword of the Crane once more and stared deeply into its light.

Yoshi's hand fell open, and the token of jade rolled to the dais. It glowed faintly, the inner light of the kami shining in the presence of Hoturi's madness.

With an angry curse, Hoturi picked up the token and hurled it across the room. The scent of burning flesh came from his hand.

"Now, cousin Yoshi." Hoturi grinned with feral passion. He held his left hand gingerly, but his sword did not waver in his steady grip. "I have a few commands for you." Without bothering to resheath his katana, Hoturi reached into his sleeve and tossed a package of papers on the floor. "You will find instructions for the court and new alliances to create. Do whatever you must, but do not deviate from these commands. You may even find," Hoturi said with foul pride, "that you could stand to learn a few lessons from the champion of the Crane."

"Hai, Hoturi-sama," Yoshi whispered, anger swelling in his mind. Never had the sons of Doji dared to give him orders for the court. Hoturi was acting fully within his rights as champion—but his foolish pride could damn them all. As Yoshi reached to place the letter in his obi, a voice came at the wide doors to the throne room.

"My lord Kakita?" Shizue called. Entering the room with a gentle bow, she walked toward them. Her steps slid gracefully across the doorway, her clubfoot moving silently beneath the hem of her long kimono.

"Leave us, Shizue-san," Yoshi choked, hoping the girl would not enter.

"Hoturi-sama?" she smiled. "I did not know you were in the capitol."

"Sister." The gleam in Hoturi's eyes startled Shizue as he turned toward her. He extended his hand, still holding his sword before him. "Come to me."

"Hoturi?" She took a few sliding steps across the floor toward him.

"Yes, Sister." Striding to her side, Hoturi reached to catch a long lock of her pale white hair between his fingertips. Instinctively, Yoshi looked away, ashamed at such casual familiarity. Hoturi continued, "You appear more lovely than usual, little one."

"Thank you," she replied, glancing uncertainly at her mentor and trying to ignore the sword in Hoturi's hand.

Hoturi allowed the lock to slide over his palm. He removed the pins that held the thick cloak of her hair in a carefully styled foxtail. As it fell, he pulled it free across her shoulders. "My poor sister, trapped behind a crippled foot and a crippled mentor."

Yoshi stiffened on the dais, the insult scarring his features with anger.

"But do not worry, little sister," Hoturi breathed, pressing the blade of his shining sword to her pale throat. Light reflected from the blade. It scattered across her frozen features, illuminating her hair with cold blue flame. "If we haven't found you a husband by the time the Lion take Kyuden Doji, I will make a woman of you myself." His lascivious hand brushed her cheek.

Shizue shuddered, taking an involuntary step backward.

He grasped the hair at the back of her neck, pulling it into a knot about his fist and bending her head back. The blade hovered against Shizue's throat for a moment more.

"Hoturi-sama," Yoshi whispered. "Your commands will be obeyed, and your men are prepared to march within the hour. Take them and defend our lands." A desperate gamble, but Yoshi had no other game to play.

"You are right, Kakita." Hoturi's hand slid slowly from his sister's bent form, allowing her to fall to her knees. Snarling, the Crane Champion looked down at his retainers. "Have the Daidoji meet me outside the stables in half that time. I will kill any that dare delay my journey. Do you understand?" Hoturi grinned wickedly, pausing for a moment with his sword raised above Shizue's form.

"Hai, Lord Champion," Yoshi breathed, bowing his head to the floor in a gesture of obedience.

Shizue too bowed her head to the mahogany boards, her heart pounding in fear. They did not look up again until the storming beat of Hoturi's footsteps had faded from their ears.

⌃⌃⌃⌃⌃⌃⌃⌃

Yoshi watched from the balcony of the Crane as the contingent of Daidoji rode from the Imperial City. Their banners waved in the light of the torches they carried. At their head rode Hoturi, a brave figure in armor of blue and silver.

"Send a letter to Uji-san," the Kakita Lord commanded. His aides hurried to obey. "Tell him the Daidoji of Otosan Uchi march to the Crane provinces, bringing all the aid we can spare. More, tell him Hoturi rides with them."

Yoshi looked down at the token of jade in his hand. The lady's legs had melted as if burned by some titanic flame. In the moonlight of his chambers it almost seemed as if she knelt in his hand, praying for mercy from the madness of a ruined world.

16   FIELDS OF THE KI-RIN

Cracking walnuts between his teeth and spitting the shells into the large fish barrel, Wayu pondered the insanity of the world. Toku ferried helmets full of the sour nuts from the Shinjo woods. Toshimoko demanded more and more of the forest's fruit. The campsite was cold and wet from recent rain, and the barrel they had taken from the last village smelled of dead fish and old salt.

Overall, thought Wayu as he spat another walnut into the bin, this is an entirely unpleasant day.

"Master," one of the men shouted, "haven't we cracked enough?"

"No!" Toshimoko shouted, rapping the man on the head with a thin cane of balsa. "Not until that barrel is full."

"But why?"

Rapping him again, the old Crane samurai rebuked his inquisitive nature. "I don't want the Unicorn to think the Emerald Champion travels with bandits and mercenary ronin." Laughing, Toshimoko pointed at Toku. "Get a large stone, as well, boy. We'll need it." He circled the fire, checking the barrel and encouraging the men. The sun was slowly fading in the sky, but Toshimoko showed no signs of stopping, and only one man was allowed to leave the group—to make food for the others.

Confused, Toku continued to split the nuts with his teeth. The Emerald Champion had gone mad, but it was his duty to obey.

A few hours of pounding later, Toku watched, amazed, as Toshimoko calmly ordered all the men to strip off their gi and hakima and hand him the garments. Over the fire, he placed a large iron cauldron—a cooking pot, taken from another village—filled it with water, and added the walnuts one by one. In went the clothes—blue, green, orange, and gray—and out they came, a dark brownish-black. The men huddled in their cloaks, exchanging extra clothing while their garments dried. The old sensei looked on with faint approval.

"Not the most attractive group," the sensei said when the men were arrayed in their newly dyed garb, "but at least you give the illusion of a unit. It will have to do."

Wayu brushed his blackened haori, tucking the long sides into his hakima to keep warm. "Shiro Shinjo is only a few miles beyond that ridge," he pointed. "We should make it to their first outpost by midmorning tomorrow." They had nearly twenty men, the remnants of the Emerald Magistrate units from Otosan Uchi to the Dragon mountains. Once, there had been more than two hundred, but now only these few remained. Toshimoko glanced through the ranks as they began to march, straightening their lines with a shout and a mocking remark.

Over the long days of travel, Toshimoko had begun to teach some of the men, encouraging them to improve their skills and rediscover their strengths. Many of the men no longer referred to him as anything but sensei, and any resentment toward the gruff old man soon died on their lips.

▲▲▲▲▲▲▲▲

The next morning, they marched into the Shinjo lands. The Unicorn plain spread out beneath the mountains like a quilted canopy. Open roads stitched across wide fields of gold and the marshy squares of harvested rice paddies. The snow of the mountains had faded away against the foothills of the Shinjo territories. On the road below, horsemen approached.

The three horses were large, their flared nostrils breathing great gasps of air. Riders in the purple and gold of the Unicorn sat atop the massive steeds, holding high banners with the Shinjo mon. Toshimoko watched as they approached, recognizing one of the men as Yasamura, son of the Shinjo Daimyo.

The old samurai straightened on his scruffy pony, wishing the chubby steed were more statuesque. The Unicorn stallions stood at least half a man taller than his own steed. Their arched necks were wide and muscular. No wonder their cavalry could ride across the empire in half the time of the other clans. Each of their horses' steps were three paces longer than those of his pony.

Yasamura lifted his fist to halt the scouts beside him. All three slowed from their racing gallop to a more sedate walk.

Toshimoko nodded to Wayu, who bellowed a command and halted the Emerald Magistrates. The sensei rode forward, his weary pony whuffling at the huge red beasts.

"Greetings, Champion of the Emperor," Yasamura called, bowing in his saddle. He was a cheerful lad. Youthful and handsome, Yasamura wore his two swords more like ornaments than the weapons of a samurai. He was still a lad, but atop his massive steed, he seemed more impressive than many daimyo in the empire.

"Greetings, Shinjo-san. My men and I," Toshimoko's sweeping gesture indicated the twenty samurai in black, "are weary, and we request the hospitality of your lands."

"It would be our honor, Kakita-sama."

Tradition served, Yasamura sent a Shinjo ahead to inform the palace that the Emerald Champion had reached Unicorn lands. Yasamura and his lieutenant meanwhile rode beside the magistrates, providing a very public escort down the wide, sloping roads. The Shinjo palace stood atop a high plain, its strange walls arching with barbarian architecture. Purple banners waved from high minarets. The road that led to the palace was lined with white stones, quartz shining brightly in the winter sunlight.

The courtyard of the structure was wider than in traditional palaces, covered in trailing ivy and fountains that trickled over carefully carved boulders. Unicorn palaces always had fountains; their fetish with water seemed to be a carryover from time spent on their journeys through the Burning Sands. The deserts lived in Unicorn history, carried over to their descendants in the Emerald Empire.

On the wide stairs that led into the inner hallways of the palace, the Unicorn Champion waited. Shinjo Yokatsu was an older man, his hair graying with the weight of many years. Though younger than Toshimoko, he had been Doji Satsume's peer for many years. Looking at his wide shoulders and bandy legs, the sensei was reminded of the past Crane Champion, remembering how the two men had struggled together against opposition from the other great houses of the empire. Yokatsu must be made to remember his alliances with the Crane, and if Toshimoko's journey was to be worthwhile, the champion of the Unicorn must renew his alliance with Satsume's son.

The Crab would not forget their war with the Crane simply because they had been beaten in the fields of Beiden.

Although the war for Beiden Pass continued, the Unicorn did not keep their armies in the pass. The massive cavalry still remained on the fields of the Unicorn provinces, awaiting Yokatsu's orders for deployment.

Yokatsu stood at the top of the stairway, three courtiers to either side and a small troop of Shinjo guards behind. As Toshimoko dismounted, he could feel the Unicorn's eyes sweeping over his men, taking in every nuance of their stance and attire. Though their dyed clothing gave them a certain unity, the men could barely be granted the title legion or even unit. Still, it was the best that could be done. No doubt Yokatsu understood the necessity.

Then again, Toshimoko noted as Yokatsu smiled, the Unicorn were hardly more educated than gaijin, and might not have noticed at all.

"Toshimoko-sama," Yokatsu's aide began, speaking for his lord as was appropriate, "you are welcome here. Your men will be given a wing of their own for their stay, and whatever amenities they require. Tomorrow, you will meet with my master."

The Emerald Champion nodded seriously. "There is much to discuss. Much to be said." Changing the subject, he said, "Tell His Excellency that it was a pleasure to meet his son. The boy seems to be growing well, and strong."

The aide smiled, "I will tell him your words, Kakita-sama. We are honored."

"As I will be honored by your lord's words, tomorrow." Leaving the modest implication to hang between them, Toshimoko followed his men into the palace.

▲▲▲▲▲▲▲▲

Waiting was the worst part of such negotiations. Although it had been only a night and a day, already Toshimoko felt as though he had been kept waiting for years. He and his men had enjoyed the luxury of the Unicorn baths, and were clean at last of the filth of travel. Outside in the fields, huge horses pranced and played while a chilly wind whipped the violet banners above the sprawling wall. Toshimoko leaned on the windowsill of his high stone chamber, looking down at his magistrates as they practiced their technique alongside the Shinjo bushi. Dawn passed, and then morning, and each hour of the afternoon seemed to stretch on for days.

When the servant finally came to the guest chambers to escort him to Yokatsu, Toshimoko nearly let out a cry of relief. Wayu smiled at the old sensei and offered the Emerald Champion his cloak. "Take care, Sensei," the young lieutenant said with a smile, his broken teeth glinting. "You never know what to expect from the Shinjo."

"I know just what to expect," Toshimoko sighed, shrugging the cloak over his blackened haori and gi. "Expect difficulty." The words were from his ancestor's treatise on swordplay, but their meaning was true even on the field of diplomacy. Thank the Fortunes that it was the Unicorns he bartered with, thought Toshimoko as he followed the servant. Other clans would have made him follow their explicit directions for bathing and purification and pray for two more hours.

Thank the Fortunes for Unicorn sense.

A Phoenix Daimyo would have met with Toshimoko in a council chamber, its arched walls and elaborate screens giving the illusion of prosperous formality. A Crab would have walked with him atop the wall and watched the Shadowlands boil in constant reminder of eternal duty. Kakita Yoshi preferred discussions in the Doji gardens when the weather was fair. The Lion might have met only on the battlefield, in a tent erected for the purpose. It was appropriate, therefore, that the Unicorn Champion was in his stables, watching the treasured steeds of his clan race through the field, their tails held high and their necks arched. These steeds were creatures of the wind, as unpredictable and challenging as their masters.

The servants announced Toshimoko's approach. Yokatsu turned from the fence and bowed effortlessly from the waist. Toshimoko returned the greeting, masking a smile as he noted that the Unicorn's boots—another gaijin affectation—were covered in mud from the fields. These muddy paths were not the royal chambers of Otosan Uchi.

"Your men are not Crane," Yokatsu began curtly, his syllables clipped.

"No, Lord Yokatsu-sama. They are Emerald Magistrates, under the direct control of their champion."

"But you are a Crane."

"Hai."

Gruffly, Yokatsu snorted. "Satsume saw no difference. Do you?" With a riding crop, he flicked a spot of mud from his boot, discomfort apparent in his motion, if not his words.

Toshimoko turned to watch the horses as they played in the wide green fields. "Do you think, my lord, that the stallions in the field think of themselves as your servants, or your companions?"

"Eh?" Surprised by the question, the retiring Unicorn Champion stared out at his steeds. "They are our companions, yes, but they obey our commands."

"So too am I the cousin of the emperor, yet also his servant. I am the Emerald Champion, and I am also a Crane."

Yokatsu considered for only a moment, a belligerent crease upon his brow. "Serving the emperor is not the same as serving the empire."

The Daidoji's words rang again in Toshimoko's ears. "No," said Toshimoko thoughtfully. "They are not the same. But so long as the Hantei remains on the throne, I serve his needs above all others."

"Above even the Crane?"

The trees shivered in a brisk wind, raining the last of their autumn leaves on the sloping roof of the Unicorn barn. A mare whickered to her foal. The golden colt replied as it chased its mother through the fields.

"Champion, my men are not Crane. They are magistrates, of all clans and all backgrounds. They are men from all the seven great houses, and many of the minor ones. They do not serve the Crane. How can I lead them, if I do not serve them as they serve me? It is bushido that a samurai does not expect reward for his labor. It is also bushido that a lord should keep his faith to his men, as they give their lives for his service."

"Words of Kakita?"

"Simple truth, Yokatsu-sama, and even Shinsei would agree."

"Then, if the emperor commands it, will you lead them against the Crane?"

His face hardened, and the sensei sensed a trap. "If the Crane attack the empire, I will defend the empire. Unto death." He did not know the words were coming, but as he said them, Toshimoko realized that he spoke the truth. Satsume's burden, he thought. Although the lord of the Crane had also been the Emerald Champion, he had never distinguished the two. Perhaps that was why the Scorpion had been successful—the champion of the emperor had been attending his own duties, stolen from the side of the Hantei in his hour of greatest need. If that should occur again, and Toshimoko was with the Crane . . . the empire could fall.

The burden had fallen on his shoulders, and it was greater than he had realized. Kakita Toshimoko looked back at the Unicorn palace, where his men marched. They practiced the lessons he had given them—swordsmanship and stature. Their dedication to the Emerald Empire had survived the fall of an emperor and the failure of their lord, his champion. Wayu shouted from the practice ground, encouraging his men to serve well, to be worthy of their sensei's respect.

It was time he stopped thinking of himself as a Crane and

thought of himself instead as champion of the emperor, defender of the empire. With their rough manners and unswerving dedication, the Unicorn had taught him a lesson. Bushido.

May the First Doji, Lady of the Crane, grant that I bear it well.

Yokatsu smiled as he saw realization dawn in his companion's eyes. The Unicorn had been deliberately leading him toward this, as one would break a foal to the saddle. With a simple gesture, the champion of the Unicorn withdrew a letter from his sleeve, offering it to Toshimoko. "This came for me today, Lord Toshimoko-sama. I thought it only fitting that the Emerald Champion should read it—but I would not dare show it to a Crane."

Concerned, Toshimoko accepted the letter—and the implication. Again, the Unicorn surprised him. Despite their crude exteriors and strange customs, the hearts of samurai still beat in their chests.

The Unicorn's letter had no mon on the cover, no distinguishing features. Opening it gently, Toshimoko read the simple words it contained.

My Lord,

> *The Crane have left the city of Otosan Uchi, taking with them all their legions here. Although they say that they will be marching toward Kyuden Kakita, I fear their objective is more sinister. Among them rides Doji Hoturi, Crane Champion and son of Satsume. From the south came reports, shortly after their journey began.*
> *The men of the Crane that follow the Doji Champion have razed two of their own villages, bringing plague and death as well as Taint. It is believed that the Crane have made some alliance with the Shadowlands, possibly to defend themselves against*

*the Crab and Lion forces. In their desperation, they
have fallen to the Dark One. I can only pray to the
Fortunes that their souls will be spared.*

I await your command in ihe emperor's city.

Ide Tadaji

Toshimoko's face turned white with grief and anger. "No,"
he whispered. "It cannot be."

Yokatsu turned back to the graying fields, watching as
the sun's glow turned orange against the horizon. "If you
are the hand of the emperor, you know where your duty
must lie."

"If this is true—and I swear in my soul that it cannot
be—then I will perform the emperor's duty." Toshimoko
handed the letter back, his mind racing with thoughts.

Yokatsu's eyes narrowed, testing Toshimoko's endurance.

The sensei continued with anger. "I am a samurai. My
soul is my own. If I am to die in the emperor's service, so be
it. But I will not turn my back on that duty, even for my own
clan." More softly, he continued, "Even . . . for my own student." Toshimoko's face was pale, his legs shaking beneath
the blackened hakima pants.

"The emperor's hand is strong once more," Yokatsu whispered, watching the anguish fade as Toshimoko recovered his
on, the face of a samurai—emotionless, stoic, and firm. "And
we shall ally with him."

"No." The word was sharp, harsh. "The Emerald Champion did not request your clan's alliance." The aged sensei
turned canny eyes to his opponent, placing the final stone.
"The Emerald Champion will be pawn to no one, not even
the allies of the Crane."

Surprised, Yokatsu raised a thick eyebrow. "Then what of
the Crane, and the Crab that fight them?"

"As the hand of the emperor, I could command your
troops to intervene."

The Unicorn Champion cawed a sharp laugh. "Command? You do not have the men to command anything, Toshimoko-sama."

"No," the sensei said with a faint smile. "But neither can you claim an alliance with the emperor's hand. Such an alliance would benefit you in the court of Otosan Uchi, whether I am Crane or Dragon or Crab."

Smiling, Yokatsu thumped his riding crop against the wooden beams of the fence. "Well played, Emerald Champion."

"Send your troops to Beiden Pass. Harry the Crab and drive them south. In exchange, my magistrates and I will grant you passage through the empire, without toll and without clan permissions. Six months of free travel, Yokatsu—such a boon could remove the only barrier that prevents your cavalry from having true power in the empire."

"Free passage through the empire . . ." Shinjo Yokatsu murmured. Toshimoko could tell the Unicorn was tempted. The man's untrained face contorted, and his eyebrows worked up and down like flying birds.

"So long as your first journey," he said emphatically, "is to enforce your control over Beiden Pass, and that you drive through it toward the lands of the Crab."

"An alliance with the Crane, paid for by the Emerald Champion?"

Toshimoko smiled grimly. "Consider it my last service to the house that gave me birth. When I leave here, I travel home—not to give the Crane the strength of the Emerald Magistrates that follow me, but to determine the truth of the accusations you have shown me. To face Hoturi, and if he has fallen to the Dark One, to see him die beneath my blade." The words were difficult to say, but they held the ring of truth. Toshimoko's face did not betray the tortured emotions that burned within him.

Nodding slowly, Yokatsu bowed to the champion of the emperor. "We leave in the morning; you for the provinces of the Crane, and the Unicorn for Beiden Pass. With luck, Toshimoko-sama, we shall not meet again."

Bowing in return, Toshimoko listened to Wayu's cries of pride in the distant practice field. "May the Seven Fortunes bless us both, my friend." With that, the sensei turned and strode back toward the palace of the Unicorn, leaving Yokatsu alone with his horses and the dying sun.

17 THE FALL OF HONOR

Uji stood on a hillock and stared moodily at the gray southern skies. Perhaps it would snow and the winter would finally come. In the distance, the clouds blew, their swollen bellies laced with bitter winds. Kyuden Kakita was not far. Soon Uji and his men would reach the safety of the fortress. He would have traded all the dry nights and cold weeks of autumn for a single day of snow. Even if it were brief, snow would have prevented the Lion from attacking Kyuden Doji for at least two months—more if the winter were heavy. The time would surely be enough for Doji Hoturi to move his gathering army before the Matsu could attack. Then, with the northern provinces safe, Hoturi could bring his armies to Kyuden Kakita and protect them from the Crab.

Uji was fifteen days out from Kyuden Kakita, his feet crunching through the thin layer of frost that spread across the ground. Fifteen days, and his men would reach the tall stone walls and warm fires of home. Seven winters as a Crane general had taught him how to encourage his troops through the cold nights and keep them marching through the short winter days.

His lieutenant, Daidoji Ritenu, paced beside him with the long steps of a jungle cat. Ritenu's narrowed eyes showed only anger at being withdrawn from their fights against the Matsu, but the young man was too disciplined to utter a word of disapproval. He knew the Crab were a greater threat—one that could not be stopped by the light snows of the south lands. While the Lion would freeze, trapped in ruined Sayo Castle, the Crab would take the villages of the Crane and warm themselves inside Crane huts—or worse, Crane palaces.

On the road to the south, a rider approached, his shaggy pony breathing great steaming trails of mist. The rider bore Kakita colors and did not appear to have rested in many days. The pony's steps were shaking, its weary body nearly ready to collapse. As the horse approached Uji, its rider swung down to the ground, barely keeping his feet beneath him. He bowed to Uji, trying not to keep his hand on the horse's saddle for balance. Despite his obvious weariness, the man was determined to keep his dignity.

Uji formally returned the bow, giving respect to the young man's house. The soldier's face was haggard. Ready for the worse, Uji squared his shoulders.

"My lord Uji-sama," the messenger said, "there is grave news."

"Speak."

"The Crab are marching east from Beiden Pass."

"What?" Stunned, Uji reached to steady himself on the pony's warm neck. A wave of sick dread passed through him. "Tell me of the battle at the pass. What has occurred that the Crab march on us so early?"

"The Crab taken Beiden Pass, my lord. They seek provisions

in order to hold the pass. The closest source of those supplies is Kyuden Kakita." The rider's words were rushed, spilling over each other with anguish and lack of sleep. "A few days past, the armies of the Unicorn marched to Beiden Pass and joined Toturi's legions there. Even now, a Unicorn contingent chases the Crab, beating them when they camp. But without the force of the Dragon and the walls of the pass to give them the advantage, the Unicorn are little more than an annoyance to Kisada's great army."

"Damn," Uji swore, turning to his lieutenant. "Ritenu, we have fewer than ten days to make Kyuden Kakita. Can the men do it?"

Stuttering in surprise, Ritenu said, "I think so, Uji-sama, but the march will be difficult."

Uji nodded darkly. "Less difficult than cleaning the bodies of the Kakita from the wreckage of their palace. Damn the courtiers. Yoshi, you fool—you've not stopped the Crab, you've released them. Whatever games you play in that court of yours, you haven't played well enough." Muttering foully, Uji summoned his men forward to give them the bad news. "Damn all courtiers and their faith in words." Fewer than five days ago, he had received word from Yoshi that the Crab had been stopped south of the pass. Something must have happened to change that. Even as angry as he was, Uji knew that it was not typical of Yoshi to exaggerate, or to fail so badly.

Something else had freed the Crab from the dictates of the Imperial Court, and whatever it was, the damage had already been done. Ten days to reach Kyuden Kakita or the lands to the south would be covered in flame and death.

"Even if we are in time, my lord, will our men be enough?" Ritenu's question was soft, meant for Uji alone. It would not do for their men to see doubt. Less than a hundred men stood with them, the remainder of all the northern units of the Crane. The group was small, but their eyes were as hard as stone.

"We will have to be, Ritenu-san," was Uji's dour response. "We have to be."

▲▲▲▲▲▲▲▲

Kyuden Kakita stood on a wide hill, the forests of the Crane surrounding it like a mother's sheltering arms. In Uji's childhood memories it had been a place of laughter. Today, the laughter was dead. The ground shuddered with the sound of marching feet.

To the north, the Crab army swarmed, less than a day from the walls of the Crane palace. The cheers and war cries of the Crab shook the heavens, and their feet echoed like thunder against the cold ground. Their general marched with his men, needing no horse to place his eyes above the rest. Hida Yakamo towered above his men. On thick shoulders he carried a mighty club, like the tree trunk of an ogre.

In gray and blue, the Crab armies chanted as they marched. The chant seemed impossibly low, like wind echoing through a thick tunnel of earth. From the woods nearby, troops carried lumber for siege engines and battering rams. The army stretched wide from Beiden, its men filling the valley passes like a swelling tide.

That was not the worst of it.

By their side slithered creatures of the far-distant south— the Shadowlands. Demons raised their heads. Great teeth clamped down on air. Wide nostrils smelled the flesh of men. Hundreds of goblins crawled and chattered among the greater beasts, cowering lest their masters reach down and tear them to ribbons for food. Behind them, more oni marched, their eyes bright and claws stained with blood. It was an unholy alliance: the empire's protectors, freed from their wall and marching beside the very beasts that they had warred against for generations.

Kisada must have gone mad.

Goblins, green and long-eared, wore mockeries of samurai armor, scavenged from the corpses of the dead. They carried weapons made of bone and charred iron, and their feet slapped the rocky ground without rhythm. A parody of the brave Crab samurai who led the way, the goblins cawed and capered. They marched only when their tremendous warmongers shoved them forward, lashing them with whips or tearing them with claws. Better the warmonger's whip, certainly, than the sharp teeth of the oni that marched at the army's rear.

Only the courage of the Daidoji men had given them the fleetness they had needed to reach the walls of the palace before the sun rose on the tenth day. Regardless of their station, their honor, or their lives, the Daidoji raced through the Kakita forest by hidden path and secret ravine.

Charging toward the golden doors of the palace, Uji screamed the name of his house.

Doji Kuwanan came to the battlements.

Uji waved his blue banner three times in the age-old signal of the Crane.

The archers withdrew from the top of the walls. Kuwanan raised a silver flag and signaled the men to come ahead. The sinking sun flashed from Kuwanan's gauntleted fist. With a wave of his hand, the Doji motioned to the gatekeepers. Metal shrieked against wood. The gates moved, opening to allow the Daidoji inside. Troops raced into Kyuden Kakita. They panted and fell to their knees well inside the palace walls. It took a few minutes for all of Uji's men to rush in from the woods, but the palace's gates remained open until all had arrived.

"Seal the wall!" Kuwanan cried.

As the last of Uji's men stumbled into the main courtyard, the gates of Kakita palace swung closed. Men slid a series of thick bolts against the heavy oak doors.

By morning, the Crab would arrive, their massive army growing in number as they swarmed down the Kakita fields.

"Where is the Lady of the Doji?" Uji panted, darkness invading the corners of his eyes. He stumbled, and Kuwanan moved to support him. Shaking off the offending hand, Uji gripped Kuwanan's wrist. The Doji prince's eyes were haunted, shadowed like the stormy sky.

Uji shook his head to clear it. "Tell me she's not in the palace. By the Fortunes, Kuwanan!"

"No . . . Uji-san . . ."

Angry and exhausted, Uji could hear the cries of the Crab armies marching closer to Kyuden Kakita's gates. "Where is Doji Ameiko-gozen? There is still time. A contingent of men can take her to Kyuden Doji, where she will be safe."

"She is gone, Uji." It was all Kuwanan had to say.

Uji sank to his knees, panting with exhaustion. The last of the gate locks slid into place. A massive iron bar sealed the thick oak doors, braced to withstand the inevitable assault of the battering rams.

Silently, Kuwanan reached into his obi, withdrawing a small pouch of folded rice paper. Opening it, he handed the Daidoji general a shining length of black hair, cut cleanly by a dagger's blade.

For a moment, Uji stared dumbly, not comprehending. Then, Kuwanan lifted his other hand.

In it was the tanto that the Daidoji general had given Ameiko.

▲▲▲▲▲▲▲▲

During the night, the Crab camped outside the gates of the palace. They waited only for dawn to bring enough light to start the siege. In somber gray and black, the Crab waited. Their weapons shone like small fires in the glare of the rising sun. Among their troops, Uji could see the mon of the Kuni and Kaiu gathered beside Hida and Hiruma forces—the great families of the Crab arrayed for battle. Yakamo led a force that numbered easily fifteen thousand men.

Uji did not fear the samurai, but the creatures with them.

An oni howled as the light of the sun crested the horizon. The beast lifted a huge, fanged head atop its long, wormlike body. Three pairs of claws reached out toward the dawn. A segmented pink tail thrashed among nearby samurai. The beast shrieked with a voice that sounded like dying children. Behind it, another oni snarled, reaching for a goblin that had the misfortune of walking nearby. A slash of dripping black claws, and the goblin was in two pieces. The oni stuffed them one by one into its mouth. Its gelatinous belly rippled with meat and armor. Its body was laced in scars laden with pus and gangrene. The demon did not seem to care. Sucking the blood from its fingers, it poked angrily at the towering worm beast and yowled.

Uji shuddered. These oni were the true denizens of the Shadowlands. At least twenty such monsters, all different, marched within the Crab lines. Another seven thousand goblin accompanied them, and at least half that many mujina—lesser oni, with fewer powers than their great masters but equal ferocity. Around them, the grass withered to brown, tainted by their very presence.

"Dear Lady Doji, protect us from Taint and lies." The ancient prayer died on Uji's lips as the swollen beast lifted another screaming creature and stuffed the writhing mujina into its wide mouth.

"To the battlements, Uji," Kuwanan said, his face as gray as the stone of Kyuden Kakita's walls. "The fighting will begin soon."

"How many men do we have?"

"How many did you bring?" Kuwanan replied, turning to ascend the stairs.

"Nearly a hundred."

Kuwanan nodded gravely. "Then we have almost two thousand—still not enough to man all the guard posts and keep the arrows firing day and night."

"Two thousand? Only two thousand? Where have the reserves gone?" Shocked, Uji followed Kuwanan.

The Doji prince pointed out toward the swollen armies of the Crab. "They have gone to feed the oni, Uji. And they will not return. A unit of Yakamo's men caught our reserves as they marched here. None survived."

Uji followed Kuwanan up the long stone staircase that led to one of the Kakita watchtowers.

Below them, the Crab began to form a front line along the road, their thick shields raised to block the fierce spray of arrows from the Kakita wall. Shields were useless on the battlefield against a sharp katana, but the Crab insisted on them. At times like these, Uji thought wearily, perhaps the Hida ways were the best.

One of the Hida rode his steed just beyond the range of the archer fire, commanding his troops to surround the gate and test the strength of the men on the walls. Uji recognized him as Hida Tsuru, cousin of Kisada and guest of the Crane at their harvest festival. Good, Uji thought, his hand tugging at his unshaved chin. Better an enemy you know.

"Surrender, Crane!" Tsuru called. "Half your garrison is dead from plague, and the rest are falling down with exhaustion. We have more than twenty thousand men, and you have perhaps one-tenth our number. There is no chance of defeating us. If you try to hold our armies at bay, you will only gain the deaths of your men. Give us the palace, and we will allow your troops an honorable death!"

"The fool," Uji growled to himself. "He knows we will never surrender the palace."

"Of course he knows," Kuwanan replied. "He seeks to build his men's courage, not to temper ours. Soon, the snow will fall, and his men will be trapped outside the palace."

"Do you think that any one of those men," Uji waved his hand at the massing Hida troops, "would not give his life willingly, and more so if he was already dying? We have plague in our lands. Some of the samurai in the palace already show signs of it. We must fight with caution, or we will lose." Uji considered his choices carefully. "You have been trained by the Lion," he began.

"And you by the oni themselves." Kuwanan snarled. "What are you suggesting?"

"That if we fight with honor, we will die. But if we fight with courage, and forget the rules of battle, we might be able to survive, and keep the palace out of Crab hands."

"Fight without honor?" The Doji prince glanced angrily at his general. "No."

Uji pointed out at the oni that had begun to claw their way toward the palace walls, ignoring the arrows that rained around them. "Your enemy will not be as polite. Listen to me, Kuwanan. You know this is the only—"

"No!" Kuwanan yelled. "My men will die like Crane! With honor!"

Unmoved, the dark Daidoji Daimyo stood his ground. His voice lowered to a malevolent whisper as he continued, his eyes never leaving Kuwanan's own. "You are commander here, my lord prince, and I will respect your orders. Allow me to speak, then, if you wish, you can remove my head from my shoulders for my failure to obey. But hear me out." The hiss became short, harsh, each word punctuated by desperate need. The Daidoji stood as straight as the ramparts of the palace,

Still furious at Uji's disobedience, Kuwanan considered his request. The Doji controlled his rage, pushed his katana back into its sheath, and nodded silently.

"Behind the Crab units there is a line of Unicorn, sent by Fortunes know what stroke of luck. They chase the Crab, but the Hida have arrived ahead of them—possibly because of some dark magic of the Crab shugenja, possibly because the Unicorn have been injured by the Crab and travel slowly. We must do two things. First, we must hold the Crab for two days, until our Unicorn allies can arrive. Second, we must injure the Crab as deeply as we can.

"Even now, the Crab search our forest for lumber to make their battering rams and palisades. In days, they will have shattered the walls of Kyuden Kakita, and we will be rats to scurry before their troops. Only if the Crab are wounded can we hope to survive—and only if we wound them deeply enough will they turn away from Kyuden Kakita and seek easier prey."

Kuwanan was grim. "You suggest using our manpower to damage the Crab as heavily as possible, to make every Crane life cost three of the Crab? How, Uji? Slaughter tactics? Night strikes? Hiding, sneaking like goblins and beasts rather than fighting like samurai? The Crab won't simply invade, steal the food and provisions they need, and leave. They are here to turn their vengeance against the Crane, and to destroy us."

The shouts of the Crab turned to roars as one of the ancient oaks of the Kakita woodlands fell in a rush of barren branches and the shriek of twisting wood. Kuwanan's mind fought to ignore the faint tang of dishonor. It was bushido that you should meet your enemy face to face on the field of battle, not skulking treacherously. Kuwanan's Lion training said that he should die fighting the Crab with every sword at his command . . . but his soul, as a Crane, whispered for a different path. Lowering his hand from the hilt of his blade, Kuwanan watched as the gray-clad Crab tore the bark from the ancient oak tree. With a mighty cry, they felled another. Uji only nodded in silence, aware of the burden that hung over the young prince's head.

"I've never been the heir, Uji-san," Kuwanan said. "The decisions I was expected to make in my lifetime were those of a soldier, and my soldier's heart cries for battle. If Hoturi were here, he would know what to do."

For once, Uji's somber attitude broke. He placed his hand on the cold stone wall of Kyuden Kakita, feeling the smoothness of granite and age. "Hoturi is not here, Kuwanan." The Doji prince glanced up at the swarthy face of his general, and Uji continued passionately, "The Crane do not need Hoturi today, my lord. They need you."

"Ready your plan, Daidoji-san," Kuwanan told him. For a moment, the young Doji stood straighter, at last feeling the weight of his burden lift from his shoulders to be shared by all those inside the palace's timeworn walls. "But first, sleep. You have spent the night in preparation, counting the Crab armies and making certain your men were well. Now it is time for you to rest. We have a few hours before the Crab strike. They must ready their battering rams and position their armies. I promise you this." He placed his hand on the Daidoji's shoulder in a gesture of respect. "The palace will still be here when you wake."

▲▲▲▲▲▲▲▲

The agonizing thud of the battering ram shattered Uji's concentration, pounding the rock of Kyuden Kakita's walls. With it came the whir of spells hurled by Crab shugenja to hold the breach wide and allow the Hida passage. Sparks flurried into the sky above the dark-robed shugenja, arching from their hands and spinning into lightning on either side of the marching Crab. Any arrows that tried to reach beyond the lightning wall were pulverized into searing ash.

Two days had passed, and only a hundred Crane had died. They had died outside the palace, not inside, led by Uji on raids of the Crab supplies and assaults against the goblins. Nearly two thousand of the dim-witted green creatures had broken and run, convinced the very spirits of the ground had come to kill them. Fear of their oni leaders had kept many of the goblins in line, but fanatical superstition had driven away the rest. Those that remained fought with blood-painted helmets and whispered of rolling ground that spoke with strange tongues.

Never tell a goblin that wet sod can be cut into man-sized strips, and never mention that the ground speaks with the voice of a Crane.

Over a thousand Crab were already sick, showing signs of the filth that had been placed in their water supply. Uji's men had hunted for anything that would spoil the Crab reserve, from deadly herbs to the corpses of small animals, and had used them with devastating effectiveness. The Hida now posted three times the guard on their provisions—more men that would not be joining the attack on the Crane.

Thus far, Uji's strategies had been successful, but there was more to do. Soon the Crab would regroup and overcome their losses. Still, there had been no sign of the Unicorn troops that were expected behind the Crab, and no sign of further Crane reserves. Uji snarled and shook his head to clear it. This was not the time for doubt.

Suddenly, a crash tore through the palace. The western wall shuddered as one of the stone supports snapped beneath the pressure of the Crab battering rams. Uji leapt from his position near the gates, falling to the courtyard below and rolling to his feet. Indeed, the western wall of the palace had begun to crack, and eager hands pushed aside the rubble.

Thum! Thum! Thum!

The stone chipped, tearing apart. Black claws dug wildly through the granite. Where the claws touched, the stone began to crack as if weakened. Granite turned pale white beneath the oni's hands. That was how the Crab burst through stone walls—they had the dark magic of the Shadowlands to help them.

Uji readied his twin swords, drawing them from their sheaths. More Daidoji rushed into position near the breach. When the oni and his Hida companions tore out enough stone to step through, the Crane would be ready.

The stone fell away in larger chunks, and the oni's claws dug deep into the weathered stone. The blackened fingers withdrew, dragging long rifts in the remaining stone. The hole was large enough for a man to duck through with his weapon drawn.

Even that was not the Crabs' plan.

"March!" called the Hida commander. He whipped one of the fearful goblin units toward the shattered wall. "March, you dung-infested beasts! On!"

Goblins skittered forward, broken weapons clutched in greenish fists. Their long ears flopped wildly beneath scraps of armor and hide.

Three Daidoji soldiers leapt to the wall, ripping into the goblins with raised yari spears. Their sharp points dug into the green flesh of the scurrying beasts, tearing wounds through the hide armor the creatures wore. With shrieks, the goblin unit disintegrated, running to and fro outside the wall and howling in pain and fear.

Now the three Daidoji stood in the open, vulnerable to the Hida on the opposite side of the gap. Arrows pierced the Crane, and they fell.

Ten more goblins forced through the gap, raising their arms to defend against the waiting Crane. While their bodies were being cut down, the Hida pushed away more stone, quickly stepping through to the inner courtyard. They guarded the position, literally throwing the expendable goblin troops toward Uji and his men. Slowly the Crane troops were pushed back.

A terrible crash broke the air as another wall shivered beneath the force of the Hida siege engines. A third ram and a fourth pounded the outer walls, still the thick stone held. Only the breech at the front of the courtyard continued to spill Crab troops.

Uji commanded four more Daidoji to his side. He attacked the largest Crab near him, cutting at the man with all the strength he could muster.

With a yell, the Crab swung a tetsubo toward Uji's head. The massive iron club whistled through the air. Uji leaped aside and then darted in with his weapon, slicing toward the Hida's unprotected knees.

Another Crab intervened, thrusting his short spear before

Uji's katana. The shaft shattered, cut in two by the Crane's sharp swords, but it did deflect Uji's blow.

The three adversaries circled. Uji kept the two men at bay behind shattered rubble until he saw an opening. In a fast one-two motion, he cut first with one sword then with the other. The first blade feinted aside the Hida's spear. The second struck flesh. The Hida fell, clutching at the deep cut in his neck.

Twisting, Uji avoided the falling tetsubo and drove toward its wielder. A second cut, while the club was still down, and the Hida fell.

Outside the palace, a horn blew. Marching feet echoed behind shouts of war. The Crab commander shouted the order to withdraw. Only a few Hida stood in the opening, their scarred faces dead and empty of emotion. One looked behind him, toward the breach in the stone. Uji took the opportunity to cut open his torso. When the Crab fell, he almost looked grateful.

Uji stepped back, his heart pounding.

The rest of the Hida within the courtyard faced the small troop of Daidoji guards. One Crab thrust toward Uji's side, but the general of the Crane stepped nimbly away and buried his own blade deep into the Crab's throat. Two more men moved from the Hida guard, swords flashing. A Crane fell to a swift strike. Something outside the wall was moving, and the sick sliding noise filled Uji's ears. He rained down a series of blows on his Crab opponents, trying to maneuver toward the breach. They held the line as firmly as a row of ancient oaks.

Another Hida launched a fierce flurry of blows toward Uji's shoulders. Each strike rung from the Daidoji's blade. One more attack, and the Hida's blade turned against his own. The sharp steel of his katana entered the fleshy torso of the Crab. The man fell without a sound. Uji stepped back.

A shadow fell across the gap in the stone wall, a shadow impossibly large and terrible to behold. One Daidoji beside Uji stepped back, unable to contain the fear that overwhelmed him. An oni stepped over the broken stone and into the courtyard. One man tried to run, his feet slipping on ground slick with blood.

Before he could take the second step, Uji's sword had cut him in two.

"There is one escape from that beast," Uji howled, grabbing the samurai nearest him and guiding the man toward the oni. "Your escape is a death with valor! If you flee, I promise you, there will be no escape from me! March forward!" Uji's voice echoed with the sound of barely contained madness.

His men flinched at the command. Still, they knew their duty. With pikes and spears raised for battle, the Daidoji moved reluctantly toward the massive creature.

Its skin was covered in tar, its long claws greasy with blood and filth. It stood almost twelve feet high, towering above the Crane legions like a giant made of black blubber and greasy flesh. Humanoid arms coiled from the wide man-like torso, its muscles standing out like ropes of thick tar beneath the creature's skin. As it roared, the scent of rotting flesh blew like a massive wind from its mouth. Chunks of its last meal sprayed upon the standing legion. Four black eyes rolled in a twisted skull, shining with a crafty intelligence. Black tar oozed from its fatty skin, dripping down legs that were as thick as stone pillars. Each step caved the ground beneath its feet, crushing earth and stone. It reached toward the Crane with two grasping hands, its iron claws as sharp as twin katanas.

With a shout, the daimyo of the Daidoji blocked one of the swift claws with his sword. The oni roared again, reaching to grab another of the Daidoji in its fist. The woman launched a fierce attack with her yari, breaking the shaft of her spear on the long iron claw of the creature's hand.

The oni laughed, a terrible sound. It lifted the screaming samurai to its mouth. Biting into the Daidoji's body with iron teeth, the oni tore her in two. Hunks of flesh belched forward with the last of her terrified screams.

Uji leapt toward the oni with both swords, cutting a massive swath in the beast's foul hide.

It roared in anger. Thick black tar escaped from the wound.

A shout went up from the assembled Daidoji. The creature could be hurt, and if it could be hurt, it could die.

Renewed strength flowed through Uji. He grinned evilly. He sheathed his katana, holding fast to his wakizashi.

The oni lunged toward him.

The daimyo dodged, plunging his wakizashi high up into the oni's fleshy back. Pulling on the blade, Uji climbed onto the creature, shielding himself from the oni's claws with its own body. The Crane general clutched his wakizashi in one hand and grasped for purchase against the creature's blubbery flesh.

It roared again. With a terrible sweep of its claw, it shattered the pikes that tore at its skin. Two more Daidoji fell, their bodies tossed aside like wooden dolls before the massive strength of the demon.

Uji stepped higher onto the oni's back, trying to draw his feet beneath him for leverage. It was no use. He was stuck against the oni's hide, trapped in the thick tar that slid from the wound in filthy bursts of black blood. Cursing, Uji reached into his obi and drew out his katana.

Howling, the oni flexed its ropelike muscles. It clawed at its own back in an attempt to reach the offending samurai. Turning from side to side, its iron claws clicked uselessly.

Uji jerked away, but before he could shift his weight, he was covered with another warm wash of tar. He clung to the short hilt of his wakizashi, lifting his katana to drive the second blade into the oni's neck.

Before he could stab with the blade, the oni turned, throwing itself against the stone wall behind it.

Uji was crushed by the sheer weight of the thing's flesh. His fingers slipped on his katana's hilt, nearly dropping the weapon. He felt a snapping in his ribcage. His breath grew short as he choked on the tarry flesh of the beast.

The oni slammed against the wall once more.

Faintly, Uji heard a battle cry, and he felt the pressure ease.

The cry came from Ritenu, the last man of Uji's legion left alive. Spear in hand, Ritenu hung from the creature's claw as it struggled to shove him into its mouth. The beast snapped its fangs together. The valiant Daidoji took his spear and drove it up into the oni's pallet. The creature screamed, shoving Ritenu down its gullet with one mighty hand and shattering the shaft of the spear entirely.

Ritenu's attack had been enough to move the oni away from the wall; enough to allow Uji to strike at the beast's unprotected neck. Even as Uji felt the pain of loss for his friend, he blessed the man's courage.

One hand clung to his wakizashi as the other swung the katana with all his strength. Uji drove his sword into the base of the creature's skull. The oni fell. Pulling himself free of the clinging tar, Uji twisted to face the wall once more, his hakima covered in grime and blood.

"The Unicorn!" the call echoed through the palace, raised by the archers on the wall. Through the breech, Uji saw that it was true—huge steeds bearing the mon of the Shinjo flooded the far hills of the Kakita, only a few minutes away from the walls.

Outside, the Crab milled in anger, unprepared to halt the siege. Uji heard the shout of the Crab commander outside the breach. "Take the food! Burn the palace! Retreat!"

Hida poured through the broken wall and hurled torches. The palace, the elegant gardens—beneath the oil and flame of the Crab, nothing was safe. The Daidoji within the courtyard fought valiantly, but as they did, Uji heard the great gates of Kyuden Kakita burst open, torn from their hinges by a final, massive blow from the battering ram.

The Shinjo were too late. Before the Unicorn could fully enter the battle, the palace would be in flames.

"Uji!" Kuwanan howled from the battlements, watching

as the Crab poured through the open gates and into the flaming palace. "We must leave the palace before it falls and destroys us all!"

"No," Uji hissed, lifting his sword again. "NO!"

Hiruma scouts, bearing the mon of the Crab forces, released a barrage of flaming arrows toward the palace. Burning shafts lit the elaborate tile roof. Pitch-covered arrows struck the already blazing wooden walls of the inner courtyard, scattering flame throughout the palace. The grass, littered with Crab and Daidoji corpses, began to catch fire. Uji's men were being cut down by the Hida, burned within the corpse of their own fallen home.

Eyes burning from smoke and tears, Uji lifted the Daidoji hunting horn and sounded the retreat.

If they were lucky, the Crane soldiers would make it through the scattered Crab lines, using the arrival of the Unicorn to cover their escape from the ruined kyuden.

Uji turned wearily, ignoring the flames that licked at the palace walls. He fought his way out of flame and chaos.

There was nothing left to save.

▲▲▲▲▲▲▲▲

One by one, the legions gathered. Eyes searched for friends thought lost. Many had died in the combat with the Crab. Many more were burned alive in the flames of Kyuden Kakita's fall. In the distance, beyond the forest, smoke still poured from the palace's northern side. Only three hours had passed, but to Uji, it seemed an eternity.

Of the two thousand men that had manned Kyuden Kakita's walls, only one thousand had survived.

"We failed." Uji's voice was hoarse from shouting, and raw from smoke and bitterness.

"I know, Uji. One day, it will be rebuilt, with twice the grandeur and beauty of the old." Kuwanan panted, sweating from the battle as he watched the Crab armies turn beneath the sudden assault of the Unicorn troops. Pointing after them with an open hand, Kuwanan said, "It seems that the Shinjo have the upper hand against the Crab."

"May it serve them well," Uji said. "We cannot help them in their fight."

"We must gather the men and make for Kyuden Doji." No smile lit the Doji prince's face as he said, "Hoturi will be gathering an army from the north. We need to take these men, and any more we can find that escaped the Crab, and meet him there."

Looking back at the ruin of the palace, Uji shouldered his father's sword.

18 THE FALLING DARKNESS

Matsu armies swelled through the valleys of the Crane, ignoring the melting snow that churned beneath their feet. The winter had been a light one, and at the first sign of warmth, Tsuko had ordered forty thousand samurai out of Sayo Castle and toward Kyuden Doji. Spring had come at last, and it was time for revenge.

The general's name was Matsu Agetoki, a fierce, bearded man with unusual red hair and brilliant brown eyes. He was portly, but beneath the flab swelled muscles as strong as an ox's. Of all the Lion, he had been the most successful in incorporating the strange battle strategies of the Unicorn, and so he led the massed cavalry of the Lion. Their shaggy ponies struggled to keep pace with his long-legged steed. Though not of Unicorn descent, Agetoki's mount had been born in the Yobanjin Mountains, bred of gaijin lineage to a foreign people.

Agetoki quieted his restless steed, giving the mount its head as he stared up the high road toward the palace at the peak of the sea cliffs.

Kyuden Doji was massive, far larger than any other palace in the empire. It was twice as ornate, filled with the gold and artistry of a thousand years of Crane. Rising atop the sheer cliff walls of an angry ocean, it had been carved deep into the stone of the mountains. Below, waves pounded the rocks. Above, clouds thick with snow and ice blew past the high towers of the kyuden. Ancient walls, shrouded in brown, dead vines, embraced three massive towers and a white fortress. Though the kyuden was not built to withstand a long siege, the land around the palace protected it. Only one road led to Kyuden Doji's thick steel gates; one road that twisted back and forth across cliffs, hundreds of feet above a blackened sea.

The sea churned angrily against cliff shores, pounding the sand. One white boulder, the size of a peasant's hut, gleamed faintly through the spray. It was known as the Champion's Stone, final resting place of the founder of the Crane. It was also the site of the death of Doji Satsume's wife, some twenty years past.

Kyuden Doji was as ancient as the oldest stories of the empire. It had been the home of the founder of the Crane, and they would not take kindly to the Lion's assault.

Agetoki smiled. That was exactly the way he preferred it. Soon the palace would rest in Lion hands, its ocean passages and ports controlled by the mighty Tsuko. With the strength of the Lion armies and the wealth of the Crane lands, the empire would have no choice but to bow to the might of the Lion.

Inside the palace, only ten thousand Crane remained. The plague had struck their lands like an oni's blow, tearing through their paltry samurai and leaving only pus-filled bodies. Especially here, in the Doji fields, the plague had been rampant. When the Lion controlled these lands, there would be a purge of fire and ash. All signs of sickness would be destroyed along with the heimin that carried it.

Inside the palace the Daidoji general, Uji, stood firm. He had brought a thousand troops, all rescued from the fires of Kyuden Kakita. Damn the Crab for not finishing the job to the south. Now the Lion had more men to fight—uphill, through cliffs and pounding surf. Still, fight they would, Agetoki thought, his massive chest puffing with pride. His men were Matsu, and Lion, and therefore unafraid of any challenge.

Looking over the reports once more, Agetoki gave another thought to the young Crane Champion and his band of mercenaries. To all accounts, Doji Hoturi had been collecting any men who would follow him, leaving entire villages empty. The reports, if you believed them, spoke of the Taint that followed the lord of the Crane, whispering that he brought death to those who refused his service. Perhaps there was one Crane, after all, who did not have a heart of silk and flowers.

Agetoki smiled. He hoped the reports were true, and Hoturi would attempt to bring his legions to the rescue of those in Kyuden Doji. That would be a foe worth fighting, rather than the treacherous and stinking Daidoji.

If Hoturi should come, he would relish the contest.

The Lion troops marched slowly up the steep slopes of the Doji cliff road, ready to fight once more in the name of their champion and their honor.

▲▲▲▲▲▲▲▲

With the ocean at their back and the Lion before them, the Crane had little room to maneuver. Kuwanan ordered the archers of the Doji to the castle's wall. The bitter defeat at Kyuden Kakita still haunted his mind. At Kuwanan's signal, the Doji closed the palace gates, confident all scouts and heimin in the area were safe within the walls of the mighty keep.

"He will come," Kuwanan shouted as he marched through the wide corridors of his childhood home. Every wall, every scent and sound of the palace was familiar—but he had never once thought he would need to defend it against a massive army of Lion. "Hoturi, Brother—where are you?"

The letter had arrived less than a week ago, commanding Kuwanan to hold Kyuden Doji at all costs. It was the only word from the Crane Champion since he had left Otosan Uchi long ago, but all the reports of the north—scattered though they were—spoke of Hoturi's armies, their great numbers and their strength. Already, he had razed three villages that had been taken by the Lion, killing Crane and Lion with a fervor not seen since the days of Satsume. Perhaps a bit harsh, thought Kuwanan, but if Hoturi had discovered that the Doji samurai of those provinces had allied with the Matsu, he could have done no less. It would all be explained when Hoturi arrived with his legions.

It would all make sense once his brother arrived.

Climbing to the top of the palace's stone steps, Kuwanan addressed the men as they prepared for the day's battle. He stood at the edge of the wall that surrounded the inner courtyard, looking down at the samurai who had gathered to defend their ancient keep. There were no gardens here, no pretty paths—only stone and sand and ten thousand bushi ready to fight against the Lion. Looking over the tiers of blue and silver, Kuwanan felt a wash of pride.

"You are Crane!" he began, his voice high and clear. "You are the cousins of the emperor, the sons of Doji and Kakita. There is no force in the empire that can overcome you. You alone have the soul of Rokugan in your hand!"

A cheer went up from the gathering. More bushi pushed their way into the courtyard.

"The Crab destroyed Kyuden Kakita with a force ten

times the size of our army there. They had oni and creatures of darkness and Taint. Yet we fought, because we are Crane, and we will not bow to dishonor and Taint." A murmured agreement came from the men, accompanied by the cheers of those who had fought at Kakita palace's gray stone walls.

"When we have turned back the Lion, we will march to the fields of the emperor, and we will demand repayment for this insult. The Matsu believe they have the strength to destroy us—but a thousand years ago, when Kakita fought Matsu, it was their ancestor who fell before his sword!" Kuwanan raised his fist as a shout went through the Kakita before him. "The Lion have never forgotten that day, and we would do well to follow their example. Let them know that they are already beaten, that their troops march in vain. Their swords will falter and break before the strength of our honor!

"Less than a day's march from our walls, Doji Hoturi brings a force of ten thousand samurai!" The cheer this time shook the palace walls. Men chanted the champion's name as Kuwanan continued. "All we must do is hold the walls, as we did at Kyuden Kakita, and Hoturi-sama will be our strength! The Lion will be crushed between his might and our walls, and they will rue the day they chose to make us their enemies!"

"Ho-tu-ri! Ho-tu-ri!"

Though all those around him chanted, Uji, the black-eyed daimyo of the Daidoji, ignored the rising sound of the champion's name. Uji turned away as the men cheered, walking toward the great gates of the castle, a darker shadow in the crowd of blue-clad samurai.

"Let the Lion know that we are not afraid!" Kuwanan could barely be heard above the shouts of the men. They raised their voices again. Every fist in the palace reached for the sky. Every face lifted with joy and righteous anger. "We will show the empire that the Crane cannot be so easily defeated!"

"Ho-tu-ri! Ho-tu-ri!" yelled some. Others chanted the

name Kyuden Kakita, as if its noble defeat were a talisman of victory. The bushi of Kyuden Doji reminded themselves of those who had already fallen for the honor of the Crane.

▲▲▲▲▲▲▲▲▲

When the Lion attacked, the Crane were ready.

Four times, the Lion hurled themselves against the Crane walls. Four times, they were forced to withdraw, their troops impaled by arrows and burning with pitch. The Crane fought like cornered tigers. Their strength unified to drive back the Matsu. Together, Doji, Kakita, and Daidoji fought. Through their unity, the Lion were unable to gain more than a foothold in the Doji cliffs.

The Lion marched up the road, using steel shields to block arrows and throwing them down when they reached the high walls. Hundreds of blue-fletched arrows thrust through the air, cascading down upon the Matsu troops. The Daidoji from Kyuden Kakita hurled spears through the Lion lines. When the Lion slowed, hot oil poured from the castle gate, rushing down the road like lava from a volcano.

Each day was torture. The Lion spent their strength against the wall, alternating legions to rest their troops. The road was covered in oil, pitch, and blood. The corpses of the dead littered the rocky ground. Still the Lion fought. They were indefatigable.

The Daidoji spent their arrows, trying to cut down the commanders of the Lion and turn their forces to chaos. The arrows began to run out and the last spears were thrown. The oil dried up. The road froze to ice, cracking beneath the tread of Lion feet and turning to hard-packed ground. The Lion advanced farther each day. Crane resistance grew weaker with each passing battle. Time was not an ally to the Crane.

Days passed, and the Lion encampment grew closer. The Matsu assaults grew bolder.

"He will come," Kuwanan said, his face blackened from smoke. A volley of Lion arrows sailed overhead, covered in burning pitch. Heimin raced from the castle with buckets of water, quick to put out any fire that threatened the castle's roof and inner buildings. Already, the few trees within the palace had been cut down for arrows and spears. The sand beneath their feet was stained with the blood of the wounded. Of ten thousand Crane, two thousand had already been lost to Lion attacks. With ladders and ropes, the Matsu had twice scaled the walls. Even though the Crane took heavy losses, they slew the invaders both times.

Another volley of Lion arrows rained down, followed by the tremendous boom of a battering ram.

"Use the last of the pitch and tar," Kuwanan ordered. "Let them remind the Lion not to approach the gates of Kyuden Doji!"

When the orders were carried out, the steel gates were blackened with fire, and the ground charred and stinking with the bodies of Matsu samurai. Even the smell of the sea below could not block the horrid stench of war.

It only kept the Lion away for a single day.

Even the stalwart Uji nearly gave up hope. He kept his sour face turned away from the men he led. It was not his place to steal their dreams of freedom and victory. Still his heart grew heavier as each Crane fell behind the walls.

▲▲▲▲▲▲▲▲

At sunset on the tenth day, a single rider approached over the Doji cliffs, galloping down the road through the Lion armies. He straddled a Unicorn steed. The puffing stallion covered the ground in tremendous strides. On the rider's back fluttered the tall mon of the Miya, the emperor's heralds. The Lion were forced to part and let him pass.

"By the Lady Doji," Uji breathed as he watched the

emperor's messenger gallop toward the leaders of the Lion armies. "We are almost beaten, and then . . ."

Suddenly, a cheer erupted from eight thousand throats, shaking the palace of the Doji. Through the midst of the Lion armies rode another army—this one led by a young man in brilliant blue armor. His sword gleamed as he rode atop a rearing black steed.

Hoturi.

As Uji watched, the herald of the emperor dismounted and spoke to the Lion generals. Something was happening, and it did not seem to make sense. At the far side of the high plain, the new Crane army slowed, as if waiting for an unseen command. They were still too distant to make out, but at least ten thousand men marched behind the Crane Champion. The Lion nearest them began to retreat into the body of the Matsu forces, shouting with fear. Hoturi's legions marched.

"What are they doing?" Uji hissed, squinting into the light. "The herald of the emperor, here? Could this be Yoshi's doing?" Barely hoping to pray for a reprieve, Uji leaned across the battlement and tried to make out the Lion's commands.

With a bow to the emperor's herald, Matsu Agetoki climbed atop his great steed and lifted his fan to command his troops.

Suddenly, one of the Lion commanders drew his sword, leaping toward the Miya herald. Before Agetoki could shout to restore order, the herald had drawn his own sword, and the echo of their blades rang out over the massed armies of the Matsu. Twice, steel met steel. The blades shone in the sunlight. The Lion screamed in fury, raising his katana above his head to complete a massive shomen strike.

Agetoki shouted another order. Three more Lion moved between the attacking commander and the emperor's herald. Within moments, the insubordinate Lion was dead. His sword was broken. His mon was cut from his corpse and cast into the sea.

With a flick of Agetoki's wrist, he ordered a full withdrawal—complete retreat and disengagement.

The massed Lion troops began to part in confusion. Entire units seemed unwilling to leave the field, refusing to march back down the twisting road.

One commander, and then a second, and then a third stepped before the red-helmed man. Each one bowed humbly to Agetoki, spoke for a short time, and then knelt to commit seppuku. For each one, Agetoki himself delivered the final blow. Thus, the Lion protested the emperor's command.

After three generals had fallen, the rest began to obey. Slowly, the Matsu armies condensed, marching down toward the valley beneath the palace. Ten legions of men lowered their banners and followed Agetoki's command. Not a single Lion banner rose again once they reached the distant plain.

At last, the wide lines of the Lion had opened enough to allow the march of Hoturi's men.

Inside the Crane palace, mad shouts of victory tore from open throats. The men at the great gates began to pull back the huge stone barriers that held Kyuden Doji's front archway safe.

It was over. The Crane had won. The Lion were driven back. With ten thousand more men, the kyuden would be safe—their supplies and armaments would reinforce the keep, and the Lion would be completely unable to restore the broken siege.

Kuwanan grinned down at his men, enjoying their fervor and their almost giddy relief.

"Hoturi!" Kuwanan shouted with the rest.

"No," Uji whispered, tugging at the stubble that had grown upon his swarthy chin. "Something is wrong. The Lion move aside too easily."

"Yoshi is a master diplomat. The emperor's own herald told them to move!" In celebration, Kuwanan pounded a fist into the stone battlements. "We have won the day!"

Still, Uji was unconvinced. As Hoturi's army marched over the wide chasm, Uji's eyes were drawn back to the Lion lines. Something was wrong. They seemed almost to cringe back from the armies of the Crane. A number of the Lion units broke, their legendary discipline failing. They raced away from Hoturi's men.

"Something strange is happening, Kuwanan. Even the Lion are afraid."

Kuwanan did not hear him. Already, the champion's brother and three of his personal guard had gathered at the gates of the inner courtyard, raising their blue banners. Their feet echoed to the rumble of drums. They marched across the stone archway to greet the victorious Crane Champion. "Open the gate!" One of the Kakita yelled.

A thousand throats quickly took up the cry. "Open the gate for Hoturi-sama!"

Kuwanan's men moved with a military bearing worthy of the second son of the Doji noble house. Kuwanan himself, despite the weariness of the battle and the days of labor, walked through the gate with a martial stride, eager to give formal greetings to his elder brother on the day of their greatest triumph.

As Hoturi approached, Kuwanan bowed from the road. The gate behind him stood open and welcoming. Crane samurai cheered from the walls.

"Kyuden Doji stands with you, my brother," Kuwanan said.

Hoturi's steed reared, its sharp teeth piercing the air as it let out a wailing cry. The Crane Champion did not seem concerned by the antics of his steed, but sat proudly, helmet off and white hair flowing in the brisk wind of the sea. Behind Hoturi, ten thousand men marched.

No, they did not march, but staggered.

Rotted flesh trickled from beneath polished mempo masks. Mad laughter rang from throats torn open by ancient wounds. Eyes gleamed a foul red beneath shadowed helmets.

Hoturi rode no true horse but a hellish black steed. As his men approached the palace, the champion looked up into Uji's eyes and raised his sword in the gesture of a samurai about to begin the slaughter.

Racing for the gates, Uji drew his sword. "Close the gates!" A few men stopped in their tracks, staring at the Daidoji Daimyo as if he had lost his mind. The long stairway took a lifetime to cross, and his voice was raw and hoarse. "Shut them out!" he screamed, his voice barely reaching above the Doji cheers. "In the name of Shinsei and the Fortunes, by the Lady Doji, close the gate!"

It was too late. The Shadowlands madmen behind Hoturi's black steed had already rushed to the gates, jamming them open and flooding into the keep. They raced to join their "brothers" within the Doji walls. Without understanding the nature of the threat, the Crane left their swords sheathed and reached to welcome their brothers. They chanted Hoturi's name like a prayer.

Just outside the gate, Hoturi lifted his sword before his brother's face. The bright blade fell. Kuwanan's blood spilled across the stones. Hoturi turned to his men and gave the command to attack.

The speed of the monsters astonished Uji as they poured into the courtyard. They threw off their disguises and attacked. The Daidoji's stomach churned as he recognized the faces of Hoturi's men. They had once been Doji samurai, peaceful northern lords dead of the plague at the beginning of the season. Now they were ravenous beasts driven by the instinct to kill. Somehow, Hoturi had infected them, given them the Taint of the Shadowlands, and raised their bodies from the dead. It was a blasphemy that must be avenged.

Uji slashed desperately. Beside him, three men fell on the blades of the undead. Rusted katana and poisoned claws tore heads from bodies. Before the corpses could fall to the ground, Uji leapt into action. With one savage stroke, he sliced through three undead, and they landed with their victims.

Behind him, the Daidoji guardsmen staggered back, drawing their swords and attempting to close the great gates of the seaside palace. They were too late. A flood of undead pushed open the Crane gates, blocking their passage with the dead bodies of the Kakita that had manned the walls.

Hoturi's troops were inside the palace walls. Soon, there would be no survivors of their attack.

Uji slashed a foe's helm, decapitating him. "Fight them!" he snarled to his samurai, cutting down another of the undead madmen. "Do not despair! We are stronger! Fight!"

Slowly, his men rallied to him. They gave their strong right arms to his service.

A Kakita samurai stood his ground against twenty undead. His bright sword flashed as he cut through them one at a time. Still, their numbers were tremendous. With no sense of honor or timing, they threw themselves on the man. The weight of their bodies bore him to the ground. Within seconds, only a few pieces of him remained, tied together by the scraps that had once been his clothing.

A bloody mist rose around the monsters. Through it, Uji peered out the gate. There, he glimpsed the black steed tearing open bodies with fangs and hooves. On its back, Hoturi cut down Daidoji as they threw themselves against him. Only sheer desperation gave his men the strength to fight. Soon, desperation would not be enough to save their lives. Something had to be done before the madman that smiled with Hoturi's face had closed all avenues of escape.

With an angry yell, Uji charged out the gate and raced down the road toward Kuwanan and Hoturi.

"Are you still moving, Brother?" Hoturi's perfect voice called over the shrieks of his men. He fought a group of Doji who guarded Kuwanan. "Still fighting me, even with your belly open on the ground? How touching—I believe I'll let you die like our father did; bleeding and wailing for his little wife."

Uji reached Kuwanan. Covering the Doji's body with his blade, Uji reached beneath his arm to drag him to his feet. "Get up," Uji growled. "We have no time for weakness."

"Leave me . . ." Kuwanan whispered, holding his stomach with one hand. "Let me die with my failure."

"Never," hissed Uji. "You are a Crane, by the Sun, and you will live like one." Shrugging Kuwanan against his side, Uji kept his katana ready in his hand. He dragged Kuwanan away from Hoturi and his undead. Uji slipped. He felt the edge of the castle road beneath his feet. Somewhere far below, the ocean waited, and foam dried on the sharp stone of the beach.

"I must tell you this, Brother, as you die in torment," Hoturi called. He slew another Doji and rode closer. His stallion's blood-covered face fought between samurai, and murder shown in Hoturi's mad eyes. "I never told you how our mother died. I wanted to protect you from the truth. You were my little brother, after all." Something sinister crept into Hoturi's voice, and he lifted the ancestral sword of his family.

"Hoturi," Kuwanan struggled to understand, half-standing beside the Daidoji general. "Why are you doing this?"

"Satsume took me out to the cliffs that day for a reason. Teinko found us there." Hoturi's legs tightened around the great beast he rode. It reared in protest. "Our mother didn't commit suicide because she was unhappy. She hated Satsume, that is true, and she would not give him her love after the day you were conceived. Two sons are required by decorum. Once those were born, Teinko had no reason to love Satsume. Her duty was fulfilled. But do not believe the courtiers and their tales of sorrow and romance. Teinko died for a very simple reason, my brother. She did it to save my life."

"What are you saying?"

Urging his horse toward them, Hoturi forced Uji to teeter atop the high cliff's edge. Waters churned hungrily below. The Crane Champion continued speaking, laughing with each step the mad horse took toward the edge. "Satsume gave her a choice: she could give him her body again and bear another son, or he would hurl me over the edge of the cliffs. A life for a life, Father said."

Kuwanan's face went white as he understood the implications of Hoturi's words. "She . . . leapt over the cliff. . . ."

"To save my life. A life for a life. She gave him a life, to save mine." Hoturi smiled wickedly, raising the sword in his hand. "She gave him her own."

"No!" Kuwanan shouted. "That's not true!"

"Oh, it is true, Brother. And you are about to join her, so that the Crane might live. Don't you see? It is time for the Crane to be reborn. Don't worry. I'll treat your precious Daidoji well. They will be honored as slaves beneath my feet." His ringing laughter was even more hideous than the death screams that echoed inside the palace, the ripping and tearing sounds that Uji tried to ignore.

Uji struck out at Hoturi's horse. With a titanic swing of his family blade, he cut its legs from beneath it. The creature shuddered, screaming with agony as it fell to stunted knees. Its teeth caught Uji's arm, nearly pulling it from the socket as the horse fought. Hoturi sloped forward, clutching the horse's mane for balance. As he did, the sword of the Crane fell from his hand and landed with a ringing clatter at the ground near Kuwanan. Uji reeled, nearly slipping from the cliff's edge and sending a shower of rocks to the waters far below.

Nearly bent double by the pain of the wound in his side, Kuwanan picked up the ancient sword. It made no sound in his hand. It did not recognize him either by its ethereal ringing note or by the shining light he had seen it give so often when his brother first drew the sword. He was not its true owner; unworthy of its call.

Beyond Hoturi, undead raced toward them, bloody hands reaching to grasp Kuwanan and drag him into their sharpened teeth.

"You cannot defeat me, Kuwanan," Hoturi said, rising to his feet and drawing the shorter blade of the wakizashi from his obi. "And when you die, your bodies will rise again at my command. The Doji will live forever, Tainted by my power. Mother would have liked that, you know. Her sons, united forever in death. You would make a strong addition to my armies." The undead advanced, preventing Kuwanan from attacking.

If he moved forward, they would kill him. He would never reach Hoturi now, never be able to save his family's honor by destroying its Tainted son. All Kuwanan could do at the end was to save his own honor, and pray that his father would forgive him. "I may die, Brother, but I will rob you of your greatest weapon. We will not fall by your hand." Kuwanan snarled, grasping Uji's obi. "Better to give our lives to the Fortunes, than to join your horde."

"So be it." Hoturi said grimly. He raised his hand. The legions of undead leaped crazily forward, but they were too slow.

Kuwanan leaped off the high cliff. Air opened around them. Far below, the swirling waters of the Crane coast crashed against unforgiving rocks. Neither man shouted as they fell through the rushing air. The waters of the ocean swallowed them.

The false Hoturi stared down from the high cliff. "May the First Doji have mercy on your souls," he smiled radiantly. Then his laughter echoed through the high plains, dancing over the corpses of the Crane.

19   DREAMS OF SILK

Darkness, thick and gentle, spread like a blanket through the long corridors of Otosan Uchi. It touched the corners of the palace with a lover's hand, caressing the hardwood floors and slipping beneath the sliding screens that divided one chamber from the next. While the palace rested above, somewhere deep within the palace's stone cellars, a soul cried out for mercy.

Swirling images of home moved past Hoturi's eyes, obscuring dreams of the palace above. Occasionally, faint strains of music drifted down through the thick stone, taunting his ears with dancing notes. Hoturi wondered if his screams were ever heard in the palace. If they were, they were surely said to come from some heimin prisoner, being punished for rebellion against his lord. There would be no rescue from this tortured cell.

Hoturi's tongue felt thick in his mouth, blackened by drugs and Kachiko's kiss. Days had passed—long, tortured days without water, without food. Each time he awoke from the haze of sleep, Hoturi scratched a mark upon the wall above his right hand. Every time she came, he scratched another. His fingers felt the long scars in the mortar of the stone. Twenty-seven. If those were days, he thought blearily, the Crane must surely be dead.

Toshimoko, Master, Sensei . . . how I have failed you.

As he raised his head to the blackness of the ceiling, a faint cry echoed from his throat. The duty of a samurai was clear—death before bringing dishonor to your clan, to those who serve you. Death moved in the darkness of the dungeon cell, but Hoturi could not call it to him.

More flashes of light came. Drifting dreams haunted him. Ameiko begged him not to come to Otosan Uchi. Her magnificent red wedding gown caught the last light of the setting sun as the Asahina priest raised his hands in blessing. Her strange green eyes, more spirit than human, teased him as he took her to his bed.

He did not love her. Her body shifted, became a serpent in the darkness. Hoturi screamed. Hands pressed cold iron to his wrists, tearing through flesh and shackling bone. Flames seared the inside of his eyelids, peeling his eyes open. Light burned him. He turned his face away. Darkness fell once more.

He saw Kyuden Kakita—no, Kyuden Doji. Armies flanked the high palace walls. Faces streamed blood. Kuwanan's head stared down from a high spike above the palace gates. The mocking laughter of a madman echoed within the walls. Golden gates opened—was it Kyuden Kakita?—and inside the flowering courtyard, Ameiko stood in her red gown. She held the arm of a man who was not Hoturi but who bore his face.

"I will have her, Father," the false Hoturi hissed. Flesh rotted from his cheeks and showed the grinning skull beneath. "I will find her, and I will make her mine. . . ."

Another scream, and the flowers around the two pooled into blood. Red streamed along the ground like serpents. Hoturi could not pull his eyes away from the scarlet rivulets. They twisted like fireworks, turned back upon themselves. When they grew still, the face of a young boy stared out from beneath their thick waters. Dairu's blue eyes stared into those of his father.

I didn't know....

The boy's jaw was so like his own, but the shape of his eyes mimicked Kachiko's catlike gaze. Their son. How had she kept him alive within Shoju's court? What had she given Shoju, so that their son might live?

She can never see you again.

A life for a life, Hoturi whispered, hot tears brushing his cheekbones. This time, though, the son had died, and the mother had lived to tell the tale—and to take revenge.

It was dark. Iron chains bound his wrists icily. Their bitter chill burned his raw flesh. Hoturi could feel the touch of silk, could hear Kachiko's laughter. He scratched another notch on the wall and felt a cool rag pressed to his lips. Drinking greedily from it, he tasted bitterness in the draught. More of the drug that kept him dreaming, of course.

In time, she assured him, he would no longer feel the sting of Aramoro's whip or the lash of her kisses on his cheek. After a few years, when his clan was destroyed and his duplicate had completed his tasks, Hoturi would be set free to wander the empire, mad and alone.

It was the madness that he feared.

Bitter draught, this time from a sake bowl. He had not been given such water in days. Hoturi coughed and choked. He tried to force the cool drink down his parched and raw throat. She must have had a special torture in mind, to allow him such a courtesy. Another dream assailed him, and he saw Satsume's face. His father stood before him in the cold cell, drawing the sword of the Crane to end his life.

"Yes, Father. It is time for you to complete the task,"

Hoturi spat. His voice was no more than a hiss in the silence of the stone chamber.

Satsume drew the sword above his head, testing the steel. "You have failed, Hoturi," echoed his voice. "But still, there is time to save your people."

"How?" Hoturi shook the thick chains that bound his wrists. "You were right, Father. Always right. I've been a fool, and I've turned my back on my clan, to follow my own goals. I deserve . . . deserve to die.

Satsume shifted, becoming Kuwanan's bandy form. The wound across Satsume's belly remained on Kuwanan's bare skin. Blood stained his brother's hakima and trickled from the ancestral sword of their clan. "Hoturi, nothing is truly lost if it can be rebuilt. Remember that, and take up your duty."

"My duty . . ."

"You are champion of the Crane, and you are destined to free them. Shinsei has sent me. . . ."

Hoturi shook his head to clear it. Shinsei? The voice of his brother became more feminine. The face behind the blue gi came into focus. A woman's face. "When the Way comes to an end . . . then change. . . . " Hoturi's lips cracked, and his tongue stumbled over the ancient words, "and having changed, pass through. . . ."

"Yes," the woman said. She transformed once more into Kuwanan in full battle armor. "You must be more than this, Hoturi. You must pass through. Will you fight beside the Crane? Do you have the courage to undo what you have done?"

For a moment, the world grew blurry. Hoturi could see Ameiko's face shining beneath the starlight, brightly lit by happiness. "I can." He threw his weight once more against the chains, feeling blood trail down his forearms, as it had a hundred times before.

Satsume raised the sword, hatred and anger in his eyes. A swift stroke cut through the air toward Hoturi's head. The

Crane Champion did not flinch or cry out. He only stared into his father's eyes without regret, without remorse. This was how he should have died, long ago, by his father's blade on the shores of Kyuden Doji.

Teinko floated. Blood surrounded her head, and her black hair cascaded over the sea-torn shore. In smoke and mist, the scene changed, and became Dairu. My first duty.

The sword approached. Satsume's face was resolute and filled with bitterness. Hoturi watched it come, his stinging eyes open against the bright torchlight.

A shattering clang, and Hoturi's wrists fell free.

Hands reached to lift him, placing a cool rag over the worst of his wounds before wrapping him in a soft cloak. The darkness swam around him.

Hoturi clawed to his feet, determined to stand. A few steps, a few more . . . Hands held his shoulders, and he leaned on a soft arm.

Satsume had gone. The light had been put out. Only the dark stone caverns stretched out around him, like the labyrinth of Kyuden Bayushi.

Kachiko . . . never again.

Hours seemed to pass in a drug-filled haze. Hoturi fell, but stood again. His eyes watered with shame. His knees were torn and bleeding. It seemed to Hoturi that the figure beside him was half-dream, half-real. She was the only solid thing in a world of shifting images and strange dreams.

She placed him on a low travois, drawing blankets over his charred flesh and putting a thick bandage around his wounded eyes.

"Are you a kami?" he asked her in a moment of clarity, but her face turned away.

"No, Hoturi," the whisper came, "only a woman, with a duty still to complete. Remember me, when you find the Thunder in your soul."

Then the darkness took him, and Hoturi knew no more.

20 OATHS

oturi awoke to the sweet smell of incense and the gentle rhythm of prayers. His eyes were thickly crusted, and his body felt as though it had been thrown down the Dragon Mountains. Agony hovered at the edges of his mind, a defeated dragon hungry for revenge. The drug was wearing thin. Soon he would be free of it. Still, its gnawing anger had gashed a permanent wound in his soul.

"Quiet, now." A hand pressed cool water to his brow.

"Dear Fortunes," Hoturi croaked with recognition. "Akodo Toturi-san?"

Chuckled laughter came, and a voice of relief. "It seems you've your wits about you again, my old friend. But have you forgotten the day in which we live? Now, it is only Toturi."

"Never to me."

"Gently, Hoturi-sama, your wounds are

still fresh. If you do not rest, the Asahina will never forgive me."

"Who?" Hoturi tried to sit up, to move, but the very thought made his mind swim sickly and his stomach churn.

"Tomo, the old man. He's come here the minute we sent for him. Your old tutor, I believe?"

"Tomo?" Down from the mountains to cure him. That was a shock, as much as Toturi's voice had been. Though the Asahina were Crane, and loyal, their path was one of quiet contemplation and the craft of magic. They were pacifists, believers in life and fervently opposed to war. Until now, their small family had remained in their quiet southern castle, resolute in their refusal to fight or shed blood. Then again, Hoturi would never have believed he would accompany the Black Ronin, Akodo Toturi—Toturi, he corrected himself. Just Toturi, now.

"Where . . . are we? Kuwanan—does he live? Uji? Kyuden Kakita? Does Kyuden Kakita still stand?"

"Sleep, Hoturi," said the deep, rich voice of his friend. Darkness began to creep at the edge of his mind once more. "Sleep now, and when you wake, I will answer all your questions. There will be time enough for answers, then."

"A Lion, worried about a Crane," Hoturi croaked weakly, amused. "The empire will surely fall around our shoulders, old friend."

"I'm not a Lion anymore, Hoturi. It is allowed." The sonorous voice continued speaking, but Hoturi could not make out the words through the fog of his tortured mind.

In time, he slept.

⋀ ⋀ ⋀ ⋀ ⋀ ⋀ ⋀

He stirred. Something cold was pressed to his face, the bandages released. His eyes fluttered wearily beneath a wet rag.

"Careful, Master," a heimin murmured soothingly. "Your eyes are only just healed enough to see. Can you tell the light?"

"Hai," Hoturi nodded gently. The swimming in his head diminished to a thin swell.

Lifting the rag gently, the heimin held a finger before Hoturi's face. "Can you see this?"

"Your hand. Hai."

"Good, good!" The heimin turned away. "Lord Tomo, he is awake, and his eyes are well."

Tomo had been his father's healer at the battle of Otosan Uchi, so long ago . . . but when his father fell, the old shugenja had been unable to assist. Nothing could have saved Satsume, not even the magic of the wise Asahina.

"That is good news." The crotchety voice came from somewhere else in the tent. Hoturi was lying on a futon that rested upon a packed dirt floor. Asahina Tomo stomped closer. He was a bent man, stooped with the weight of years. A sparkle still lit his pale blue eyes, and his long fingers tugged at his gray beard with quick dexterity. "Can you see me?"

Though his vision was still blurred, Hoturi could make out the faded blue hakima, and he nodded. "You look well, old father."

"Bah." Tomo reached in his belt pouch and drew out a small sphere of crystal, pressing it first to Hoturi's forehead and then to his hands and feet. "No more swelling," he said gruffly. "Get Toturi," Tomo said to the heimin. "He wanted to know when our lord awoke." Bowing quickly, the man nearly danced from the tent with glee. "Happy to see you awake, you know," the old man continued, putting away the tiny sphere. "I suppose we all are, around here. Good to know you're . . . well. Good to know you're you."

"What?" Hoturi said, confused.

"Enough trouble out there, you know. Should have stayed in my little hut on the Asahina compound. Coming out here to take care of you, boy. Don't like being down here, with wars and all the fighting. Can't you get sick closer to home?" The old man's good-natured banter cheered Hoturi, and the lord of the Crane smiled weakly.

"I'll try, next time. I promise."

"Hmm. Hold you to that, yup. You see if I don't."

Within moments, the tent flap opened, and three men entered. One was Toturi, a tremendous man with broad shoulders and a wide smile. Toturi moved with the grace of a bushi, yet spoke with the cultured voice of a courtier. It was strange to see him here—stranger still to see that his once-gold hair had again grown black, the dye faded and almost cut away completely. No more a Lion. Toturi smiled broadly and knelt beside the futon with his swords at his belt.

Behind him came Kakita Toshimoko, dressed not in the blue and gray of the Crane, but in strange blackened garments, covered with a large cloak of the emperor's green and gold. He looked at Hoturi once, as if to reassure himself that the man on the futon still lived, then quickly looked away.

Behind him was another man in blackened clothing, also obviously dyed with walnut stain. The man was unfamiliar to him. As he bowed at the tent's flap, he introduced himself to the lord of the Crane.

"Ichiro Wayu, Hoturi-sama, second-in-command of the Emerald Magistrates."

"A magistrate?" Hoturi whispered in disbelief.

"Hai, my lord." Wayu drew a pendant of jade from beneath his darkened gi, the symbol of the Emerald Champion's men clearly carved into the intricate token. "And Toshimoko-sama's first lieutenant. I speak for him," the man glanced at the old sensei, "because the Emerald Champion's legions must not be swayed by house or clan."

Toshimoko nodded. The wrinkles around his eyes deepened with age and care. "It is enough that I am here," he said warily, not looking at Hoturi. "Let Wayu speak for me, so that it cannot be said that I speak as a Crane in this matter."

Hoturi looked up at his old mentor, suddenly noticing the signs of age that curled at the edges of Toshimoko's lips.

"Hoturi," Toturi began gently. "There is much to say. You are feeling better?"

"Yes. In a few days," Hoturi pushed himself up from the cushions slowly, testing his strength, "I should be able to ride."

"Good. You . . . are needed." A troubled look crossed the ronin's face.

Outside the tent, the guards softly closed the flap, and the brown silk lessened the brightness of the sunlight. "Kyuden Kakita?" Hoturi guessed. "The Crab have moved south?"

Glancing at Toshimoko, the ronin general answered. "Hai, Hoturi-san. Kyuden Kakita . . . has been taken. Burned by Kisada's armies." Seeing Hoturi blanch, his pale face growing even paler as he accepted the news, Toturi continued. "To the north, as well, the Crane fare poorly."

"Poorly?"

"The Lion . . . Kyuden Doji was assaulted some time ago."

"Did they take it? Kuwanan . . . ?"

"The Matsu were commanded to retreat. The emperor's herald arrived," Toturi continued, "with an order from Empress Kachiko."

"Dear Fortunes, no . . ."

"There is more, and you must hear it." Without preamble, Toturi spoke. "Kyuden Doji was assaulted by a force of Crane under your banner. They were . . . undead. Torn from the ground by dark blood magic, maho, and foul Shadowlands Taint. The madmen attacked Kyuden Doji, and they destroyed the Crane forces there."

"My banner." Hoturi said bitterly. Understanding tasted like bile on his tongue. The tent was silent as the assembled samurai allowed Hoturi to accept the information. When he spoke again, his voice was like ice cracking beneath a soldier's heel. "You do not believe that I have led them."

"No, of course not," the old Asahina said grumpily, stirring the fire with a riding crop. "Foolishness."

"It's not foolishness, Tomo-san," Wayu said cautiously. "There are many who do believe it, Hoturi-sama. Those who believe it curse your name and slander your clan. The Crane are dying."

"Because I am destroying them."

"Not you, Hoturi. Something that looks like you." Toturi's dark brown eyes turned sad. "What do you know of this?"

With halting words, Hoturi told them the story of the Egg of Pan Ku and Kachiko's treachery, leaving nothing of his own failure out of the tale. Bushido demanded that the whole story be told, even the darkest and most dishonorable parts. As Hoturi continued, he grew stronger with anger and pain.

Toturi's face darkened with thought. The tent in which they sat was quiet save for the faint brush of wind against the silken walls. The low table on which a warm teapot rested shone with care despite the deep scars in the hard wood. By a small covered fire, Asahina Tomo rested his old bones, enjoying the warmth of the flames against the cold winter's afternoon.

Hoturi spoke until the sun had gone down and the red glow of the fire was the only light left in the tent. When he had finished, the four samurai considered his words quietly. Silence fell like a blanket over Hoturi's shame.

"Can you prove this?" Toturi said.

"The only witness is Bayushi Aramoro. But I do not wish to assault the empress on her own field." The champion of the Crane winced, pulling his wounded arm forward to support his weight. "Even if I could succeed, the false Hoturi would have destroyed the Crane long before the charges were issued."

Across the tent, Hoturi could see disbelief in Wayu's eyes.

"Do you believe that I have done this to myself? That I would assault the Crane, or that I would lead an army of Shadowlands madmen against my own brother?" Enraged, Hoturi tried to stand, but his legs were too weak to support his weight.

"If you believe that, Toturi-san," the champion of the Crane looked toward his childhood friend, "then kill me now, and spare me your falsehoods. I will die as a Crane—on my feet."

"No, Hoturi," came Toshimoko's weary voice. "Your tale may be true. The Shinjo Champion said as much when I visited their lands. Their councilor, Ide Tadaji, received a missive from our own Kakita Yoshi, speaking of your mysterious disappearance and telling tales of a strange madness that had gripped you when you returned. He too spoke of Bayushi Kachiko's treachery, though he knew of no way to prove it other than to face you on the field of combat."

Tomo interrupted with a cackling laugh.

Concerned he had said too much, the old sensei stepped toward the fire.

Toturi spoke next. "The false Hoturi's men are arrayed through the fields of Kyuden Kakita, burning each village and taking the able-bodied men for his own troops. It is said that even those who refuse to join him eventually become part of his legion. The dead rise and follow his command. He will not reach the Asahina fields soon, but when he does, he will have ten times the forces we can gather. Each day he grows stronger. The Crab have been driven back from Beiden Pass, and we can leave it safely in the hands of Yokatsu's men. My troops could leave within two days."

"Then you believe me?" Hoturi said quietly.

"Let us say only that I believe the messenger that brought you," Toturi replied as he looked away.

Suddenly, the woman's face became clear in Hoturi's memory. His eyes widened with understanding.

Toturi continued. "The samurai's name was Akiyoshi, once an Akodo under my command." Toturi's eyes asked for his silence. Hoturi nodded once. The name was a false one, meant only to cover the messenger's true identity. Leave us this secret, Toturi's eyes pled of the Crane Champion. Let the world believe her dead.

Changing the subject before the others noticed Toturi's lingering sadness, Hoturi asked swiftly, "Is my brother alive?"

"Barely, my lord," Tomo cawed from his fireside cushion. "Alive, and Uji too. Both nearly died, escaping Kyuden Doji. Now they gather what troops survive in the deep Daidoji lands. The armies ride toward the Asahina fields, but my family refuses to help them."

"There is a time for war, Tomo. The Asahina must realize the error of living a hermit's life."

"Shinsei once spoke as you," Tomo said thoughtfully. His pale eyes glinted in the firelight, "But he couldn't get them out of that library, either." The old man's grin was nearly toothless, pink gums shining wetly in the firelight.

Hoturi's face fell, but his stubborn chin refused to lower. "My honor has been destroyed with the lands of the Crane. All the pride and tricks I used to bring my clan to glory have been stripped away by this . . . mockery of my life. There is nothing left for me but to fight him. No matter what the Asahina say, they will obey their lord."

With steel in his voice, Wayu spoke from the rear of the tent. "Perhaps you samurai can believe this man, but I cannot. I must recommend that the Emerald Champion's men remain here, in the pass. I cannot say with honor that the rumors of Hoturi's fall to madness have been disproved."

Hoturi looked up at the wiry man in black, testing his resolve. "The emperor's legions cannot support their cousins?"

"I serve the emperor, not the Crane," Wayu replied angrily, stepping forward and deliberately standing over Hoturi. "If the Crane are not strong enough to stand on their own, we will not be their crutch. Let them fall."

Behind him, Toshimoko did nothing, unable to place himself between his clan and his duty to the emperor.

Enraged, Hoturi pushed himself to his knees, reaching for his swords. "Say that when I am on my feet, magistrate, and we shall see who will fall."

"Do what you will, Hoturi-sama, but I speak the words of

an empire that believes you have gone mad." Wayu's expressive face was immobile. "The Shadowlands have made another Hoturi, you say, and he ravages the lands of the Crane. It is an easy excuse for treachery. Worse, what makes us believe that if one such copy can be made, that they have not made two?" He stared down at Hoturi, his body stiff. "Who is to say that you are truly Hoturi, as well?"

Hoturi knew he was being manipulated. Part of him hated the magistrate for it. Yet he saw the truth in the man's words. When he spoke again, Hoturi's voice was curt and controlled. "No matter what you say, no matter if I must ride against ten thousand madmen, I will fulfill my duty to the Crane." A wave of fear and regret washed over Hoturi. Shame showed plainly in his clear blue-gray eyes. "My duty as champion demands that I protect them, even if I must stand on that field alone. There is no other way to save my honor—no other way to reclaim what the false Hoturi has stolen from me."

"You would go alone?" Wayu asked in disbelief.

"To save the Crane?" Hoturi looked up and reached out his hand unsteadily. "Give me a sword."

Wayu only stared at the Crane Champion for another long moment before turning away. "We shall see."

"There is a strength in names, Hoturi-sama," Tomo's voice rose with the crackling fire, ignoring the tense conversation. "This creature, this false Hoturi, has stolen yours. You will not be whole again until it has been reclaimed. And because you are the lord of the Crane, you are the Crane. If you fall, we fall."

"Then I must not fall." Hoturi said.

"No, Crane Champion," Toturi said, rising. "We must not fall. For if we do, more than the Crane will be slaughtered. The empire itself is threatened by this rising evil. It is the duty of every samurai to see it destroyed. The question, Hoturi-sama, is how do we get you to the Asahina lands without the false Hoturi becoming aware of your presence? There are still many who would seek to kill you, for his deeds."

"Don't worry about that, Toturi-san." Hoturi smiled wearily. "I have traveled as a ronin before. It is time to do so again. This time, not to hide my honor, but to give it for my clan."

From his corner, Tomo nodded thoughtfully, watching the smoke rise from the small cooking fire.

21   HOMECOMINGS

When one eye is fixed upon your desti-nation, you have only one with which to fol-low the Way. . . .

The words were simple, but they held great meaning. Carved on the doors of the Asahina shugenja school, they were meant as a benediction to study and dedication. Yet, to some, they seemed a prayer for the outside world to turn away, leaving the Asahina alone with their contemplation and their false peace.

"My lord Asahina?" gasped a young student. He stuck a bald-shaved head through the doorway. His eyes were filled with the blank stare of a child.

"What is it, Sembi?" Asahina Tamako irritably raised his eyes from his parchment. Too many interruptions and too many rumors. It was bad enough that the Crane had gone to war despite his urgings, but worse that they would dare bring their terrible battles to his very door.

"Three ronin, my lord, on the doorstep. Three men, and they are," the young man ran a damp hand over his bald forehead, "very eager to see you."

"Do they bring knowledge of any sort? Anything worthwhile?" Tamako's brush continued in its slow, deliberate pace over the rice-paper scroll, copying the words of Shinsei's Tao into an elaborate poem of peace.

"They said only that it was important."

"Turn them away. There is enough to do here without such uninformed interruptions." Sniffing broadly, the daimyo of the Asahina scattered sand across the parchment to dry the ink.

The boy bowed hastily, his wide eyes fearful. He went slowly back to the gates of the Asahina compound.

Shortly after, there was a fierce pounding that echoed through the long stone corridors of the compound, nearly shaking Tamako's brush free from his hand. Ink slid across the carefully prepared scroll. Angered for the first time in years, the daimyo of the Asahina drew himself to his full height and marched out the library door to see what had disturbed him. The disruptive student would pay for his insolence with days of prayer and fasting.

Tamako was completely unprepared for the sight that met his eyes. Three men, dressed in the garb of ronin, stormed through the open halls. Students fled to get out of their way. The ronin did not raise their swords. Nor did they seem to threaten, but their firm step would not be slowed by prayer or pleading. Before them scurried the young student who had come to Tamako's door, his eyes white and rolling.

"Master!" he chittered, wringing thin hands, "they would not leave . . . as you see. . . . I could not make them."

"How dare you!" Asahina Tamako felt the words to a prayer of restraint come to his mind, but cast the spell away with an arrogant thought. "This land is sacred by the decree of the Crane Champion and the dictate of the Emperor Hantei himself! No weapons are allowed here!"

"By the command of the champion of the Crane, I say they are not proof against the maho that stalks this land," one of the ronin said, removing his hood. Tamako staggered backward as he recognized his own lord, Doji Hoturi. "And if I must command you, I will. But you will hear the words I have to say, or by the Fortunes, I'll see you cast out to the monasteries of the Crab!" Hoturi's voice was commanding. His presence filled the narrow hallway.

Tamako leaned against a nearby wall, his chalky face blanching. "Hoturi-sama . . ." At his side, the student hopped from foot to foot, waving his arms toward his master's face to give him air.

Annoyed, Tamako batted at the offending limbs. With a disdainful gesture, he waved the student back into the hallway. "You must forgive me. I did not recognize you without your guard."

"The undead, you mean?" Hoturi had caught the implication in the old man's words. "That will be explained, soon enough. Know that you need have no fear of me or of my companions."

Tamako glanced at the two ronin. "May I guess that these samurai are the esteemed champions of Phoenix and Unicorn?" he said, sneering slightly at Hoturi's ruse.

"No, Tamako-san," Toturi said as he removed his hood. "I am champion no more."

As Kakita Toshimoko's smiling face emerged from the third hood, Tamako's wide eyed student choked a gasp. He fell heavily to the floor in a dead faint.

Tamako glanced first at one face and then the next. "You . . . you travel in distinguished company, as always, Lord Hoturi." His voice was weak and confused, his eyes darting back and forth like those of a trapped animal. Around them, Asahina students scattered through the halls. "Your brother is here. By the strength of our healers, he lives, though his wound was grave."

"Take me to him."

"Of course," Tamako said, waving one of the other students forward. The boy on the floor would need care before he was sentenced to four days of prayer for humiliating his lord in such a fashion. Gathering his robes about him, the Asahina Daimyo looked nervously about, as if seeking an escape. Finding none, he sighed and turned toward a long stairway of stone. "This way, samurai."

They walked through the stone corridors of the Asahina compound. The home of the Asahina was nothing like the opulent palaces of the Doji and Kakita families. It was solid, stoic, and boring—as befit a family of scholars and peacemakers. Yet behind the thick stone walls of the library, an army could stand for days, if need be.

The chamber that Tamako opened was sparsely furnished. The mahogany floor glinted. No tables rested in the room, but only three futons unrolled on the floor. On one lay Hoturi's brother, Kuwanan. His skin was chalky against the dark covers. At his side, two Asahina healers knelt, replacing the bandages that bound his torso.

As Tamako entered, Kuwanan looked up with bright eyes. "Nearly healed, my gentle friend," he said cheerfully.

"You have a visitor, Kuwanan-sama. . . ." Tamako began, unsure.

Hoturi stepped past the Asahina, lowering his hood so that his brother could see his face.

"Dear Fortunes," Kuwanan's eyes blazed with hatred and anger. "What courage it must take, Brother, to follow me so far south. Or have you captured the Asahina, as well?" He stared at Tamako and the man took an involuntary step backward. "I heard no sound of fighting."

"Kuwanan-san, you must be willing to listen."

"No, I have listened enough." The healers raised their hands in protest as Kuwanan stood, testing the strength of his bandages. "I have seen your slaughter of Kyuden Doji, Brother," the word was a sarcastic slap. "And I do not believe there is anything more to say."

Hoturi took a step forward.

Kuwanan leaped to the side and drew the Crane ancestral sword from the dai-sho holder that had rested near the bed. The bright blade shone in the light, making strange patterns against the cold stone walls.

Hoturi instinctively reached for the hilt of the sword Toturi had given him, but did not draw it from its sheath.

The healers shrieked. Tamako stepped between the dueling brothers, his arms outstretched.

"There will be no war here!" the Asahina said angrily, sounding like the daimyo of his family and not a humble librarian. "No blood will be shed in this place, or by the Fortunes, Lady Doji herself will turn her face from you!"

"You say you do not want war," Kuwanan said bitterly. "Yet you bring war to my chamber, Tamako. This man has destroyed the Crane."

"You are wrong, Kuwanan." Hoturi's voice was calm.

"Kuwanan-sama!" The Asahina stared at the ancestral blade in the samurai's hand. "My healers dragged you and your companion from the sea beneath Kyuden Doji. Brothers of my temple saved your life from the grievous wound. If you have honor, you owe it to me. You will put away your sword, and you will not draw blood in this sacred place!"

Kuwanan flinched, his eyes narrowing. "I owe you, Asahina, and although you are a vassal to my house, you have a debt of honor from me. But this man has lied to you. He says he comes to bring peace, but I have seen his 'peace' covered in blood on the gates of Kyuden Doji!" Kuwanan moved, striking toward Hoturi.

With a deft step, the Crane Champion avoided his brother's strike. Faint remnants of poison still slowed him. His hand remained on the hilt of his own sword, but he did not draw it from its sheath.

"No, by the Fortunes!" Again, the Asahina stepped between them. "This is a house of peace!"

"Our mother died to save your life, Hoturi, and this is how you have repaid her?"

The words were a blow to the young lord of the Crane, and he stiffened. "How do you know that?" he whispered, disbelieving.

Kuwanan laughed. "So sincere. You told me yourself, when you slaughtered the Crane at Kyuden Doji. Did you have any mercy for her, or did you push her from the cliff, as well?"

"No, by the Sun, Kuwanan! It wasn't like that!" Hoturi's voice was choked with emotion. "I never told you because I knew you wouldn't understand. She gave her life for me— because she knew Satsume would kill us both if she refused."

Doji Kuwanan stepped back from the Asahina, the ancestral sword of the Crane silent in his hands. "Your life for hers. The Fortunes have mercy on us all, for being bound by duty to a damned honorless dog. You should have been the one pushed from the cliff, Hoturi."

Without thinking, Hoturi drew his sword, turning the blade in his hands. "Kuwanan, you have been deceived. The Hoturi who spoke to you, who destroyed Kyuden Doji—it was not your brother."

The Asahina stood as stiff as marble between them, his cold eyes unafraid.

"You are right, Hoturi." Kuwanan said angrily. "He was not my brother. You are not my brother. You have led the Crane to their death, and I will die before I turn this sword to your hand again." He held the sword of the Crane before him as a steel wall, ready to kill. "The Crane are better off without your service, samurai."

Staring past the Asahina's outstretched arm, Hoturi lowered his sword and placed it in its sheath. "Then, Kuwanan, you must kill me. If I cannot make you believe, perhaps my death will prove my words." Hoturi placed his hand on the

Asahina's shoulder, pushing the man aside with a strong shove. "But kill me, knowing that if I could have done so, I would have gladly traded places with Teinko. I tried . . . I tried to catch her, but my grip wasn't strong enough. Satsume watched as she jumped. Just watched. He did not even stay to see her strike ground. But I did. I saw her face on the rocks below. She was happy, Kuwanan. She was free of him at last."

Kuwanan's sword shivered in his hand. Tears filled his eyes. "No!" he howled, ignoring the pain in his side and forgetting the Asahina who tried to leap before his sword. "NO!" The sword fell with a single strike, arching toward Hoturi's neck in a powerful blow.

Hoturi simply stood, hands silent at his sides. He did not draw his blade, even to defend himself.

Kuwanan's strike carried true, swinging toward Hoturi with the fury of a Lion.

At the moment the ancestral sword of the Crane touched the flesh of the Crane Champion's neck, it released a single chime of such beauty and joy that Kuwanan's hands opened on its hilt and he staggered back.

The strike froze before it could be completed. For a moment, the sword hung in the empty air. Its ringing chime echoed through every hallway and chamber of the Asahina temples. The sound was a pure note of ultimate truth. In wide libraries, students looked up from their work, hearing the sound. The Daidoji who prayed in the temple's heart leaped to their feet with hope.

Stunned, Kuwanan fell to his knees. The sword swung slowly to the ground, landing gently at Hoturi's feet. Its note faded.

"The sword knows its true owner," Daidoji Uji whispered from the doorway behind Toturi. No one had seen him arrive, but he stood with the others, watching in awe. The sword glowed for a moment with a crystalline light, the echo of its note fading from the air. "It would not ring if Hoturi had truly dishonored himself . . . if he were not truly the champion of the Crane. It is true." The dark-eyed Daidoji fell to his knees in reverence. His face glowed with renewed hope.

"Hoturi . . ." Kuwanan whispered.

"Brother," Hoturi reached for the sword at his feet, listening to the faint chime as he grasped its hilt and raised it to meet his eyes. "Can you believe me now?"

"Hai." Kuwanan bowed in shame. "The creature at Kyuden Doji . . . was not you."

"No, Kuwanan. And it is time we destroyed that creature and freed the Crane. I will need you, Brother." Hoturi took in the room with a single glance. "I will need all of you. This is a war not against men, but against evil itself. It is battle not against enemies of the Crane, but enemies of life—the very thing that the Asahina strive to protect. The armies of the False Hoturi are undead, stolen from their graves and from the afterlife of Jigoku and thrown against helpless men and women. You say that the Asahina are peaceful, Tamako, that you respect all life—then defend it now, and put aside your reservations."

Tamako sank to his knees, unsure what to say. "The creatures you fight are undead, stolen from the eternal wheel of reincarnation, a blasphemy against the Fortunes and the spirits. They are abhorrent, even to us. But we have no weapons, nor skill or will to wield weapons."

"Then use your magic to fight them—or, if not to fight, at least to help us in our battle. Your spells, your healers, all these can be turned against the monsters that destroy the land. These creatures have blasphemed the Fortunes and slaughtered peaceful heimin across the Crane lands. Think of them, their lives wasted against undead servants of the Dark Lord. Can you ignore their cries for help?"

Tamako tilted his head and said, "We cannot allow innocents to be sacrificed to our arrogance, but it is better to allow an unjust sacrifice than to cause one."

Hoturi knelt before the daimyo, bringing their eyes level.

"I do not ask you to fight against humans, but against demons. These are the same monsters that your family fights every day, kneeling in meditation for the salvation of mankind. Can you turn your back to us as we fight them now?"

At last, Tamako nodded. "You respected our temple and did not strike, Hoturi-sama." The Asahina's voice was shaking. "Even when your own life was in danger, you put away your blade. For that, I can respect you. Though we do not approve of fighting, the Asahina will repay his respect with their own. But there can be no fighting in the temple of the Asahina, or the Fortunes will turn their faces from us forever."

"You are right, Tamako-san." Hoturi rose and stepped to the window. "The Crane have hidden behind too many walls." Lifting the Crane ancestral blade, he pointed out toward the golden fields that surrounded the compound. A great torii arch stood on the horizon. "This battle will not be fought behind the gates of the Asahina, but there—on the Fields of the Golden Sun, that Amaterasu herself might know the valor of the Crane."

"My lord," Uji said from the doorway, not wishing to disturb the champion but knowing where his duty rested. "I have failed in my responsibility, and I humbly beg your permission to commit seppuku."

"How have you failed me, Uji?" Hoturi asked softly, not understanding.

With catlike grace, Uji stepped from the doorway. He reached into his belt and withdrew a long, shining lock of jet-black hair. "I have carried this since Kyuden Kakita fell. Where I could not protect her, I thought to save it . . . at least, so that something of her survived to greet you when you came home once more." Uji raised his dark eyes. For once, his stone face bore a hint of genuine grief. "Your lady, my lord. She is . . . gone."

The news struck Hoturi like a blow. Where he had

thought himself numb from the thousands of deaths at Kyuden Kakita and Kyuden Doji, the sight of Ameiko's hair brought tears to his eyes. "Ameiko . . ."

"I allowed this to happen, Hoturi-sama."

"You allowed nothing. I was not there . . . when she needed me most." Hoturi took the hair from Uji's hand and touched it softly. "Forgive me, little one. I should have loved you for your imperfection, rather than despite it. May you have mercy on me for not understanding your true nature." Hoturi tied the lock of hair to his obi, touching its softness once more with a shaking hand. So much had been lost, and all because of his own pride. Looking up at Uji, Hoturi said, "No, Daimyo-san, you have not failed. You may not take your life. It is still too valuable to be lost. Tomorrow we fight this false Hoturi and his men, and we will have need of you."

"Hai, my lord." The sorrow in Hoturi's voice was echoed in the somber tones of the daimyo's assent.

Looking out the window at the golden plains of the Asahina, Hoturi could have sworn he heard a fox's mournful howl. Then the lands were silent in the coming twilight, absolutely still beneath a fading sun.

22 SOUL OF THUNDER

Strengthen the spirit as well as the body, and the depths of the soul will become the steel of the blade. . . .

Kakita's words rang in Hoturi's mind as he reached for his armor. He drew smooth blue laces through the enameled metal of his breastplate. The wide shoulders, edged in soft feathers from a long-dead crane, gave the appearance of wings. Hoturi reached for the silk cord that bound his white hair beneath the metal mempo. He tightly tied back the long strands. There must be no error today, no mistake. Any flaw in his technique or his strength could cost him more than his own life.

It could be the death of his family, and the final chapter to a thousand years of Crane history.

For them—for his brother, the spirit of his ancestors, and those samurai who still lived and camped on the Asahina field—Hoturi must be everything they believed him to be. He pushed Satsume's voice from his mind and lifted his helm. His fingers brushed the smooth hair at his belt one final time before he stood. No time remained for doubt or indecision.

Tamako's students slid the screen door of the chamber slowly open. They looked down at the hard stone floor as he stepped by. "My lord Hoturi-sama?" The Asahina coughed, huddling in his robes and tugging blandly at a long braid of his black hair. "Lord Uji-san has assembled the men."

Hoturi lifted the beaklike mempo of his armor and brushed his fingers over the cool metal mask. A samurai's armor was designed to be impressive, to strike fear into the hearts of opponents and to give courage to one's own men. It also invoked the spirit of the ancient kami, the first of each clan.

Lady Doji, forgive me, Hoturi thought as he replaced the mempo on the wooden armor stand. Today, I cannot hide my face. I fight myself. I must be willing to accept that dishonor without shame.

Without looking back, he followed Tamako from the room.

▲▲▲▲▲▲▲▲

Two thousand Daidoji stood upon the golden plains. The Fields of the Sun were covered for the first time in steel and war.

Uji, commander of the Daidoji, looked up at the Asahina temple upon its singular hill. He wished for its stone walls and twisting corridors. There, the fight might have been even. They might have had a chance.

Over twenty thousand undead marched on the roads to the north. Their rotting flesh sloughed on Crane land. Their leader, white hair shining above his black stallion, cheered them on with howls of rage.

Uji closed his eyes, remembering the madness that had shone from Hoturi's face as he forced them from the cliff. Uji's wounds, barely healed, still felt the crash of rock and surf.

The Crane troops had been told that the undead were led by a false Hoturi, but for most of them, this was the first time they saw the truth.

One of the men stepped before Uji, kneeling as his lord opened his eyes once more. "Our true champion has arrived."

The Daidoji Daimyo looked up from his reverie to see a parade of figures emerge from the temple gates. The Asahina shugenja walked in slow columns, their prayers whispering to the heavens in remorse and piety. But the figure that caught Uji's attention was not dressed in the wide robes of a shugenja, nor in the hakima of a courtier.

Doji Hoturi, champion of the Crane, stood in his father's armor and gazed out on the field. His face was uncovered, and his white hair was bound in a samurai's topknot. At his side hung the sword of the Crane. Its ancient hilt was wrapped in new silk. The battered saya shone with care.

As the troops noticed their commander, an audible whisper flowed through them. Some shook their heads in shame, fearing the demon that had destroyed them at Kyuden Doji and trusting only to their oaths to the Daidoji family. Fully one fourth of the men had asked Uji's permission to commit seppuku when they were told their leader would be Hoturi. Uji had refused them all. It was better that they live to see the battle to come. Then, if they had been deceived, they could die in honorable combat, defending the Crane.

Smoke from the north began to rise, and Uji heard the marching beat of drums and thickly sandaled feet.

Hoturi, too, heard it. As Kuwanan knelt to receive his orders, the champion of the Crane reached for the sword at his side. He drew it forth, and the echoing chime reverberated through the field. It seemed to gain strength from the whispers of the men. It gathered their doubt and changed it to a single ringing note. Each man raised his weapon to salute his commander. Their fears began to vanish beneath the light of truth.

The sword's note faded. The drums ceased. In the silence, Hoturi lowered his sword. A golden ray of sunlight pierced the stormy clouds, sweeping across the battlefield with the light of Mother Sun.

From the hills to the north of the plain, a black tide rose. It rushed down the plains with stomping feet. Broken weapons and mad shrieks drowned the sound of Hoturi's sword. Upon the top of the hill, surrounded by thousands of crawling, running, bleeding corpses, a single figure on a jet-black steed raised his hand in war.

"It is time!" Hoturi shouted from the gates of the temple. "Show them what it means to be Crane!"

Uji screamed a wild battle cry, sending his men forward through the thick grasses that waved waist-high around them. The field of Daidoji was weak to the right, and Uji knew it. Seeing the defensive line breaking, the false Hoturi punched his fist to the side, commanding a legion of men to take advantage of the flaw.

Exactly as Uji had planned.

He lifted the horn from his side. In a long, bloody line, his men clashed with the undead horde. Uji blew a high-pitched tone from the instrument. The lieutenant to the right flank raised his fan in understanding, and the Asahina shugenja ceased their chant.

The golden field shimmered. Waves of light rippled through the high grasses and changed them to armored forms. The illusion of an empty plain faded away, and the Crane hidden beneath its power rose to join the battle. Behind the vanishing illusion, a thousand more Crane—two, no three thousand more—lowered their pikes to receive the undead charge.

With a scream, the undead slammed into the spear points, impaling themselves on the thick iron shafts. The illusion shimmered once more before vanishing completely. Rows of marching corpses were slaughtered by an enemy they had not known existed.

A cry rose above the fray: "Who are we?"

"Kakita!" came the proud response.

The samurai dropped pikes covered in black blood and reached for gleaming katanas. Raising his sword to join the fight, Uji smiled. That is what it means to be Crane, you filthy eta. It means you never fight alone.

Hoturi led the second wave himself, marching his men down the field behind the Daidoji. The archers at the rear lifted their bows and sent arrows arcing toward the enemy. Under their fire, Hoturi's Doji guard leapt through the high grass and joined the fight. They were few, but stalwart, and their swords cut through the sluggish legions of the false Hoturi like sickles through rice. Still, it was not enough. With determination stolen from the gates of Jigoku, the undead relentlessly advanced, tearing with clawed hands and slashing with broken swords.

Another horn trumpeted. The Asahina chant from the temple gates gained volume. The clouds above the plain began to open, pushed by an unseen hand to allow the sun's light through. Threads of gold pierced the storm, but the clouds stubbornly refused to part. More voices joined. Students, teachers, and every master of the Way stood as one before the gates, lifting their voices to the sun and beseeching the kami to hear their prayer. Again, the clouds began to part. Again, they were forced back, the light of Amaterasu forbidden by darker magic.

Beside the man on the jet-black steed stood a dark-robed figure whose hands were circled by a powerful glow—a bloody aura of maho.

"Necromancer!" Hoturi shouted to Kuwanan, pointing with his blade. "A strong one. This is his storm!"

Kuwanan nodded. Together the two men charged the hill. They cut their way, step by laboring step, through the massed undead. More Crane samurai joined them, supporting their charge. They advanced up the churned dirt of the golden field. Every inch they gained was another swing, another dying corpse or injured Crane.

With horror, Hoturi realized that he recognized many of the faces of those who stood against him. Stolen from early graves, their putrid corpses opened gaping mouths as if to speak, but only burbling gasps came out.

Omoru, Hoturi thought, drawing his blade from one fallen man to slide it through another's grime-covered neck. As Oromu's head fell at the feet of the Crane Champion, Hoturi was overwhelmed by a memory of the man's palaces, his ten daughters, and their plump mother. He had been a vassal, a friend. He had died of plague, not nine months past.

Two more took his place, their tattered blue garments hanging with soil and ash. There had been no time to burn the dead. They had died suddenly, the plague sweeping over their provinces like fire through thick brush. The two new monstrosities reached for Hoturi with new strength, and a thousand more stomped fleshy feet upon the cold ground.

Not twenty thousand undead, but twice that number.

A gust of wind screamed through the field, churning the high grasses in its passing. The undead swarmed over the hill like a great mass of black beetles, leaving torn ground and fallen bodies in their wake. The full might of the false Hoturi's army had arrived—and it was made of thousands of fallen Crane.

The fallen legions of Kyuden Doji howled vengefully, their rotted eyes peering out from bare skulls, their teeth tortured into fangs. Each one limped eagerly toward the fight. Uji's line began to buckle. They fought friends, companions, brothers and sisters—those fallen and left behind.

"Doji, help us," Hoturi breathed, lowering his sword in shock. "We fight against ourselves."

But before the Daidoji could begin their retreat, another call echoed from the field. To the west, a smaller force marched. Their black banners waved in the wind. Leading them rode a tall man in an emerald-green cloak. He lifted a golden fan that bore the mon of the emperor. Perhaps three hundred men followed the grizzled sensei, their black cloaks unfurling as they marched. These were the Emerald Magistrates, a new generation of guardians for the empire.

"Toshimoko," Hoturi whispered. He repeated the name with a yell strong enough for ten men. "Toshimoko-sama!"

"Toshimoko-sama!" echoed Kuwanan. His stoic face broke into a grin.

Beside the Emerald Magistrates marched Toturi's ronin army, their scattered colors dyed a matching black. Only Hoturi could tell that the tall warrior who marched beside Toshimoko had once worn Lion colors, or that his newly shorn hair had once been dyed a bright Akodo gold. For now, it was enough that the Crane saw their brothers-at-arms in the Emerald Champion's guard.

Toshimoko commanded the charge with a sweeping arc of his blade, which cut down the first zombie with a perfect strike. At his command, the black-garbed samurai charged to the field, covering the hills with another shade of darkness. Peeping sunlight glinted from shining blades.

The dark rider turned his fanged steed to ride down Daidoji troops. The necromancer, absorbed in his magic, did not move from the hillock. Above him, the storm boiled and blew. Clouds chased sunlight through the sky.

A great wind lifted ten undead from the ground, hurling them toward a line of Daidoji pikemen. Uji was among them. His enemies screamed and twisted upon his spear. He hurled them off and quickly rejoined the attack.

Above, the storm clouds began to break apart, bombarded by the relentless prayers of the Asahina. The blazing rays of the sun began to cut through the undead, leaving them screaming with pain from Amaterasu's pure light.

With a victorious hurrah, another unit of Daidoji charged the horseman, hoping to overwhelm him. The false

Hoturi simply smiled widely and countercharged. His steed tore through flesh and bone. Before they could even reach the rider, the Daidoji had to face the onikage, blood steed of the damned. For a moment, Hoturi thought the Daidoji might bring the monster down, but then the sky grew dark once more.

Another wind began. A bluish smoke churned in the center of the field, rising into a tremendous pillar of mist and swirling color. On the hillside, the necromancer's pained face smiled. He raised a bloody knife from a fresh cut on his arm. He cut once more. The smoke thickened, blocking the sun's rich light. A pall passed over the field, covering the battle in choking darkness.

Kakita gagged, raising their swords only to fall before the false Hoturi and his army's renewed assault. Daidoji turned blue as they groaned for air. Galloping amid them, the false Hoturi raised his sword and cut a Crane soldier's head from his body. The onikage plunged through the rest of the unit with a dashing sweep.

Gasping for breath, Hoturi shot a glance back toward the temple. Asahina Tamako stepped away from the knot of chanting priests. He raised pale hands to his shoulders on either side, stretched his arms out as if in benediction, and whispered prayers to the spirits of sky and air. He looked down upon Hoturi. Smoke clutched the champion's throat, choking the life from his body.

Now, my lord, the whisper was carried by wind and feather. *Leap.*

Trusting his vassal, Hoturi did. The force of his jump carried him above the stench and through the smoke. He landed on the far side of the field, beyond the zombies. Hoturi looked back at Uji and the Daidoji guard. The Daidoji shouted, rallying his men against the undead, and raised his spear to Hoturi.

Nearby, the False Hoturi raised glowing eyes. Hoturi saw his own face smile. Jerking savagely on the horse's reins, the evil samurai turned the beast from the Daidoji and spurred it toward his foe.

The field was chaos. High grasses caught at Hoturi's feet and the smoke burned his eyes.

The false Hoturi charged, undaunted. He impaled three Kakita duelists with a single thrust of his yari. The spear caught against the third man's collarbone, snapping the shaft of the yari in two. Throwing away the useless weapon, the False Hoturi reached for the sword at his side and lifted it free.

A bold Daidoji intervened, leaping for the man. The false Hoturi caught him and spun him about. With a single cutting pull, the horseman tore the Daidoji's belly open against his sword. As the soldier fell, the evil samurai lifted his bloodied weapon to point at Hoturi.

The champion's eyes never left those of his insane double, understanding the meaning behind the stroke.

Satsume's wound.

The False Hoturi's back banner snapped in a sudden gust of wind. The silver mon of the Crane fluttered angrily behind him.

Hoturi stepped forward to accept the challenge. He advanced over the corpses that littered the field and shook black blood from his sword. The enchanted weapon rang softly in his grip. The blade trembled with an eagerness he had not felt before. Its note chimed with increasing pitch, sliding up the scale of audible notes with a swift and almost intelligent howl. The sword sang angrily, prepared for combat.

In the wide field around the two combatants, the Crane armies fought for their lives. The Daidoji had caught the first wave of undead, but the creatures of Kyuden Doji had beaten them back upon the plain, to the base of the Asahina hill. Though the ronin army hounded the zombie army at every turn, the overwhelming numbers were beginning to tell. Even Toturi appeared haggard.

Still, the Emerald Magistrates did not lag. At last, after

having been so long denied their place, they fought for an empire that truly needed their strength. The pride that shone on their faces did not leave them even in death. As each magistrate fell, the rest of Toshimoko's men redoubled their efforts, standing side by side against the demon horde.

"Watch them, Father," the sick voice of his double hissed to Hoturi over the snorts of his demon horse. "Watch them die."

"No, I will watch you die," whispered Hoturi, taking a duelist's stance behind the ringing sword.

"You've killed one son, Hoturi," his own voice echoed with perfect timbre, and his own face smiled beatifically. "You don't have the strength to kill another." This time, Kachiko's voice purred madly from the man's lips, "My love . . . come to me. . . ."

Sick to his core, his stomach churning with shock, Hoturi raised the sword of his clan and charged.

The horse's head spun. It reared in surprise, and its iron hooves blocked his blow. The Crane Champion's move had been sudden, but the onikage was battle-trained. It kicked at his head.

He ducked the blow and lunged toward the man that clung to the maddened creature's back.

Its fangs bared, the horse lashed out, sinking iron teeth into Hoturi's shoulder. Metal shrieked against metal. Hoturi gasped with pain. Fangs cut through lacquered armor and tore into the flesh beneath. Hoturi punched with his other hand, trying to reach the creature's nose. The blow connected, driving the fangs deeper but injuring the creature enough that it pulled its face from his arm, releasing him.

Staggering back, Hoturi took another stance. Fresh blood trailed down from his shoulder, feeling the pull of muscle against bone. The wound was deep.

Laughing, the false Hoturi twisted the reins back and forth, teasing the giant steed with its own lust for blood.

The horse leapt toward the Crane Champion. Its hoof

caught Hoturi's shin. With a powerful kick, the beast knocked him to the ground.

He struggled to rise, still grasping the ancient sword.

Above him, the doppelganger released the reins. "Kill him," he snarled. It leapt forward.

Hoturi lifted a spear from the ground, tearing it from the hand of a dead Daidoji and bracing it against the cold, hard soil.

The spear slid between the horse's legs, through the barreled chest and the wide body, seeking the heart. It plunged with all the power of the demon horse's lunge. Shrieking in anguish, the creature staggered forward a few more steps, unable to comprehend the pain. At last, it collapsed.

The false Hoturi spun in his saddle, leaping from the steed before it could crash to the ground. Enraged, he lifted his sword—a black blade, dull and foreboding.

Despite his wounded arm, the son of Satsume lifted his own katana and heard the faint whisper of song within the steel.

"No more," Hoturi said, staring into his own eyes. "There will be no more slaughter."

With a snarl, the Egg of Pan Ku charged. Hoturi saw his own face contort with rage and madness. Two swords struck. Metal rang as both samurai thrust and spun.

The movements were precise. The swordsmen had learned from the finest duelists the Crane Clan had to offer. Hoturi knew his opponent's moves almost before they were made. From intricate footwork to ringing steel, his foe's technique perfectly echoed his own.

The false Hoturi's black cape swirled, hiding his movements, but the young champion did not need to see his stance. He knew the dance of strike and feint. He could not be confused by the blur of fabric. As they fought, Hoturi felt a kind of trance fall upon him. The clear sound of the sword in his hand grew, ringing with purity whenever it deflected the Black Crane's blows.

The false Hoturi screamed. His blade began to glow, first faintly and then brightly as his blows rained down on Hoturi's swift defense.

Hoturi drew back, dazzled by the black radiance. He stared at the rabid glow in his duplicate's eyes. Lunge, twist, evade, slice, and lunge again—an intricate interplay of deadly katana, capable of cutting through the hardest stone.

"Tired, Father?" The false Hoturi drove in, slashing at his knees with a savage strike.

Nimbly, Hoturi stepped out of the way, but felt the cold steel of the blade close to his flesh.

Angling his sword, he turned the blow and stepped inside the Black Crane's defense. His fist delivered a brutal punch to the wide chin.

The false Hoturi staggered back, bringing up the strange black sword. The tip of the obsidian blade caught Hoturi just behind the knee.

The Crane Champion staggered. Steel and grass, twisted together from the day's battle, curled around his ankle and dragged him to the ground. Hoturi wrenched his foot free, attempting to find firmer ground, but his wounded arm faltered. His balance lost, Hoturi fell hard to the side. Rocks beneath the grass drove into his skin. The impact ripped bone from tendon. Hoturi gasped. Pain lanced through his wounded shoulder.

"Wonderful, Father," the false Hoturi taunted, cutting lightly at Hoturi's face with his obsidian blade. "On your knees. It is where you should have been, long ago."

Hoturi dived to the side, ignoring the raw pain in his arm, and twisted away from the strange katana. He lifted his weapon once more and lunged onto unsteady feet. Blood stained his right palm, covering the silk wrappings of the ancient blade. He did not care. Pushing forward, he caught the false Hoturi's knees in his arms and twisted them both to the ground with a rough shove.

The false Hoturi's blade swung from his hand, dropping

to the side as they fell. The Black Crane gave out a gasped laugh, clutching for his weapon. It was beyond his reach.

Hoturi gulped, each breath stabbing fire through his shoulder and lancing pain through his injured side. With the hilt of the Crane katana, he plowed his fist into the false Hoturi's face again, feeling bone crunch beneath his strike.

The son of the Egg of Pan Ku lifted Hoturi from atop him and threw the Crane Champion to the side. The creature lumbered to his feet and grasped the obsidian hilt.

With a fluid motion, Hoturi stood, feeling his feet against the hard-packed ground. His mind was clear, his body relaxed, his stance true. Even his shoulder, still inflamed, rested for a moment. The single, strong stroke of the Kakita duelist struck purely. His sword rang as it sped toward the false Hoturi's throat.

It cut through armor, through steel and through bone, cleaving into the soft flesh of the false Hoturi's throat and snapping the spine beneath with a mighty cut.

The figure wove. Its head tilted crazily. Mad eyes flashed one last hateful glance at Hoturi's stoic form. Their gazes locked in one last moment of anguish. "Now you see yourself die," it mouthed.

As the head rolled upon the ground, its laughter began to grow with demonic madness. Soon it filled the air around the combat and echoed the drowning song of the Crane sword. The body wheeled for a moment, hands still reaching for its weapon. The corpse then fell to its knees beside the howling head. It toppled to a ground slick with blood and crushed grasses.

In only a few seconds, the features began to melt. Fingers dissolved into maggots that writhed and shook. The face oozed like wax beneath a candle's flame. The body slumped into the ground. Flesh turned black and acidic. Bugs swarmed from every opening in the lacquered armor. The face sank into a burbling, choking mask.

The Crane Champion staggered to his feet. He stared in

revulsion until there was nothing left of the false Hoturi save an empty suit of armor, a wormy sludge, and the shattered remains of golden eggshell where the beast's heart had once lain.

Around him, the smoke of the battlefield had begun to clear. The noble chant of the Asahina shugenja continued. The wind began to rise. Patches of sun scorched the bodies of the undead. They crumpled under Amaterasu's gift. The cloying smoke began to dissipate, and on the far hillock, Kuwanan lifted the necromancer's head for all to see.

The battle had been won. The Emerald Champion's men surrounded their leader, cheering with the relief of hard-fought victory.

Hoturi reached to touch the soft hair at his belt. "For you, little one," Hoturi whispered, tears filling his eyes. "For you, and for the clan we both love." As he turned away from the battlefield, the first spring breeze brushed warmly against his cheek, like the touch of a remembered hand.

23 A FRAGILE PEACE

Hoturi paced through the long aisle of Kyuden Kakita's tattered gardens, watching as architects argued about replacing the stones and scouring the broken timbers before they raised the new wall.

The spring's warmth felt good after the long winter chill. The snows were melting from the high hillsides of the northern provinces, bringing fresh water to feed the rice fields. Soon the Crane lands would be prosperous again, bearing enough rice and grain to feed the empire.

The rebuilding of Kyuden Kakita was a great task for the Crane, and one in which they all took pride, but healing the scars left behind by the False Hoturi would take more than mortar and stone. Those wounds would remain deeply imbedded in Hoturi's soul until the Crane were truly safe once more.

"My lord?" Yoshi's voice was bright, the courtier's lilt drifting easily across the garden.

Hoturi looked away from the scrambling heimin on the inner wall of the ruined palace. He smiled as his old friend approached.

"Yoshi-san," Hoturi smiled. "Greetings." In response to the courtier's graceful flourish, he bowed. Seeing that the courtier was not alone, the champion of the Crane nodded politely to old Asahina Tomo, following shortly behind Yoshi.

"Let me see your wound," the old man croaked, lifting a wrapped bundle of herbs. "There's more to be done, and I won't have the emperor saying his cousin healed crookedly!"

Hoturi smiled at the strange old man's attentive concern. He nodded and lifted his gi from his shoulders so Tomo could see the bandages.

As the old healer cautiously removed the wrappings, Yoshi knelt near Hoturi. He looked with casual interest out at the builders. "The palace will never be the same, you know. That front wall is two hand's breadths to the right. Its not symmetrical anymore—"

"Of course not," Hoturi said, wincing at the too-eager Asahina's touch. "It is not the same palace that it once was. But it will be reborn."

Yoshi smiled, the imagery delighting him. "Born from flames? That's a Phoenix's duty, not a Crane's."

"Born from dishonor to honor, Yoshi-san." He tilted his head to allow the cool wrappings to be replaced with a fresh layer of sweet herbs. "The Crane have been obsessed with their own perfection for too long. Let the new kyuden show the empire that we have things to think about beyond the end of our noses."

A laugh broke the garden's silence. "Well said, Hoturi-sama." Old Toshimoko strode through the palace's open archway, passing artisans who carved elaborate tracery on the wood that would become the new gate. Standing stiffly in the green of the Emerald Champion, Toshimoko affected a solemn bow, belied by the mischief in his smile.

Hoturi and Yoshi both bowed in return, pleased to see the sensei. "What news from Otosan Uchi?" Hoturi asked simply.

"Ten new legions of magistrates, from every corner of the empire. With the victory over the Dark Crane at the Asahina temples, half the empire wants to join the fight."

"Hmm," Hoturi smiled. "More likely, they all wish to take the opportunity to study with you, Sensei." He motioned to Toshimoko to rest nearby, and continued, "And don't you wave that golden fan of yours at my Daidoji samurai. Uji has his hands full trying to build up the ranks before the Lion rally again."

"We have plans for them, if they should try," Yoshi said smugly. "Toshimoko's victory has brought the Crane many new allies in the Imperial Court. With the spring thaws, the Phoenix will be sending ambassadors to aid us in rebuilding Kyuden Kakita."

"A legion of 'ambassadors,' eh?" Toshimoko laughed. "Old tricks, Yoshi-san."

"Rebirth does not mean throwing away the old ways, Toshimoko-san." Noting the sensei's new rank, Yoshi bowed in friendship. Toshimoko returned the faint bow with a grin. "We are still the Crane."

Hoturi smiled at the banter of the two brothers, listening with half an ear to their pleasant conversation.

When the Lion come this time, he promised himself, the Crane will not bow to their armies. Instead, we will meet them on the field with courage and honor, and we will bring victory home.

He gazed out into the gardens of Kyuden Kakita, looking at the old trees that spread their ancient branches above the twining ivy. That much, at least, had survived. No matter how long it took to return the palace to its former splendor, the beauty of the Crane still lay not in gold or art, but in the soul of its people. Reaching out softly to cup a blossom on the branch of a flowering cherry tree, Hoturi smiled sadly. One petal of the flower had browned, leaving a faint stain on its perfect form.

"That one's wilted, my lord," Yoshi said, noting his movements. "Best to leave it for the gardeners. They will remove it, no doubt."

"No." Hoturi spoke clearly into the quiet of the afternoon. "Tell the gardeners it is not to be touched. Leave this one . . . to remind me of the nature of my soul."

▲ ▲ ▲ ▲ ▲ ▲ ▲ ▲

In the forests of the Kakita, the sun burned an orange glow over twisted vines and thick bramble, illuminating the form of a young fox that lagged behind the rest of her pack. With one last adoring glance through the trees toward the prince in silver and blue, she raced after her companions, white breast shining in the sunset and green eyes pale with joyful tears.

It's all true.
It's really happening.
It's not paranoia.

**Reality and nightmare collide when dark forces converge
on a world that seems so normal.**

DARK•MATTER™

(oNe)
In Hollow Houses
Gary A. Braunbeck
August 2000

(two)
If Whispers Call
Don Bassingthwaite
December 2000

(Four)
Of Aged Angels
Monte Cook
July 2001

(thReE)
In Fluid Silence
G.W. Tirpa
March 2001

(fiVe)
By Dust Consumed
Don Bassingthwaite
December 2001

The Hoffman Institute may be our only defense against the
Dark Tide, but is it part of the solution, or part of the problem?
For a team of investigators with their own connections to the
unseen world, the answer to that question may be a matter of
life or death, sanity or insanity.

Contemporary dark fantasy from the publisher of MAGIC: THE
GATHERING® and FORGOTTEN REALMS®